I0775675

Wareham, MA

ISBN: 979-8-9859692-7-6
Library of Congress Number: 2023907124

This book was originally published in French as *Vidures* © by Actes Sud Editions in 2011. Permission was given by Actes Sud to publish this English translation of the book.

The foreword has been edited from its original publication as an article titled, *Trashland: an Armenian Dystopia*, by Christopher Atamian in the *Armenian Mirror Spectator* on 08/31/22.

Cover Design: Nauset Press
Cover Image: *Lying Pig* (1812) by Jean Bernard (1775-1883). Original from The Rijksmuseum. Found on rawpixel.com.
Copyright © Illustration 2011 by Mkrtitch Matevossian, page 98
Copyright © Sheet Music 2011 by Gerard Torikian, pages 128-9, 167-8.

Trashland

Denis Donikian

Translated from the French by
Christopher Atamian

NAUSET PRESS, WAREHAM, MA

The world has gone mad
And my soul weighs heavily on me.
Neither good nor evil exists
In this infernal world.

— Rabiz Song by Tatoul Avoyan

Every pig has within him a man who slumbers.

— Pierre-Henri Cami

Foreword

*I*n a disremembered corner of Asia Minor, amid the ruins of a former Soviet Republic-turned-capitalist hell hole, in a land where a brutish individualism has taken hold and a handful of oligarchs live in unimaginable luxury as the rest of the country starves; here atop a hideously smoldering trash dump where the denizens of the model Nubarashen community are reduced to foraging with rats and dogs for food, begins Denis Donikian's remarkable novel *Trashland*.

Trashland starts off with its hero Gam—which in Armenian means both "I exist" and "or else"—a clever play on words, standing atop a hill as he relieves himself on the Armenian capital of Yerevan below. He then joins some trash pickers and mourners following the burial procession of a woman named Anna, who turns out to be his mother. Once a muckraking journalist nicknamed "The Hedgehog," Gam fled a life-shattering earthquake in his home city of Gyumri into a life of subsistence, living in a small hut near the garbage dump. Here he has escaped society, only to later be tailed by the henchmen of the Armenian government. Hook and shoulder bag in tow, he joins Roubo, Lousso, and their motley group of friends to pick for food in the trash daily. When the government henchmen arrive, they inform the trash pickers that the Japanese have been hired to install an efficient incinerator system. Everything—and everyone—must go. The rest of this tale involves many remarkable twists, turns, and ironies. Coincidentally, the great Armenian writer Vahan Totovents wrote about trash pickers (or *kulkhan beyi* in Turkish) in his 1930 novel *Life on the Old Roman Road*. It's a sad but telling comment on how that part of the world has gained precious little social equity over the past century.

Few novels deliver quite so biting, acerbic, and at times lively societal criticism. *Trashland* serves as a dirge (and underneath it all, a paean) to a country abandoned to its worst tendencies. Where, in real life as in fiction, women forced to prostitute themselves with their historic enemies in Turkey, journalists who openly criticize the country's corruption, or anyone who blatantly disagrees with the government are "disappeared" or "suicided" off the frightening Kiev bridge with alarming regularity. *Trashland* owes a debt to both Golding and Orwell. Instead of an island, as in *Lord of the Flies*, Donikian presents an Armenian trash dump. Instead of an allegorical animal farm as described in the eponymous novel, the author gives us a whole country turned into a slaughterhouse, its people no better than farm animals to be exploited, metaphorically consumed, and then finally, their husks discarded. In these pages the reader also meets the first three Oligarch Presidents of Armenia, here given clever pen names: The Scholar (Levon Ter-Petrossian), The Cobra (Robert Kocharyan) and The Samourai (Serzh Sargsyan), while the fourth politician portrayed, Pasha Nikolyan represents a spoonerism of the current President's name, Nikol Pashinyan. The pig that the ragpickers roast and ceremoniously eat at one point is named Bella, a witty and barbed send-up referencing Kocharyan's wife, Bella Kocharyan.

Trashland was received with dismay by many of Armenia's so-called intelligentsia. Everything from the title to the brutal honesty of its narrative took many by surprise. Just as Junot Diaz's *The Brief Wondrous Life of Oscar Wao* takes a candid look at the Dominican community in New York City and the Dominican Republic, *Trashland* offers an insider's view of an often-insular society. As a diasporan Armenian, Donikian writes from a privileged vantage point. Playing devil's advocate, he has superseded the expectations assigned to diasporans as cash cows to be bilked for imaginary projects or retirees who come to spend their hard-earned money in their golden years. To cross this line, one must love one's people and community. To lay bare its deepest wounds and expose its most deep-seated corruption—those are the signs of a true patriot and humanist. Marc Nichanian has noted that Armenian writers of the diaspora labor within a self-contained world with an imaginary and yet very real curtain separating them from Soviet and now independent Armenia on the one hand, and the rest of the world on the other. Let's hope that *Trashland*, published first in French by a leading publisher—Actes Sud—and now picked up in its English translation by the fine independent publishing house Nauset Press, will help to pull back this curtain. And perhaps, Oz-like, reveal the underlying reality of this fascinating and complicated culture to the world at large.

Trashland is a liminal novel, written from a perspective straddling the thin line between insider and outsider. Denis Donikian was born in 1942 in Vienne, a small city just south of Lyon, France. He grew up in Le Kemp, a former armaments factory housing workers who were all Armenian Genocide survivors. He studied first in France and then in Soviet Armenia while still a young man. He has spent the better part of his adult life writing about and critiquing life in both the Armenian diaspora and the Republic of Armenia. Donikian has published some forty books, including several tomes of poetry. His extended poetic essay *Paradjanov's Horses* to this day remains singular for its beauty. He has also flexed his creative passion outside of writing by exhibiting his wonderfully quixotic sculptures influenced by First Nation totem poles. Donikian's recent *Small Encyclopedia of the Armenian Genocide*, a monumental six-hundred page thematically arranged history of the Great Catastrophe or Medz Yeghern, is both a devoir de mémoire and a homage to his parents who survived the event and managed to transmit Armenian culture and language to their son. The better part of Donikian's oeuvre then, including his journalistic work at www.yevrobatsi.org, where he was my brilliant editor in the early aughts, has been a comprehensive critique of the Armenian world and a quest for justice for the Armenian people. His work is living proof that the two are not mutually exclusive.

Trashland transmutes a hodgepodge of styles—poetry, prose, direct address, third-person narration, and inner monologue—into a lively and dynamic text. The novel was published a decade ago in French, and now a new generation, dubbed Generation Independence, has emerged in Armenia and is equally critical of its social ills. Writers such as Aram Pachyan, Anna Davtyan, and Armen Ohanyan have exposed everything from corruption in the army and society to warped gender relations and the persecution of sexual minorities with an eagle eye and acid pen. But before they came along, Donikian and a few others, such as Violet Grigoryan, were lone wolves in an otherwise empty forest of pallid acquiescence. They helped to pave the way and we are grateful to them.

In his 1844 book *Armenia*, the English writer Lord Robert Curzon, who had spent a year stationed in Erzerum, writes that as recently as the 17th and 18th centuries, Armenians dominated the world's most coveted trade routes from Asia to Venice and Western Europe along with Sephardic Jews. They lost out to these rivals for one simple reason: the Jews formed alliances and came together. At the same time, the individualistic-minded Armenians refused to do so with the same willing and cooperative haste. If Donikian's novel represents a social barometer, little seems to have changed in the Armenian world. One of his characters in *Trashland* describes his fellow Armenians thus: "Savages, that's what. Too busy waging war against each other. Whether we like it or not, we're unable to communicate without ending up at each other's throats. The political murders should be enough to prove my point, no?" Donikian's novel transcends the simple parable of Armenian life. It serves as a metaphor for the human condition and for the ruthless way in which the powerful, regardless of the country or community, will abuse the weak and less fortunate. The one true ray of hope that Donkian gives his reader lies in how the trash pickers—the most dispossessed of the dispossessed—come together despite desperate circumstances. And the open-ended final chapter leaves one wondering if and how Gam will prosper despite all the adversity that life has thrown his way. Let's hope that Donikian's universal message rings far and clear—past Armenia and its diaspora and on to the greater world beyond. *Trashland* is a wake-up call, a bracing reminder of the writer's vital role in society.

—Christopher Atamian,
New York City, New York

1.

Dèr voghormia! [1]

Dèr Voghormia!

Naked with legs spread, Gam[2] pointed his sex at Yerevan[3] and pissed. Feeling lighter and refreshed, he repeated out loud: *Der Voghormia!* The dawn had already emptied the sky of stars and flickers of light still dotted the city. It was always the same before daybreak. Gam directed his flow towards the swamp below, imagining that he might somehow be able to fill it. In truth, he was aiming at a specific target: an anthill that he could never get rid of. He had held it in all night again so that he might destroy the anthill in a flood of urine. That was his ritual. *Go to the ant, thou sluggard,* he repeated inside his head. Barely awake, he couldn't resist pissing on them again. In this way he'd made a brown spot around the anthill. The grass surrounding it had died. And, on this day, his eyes half-closed and subject to the light's increasing pressure, Gam had trouble distinguishing one and from the other, because the ants had been driven crazy by the urine he showered down on them. He had chosen the exact moment when they were cleaning their den before setting out to gather some food. Now

---

1   *Lord have mercy!*: A liturgical chant, but also an intimate supplication made by a man to the divine Master of the visible and invisible worlds.

2   Djohar, our character's grandmother, pronounced his name Gam. She did so in memory of her husband Gamo and for the ancestral lands from which they had been chased before they ended up in the ones where the current story takes place. And that's why they continued to say *Gam* in her family, while in this new country, the correct pronunciation was *Kam. Gam/Kam* means *I am, I exist,* but also *or else,* as the reader will observe in Chapter 29. Here, we prefer the spelling *Gam,* rather than Kam.

3   Pronounced Erevan or Yerevan.

they panicked and ran amok in every direction. The knowledge that each morning at the same exact time he could at a whim disrupt their peace amused our all-powerful pisser to no end. Gam's internal clock forced him out of bed before 6 A. M. *Hey you slacker, how long are you going to sleep?* He heard himself say inside his head. Emerging from the muffled darkness within his brain, he would stagger towards the door, outlined in light like some automaton eager to set in motion his murderous release. He was convinced that by pissing on the ants, he would create a disruption in their daily physiological routine. And so, the liquefied air beat down on them in acrid, hot torrents. And the earth rent. The flood devoured their nests and the ants died in great numbers. His head kept repeating *Chârt! Chârt! Chârt!*[4] like the sound that bags of blood make when you pop them open with a blade. Gam smiled. The desperate ants sank into the mud and their underground tunnels collapsed. The ants, usually so lively, turned clumsy and sticky. Thus, the great catastrophe descended on them again. And it was Gam, ruthless sower of chaos, who set it all in motion. Being human, he couldn't hear the terrified chirring that the ants emitted, which resembled those made by any other living body repeatedly being bruised. The ants cried out in a horrible stupor. Fall ants, like our men and women fell! *Der Voghormia!* he repeated. He saw the moans of hands torn apart, stupefied. The mouths of horses deformed by fear. Women whinnying from pain. Giant mouths, silent wounds. Children like limp dolls. He saw broken things, fragments, lightning that streaked their beings. A sudden flash of light, then sharp teeth spat out from some apocalyptic light. *The same eternal crimes committed in a distant corner of the world enveloped in silence*, Gam said to himself. A scene from a film had lodged itself forever inside his brain, slowly decaying ever since childhood. In it, people are being taken out of a shack, one by one. The sky throws its claws at their eyes. They think that they've escaped, but suddenly they find themselves in a narrow corridor surrounded by men and women with hatred etched on their faces. Fists, feet, sticks beat down on them. They try to shield themselves with their arms, but the onslaught continues, pummeling them repeatedly. This goes on for another

---

4   Onomatopoeic. The word also means *massacre.*

twenty meters until they reach the edge of a cliff. And then someone grabs these human playthings and throws them over the edge, as if they were mere garbage. A scream as they plunge, a scream that wails all the way down until they finally crash. As they fall, you hear a scream repeated within you as well. *Eternal crimes committed in a distant corner of the world enveloped in silence.* And when Gam reads similar things about his own people for the first time, his eyes have already witnessed the same bloody scenes. Pushed along, chained on a road bordering a cliff: when they reach the end of it, they are all slaughtered. Knifed in the stomach. *Chârt! Chârt! Chârt!* Then they throw the half-dead bodies down to the bottom of the cliff. They fall limp, on top of a heap of cadavers. *Der voghormia! Der voghormia!*

Alternately squeezing and shaking his now limp penis, Gam tried to eke out one last drop. Planted firmly atop an earthen mound, he assumed the stance of a tribal God. A look that defied the world. He gazed down at Yerevan with contempt. The monstrous City's skyscrapers and scaffolding rose to the sky. It stuck out its metal and concrete claws at him. Without wasting any time, the surviving ants were already at work recuperating from the chaos caused by the shower of urine. They evacuated the dead bodies and cleared the entryways. Some ventured into the galleries to create new openings. Others took over and when the opening was finished, rushed in by the dozens. *Ants don't remember their past misfortunes,* thought Gam. Instead of fleeing a particular area where they are periodically destroyed, they become attached to it, even if the next day they are once again subjected to the same destructive storm. Oh ants! Ants! How similar you are to us, are you not? We share the same sense of mourning, as pronounced as our will to live. Flee already! Clear out! Go anywhere and escape this insanity that descends upon you daily from the sky above!

Gam returned to his hut. The sheet metal on his door emitted a plaintive creak. *That's the noise my house makes,* he thought. Suddenly daylight streamed into the room and projected itself onto the back wall where two portraits, one of Stalin and the other of Jesus Christ, hung above an old metal bed about a meter apart from each other. Gam drank a glass of water, made a smacking noise with his tongue, and then dove under his covers with a sigh. And as he fell into a deep slumber, words began to surface from within him—always the same words which helped him to escape from his lonely state of being.

> *Your breasts are grapes in the palms of my hands*
> *Your skin velvet, vibrant with confusion*
> *Your forehead...*

Erotic songs and dreams of a life that emerged from the darkest of crime scenes. Now he sees himself. His eyes sparkle. He is dressed in pristine clothing, for the pure joy of it. Triumphant at having finally unearthed the object of his sad desires. The trash has delivered its gold unto him. The gold which sets you free. And so, Gam dances. He rejoices. He turns in every direction and flies through the same air that serves to set ablaze the trash below. Gam in Majesty flying high above the chaos and the stench beneath him. Envied by all, famous, transformed into a God by the miraculous power of his faith. Gam.

Two hours later, he slipped on his shirt and pea jacket, which reeked of smoke. Next, he put on his soot-covered boots and tore into a piece of lavash bread with his teeth. The bread cracked in his mouth. He gulped down a large glass of water before starting to chew again. And after deciding that his two-day-old beard did not yet need his attention, he grabbed his hook and *meshog* that lay near the door and went outside. Without them he was nothing. The hook he used to dig around, the bag to gather his finds. His shack was held up by the wall of the house. The owners had constructed it out of random bric-a-brac as a storage room, and at the request of a common friend, they had given it away for nothing to Gam. Or possibly they had done so out of compassion. Knowing that he usually dug up his food from the trash, they never failed to offer him a part of their own meals. In exchange, whenever he had time on Sundays, Gam would till their garden's soil.

To come down from the small hill that he lived on and reach the Nubarashen highway, Gam had to take a dirt road. He snaked through the dry grass, avoiding the ruins of a factory that had never actually functioned. He looked down at

Yerevan's last dwellings, which were located at the foot of a series of smooth hills that rose to increasingly desolate heights. And behind these hills, in clear weather, the white island known as Mount Ararat would emerge, floating atop an eternal space, wedged between men and the sky high above.

The *meshog* firmly positioned on his shoulder and carrying the hook with his other hand, Gam began his descent. Halfway there, one could see the entire road all the way up until the garbage dump. On that particular day, it was blocked by a funerary procession some thirty meters long. Dogs trotted ahead, egged on from behind. Some turned around from time to time and looked furtively behind them, to stay apace with the head car that was transporting the deceased. *God only knows what's going to come my way today,* Gam said to himself, upset by the idea that he would be condemned to walk behind the crowd of people accompanying the coffin. You don't pass a dead person being led to their grave.

2.

The 21st century, the Century of Love

Gam had just made it onto the highway, and as expected he found himself rear-ending the funerary procession. A group of retired medical workers walked directly in front of him, some bald or almost so, others completely white or grey-haired, all dressed in wedding finery. Out in front, people had to endure the full musical assault of the nasal drone that two zurnas[1] were emitting. Despite this they chatted away as if they were at a local outdoor café. That was the best way to ignore the fatigue that overcame their old bones at the bottom of hills. The one that snaked its way up to the cemetery was truly daunting:

---

1   Traditional musical instrument, a type of eight-holed oboe with a ninth hole underneath that produces a sharp ear-splitting noise.

a single, remarkably long, steep, and uninterrupted road. Walking behind the queue, Gam could still make out the open casket lying in the back of a van. The men of the new republic were so pot-bellied that they would have gasped and wheezed and risked suffocation had they been obliged to follow the custom of carrying the dead woman on their shoulders. The *ancien régime* on the other hand had kept its men thin, expecting them to respect tradition and forcing them to take care of the deceased themselves until they reached their ultimate resting place without the risk of fainting from the strain—no one owned a car anyway. Gam couldn't help but listen to the yapping that emanated from the rear. No one seemed worried about his presence, although he might easily have created some suspicion. They were too busy summing up the new republic. From their puffed-up chests, resigned anger escaped, from their bitter lips vengeful cackling. The anger and cackling soon died down and the occasion turned serious once again. But the more the hill tortured their bodies, the more their tongues loosened. This contagious frivolity even reached the head of the procession. Gossip, lamentations, asides, and stories of all types began to jump with impunity from one whispering quartet to another. The whispers grew louder until they could no longer be considered whispers. And while Gam followed alive and well in his work boots, his mental faculties remained foggy from the previous night's dreams. Suddenly he perked up when he heard the old men and women discussing someone named Anna. Could they be talking about his mother? And what did she have to do with the Cobra? This nickname had been given to the second president of the republic by the perpetually disgruntled. The Cobra had followed in the footsteps of the Scholar before himself yielding to his protégé, the Samourai.

"We're going to miss Anna," said one of the pensioners. "We're going to miss her."

"We're sure going to miss her!" The others all agreed. "She told it like it is."

"Yessir, she spoke the truth," they added in unison.

"And on the square behind our Opera, she shot rubber bullets at the Cobra."

"Rubber bullets, she shot."

"A thousand rocks at a single tree."

"A thousand rocks. One thousand. Yes," they all chanted together.

"A thousand rocks at the Cobra."

"The one who poisons the weak and chokes the powerful."

"The poisoner. The choker. Yes," they exclaimed together again.

"That *bozi tegha*," [2] someone else let loose.

"Do you remember that poster? *The 21st century, the Century of Love!* They preached that we were brothers, while they dispersed our meetings with billy clubs as if we were insects."

"That evil man rules with an iron fist and the people tremble."

"They tremble. They tremble, I tell you," they all repeated.

"Yesterday, while people were out shopping, the Cobra was playing basketball. And while the people were celebrating because they were able to put a meager piece of bread in their shopping basket, he was celebrating the fact that he'd gotten a basketball through his."

"The evil one rules with an iron fist, and the people tremble," they all agreed.

"They tremble."

"And yet his wife's name is Bella, as if he lived under an unlucky star. He's the one who should have had the bad luck—*Bad Luck Bella*." [3]

"Bella belonged to the Cobra, while the scorched earth, the thirsty earth belonged to us. We all lived through a nightmare. The dark night, the stench, the dreadful insanity ..."

"All ours. All ours," the crowd intoned and continued: "But our Anna knew all these things."

"She called it like she saw it.'

---

2   Son of a whore.

3   Calling someone *Bella* is like accusing them of being bad luck.

"Yes, she knew, she said things out loud. She spoke straight to our hearts. He'd barely been elected President before the Cobra rushed to bring us all the rats that belong to his race here and send our children to get killed defending his fiefdom in Kakabakh."

"He's also the force behind Idi Gago's rise in politics. Our own Idi Amin. Important and fat men, those two."

"Circus *tsouls*."

"You go and try to close the top button on one of their shirts with those thick bull-like necks of theirs. Impossible. A black soldier and a white weightlifter."

"Cobra always loved sports and athletes. But our Idi Gago, he's a White Man who entertains African-sized dreams. He even transported jungle animals in cages to the palace that he built for himself."

"Nothing to do with our Noah's Ark, of course."

"Once, he was so bored with Armenia that he fed a donkey to his two lions."

"So what?" A few others retorted.

"Well, what do you think? People shared the video of that bestial act. It went around the world. The donkey survived, but our image in the world suffered."

"All of these things, Anna spoke out about them."

"She said that to make their fortunes, our big shots had taken from some without giving anything to others. Nothing scared our Anna."

"Yep, she told it like it is," they all intoned.

A dump truck full of garbage piled high passed by the procession, dumping greasy papers and plastic bags on the row of mourners. Instinctively panicked by the stinking mastodon's sudden surge, they turned their heads away or buried them into their now upturned collars. Gam was enraged. He was already late for his daily pickings. Intrigued by this Anna whom these old admirers missed so much, he kept his ears pealed to hear their next words. Could this in fact be his mother? Unless the dead person in the coffin being carried in the van was someone else? Anna apparently just let herself die, then. And without informing me that she was ill, he thought.

"Don't spit on people who belong to his race, they are lurking everywhere," a smooth-talking anti-Cobrist replied. He lowered his tone and nodded in Gam's direction.

"The basketball-playing president doesn't like it when you talk about his people as if they were feuding brothers. He might even convince the Samourai to legally remove the few crumbs of liberty that we have left."

"Perhaps he'd justify doing so out of racial discrimination," another person added ironically." In the end this *kapiki vor* 4 wanted to pass a law that would punish anyone who said anything to turn people against each other. Off to prison, those *barab glir*, those limp dicks! All he did during his entire mandate was fatten the coffers of his clan, that donkey ass!"

"We're one people," he warbled at us! "In reality, we're only a people in our poets' hallucinations! They drummed these narcissistic slogans into our ears to cover up our mutual repulsion for each other! And only for that reason!"

"But what would we be in the end, without the lies that poets sing?" A grey-haired man exclaimed, indignant. "Savages, that's what. Too busy waging war against each other. Whether we like it or not, we're unable to communicate without ending up at each other's throats. The political murders should be enough to prove my point, no?"

"Let's not exaggerate. Which one of us would go after you because of the anti patriotic drivel that you're spewing?"

"Anti patriotic? Anti patriotic? I think that I'm a hell of lot more patriotic than some *vôr lzogh* five like you! Show me another nation where seven deputies can be gunned down at once in parliament!"

"Hey calm down, will you? You're forgetting that we're here to bury our Anna," asserted another grey-haired man, as he tried to intercede.

"Truth be told, we're way too old to be tearing each other apart like this,

---

4   Literally: monkey's ass.

don't you think? We've lost our edge. And when the wolf gets old, even stray dogs laugh at him."

"All the same, to say that we are one people is a cheap form of mysticism. It suits our politicians' agendas. The other day on T. V., they profiled some petty thieves up close, in such a negative way that it made you want to spit on them. And what crime had those poor guys committed, I ask you? Not one of our presidents could create any jobs for them. So, they stole a bit of iron or copper from abandoned factories to resell it. What's the harm in that? They have to feed their families after all, don't they? They didn't steal to buy themselves a Hummer or a jet plane or to go gambling in a casino. It was to feed their families. I call that a moral theft, while our elected looters continue to grab the bread from our mouths with complete impunity."

"And when a radio station uncovers just how much money our rapacious presidents have stolen, they cut off their signal."

"They cut off their signal," everyone concurred, "Yep, they cut off their signal."

Gam weighed each word that he overheard from these malcontents as it escaped from their mouths. With his hook in one hand and the other hand holding on tightly to his shoulder over his *meshog*, he looked both mysterious and menacing. The veterans were starting to wonder if maybe they wouldn't be better off staying silent. After all, who was this intruder walking behind them? And where was he off to, just like that? Some reassured themselves with the thought that he probably worked in the cemetery. Seeing him in his boots frocked like some country simpleton and judging from the acrid odor that grated at their nostrils, others had concluded that Gam foraged in the garbage dump. And while they devoted their time to dishing out their political prattle as their bodies continued to painfully climb uphill, the procession was slowly coming apart from head to toe. Groups formed, creating gaps that were filled with echoes of voices and laughter. Now the *zurna*-saturated air flamed under the azure sun. And their brains slowly began to boil. Some dogs had come down from the hills and enlarged the group, instinctively walking ahead of the van of the deceased. Gam recognized a few of the ones who routinely frequented the garbage dump. A large redhead with a tufted tail led the procession. The others, empty-bellied, frolicked jovially from behind. Some frolicked so much that they seemed to be dancing. By Jove, they're dancing! Gam said to himself. They're dancing!

"Stop pissing on the Cobra president!" one of the veterans of the democratic regime exclaimed, indignant. "He certainly enlightened us more than his predecessor, the Scholar. Now our streets are well-lit. Power shortages are rare ..."

"But we're still in the dark."

"And how did the Scholar manage to read anything at all if there was no electricity, since his minister was selling it off to neighboring countries?"

"He had his own inner light, of course."

"In any case, I wouldn't want to be the last person left to turn off the last light on my way out of this country."

"My God, what are you all complaining about? At home, we have pure air and water! What do the people want?"

"The city air makes me sick. As for water, if you have any in reserve in your bathtub, it's like having gold stored in a bank!"

"Ah, so that's what you think, is it? When they devalued our money, we experienced a real financial earthquake. Our savings melted away as quickly as the snow from Massis 5 inside a stove. We were barely left with crumbs! Crumbs, I tell you! This country can take anything away from you overnight."

"For example, the hike in food prices. Twenty drams 6 more, that's about 30%. They increase our pensions, but they also hike up the price of gas, electricity, and water. The result: we still end up being cheated."

"In our markets, people even older than us sell plastic bags just to survive. You have to wonder what President Cobra was doing during his mandate."

---

5   Another name for Mount Ararat.

6   The Armenian national currency *dram* is pronounced somewhere in between *tram* and *dram*.

"But we already told you what he was doing: he was playing basketball! And when he wasn't playing basketball, he was water skiing. Our Cobra loved speed. Unless it came to passing any needed reforms—then he took his time."

"So much so that we never saw any."

The line took up half the road and buried itself within the hilly solitude. To its right and out in front, a row of dilapidated electric poles. Some bent over onto the road, their heavy wires dangling. Here and there, the skeletal remains of an old billboard. And more and more papers and plastic bags, blue ones and white ones, attached to the embankment's red grass, announced that they were nearing the garbage dump. A large pipe which was meant to provide gas to far-away stagnant villages, ran alongside the road before disappearing into the hillside. It hugged the terrain and avoided obstacles by bending at right angles in one direction, then in the other, or upwards instead. Towards the far end of the land, smoke began to rise between the back of the hills and the sky.

Despite the effort required to descend the steep downward slope, the mourners walked as if they were celebrating. The duty to be sad melted away in the animation that flitted from one group to another before it came crashing down into the next of kin's dark zone just behind the van. Young women who had taken off their high heels to avoid twisting their ankles fanned themselves with their hats, much to the consternation of those who had worn doll hats. A few, who hadn't anticipated how steep the hill would be, panted inside their own fat as they held a dozing child in their arms. Some men had done away with their jackets and were undoing the knots on their ties. Kids were playing tag within the ranks. Apart from the garbage trucks that were beginning to multiply, police vans were circulating, closed like sardine cans. Cabs passed by, some as yellow as the dying grass that lay all around. A carload of tourists wound its way up the column and disappeared into the heights. This elicited a whole new round of commentary:

"What on earth is so incredible here that it would attract these insects?"

"They want to contemplate our beautiful mountain," suggested one of the bald men towards the back of the line.

"Or see for themselves how the model city of Nubarashen has become a mirror of our decay," answered his neighbor.

"It's all very interesting. Fascinating, really. When you consider that they're going to have to penetrate deep into Death Valley. The cemetery on one side and the garbage dump on the other." At that very moment, rising towards Nubarashen, a huge 4 by 4 with opaque windows passed them by. It was hard to imagine such a jewel in this moribund neighborhood. And Gam began to worry about seeing the head of the psychiatric hospital roaming around these parts at such an early hour.

3.

The sky glides by and my eyes remain shut. Are they dead, my eyes? Who can say?

Dead to you. But in my case, they still let me look up at the azure sky. Livelier than ever over Yerevan. Dreamier than it would have been inside my soul. Perhaps this is the last sky I will encounter before they cover me up for good and throw earth over my body. They'll throw it on me by fistfuls. All of them, one after the other. I'll hear it as it hits the wood. Even the children will join in. Their mothers will carry them, so they don't soil their shoes. They'll each have a stone in their little hands. Then they'll let it go. *Here you go, old lady, this is for you!* the spiteful ones will think as they complain about having dirtied their hands. Their friends will rain earth down onto my casket. *Aufwiedersehn*, loudmouth! they'll be thinking inside their heads. Not a single cloud, not one. Only the deep blue sky. I lose myself in it. No anxiety. On the day of my burial, the sky will have shone blue. From time to time, it rocks a bit when the road gets bumpy. On one side the hills rise. On the other, the last urban neighborhoods spread outward. Sometimes the electric poles pretend that they are going to collapse onto the van. Then they immediately straighten up again. And again, the light hits my skin. A light that blindly protects the land like a faithful dog. When I was alive, it was this same sky that made things bearable for me. Its gentleness and its strength, covering me. An infinity so discrete that a human being can't hear it anymore. Tourists come and go to see the beauty of this land. But they forget about the skies that cover it. The same one as on that fated day. I lay in the grass with Garen on a hill in Dilijan. Flowers everywhere. Not like the ones that are suffocating me now inside this box. Live ones, with insects and bees.

The springtime lived within each of us. It was a Garden of Eden, before I came back down to Earth again. I had to leave my parents then, so that I could become your mother, Gam. And now here you are trailing behind me in the last row at my burial. Why so far away? And why be such a stranger? Am I not the person who brought you into this world? You barely recognize me. We met on this road again purely by chance. As if your dead mother had come to get you. What kind of son ignores his mother, even in death? Since you disappeared on a whim one day, you never once made contact. You left to go live with other people, but you always stayed a part of me. And I lived all my days this way, in darkness. The garbage trucks climbing up to the dump go by so quickly. They let things fly into the sky like butterflies. First a breath holds them still. Then when the truck has gone by, they glide in the air. The heat that builds up on the road keeps them afloat. And little by little they disperse, as if by some invisible fancy. Pieces of paper dance in the vast daylight. One of them hangs above my head. An angel's feather. Sometimes, it seems to fly of its own volition. To one side, then to the other. A car goes by, and it gets blown farther astray. I lose sight of it. I desperately look for it, for this duvet that played with my eyes. But soon enough it finds me again. My gaze follows its path as a feeling of complete peacefulness settles within me. It's as if it were searching for me. It comes nearer. The corner of a sheet of newspaper, the daily *Zhamanak*. I only started to read it for your articles. A large brown grease stain covers the article's title. It falls onto me and sticks to my forehead. And now it blocks my view.

4.

(Celebration and mourning: the procession of the living stops in front of the cemetery. In between the third entrance and the garbage dump, some cars are barred from going down, others from going up. Garbage trucks, buses, a passenger car, a military van, a couple of taxis and the psychiatric hospital director's black four by four... Probably some type of obstruction blocking the road. But what could it be again? A crushed dog with its entrails exposed to the sky? A garbage truck that rolled over onto the walkway? Horror of horrors! The line of mourners is standing still. People wait, then take a few small steps, wait some more, then start to ask questions again and to complain. Some children scream, others run towards the front of the line like scouts, sliding in between people as they approach the mortuary van to see with their own eyes what or who is causing the traffic jam, and bring the news back to their parents. In the back of the line, the mourners concoct myriad explanations, grumble, and then throw out different hypotheses: they'd all like to know what is causing the dead woman to wait at her own burial.)

Young woman: "If I were the dead woman, I'd lodge a protest. It's a disgrace to block access to the cemetery to a citizen of our good country!"

Woman: "No kidding! What are they going to do, let her decompose inside her casket? The heat's already made the flowers dry and rot. It's disgusting. Where's the police? Never where it's supposed to be, that's where! But when they want to slide your money into their back pockets, they know where to find you. And what is the President doing, I wonder? I'm sure he's hanging out with his cronies at some international meetings.

Diplomacy, my foot. While we're stuck here in desperate straits. If the dead can't be buried correctly and on time, then the living have nothing to hope for anymore in this country."

Young mother: "Nothing whatsoever. If you can believe it, when I gave birth, it was the exact same thing. I got stuck in traffic. I mean the taxi did. And nothing could get us out of it. I had to squeeze something in, that desperately wanted to come out. I was weeping. Today, with the increase in the number of cars, women can't even get to the hospital on time to give birth. The more they're in a hurry on the inside, the more things slow down on the outside. You can't stop whimpering from pain. As for a woman in labor ready to burst, as was my case, she may as well just die in her seat. The slower we went, the more my cab driver would rant. He was terrified that my water would break and leak all over the place. He kept yelling: 'Let me thorough, will you, I've got a pregnant woman who is about to give birth all over my seats!' Talk about going into labor! I kept clenching my fists and teeth. I didn't want my child to become a cab driver when he grew up because he'd been born inside a taxi! I was dying from pain. I opened the windows, but the gas fumes made my stomach turn. My legs were spreading by themselves. *Hold it in, little lady!* the guy kept telling me. *We're almost there. I'm begging you. You're not going to leave me like this? What would my boss say? If he sees that the back seats are all bloody, he'll kill me on the spot. You go and try to find another job after that! I don't know why I ever picked you up.* He was honking and trying to sweet talk me at the same time. But instead of calming me down, he was making me more and more nervous. All my body could think of was how to make the pain go away. *Let me out! Let me out!* it kept saying. How could you not listen to this voice that kept asking to get out? I was in pain. And I had the impression that my child was playing the drums inside my stomach. *Why are you keeping me inside, sweet mother? It's time now, let's do it! Let me leak out into the world.* My stomach was boiling over like soup."

Women: "And then what happened? And then what?"

Young Woman: "And then what? I just let everything go. And my little Arshak was born inside a taxi. Arshak was the driver's name."

(Now the group up front also began to stir. A truck was blocking the entrance to the cemetery, facing the dump. All the drivers—trucks, buses, vans, taxis, the military jeep, and the head of the psychiatric hospital—had left their vehicles and were standing around trying to find a solution to their conundrum. They threw their arms in the air, frowned, and tapped the asphalt with their feet. Meanwhile, Anna tried to grab one the last piece of sky from behind the scrap of Zhamanak stuck to her forehead.)

Anna: "Enough already! I want this all to end! Someone remove this blasted piece of paper from my face already! It's blocking my view of the sky! That word *Zhamanak*[1]... That's all I can see at this point! But I have nothing to do with time anymore. So please, give me back my sky. Just a small piece of it. After that, who knows what's in store for my soul? Which Cassandra dropped this bloody piece of newspaper over my eyes? And those musicians who won't stop their annoying noise! You'd think that one of them would remove this bloody paper? What the hell are they all doing? What are they waiting around for? All these people rotting away at my funeral. Not to mention that it's already beginning to stink like decaying flesh around here. How long are my friends going to have to smell this vomit?"

(The people in the funeral procession began to crowd around the cars. They all tried to get a look at what was causing the traffic jam, but only a few of them could make anything out. Some stood on the tip of their toes. The chosen ones informed the blind that a naked man was laid out on the asphalt with his arms crossed. Dead or alive? No one could tell if the dying man belonged to this world or to the afterworld already. The children had wandered far away from the inner circle that had formed around the

---

1   Time.

body blocking the road. The women turned away and closed their eyes to avoid looking. Others, younger, stared at the black dot of a funeral. The dead woman was thinking inside her box, the newspaper still stuck to her forehead. The elderly or those who had arrived too late resigned themselves to commenting without having seen anything whatsoever.)

Bald man: "So now they won't let us into the cemetery? It's not like we're going to spend all day there. Even Jesus Christ wouldn't feed us here in the city's sewer, with corpses on one side, and a trash dump on the other."

Another man: "Depends. It might be serious. People are saying there was an accident. Some guy got run over at the crosswalk at the cemetery entrance by the sewer. No one will even touch him, he's so... Otherwise why would so many cars be stuck like that? And the trucks can't even dump their trash anymore."

Bald man: "It's more like we're the ones who can't unload anything anymore. What about the dead woman we have in this casket! We have to bury her eventually, don't we? But today there's no more respect for anything. Even dead people must wait around twiddling their thumbs. Like the guy who got run over, probably. None of this is a good thing. So long as they don't make our procession go by the garbage dump. Look at all those people who must make their way through the garbage dump and go back down the other side to find a way into the cemetery!"

Other man: "Plus there's the fact that they're burning their refuse. Walking through smoke. And what horrible smoke! It's so thick it gets stuck in your suit. That's not for me. They say that the dumpster guard lets his pigs loose there to eat. Ugh! Ugh! A thousand *ughs!*"

(By now, the trucks making their way back up the road to the city had formed a litany of distress. Their bellies full of leftovers from the feast and unable to find an opening on the other side, the drivers unloaded their cargoes to get as close as possible to the calamity itself. Gam, who

had stayed behind, recognized them as they went by. He identified each one according to the neighborhood they came from. Trash from Malatia-Sebastia or from Nork-Marash, Arabkir and Shengavit, from Zeitun, Davtashen, Avan and Kanaker. The only missing trash belonged to the rich, in the City Center. But also, the trash from Ashapnyak, and why not Khatcho's trash and Levonchik's?)

Malatia-Sebastia truck driver: "They say that a guy in a beard is laid out like a cross on the sidewalk. Let's have a look!"

Avan truck driver: "A bearded guy laid out like a cross? But what on earth can that possibly mean? Meanwhile our trash rots in place. It's our Dro, he's the one who's going to be furious. We're going to clog up the trash dump by unloading everything so close together. And he'll have to work double time with his digger to take care of everything that's being dumped together. Not to mention the fact that they still haven't picked up the trash today on some of the city's streets."

Arabkir truck driver: "And all this thanks to some guy who's carrying on like a madman."

Avan truck driver: "A madman or a prophet."

Shengavit truck driver: "Well if the guy's crazy, they should just lock him up once and for all! There's a loony bin for that in Nubarashen. And if he wants to play the prophet, let's lock him up inside the prison where they put all the politicians instead."

Malatia-Sebastia truck driver: "Our guys don't dare touch him. Only the police can. Our people just like to listen to prophets. People are craving something new—any two-bit huckster who comes around and pretends to have some type of divine inspiration satisfies them. He plays with your mind and before you know it, he's the savior of the nation! And if he claims that he's going to cleanse the temple of all its merchants, everyone believes him. People even forget that he's the person who put them there in the first place. And that's why some people produce trash and others consume it."

Avan truck driver: "Personally, I don't need any of that. I take care of the city's manure and that's all. Crap—the only authentic thing in this entire country. And here we are, stuck for good."

(Gam follows the current. Why not squeeze by to get to the trash dump? But what's the use if the trucks are all stuck at the entrance? For a while he lets himself get carried by the people who all lean towards the savior lying on the asphalt in the shape of a cross. Then his curiosity takes him in the direction of the dead woman instead. He removes his bonnet out from his meshog and pulls it over his head. Hides his eyes behind his black glasses. Is it really Anna, his mother? Sleeping in her flowered craft that flows by under the sky's blue ocean? Mother, is that really you in that box? Her face is hidden under a piece of newspaper. Fallen from the sky, this piece of Zhamanak. An old issue stained in grease. Gam pinches it carefully between his thumb and his index finger. A sigh rises within him. Anna.)

Gam: "My little mother. Sweet mother. So, this is how I had to see you, dead, asleep without any chance of waking up again? Truly dead. This is how I see you again, purely by chance as I walk down my path in life, while you are at the end of yours, where our sky turns dark. Your son let you die alone, your lost son, hiding God knows where, in some sordid hole. And for so many years he was like a hole inside you. And you became a living tomb before ever seeing your real tomb, so suddenly did he leave you. He left to forget himself somewhere. And now he returns, so dirty, stinking, and unshaven. He wanted to destroy his links to the past, his habits, his warmth at your side. Simply trying to survive. To survive as far away from you as possible, so that you wouldn't know how distressed he really was. He couldn't stand the city that encroached on him from all sides anymore. Your son couldn't stand it anymore, mother. They were looking for him, they wanted his skin, he'd gone too far.

People continued to babble endlessly about the man on the road, crying out *ahs* and *ohs* and *eys! Heys* and even *hmms* that fused together and whispered in every corner. Indignation, hysteria so fixated on the event at hand that Gam didn't risk being recognized by any of Anna's family. But behind his beard and hollowed out cheeks, a familiar face might easily make out his traits of yesteryear. People elbowed each other aside to view the performance. They stood in place looking at the scene, which says a lot about the craziness of the situation. Even the dogs who were able to push past a forest of legs in front of them attempted to sniff around, hoping to find some free meat before entering the main dump. But they seemed to be aware that the man lying on the ground was still alive and only fooling those around him by pretending to be six feet under. Were they the only ones to realize the truth? Could the people in the procession really not know? Listening to the whispers that traveled from one woman's ear to the next, one might have assumed that the man lying down still had some days ahead of him as his third leg stood up high and mighty in the morning air. The musicians seemed to have forgotten that they were meant to be playing in the dead woman's procession and clambered up onto the truck to get a bird's eye view. Meanwhile Anna continued to talk to herself inside her flowered window box, finally able to enjoy the sky once more.

A voice: "You'd think he'd cover himself up? Put a newspaper on top of himself, at least!"

Another voice: "Hide your thing at least, shame on you!"

Third voice: "But he's dead, can't you see?"

First voice: "What do you mean, *dead?* With an Eiffel Tower like his? His eyes may be closed, but he's sticking way up, down there! Hey look at that! Did you see him smile?"

Woman's voice: "If you tickle him, he'll wake up all of sudden, you'll see."

Man's voice: "Watch out for the dog! He could snatch his sausage! Push him over, I tell you, push him over!"

Another woman's voice: "What a place to croak, a few feet away from the cemetery."

Neighbor: "... and from the garbage dump. This guy knows what he's doing, I tell you."

A previous voice: "And when to do it! I'm beginning to doubt that we'll even be able to bury Anna today after all."

(Having arrived at the front of the line, Gam could finally make out the identity of the man lying on the ground, causing so much consternation. The intruder lying with his arms crossed, naked and pretending to be dead. And his piece that seemed in search of God knows what, continued to stand up straight like the Statue of Mother Armenia. Gam recognized him right away: Tsknors, the fisherman. The guy who was always talking in proverbs that no one else could understand. Always making himself seem more important than he was, solemnly dealing with the world around him. His head lay on top of his long hair. His body immaculate, but his hands greasy all over. He'd even slathered the inside of his arms with red jam, like blood. Suddenly Gam heard distant cries. He raised his eyes to the sky in time to see a seagull chasing a dove that had wandered into the garbage dump.)

Voice from the crowd (addressing Gam): "Do you know this guy? You must no doubt work at the dump with him, no? So, take him along with you, let's get it over with! There are people trying to work here. And others whom we'd like to bury, once and for all."

Gam: "Others?"

Another voice, the bus driver's, in fact: "He wants to discuss the dead woman, who's rotting in the sun."

A truck driver: "Hey it's Tsknors! Gam! I recognize him, it's Tsknors."

Gam: "You want me to pick him up or something? That's up to him. Who am I to touch even a single hair on his head?"

Someone from the procession: "If he's dead, let's throw him in a hole. There are enough on sale in the cemetery."

Roubo (the cemetery guard): "Whoa, not so fast! You don't just dig a hole like that in a cemetery! You must go through the cemetery's *orders* department. And throw some money over here as well, while you're at it!"

Random man: "But you can all see that he's still breathing. This guy's still alive. All you need to do is send him back to the city."

Policeman: "Yeah, except that he's capable of starting all over again. Better bury him right away. All we have to do is carry him back up to Nubarashen. We've got jail cells in our prisons for this type of guy."

Insane Asylum Director: "Well I agree, this guy isn't normal, that's for sure. He's probably lost it completely. But from there to throwing him in jail for disturbing the peace... Let's see. I mean, he's a man after all, right? He's our brother, right? Let me take him back to our place and that'll be that, okay? And anyway, we lost one of our patients this morning. Every time we take roll call, there's another guy missing. Just disappeared. This one will do until we find the other one again."

Two soldiers dressed for kitchen duty, stood ready to grab the delinquent. Suddenly Tsknors dodged their outstretched hands and with one mighty leap was off, as if his tail were on fire. Crazed beard and perfectly smooth body, like a newborn. He smiled at his would-be jailers, then tore a path across to the entrance of the dump under the carved lion's head underneath the city's name. The pebbles on the road took him by surprise and stung the soles of his feet all the way up the rest of his body as he danced around like a devil walking on fire.

Tsknors: "He who hasn't been born can't know death. He who hasn't suffered can't know his own heart. He who has known his own death can be born at his birth."

5.

*T*sknors was a real comedian. Gam couldn't be sure of anything when it came to him. Who knew if Tsknors hadn't been hit by a car and then pretended to be dead? Or if he hadn't visited the first few phases of the sweet hereafter while he lay on the ground and then come back to life, as people sometimes say has happened to them? He'd recognized him from his beard and long hair. There was no doubt about it. It was Tsknors from the garbage dump. But he seemed somehow transformed by the chaos that his "death" had created on the road and in people's minds. As if he'd left the shell of his former life as a trash picker on the asphalt to take on God knows which new form of bodily existence. Gam knew insignificant details about his life as well as major ones. For example, that to feed himself, he had begun life as a fisherman at Lake Karnouti, Lake Arpi and Lake Abaran. That he'd come to be known entirely by his nickname. But he also knew that he'd gone out fishing with his brother Sako, when Spitak-the-White had crumbled. The rock slides made orphans out of them. Since everything else in the region was destroyed, Tsknors turned to the garbage dump for salvation. He renamed it Marlboro Land. He worked there like a madman, resold iron, aluminum, or bottles and nourished himself from his finds. At least he was free. Unlike Sako who had to sell his voice to the priests in black and to the glory of God for a few crumbs. Tsknors was a lively young man, and well past his teenage years when Gam met him for the first time, had a sharp eye and a sly mind. When it was steaming hot out, he'd work bare-chested, sweating under the heat from the incinerators. Muscles on fire, and in the afterglow of the sun's rays, steel-colored skin. At times the golden light and the white steam made him look like a God with volcanic lips. According to Sako however, Tsknors hadn't always been a simple bag popper. "He worked for a while as a stone polisher. He cut stones into pieces using a mechanical lathe. While the city was tearing down its old buildings and erecting sky-high new ones, you might be asking yourselves why Tsknors wasn't at work on one of the construction sites? Simply because in this country where industry is the only way to make money, you can exploit the working man without mercy, while those who aren't well-connected or who don't have the right last names are simply disposable, naked—human trash."

So why did he leave Gyumri for the capital? That's a long story, as told by Sako, whose words slowly took on the drunken quality of legends: "At the time, our President the Cobra was making us believe one tall tale after another. Especially during TV appearances, as the Grand Commissioner of the Greatest of all Governments which only wanted the greatest of all things for our country. Until the day when one man rebelled against all his bragging: Khachadour Vahanian, also known as the Shield of the Holy Cross. At the time the latter headed a TV station in Gyumri called *Lola*. Was the name an homage to a beloved or to his trusty steed? No one knows. If Cobra said white, Holy Cross said black. And at the time, the Cobra's biggest enemy was his predecessor, the Scholar. If you'll remember, the two men had fought tooth and nail for the right to lord it over the common people. The Scholar had called on all his forces from Aleppo and the deserts of Syria, but the Cobra had all Kakabakh behind him. Their battles became so intense that they covered the country in a layer of dark dust. And their fights in front of the Parliament gates became so pitched that Mother Armenia ended up naked from their blows. Shown the door, the Scholar had to take underground tunnels to escape the country. Debased and vanquished, he returned to his studies. Centuries of dust still covered his old parchments. From then on the Cobra felt completely at liberty to attack his political enemies, just as powerfully as he did those that pressed against his country's borders. Even if this meant putting the good people through a grinder and machine gunning any well-intentioned savior to death. An ominous silence descended over the entire country. The people became resigned to the situation at hand, or else used their cunning to survive and gossiped only behind closed doors. But suddenly one day the Scholar started to throw bitter, poisonous darts at the Cobra in a fancy midtown hotel. And who could blame him for not being able to hold it in any longer, the Cobra conceded? Except that the Shield of the Holy Cross, that monster, reprinted the entire pamphlet! Cobra lost his cool and spat his own venom out at everyone. The President's henchmen backed down as the Cobra went crazy. His wife Bella—and God knows the smut that could come out of *that* woman's mouth—turned the lights off and went to lie down on the living room sofa, her face buried behind cushions. "That damn bookworm! Let him jack off all over his manuscripts!" Lola's only answer to the proceedings was to talk to Pasha Nikolian, the *wünderkind* editor of *Zhamanak* and the Scholar's golden boy, for his live analysis. Cobra had already started selling houses to homeless Spitak Earthquake victims that had been donated to the city by European charities. The Mayor of Gyumri however was wont to point out other pressing concerns—such as the city's children whose lungs were blackened by the soot from the plastic they used to heat themselves. And while Cobra was erecting his pyramids in the heart of the capital city, the Shield showed him people who spent the winter living off his false promises. In short, a battle emerged between Yerevan, the Capitalist Capital, and Gyumri, the shining diamond of truth. Until the day that Cobra, frothing at the mouth, sent his fiscal cavalry to the recalcitrant one before using Armenia's Kalashnikovs to machine gun his successor, the Samurai. Since Cobra couldn't hunt men in his country, he took off for Africa to shoot Lions. In the meantime, our Shield of the Holy Cross had been summoned to Yerevan. He had barely entered his office before the Gladiator of the National Audiovisual Commission threw his fiscal net at him and threatened him with his trident: "Either you calm down, or I'll bleed you to death!" Once they had let him go, the Shield returned home to Gyumri, thought things over, weighed his options, equivocated, slowed up, confronted him, and then, standing on top of a low wall at Town Hall Plaza announced: "The role of the media is to present all of the aspects of public life in an objective and diversified way." He might as well have aimed war cannons straight at Yerevan! The fiscal administration's big Gladiator calmly picked up the ashes that had fallen onto his accounting notebooks and then exploded! His helmet jumped up to the ceiling under a huge surge that erupted from his brain. Six days later agents from the IRS broke down the doors at Lola's: exams, accusations, payments. It was decided that the Shield owed 26, 458, 500 drams. To whom? Why? How? The verdict against the undeniably guilty is inarguably irreversible. Shield bent, but he didn't break. That's when he decided to address the people with the idea of a telethon: "They want your skin. They want to crush you. I have nothing. I don't have anything more than you do. So, donate and let's be free!" Tsknors understood what was at stake and duplicated himself like a madman from Sassoun. One day long ago, before the great earthquake and the outbreak of War, all the way the back to the debates around independence, his father had told him: "After I am gone, never forget to combat injustice." Tsknors thought that he had raised enough money for his defense. His glibness convinced tens of thousands of families to donate, from everywhere around the world. One American guy even sent in 10, 000 dollars. The last donor was an old lady named Yerdjanik Yerdjanikian: "In the end, Tsknors told me, it's people like Yerdjanik that the Samurai is trying to destroy." But the Samurai fought back with a campaign of harassment that involved every type of administrative trickery imaginable.

The mayor took back the TV Tower from Lola. Without a tower, no TV station. The Shield found another place to build a tower, but local metalworkers wouldn't sell him any iron. No tower, no... On his end of things, Tsknors redoubled his efforts, found the iron that he needed and soon built a new tower. Tsknors took advantage of his new position as a TV personality to attack the Mayor's Office: "He who doesn't get spit on, does he deserve to be swallowed up?" "Tall as a giant, dumb as a mouse." The point is that this mayor had always ignored our demands for better housing. But one day, some random guy hung a tire from the tower. People got all emotional. A month later the tower caught fire and burned to the ground. The police stopped looking into things in mid-investigation. In the meantime, the Shield, who was a chemist by profession, had rebuilt a soap factory. If he sold the factory, he could relaunch *Lola,* but he couldn't find a single buyer. The authorities had ruined his sale, so Shield gave up. At this point Tsknors, who was being hunted down by the mayor's henchmen, went into hiding in the trash dump. We were camping out at the time not far away in an abandoned factory. One winter night, dogs started to bark. We ended up wandering around the sad, cold, endless countryside, frozen to the bone. That same day, Tsknors got on the bus for Yerevan. The priest of the Church of the Holy Sign let me sleep within the church walls. But soon thereafter I also left for Yerevan. And just as he told me I would, I found my good old Tsknors at the Nubarashen trash dump."

6.

*O*nce Tsknors was gone, the muddled mess of arguments and protests continued. Several camps opposed each other: those on their way up, those on their way down; those who sided with the cemetery and those who favored the trash dump. Crowds, cars, taxis, delivery vans, buses, trucks, dump trucks and hearses formed one large jumble of metal and flesh: "Get out of the way so I can squeeze in, you *bôzi lakot!*"[1]

"You're the son of a bitch! Can't you see that there's nowhere to get by on this road? Who taught you how to drive, your donkey or what?"

"Which way is the goddamn cemetery?"

"Over here! Over here!" The dump trucks and the buses crisscrossed each other in front of the collision. People stood side by side, shoulder to shoulder, or almost.

"Stop shoving already!" A woman from the procession who was probably being felt up gave the evil eye to a man who couldn't stop pushing up against her backside.

He raised his arms up immediately to proclaim his innocence: "Little lady. None of this is my fault. They keep pushing my ass forward."

Children were screaming: "Mommy!"

And the mothers were screaming their runts' names out: "Abo!" "Maro!" Wives were calling out to their husbands and husbands were searching for their wives. And behind the bus windows, the crazed faces floated above the heads of those who were turning every which way to find an exit. But neither Tsknors nor

---

1   Son of a bitch.

the dogs had taken the wrong direction. The smell of the place remained permanently in their bones, while the odor of burning rot was getting to them as well. Their nerves frayed. Some women in the procession had fallen in step behind them. Their eyes fixed on Tsknors' ass cheeks, which he moved around despite himself as he jumped around on the parking lot stones.

One of them said, astonished, "What on God's Earth is happening to me?"

"My stomach's on fire."

"What's wrong with you? Look up at the sky instead of staring at her *vôri,*"[2] a neighbor replied, as she released a series of petulant *eehs!* and *ahs!*

"Nah, I think that I ate too many apricots yesterday! I like them when they're ripe and this is the result!"

"Ripe, everyone likes apricots when they're ripe! Myself, I like them when the slit is perfectly formed and it's almost split open. And it's calling to my tongue. Ah, Madame, slits when they are just barely open!" And the angry guffaws started again! Another group of women was having a hard time on the Nubarashen slope.

"But where the hell are you going like that?" one of the truck drivers screamed at them. "To hang out with the crazies?"

"No, to see the dead. We're looking for the entrance to the cemetery, answered one of the lost ones."

"The cemetery? You just passed it! Just walk down a few meters. The entrance will be on your right. The guard's name is Roubo. You can't miss him, his head's a bit beaten up. But have no fear, he's no devil."

"Let's hurry up," said one of the women, "otherwise we're going to miss the burial." Gam was losing his wits as well. The general confusion was making him dizzy. And supposing it wasn't his mother in the casket? He hadn't seen her in so long.

He'd probably made a mistake, substituting her face for the last picture he'd seen of Anna. A picture from before he'd become a self-imposed recluse. Gam

---

2 Little ass.

didn't know that the day he disappeared, Anna's body became covered with red rashes and then dead skin, though her face was left intact. Her legs would itch so much at night that she would leave them exposed in the sun during the day—doctor's orders. Gam had gone so far away, and in leaving her, had abandoned her to this hole that she was creating as she scratched away at her skin. There was no address to give her, as no one knew where he was hiding out. Then as the days dragged on, the desire to return abandoned him. As if in a moment of weakness, he was afraid of abandoning his need to erase himself. The hours that followed were ones of deaf agony for Anna. Gam realized then that he'd left her no way of getting in touch with him. None of his friends who knew her had been informed of his hideout. He'd eliminated all the trails behind him and padlocked any exits. And now here she was again on his path. His mother had come to join him in a flowered casket, floating under an immobile sky, amid the most beautiful weather, on her last day on Earth. His mother, if it was indeed her, the woman who had brought him into this world.

"Who's the woman being buried?" Gam asked a man who hadn't shaved in three days as a sign of mourning.

"Anna Ananian, Garen's wife. But he was taken by the Earthquake."

"Are you sure?"

"And how! Of course, I'm sure," the man answered. "We were neighbors. Towards the end when she was weak, I was the one who went to the market for her."

"She had no one?"

"Yes, she had a son named Gam. But he disappeared out of the blue one day without leaving any trace behind him. That's what really got to her. She barely spoke about it. But I could feel that was the reason. His absence. She'd made it into an almost mute obsession if I may put it that way. You know how our mothers are here. Children, especially their sons, give them their life force. Well, that was certainly Anna's case. And by leaving her, it's as if he abandoned her to be devoured from within. I understand that if children leave, it's usually against their will. This country is built to make them leave."

Gam froze on the spot, unable to process the confusion that he was feeling. Suddenly things began to spin in front of his eyes, in an upward spiral, pulsing to the rhythm of his heartbeat, ever upward. Once, twice, three times. Without stopping, starting over again, taking on its monstrous forms, trailing behind, pulled apart, others falling one on top of one another accompanied by horrific cries and zooming sounds: *Mnnnnn, womennnnn, coituuures, vorbillaaard, garrbugtruckkkss, vannnsss, bbbbusbusbus.* The bearded man grabbed him by the arm.

"You're about to pass out. You, come over here."

He dragged him towards Roubo. The guardian was directing traffic with his arms as if he were attracting customers to the county fair:

"Come this way my friends! The cemetery's right over here! Come this way, my loves!" They sat Gam on the stool that Roubo had abandoned, with his back against the cemetery railing. Roubo turned around with an evil look in his eye. He'd recognized Gam: "Let him rest up a bit," the bearded man suggested. "Let him get his strength back. Let him get his strength back before he returns to his smoking, stinking garbage dump!"

At that very moment the hearse got stuck at the entrance. Hence the dead woman passed right underneath Gam's gaze for a second time. And this time Gam saw her, the way she was ascending into heaven, with the face of a woman who's struggled and given up, after a thousand and one heartaches.

"Are you sick, my son?"

Gam slowly stood up and approached the van. And under the piece of *Zhamanak* newspaper that covered the part of her face on the side opposite him, he could see her almost entirely, surrounded by irises, gladioli, and daisies.

7.

You're in pain. Everything inside you is jumbled, but that's just the beginning. You take your regular path for the day and on your way to work run into your own mother's funeral procession, though you can't even be sure that it's your mother. You follow endlessly behind the procession and the more you walk the more you learn that it is in fact your mother that they are taking to be buried. But your body refuses to believe it. And my body sees you. My body which you saved by living inside of it, like the doctor recommended. It carried you within and you made a hole in it and then you ran away. And now it sees you. You came closer to the coffin to make sure that it was really me. My face isn't the same as the day you ran away when I was alive, still living. Alive yes but before its very eyes, your life quickly came to an end. And now here we are together again. Your head hurts, I know it does, even if I can't feel pain anymore. And I'm here, and you're here, and we're walking one behind the other. I'm headed towards a place I already know, and you towards the great unknown. And yet I'm your Anna, even though I'm no longer of this world. I remember my fingers playing Komitas[3] along with yours on our piano at home, that fated *Krasny Oktyobr!* Capricious and stubborn that piece, but your father preferred it to the Czech composer Petrov, it was more docile. But one day your fingers gave in. They suddenly felt frozen and lacked the joyful ease of your adolescent days. They had hardened, like the world around them. And instead of dancing over the keys, they hammered down on them. You weren't in sync with the music anymore. No, you weren't with us anymore. Like the day when your body separated itself from your dad's when he took you to the parade in his medal-covered vest. Those

---

3   Famous priest, composer and musicologist.

endless decorations which he insisted on sewing on himself, to make sure they would line up in a perfect row on his chest. Not a single thread was allowed to stick out. He handled his scissors as if he were mowing a lawn. And since he limped, the medals clinked every time he took a deep breath. He squeezed your hand tightly and you would leave together, on fine Sunday mornings in the October sun, off to Liberation Square. Years later, something hardened inside you. And now you don't even recognize your own Anna. Do you remember your grandmother, Djohar, Garen's mother? Frail and black in her everyday clothes, she went about her daily chores as slow as a sloth. She would take any opportunity she could find to feed you from your baby bottle or to nestle your little baby's body in her arms and rock you back and forth. God knows if she wasn't trying to fill some hole in her own life story. Her story from *over there*, from the other side of the border, from where she had been chased. Your eyes almost closed, her mouth would start to sing a few words, always the same dark tunes, composed of all those bloody scenes that were lodged inside her head. *Lala, lala*, she would sing, *to grow, drink your milk. Lala, lala, my child who died in my arms. Lala, lala, I left you in the woods. The wolves took you, they let me be. I walked, I walked. Lala, lala. The path grew long without you. Other mothers held you in their arms. Their milk didn't flow. Lala lala. Whoever didn't experience it won't understand how I lost my child in my own arms. They ripped stomachs open. They threw children again the rocks. Whoever didn't experience it can't understand. Lala, Lala drink up your milk so you can grow strong. I saw death drink up our life.* Moaning that eventually put you to sleep, but which made bloody tears fall within you, a black blood that flows within your veins. Djohar refused to let go of you. She would put on her wicked witch look, so different from her usual air, ready to claw at anyone who came close to her, even myself or Garen. There was no way to keep her death-filled lullabies away from you. Her memories were eating away at her body. Until the day when she fell forever into the void. She became a rag and then suddenly died. You were already a young man when the catastrophe arrived. Remember the catastrophe. Stones rained down on us from on high. How could we save ourselves? We were caught like drowned rats.

That's probably the same day that your habit of scratching at things was born, of staring at the stones, of boring a hole into anything that suffocated you. The country was coming apart at the seams. Until then, everyone thought that the country was solid enough, but it had started to rot long ago. The ground opened beneath, and our roofs fell in on top of us. Suddenly the worms started to dance, crazed. Have you ever seen worms dance? They look like they're kissing and embracing while they move around, demented. I was in the kitchen. The table was already set. You were walking down the street to meet your friend Garnik, to lend him your Dante book. Suddenly a shock wave hit the ground. The earth cracked and then split open. Shaken, it lurched from side to side. Everything crumbled and remained on the ground. What crime had our homes committed that they should be tortured in such a way? The walls groaned and ripped open. The earth rumbled. Things began to collapse one after another. You fell to your knees. You had no idea whom to pray to so that it would end. The snow was blanketed with dust. Your head, your head... you grabbed it between the palms of your hands to close off your ears from the outside noise. Not far from you lay Saint Savior Church. Something collapsed and suddenly it was cut in two. A house bent in two, while others collapsed. A second tremor hit, and cracks appeared in all directions. The more modest homes were swept away all at once. A moment later, you had the impression that someone behind you was calling your name. A fallen man seemed to be lifting his arms towards you, only to suddenly disappear brutally when another wall collapsed on top of him. A woman ran down the street, her hand stuck to her forehead. People rushed behind her, terrified. "Everything is ruined," one of them shouted. "Everything is ruined!" Life suddenly returned to your body, but you were seized with terror. You began to run, to sprint towards your home. People were walking back and forth on top of piles of wood and stone. They were screaming names out at the top of their lungs, peering into openings. You recognized the façade of our house. The roof had fallen in and you could see the crumbled ceiling through the living room and kitchen windows. Desperate, you screamed out "Mother! Mother!" A few minutes before the first tremor, your father was putting on his coat while you were going out the door. But he'd stopped to get his hat before going out to buy some matchsticks. And now before your very eyes—the crushed carcass of our *Krasny Oktyobr*. You thought I had also fallen victim. You cried out again: "Mother! Mother!" No noise. No human sound. Pieces of wooden beams blocked your passage. You began to push them aside, in the hopes of reaching the living room and kitchen. You asked for help, but the passers-by, too zoned out by the collapse, didn't hear you. In the distance, cries pierced the silence and cold attacked the city, beneath a sky as blue as today's. Every piece of wood or sheet metal, every stone that you were able to remove made the rubble sink more into the ground. You tired of repeating the same gesture over and over again. The rooftop snow had cracked, scraps still hung intact from planks, while others folded or turned to dust. You called out to your Anna, begging her to say something, to make the faintest move so that she could guide your movements. Which pit had she fallen into? And in what state of fright? As if suddenly her home had betrayed her. You pushed aside plaster and pieces of roofing and iron with your bare hands. The world itself seemed heavy, and everything around you appeared to have been crushed. And your Anna underneath, engulfed in a pile of bad luck, didn't have the strength to appeal to the light, to move back up to the light that had been stolen from her. At the first crackling sounds, I dove under the table. Nothing could make that oak table give way. Then beams collapsed on top of the first piles of rubble. The table held sway. In the living room, our *Krasny Oktyobr* let out a deep moan. The echo from his cry reached your unconscious Anna in the most far-off lost depths of her soul. I came back to life surrounded by black and the smell of the demolitions, surviving on the small pocket of air that that the safe place I had found offered me. Life outside remained silent, closed in on all sides. Some rubble had slid into the refuge, while the dresser that had fallen nearby kept out the rest of the debris. I hit the oak with a brick. But the sounds I heard were muffled on the inside. I started to scratch my way out. And soon an airway opened. I clawed some more, and the hole grew larger, letting in the cold and your cries. You tore away pieces of planks and dug randomly through the piles of stones. You got rid of obstacles in front of you. And now you heard.

The thumping on the oak wood. It resonated within you and grabbed your heart. You strained your ear. Suddenly a fire truck siren invaded the city and crowded out the noise coming from the rubble. You were compelled to start rummaging again. The stones slid into the cracks, but the gaps became larger by the minute. You called through one of the ruins for your mother, who had fallen into a state of numb drowsiness. The stinking blackness played with her senses. She had to make a concerted effort to strike the wood repeatedly, once, and then twice more against the table leg. This time, the sound made its way upwards. Soon the top corner of the dresser appeared, its dark lacquer instantly recognizable. Worm-eaten wooden planks broke apart in your hands. This is what we lived in, one of those Gyumri residences that made people look up when they walked by. Beautiful, sturdy, indifferent to the country's problems. But an illness had been developing within its body for a long time now. An intimate lie that was eating at it from the inside and finally conquered it. You stuck your hand inside one of the gaps, extended your arm, and searched as far down as you could into the unknown, the skin on your hands searching out your mother's. Finally, the moment arrived when the silk from her hair touched your fingertips. You pulled on a mesh hard enough to finally wake her up. Your mother, bent under the table, turned around, grabbed your hand, and kissed it. She told you that she would wait for you for as long as it took. And I waited, I waited for you. Until the moment when you lifted me out of my hole with the help of others. You carried me out onto the sidewalk. You wrapped me in a blanket and sat me down on a chair that a neighbor brought out. I looked around. Private belongings stuck out haphazardly from furniture. People walked around dumbfounded like zombies, their arms extended in front of their bodies, wrists bent, wobbling from side to side without knowing which way to turn or look. Suddenly I yelled: "Where is Garen? Where is Garen? I don't see Garen!" You suddenly found yourself reflected in the image of the man who had cried out behind you. And what if it had been him that the wall had taken down as its crumbled? I couldn't recall the dry cracking sound that the door made when your father closed it behind him. Was he still in the house when everything started to collapse? You didn't know where to look anymore, in the street or under the wall or in the pile of stones where the two rooms met. It was impossible to share you, for you to be in two places at once. And then you threw yourself onto our rubble, ripping it apart at will with your bare hands, and stopping every now and then to listen and start anew. You dug, driven crazy perhaps by the idea that your father was squirming in pain right there in the very same spot where you'd seen him disappear when the wall collapsed. I could see your tears, the foam at the corners of your mouth, I heard you calling after your father as he limped away in the street wearing his jacket with all the military decorations. And I saw you vomit on top of the remains of this sturdy, beautiful house which had been unable to resist the ground's swaying. There were only a few diggers, and they were so busy in the school district, that they never reached our neighborhood. The only ones to appear came later, to sweep the debris from the middle of the roads. They never uncovered anything that even resembled your father. Decorated or not, he'd probably been swept away with the rubble. The guy driving the digger must have scratched open the concrete, filled his truck and peacefully carried him away on his way home. No one ever touched the rubble of our house. The day came when I asked you to stop searching for him. Garen had probably found his grave all by himself as if he knew that the afterworld wouldn't belong to him. But he was still your father, the decorated gimp whose disability nasty children made fun of and unconsciously pushed you to imitate. And this time, you were the one who felt as if you were abandoning him to the Earth's ruins, like your Anna demanded of you. But this thing of digging towards him would never end. Your Anna was wrong that day in thinking that a new page had been turned. I remember the road from Gyumri to Yerevan, the death and the ruins that remained behind us. A winter without Christmas. Broken stones dotted the countryside. The bus was heavy due to the rocks that had been emptied left and right. Not a single tree remained. Only stretches of grass. God knows—whoever had created the world had bequeathed all these stones. A country that looked like a dump in every direction. Acres of land, all unfarmable. After the urban devastation, the desolation of a road that we took without knowing what sort of new collapse awaited us. But despite its harsh quality, the capital was still charming and held our interest. What did we save from all our debris? Some books, some family photos, and those two portraits that you took before leaving me: Stalin and Jesus Christ. Stalin to remind you of your father and that world which engulfed him. Him and his medals. Was he the right man for me? I can't even remember if I ever loved him. My parents picked him out for me, according to tradition. We don't like to keep girls around too long, where we come from. And they didn't like the racy crowd that I was spending my time with. Garen extinguished me all at once. People thought that he had a future within the state apparatus. The man limped over to me. I always kept this picture of a puppet in my mind. Loved him, no. But we went forward together honestly. And he never forbade me from reading the Bible to you. He hoped that school would kill God within you, without him ever having to intervene. And that's why you left with those two portraits in your arms. These flowers, all these flowers... I can smell the white, yellow, and mauve ones. But I can also smell the stench that the dump is blowing towards us. A grey stench that eats away at the cemetery air. It's beyond me how you can do that, work with all that garbage. One wonders what on Earth you could possibly be looking for. Unless you picked the dump to hide out there. Who is chasing you down? Have you broken the law? How can anyone run away from their own mother to take refuge in that cesspool? And every day you came here amidst the smoke to dig and tear open plastic bags. I wonder if I had known, would I have had the courage to come rip you away from the oily grasp of all this decomposing matter? This black air is so heavy and becoming heavier and heavier. Who knows if I will still smell it once I'm deep inside my pit. Leave me my flowers, let their perfume surround me! Let me disappear inside them! Let me be invisible! Look at the children. They're holding their noses. The adults are content to make faces. You'd think that I were the source of this stench. Your mother...

8.

Today from the huh-eights of the mother verb
A glorious huh-imn resonates in the spirit of a glorious u-nion
Immaculate mother, tell you-our only son to intercede
And give succou-our to the oppressed
We the hungry glorify you knee-eeling from the de-ehpths
Isaiyah-ah annou-ounced you as the recepta-acle
Of mankind's unshaka-able fai-yaith

Wearing a cone-shaped hat, wrapped in a carbon-colored silk cassock, and sporting an immaculately groomed coffee-colored beard, the priest baritoned a *sharakan*[4] into the air. Rigid as a bronze statue within his religion, he kept his book of sacred recipes open with one hand, while holding the other aloft in the air at the same height, his pinky raised and ringed in gold, weighed down by an enormous ruby that flickered on and off in the changing sunlight.

The box of flowers had been laid on the ground next to the pit where it was to be lowered. Gam had no doubts anymore. At present it was certain that Anna was the box's resident. As he had crept up to her side, between door and tomb, the visible part of her face had spoken to him. About the house in Gyumri, beautiful and fragile, about Garen and his medals, about the earthquake, about the destruction in general, about his obsessive need to dig things up. But now that Anna had disappeared under her flowers, the piece of *Zhamanak* that covered the side of her face remained, as no one dared to remove it. And what if this brought bad luck? The newspaper article's title blazed triumphantly amidst the

---

4   Melodic liturgical chant that buzzes around the vowel "ou."

irises, gladioli, and the large daisies. With the lightness of a feather, he brushed up against the outer skin of an organic flow.

As the priest psalmodied into the air *We the hu-uhngry glo-o-orify you, kneeling from the dai-ais,* he looked over at his acolyte, a young novice with pink cheeks and peach fuzz. This was the signal for him to push a gold-plated tray in the dark among the overburdened, the thirsty, and the prostrated. He was a great singer of psalms that priest, using a tome of secular traditions and wearing his sorcerer's cone as he watched the uninvited Gam from the corner of his eye, whose clothing, gate, and smell seemed to collide with the seriousness of the moment at hand. And while he made cavernous sounds with his voice, he wondered what links this nobody with a *meshog* slung over his shoulder who did God-knows-what-vile-job for a living, might have with the defunct. *Isaiyah-ah* what a bizarre disgusting guy he was—and suppose he were a spy? *—like a recepta-acle-* well-dressed, perfumed, who knows?

Yes, he found this man who had come from God-knows-where and God-knows-how, rather strange. Gam didn't shed a single tear. Closed like a stone column, he was content to simply be there, a body among others, both dead and alive.

Others besides the priest were interested in Gam, including a few busybodies who would have grilled him alive: "You wouldn't by any chance be? It's just that you look so much like... But it's been so long. Your memory always plays tricks on you."

And Gam remained stuck in place, mute, his eyes fixed on Anna. *Immaculate mother. Immaculate mother.* He felt that the priest would also like to interrogate him and to find out if he was related to the dead woman.

The moment came to screw on the lid. Two men who worked at the cemetery, dressed like a bunch of ragamuffins, just recently emerged from the straw matting, with sunken cheeks and a depressed look on their faces, started to pinch the stems of the flowers with their large fingers, delicate as fairies. Anna looked beautiful, asleep in the blue dress that she usually wore in the summertime. Gam would later hear that she had asked to be buried in this dress. The wooden cover made a somber noise and fell exactly into place. Once Anna was gone, all that remained was an image of those that she had spent time with. The screws were inserted in place and turned. Then two men who were meant to descend into the hole with the coffin grabbed the ropes incorrectly and the coffin swayed back and forth as if it were a rowboat on choppy waters. The rascals! They were letting go of the dead woman in the same way as a garbage truck dumped its trash. The indignant crowd *ooed* and *ahhed*. Gam refrained from complaining. The coffin had turned onto its side. He imagined Anna's body being thrown from left to right, as if someone had turned over her chaise lounge onto the sand at the beach while she was taking in the sun. Her nose was crushed against the coffin wall, her hands disjointed, her legs piled one on top of the other. The two men started to lose their cool, each one accusing the other: *"Kunem Meret!"*[5] The other workman, with a confused look in his eyes and limp hands, mumbled some excuses as he searched for the ropes. He was finally able to grab them, but instead of lifting them straight up, caught by the weight of the coffin, he tripped and fell into the pit. The people standing around the pit moved in to see what happens to a live man who falls into a tomb that he wasn't destined for: "Tiko!" the unlucky man screamed. "Get me out of here! I'm not dead, okay Tiko?"

"Well, of course you're not dead, *dm'bo!*"[6] A ladder was hurriedly lowered into the pit. The workman had barely emerged from it when Gam placed his *meshog* on the ground and took the incompetent's place. His hands tightened around the ropes that were wrapped around the coffin, and that's how Anna was lowered into the ground, with all the solemnity required of the occasion, although no one knew whether her body had recovered its original place, so that she could sleep peacefully for the rest of eternity. Every fistful of earth that was thrown onto the coffin crashed noisily against the wood. Gam, having remained by himself, waited for the two men to fill up the hole. With what was left over they formed a small mound on which they lay the irises, gladioli, and daisies.

---

5   Fuck your mother.

6   *Idiot, imbecile.* (Pronounced dem'bo, making the consonants vibrate like the skin on a drum.

It was over.

Anna was now resting among the tombs, between two other dead people. Names which they recognized too well, given the bad luck that they had encountered: Levon Loulian on one side, and Slavik Djiloyan on the other.

Under Levon Loulian's name, the following words were engraved in gold capital letters:

AN INNOCENT CITIZEN DEAD

AT THE HANDS

OF HIS OWN COUNTRY

Yes, Gam understood why it said *dead at the hands of his own country*. Slavik Djiloyan known as *Djilo* (1940-1975), engraved on a white marble square. Gam recited these words to himself:

> *We were kissing*
> *So hard*
> *That the law finally took notice*
> *The men got together*
> *Outside*
> *Their four walls*
> *Kissing wasn't allowed*
> *That's why they dragged our kiss*
> *To court*

He wondered who could have been responsible for erecting a stone phallus whose tip had been worn out in some secret ceremony, in front of this plaque.

You're in good company, mother, he thought.

And instead of returning to the garbage dump he climbed to the cemetery heights.

9.

G am reached the last tombs. The poorest and the most naked. On a black slab, the first and last names of the defunct, their birth date and when they died. That was all. Leftover flowers that mixed their dry redness with the ocher tint of the earth stacked into piles. Beyond these tombs, the hill's smooth flank. *Why did I climb all the way up here?* Gam asked himself. From these heights, he could see the entire cemetery below him, to his left the garbage dump and far in front of him, the City. The sky was shining bright and cast its blue everywhere. In the air devoured by fire, things began to vibrate as if caught in small quakes. And what if this anxiety came from within me, he thought? The people who had accompanied his mother were grouped in front of the entrance, waiting for cars and buses. His mother. Lost forever. So now he found himself forever without his mother. Alive, she unknowingly supported him, especially in these times when they were no longer together. Just the thought that she was alive somewhere in the world was enough to keep hope alive within him. What was it that he hoped for still? What was the difference! Now he narrowed his view on the city. He dug into it with his eyes, with such intensity that he couldn't make anything out precisely, only walls that seemed to rise like funerary stellae. The city trembled, throbbed, and burned without consuming itself. The cross on top of the cone-shaped roof of Saint Illuminator's church emerged from the inferno that the city's sounds created. Soon, they multiplied and transformed themselves into a thousand crosses standing up all over the city. And the green masses from the gardens panicked, swarmed in dark clouds, and crawled into the tiniest streets and recesses, their hands searching out prey, puncturing remains and setting free noxious gases. As if instead of receiving its usual shit, the dump itself had spread all over the city and taken hold of it, redistributing its vomit, scrap iron, greasy trash, its inhuman paperwork and crumpled up newspapers, its signed and countersigned police reports, its used toilet paper, its unrefined oils, heavy grease, cement, rust, and stained earth... so that it would become congested with all these things and drown in them.

Gam felt the pain which prevented his eyes from recognizing the exact details of the panorama that appeared before him. But he didn't try to take his focus off it, as he did when menacing visions filled his spirit simply by forcing him to concentrate on a more everyday, prosaic reality. He let this distraction deform the landscape before him into a monstrosity that appeared suddenly from within its own mystery.

The tombs rose towards him. Before, he had seen the cemetery like a cloth that covered his part of the valley and the hillside in a relatively simple geometric pattern. Now the low walls and upright stones jutted out at angles and reduced the distances separated them like a wedding train billowing long folds behind it. The black headstones pushed upwards. At the same time, the dead appeared in engraved portraits against black marble slabs. The faces intensified and covered the city. But wasn't the city creeping up here? The city from before, with all its human history discharged here as little by little it reached part of the lost sky? And now time, once so clearly delineated, became unclear. No more boundary existed between the urban space and the necropolis. Mortuary stellae as tall as skyscrapers. As if blood and skin, life and death, were intertwined. As if death lived within men's souls. An anxious death, whose energy lived within the very fibers of their souls.

A man chasing his dream, Gam! What a mess! This aberration that devours shapes came from within me. I'm like a witch whose eyes make the mold sing. What's this knowledge that blurs all lines? And these black headstones as tall as buildings? How to heal from this mess?

But now the cemetery crossed the road. It spread toxic waves onto the dump area. And the dump's smoke mixed in with the sight of arms reaching into the chaos and getting lost beyond what the eye can see, into burning or decomposing waste. Pig cadavers, dogs, swallows, insects, and rats lay among the cartons, glass and plastic bottles, packaging of all sorts, clothing, and scrap metal. And soon, endless numbers of zombies, dried out by their unquenchable thirst, a century of vomitoria, and the smoke created by flesh that was burned, one after another. And ash, light and warm, that filled and darkened the air: a terrifying silence.

This is how things grew under Gam's watch. Everything appeared bewitched. The landscape, hollowed out, shaken up and walled in by men and subjected to constant activity, had become a wild swallower of souls. His own soul was not exempt from this unquenchable hunger. Despite the fact that the City had been separated from the cemetery and the garbage dump from the cemetery and the City from the garbage dump, they all melded together in Gam's eyes. Rot existed within the City, while life existed inside the cemetery and energy within the garbage dump. It carried and swept everything along its path leaving behind traces, which Gam pumped and suppressed within his own heart. A permanent flow which drowned all boundaries and blurred the world for the men who had to move along gypsy-like from one spot to another to sort, bury and survive.

God help me escape from this nightmare! Gam thought. Let him save us from the days when the City, the dump and the cemetery were all located in the same place. Millions of men parked in place, their consciousness reduced to the state of trash, bogged down in a mixture of hatred and mud, permanently hungry, and constantly targeted. An untold number of deaths.

Gam turned back and took the road that led to the entrance. All he needed to do then was cross the road to penetrate the garbage dump's main area. A dump truck, overflowing with filth, hurried along as it swayed in the dust. It would soon disappear behind a mass of red clay and roll onto the plateau of trash before emptying its cargo. All one could make out were streams of grey smoke that fell apart as they rose into the air. In the distance the great cliff rose and closed off the garbage dump to the south. To the east, the winged crest of Mount Ararat emerged. And Roubo the guardian, sitting with his back against a pillar, was still smoking one of those cigarettes that his fat fingers had trouble rolling.

10.

Roubo:

> *"I like your softness, oh pure Diamond,*
> *Take my darkest smoke*
> *Devour my trash with your flames*
> *Place your sun in my bones ...*

Hey there Gam, you who have just lost someone I assume was dear to you, take pity on your brothers and sisters who slumber beneath. And since you're meeting with your boss Dro, tell him that he can keep his smoke to himself. He's poisoning my domain. Vade retro, toxic Dro.

> *A thousand ills surround me*
> *My mouth is sour and my body incurable*

Tell Dro what I just said, otherwise I'll send my army of zombies to march on him. One night, I'll make them cross the road and enter his room and then creep through his nostrils into that son *ishi kourak's*[7] brain while he snores."

Gam: "You shouldn't blame Dro. Blame whoever placed the cemetery and the garbage dump next to each other, rather. The minute any north wind appears, you get completely poisoned. But think of us! We suffer those fumes on a permanent basis. You never get used to the smell of rotting trash, trust me."

Roubo sucked on his cigarette like a baby feeding from his mother's nipple, eyes half-closed. He chewed on the smoke, his face hollow from missing teeth

---

7   Son of a donkey.

and the remaining ones covered in nicotine. This morning, as usual he was unshaven, so that his hair formed a continuous mass down his neck and onto his chest, while more hair exploded from his ears like neglected weeds and others protruded from his nostrils, his uni brow prominent as well, the whole growing like some wild vegetation.

Roubo: "Well I, Roubik, am the cemetery guard. Okay. And who exactly am I guarding this cemetery from, might I ask? Well, obviously from people who have something against our dead. Those people who stop them from breathing properly, like your friend Dro. Closing an entrance gate isn't all that it's cracked up to be. I can stop the living from entering, but I can't stop the dead from passing through its walls."

He stood up and placed his hand on Gam's shoulder.

Roubo: "Gam, City dweller, come close so that I can whisper a secret in your ear. The dead... The dead are so clever that they make and pack their suitcases every night. Where are they going? Well, your guess is as good as mine. A people that celebrates its dead four times a year and that comes together a fifth time *en masse* at the Genocide Monument at Tsitsernakaberd, a people that has mourning built into its soul, its victimology buried deep under its skin, how do you think it gets this way? Because of them, that's how."

Roubo waved his extended arm to indicate the entire cemetery.

Gam: "And how do they achieve this exactly? Do they take the night bus? Do they wear the latest fashions to avoid detection? Or do they go in through people's nostrils, like they do for Dro?"

Roubo: "Don't make fun, Gam. You also carry death around with you in your bones. You even make your daily living off it, now don't you? You eat it. And you breathe it in while you slave away in the garbage dump. As I hope you've noticed, some of these tombs are upside down. I'll even give you some names, oh ye man of little faith! Moushegh Markarian, Kerop Stepanian. Theirs tombs are sunken, their enclosures broken into pieces and their headstones have been turned over. But the worst of it all is that we lost them. No trace of their remains. Fell out the bottom. What on earth are you supposed to tell the families who ask where Moushegh Markarian and Kerop Stepanian can possibly have disappeared? I show them the large scar that marks the eastern flank. Over there, fifty meters above the dead bodies that are highest up. I mean, I must give them some sort of scientific explanation, or no one would come to be buried here by me anymore. Does 1988 ring a bell? That's it! The earthquake. The earthquake's to blame. It came all the way to us. In certain places the low walls were literally ripped out like teeth. Can you imagine what power lies beneath this earth!"

Gam: "And they believe you?"

Roubo: "Come on now, Gam! Gam!"

> *Because you are light and hope*
> *I am only darkness and insanity*

Of course not! We'd have to be a scientific people for that. But no—what excites us is the supernatural. We revere the earth, little Gam. It may mean twaddle to others, but for us, it's the truth."

Gam: "So then why bother telling them that tall tale about an earthquake from afar?"

Roubo: "Because I like them to believe my own version of things. No kidding! Right after that, I get them with the story of the dead packing up their bags in the middle of the night. It's those nosy women ecologists who gave me the idea, truth be told. They stand and weep in front of the black pit a bit father up. During the Soviet days, they dumped five hundred tons of some toxic substance into it. They used it for agriculture. Until the day that it was banned. But how to get rid of the waste? By dumping it in the pit! And instead of cementing it over with asphalt, the authorities contented themselves with covering it up with dirt. That was in 1972. And then in 1985 despite the protests from those women, the new authorities built the cemetery there anyway. That's where they escape from, my dead people: that pit. They take a ride around the city and then they're back in place by daybreak. Death is here, now, among us. The dead spread death wherever they can. They dust over our words with it. Don't you see, death is the basis for how we survive. Without the Maccabees that unknowingly penetrate our lungs and from our lungs into our blood, tell me how we would still be alive after everything that men have done to us? It's a sign, isn't it? But not all our dearly departed have such good intentions. There are Cains among us who hold a grudge against their brothers. You want proof? My water. That water that you see right there flowing from my fountain. Clear, innocent, water that offers itself up to you like the freshest of virgins. Well *fuck your mother!* The mother ecologists insist that it can kill you. I give it to my cat, and he's still alive. And by the way, you take some from me on a regular basis as well, and you're still here, aren't you?"

He showed Gam a curved hose in the shape of a beak that came out of the ground. It spat out a water so pure that you felt compelled to put your mouth to it.

Roubo: "So what's the deal? Am I supposed to die of thirst perhaps? How am I going to snuff out the butt of this cigarette of mine, if not by drinking some of my water? Okay, I admit it, I always alternate between a mouthful of water and a glass of *oghi.*[8] Dro makes it himself. And when it comes to *oghi*, Dro knows what he's doing. Alcohol kills germs, it cleans you out from top to bottom. It's not like our nationalized, industrially produced cognac. With Dro, it's all organic."

Gam: "And what do the women ecologists say, to make it so that no one drinks from your water?"

Roubo: "My cemetery water? Those busybodies would be better off preparing dinner for the men who put bread on their table, rather than mucking up everyone's life, fuck their mothers! They kill themselves

---

8 Eau-de-vie.

trying to make me think that this water is anti patriotic. They lie as well as the people who fooled us with their silver tongues and massacred us in 1915! Their theory is that because of all the mudslides and rain, the Soviet's poison chemicals bathed the dead. All this on their way to eventually landing inside the body of water that you must have seen on your way here. Except that on the way down from the cemetery, the trees are watered from there. You go tell a child not to bite into a ruby red apple or adults not to pick their fruits to sell them! And when a mother is breast feeding her baby, she thinks that she's nourishing him. Well apparently, not! These women will tell you: they're poisoning them. We start by poisoning the earth, then the fruits, then the babies, the villages nearby and then eventually even the City. That's what they say. Me, I've never believed it. As if the dead had anything to do with it. But who knows? Until someone proves the opposite. Right? Who knows? Sometimes doubt overcomes me. And what if it were true? What if that which appears to be pure and seductive, actually kills you instead? Like a scorpion which looks harmless on the outside but carries deadly poison on the inside."

Gam: "No one knows, in the end. Who's wrong? Who's right? We know absolutely nothing. So, we can invent everything. Your dead people, for example, who play with our lives. Maybe that's why we're not extinct yet. For a people that has experienced the Apocalypse, we're remarkably alive and kicking, all told."

Roubo came back to sit on his stool, which over time he'd broken apart. Always at the same place at the foot of his pillar. Like the neuronal center of the area that separated the crazy road from the quiet, peaceful.

Roubo: "And now, tell me Gam! You have no idea anymore where you belong, isn't that true? You can't choose between this garbage dump where you dig, or the cemetery where you just buried one of your loved ones, or the City where you never go anymore. All these things are in your blood. Look at me! I'm also living amid illness. Sometimes when the clouds fill the sky, I ask myself all sorts of questions. At those times I think that my dead, at least the evil ones, try to fool me and make my mind surrender. And when my mouth starts to burn, I run towards this same water that you see now. It overcomes me. I feel it flowing inside my body. Contaminated or not, who cares: I drink, and I drink. My organs feel such pleasure that I have the impression that they are thanking me. I don't ask a lot out of life. I just need money. People pass in front of me. Lots of City people. If I had kept count since the beginning, they would number in the thousands. They go by again and again. I don't try to shake their hands. The look in my eyes should be enough to make them understand that watching over their dead is hard work. But they don't like my Cerberus-like mug. It gives them a preview of what the Last Judgment will be like:

Woe unto me who have sinned

I angered my creator

Woe unto me, who was given a thousand talents

But have nothing to pay anyone back with.

Woe unto me for I was crazy

And I ignored that people could see my faults

I will burn in Gehenna

My body that I fattened

Will make the earthworms grow strong.

Thankfully in the summer these processions resemble fashion runways. I keep my eyes open as if I were at the movies. I suck the women's breasts with my eyes as they go by. I don't miss a single one of them. I know that I irritate my creator. That I am already burning in Gehenna. Who cares? I savor my pleasure. I have so little of it. Any *koukla's*[9] neck makes me lose my wits. I get hard and then soft again. With their

---

9 *Doll,* as in pretty woman.

sad faces but stunning bodies, those *tsitsernaks*[10] drive me nuts!

> *Your eyes are black,* gakavikuss[11]
> *Your brow open, your cheeks pink.*
> *And the whiteness that you conceal!*
> *Your two melon breasts*
>
> Seksot' bala ess, ikôna,
> Ari, yaress, kéf anen'k.[12]

Dro is the one who mixes in *Koutchak*[13] whenever he feels like it. I even heard him sing some verses to your favorite sow, Bella. Sometimes I wonder if he isn't the type to like four-legged animals a bit too much, if you know what I mean..."

A car door slammed shut just then. Roubo turned his head. Three women emerged from the car. All wore flowered dresses: one red, the second one blue, the third one black. The first one, in black, was so fat and round that you would have thought she'd been blown up like a huge hot air balloon.

Roubo: "Well there they are, my *bloti seghan!* (This expression was used for callipygous women whose rear ends could serve as betting tables.) They're going to whimper over his pit. Go on my *lâtchâr,*[14] the road is free! I don't need to come along with you, you know the way."

The three women strode by confidently, a superior air etched on their faces.

Roubo: "You're lucky Gam. It's our women ecologists. Now you'll be able to hear their prognostications. They're going to spit on their black sheep. Follow them if you want. They're going to wet their slits. The

---

10   Literally: swallow (bird); here: ladies.

11   My little quail.

12   Sexy lady, you're as beautiful as an icon/Come now honey! Let's have some fun!

13   Nahabet Koutchak, a famous ecclesiatical figure, author of short poems that said quite a lot about the most intimate conflicts of the flesh and of the spirit.

14   Cry babies.

one in black is Irina, a Romanian who married one of our men way back when. When she was young, they chose her to represent Romania in sporting competitions. They steroided her up to death and now she just keeps gets fatter."

11.

Gam hesitated a moment. His day was meandering along with random events delaying his work at the garbage dump. The funerary procession, his mother's funeral, Roubo's ramblings... And now these grumblers who had come to spew their venom into a pit full of poison. But Gam had kept his hunter-like curiosity. Sniffing out brute stupidity was more interesting to him than rejoining his filthy garbage. And yet no one awaited him there. The female triumvirate followed a well-established itinerary, Irina in front, a Goddess with her stomach pushing forth like a ship through the cemetery tombs. A flock of geese marching in triangular, military precision towards those terrible forgotten items of modern industry. Gam followed some twenty meters behind them. As they reached the first slopes, they slowed their pace. For a moment the sun enveloped them, piercing them with its impudent rays. But what did Gam notice now? Underneath their dresses, the three graces advanced buck naked. They sparkled, like flowered meadows glimmering under God's light, their epidermis dotted with tiny roses, violets, and daisies. It mattered little that their bodies weren't those of Goddesses. All three were past forty, their mid sections blown out by multiple pregnancies as they dragged their backsides behind them. But their determined look mastered one's gaze: they were made of gold and emerald. *Nude,* Gam thought, *not to fight the heat, but rather to appear naked before their pit with the bodies of angry mothers, ready to accuse the guilty cesspit with their complaints.* An open wound, this cesspit. A dark den. Their thirsty and mute lips, transformed into rose petals by the light. A sword had apparently rent the earth there. But which sun would still dare to pulsate its pleasure into its depths? The three women set themselves in motion at once. One took some matches from her pockets, the other some paper, the third incense. In a dish hidden by the vegetation, they burned the tear-shaped resin. Then they formed a semi-circle around the center of the opening, Irina in the middle. Dignified, their gaze centered on the sadness of the pit. Gam observed them, hidden by the back of a tombstone carved in grey marble. Forced to walk on top of a tomb—Araïk was the dead man's name. He crushed the dry earth beneath him with his stinking boots, which released sounds like empty and deaf words. *Excuse me, Araïk-djan,*[15] Gam said to himself. *Please excuse a rogue like me for crushing the earth around your gravestone. Tomorrow I'll drink some Areni wine in your name.* Suddenly, the silence now broken, Gam heard, *Hee! Hee! Hee! HeeHee! Hee! Hee! Hee! HeeHee! Hee! Hee! Hee! HeeHee!*

A heavy, whiny soul-crushing music, a dark creaking noise begun by Irina, synchronized concerted screeching, an *ad hoc* drama hiccuped like Morse code. From this magma, once everyone's spirits had warmed up, Irina started to utter parts of sentences that the wind happily carried to Gam's ears, which he was extending past the tombstone:

WOMAN ECOLOGIST IN BLACK DRESS

"This week, Lusiné, cock upside down, cemetery, gave birth, deformed child, Why, shadow mouth?"

WOMAN ECOLOGIST IN BLUE DRESS

"why... shadow?"

WOMAN ECOLOGIST IN RED DRESS

"Why a malformed child this week and my neighbor Garineh's yellow dog dead last week?"

WOMAN ECOLOGIST IN BLACK DRESS

"Black pit in our beloved earth, our father gave... poisons. And now you vomit them back at us. What our father did unto you, now you do unto us."

WOMAN ECOLOGIST IN BLUE DRESS

"Yes, ourselves... Man spat on the heavens, and heaven has spat... on us."

---

15   Placed after a proper noun, means "sweetheart."

WOMAN ECOLOGIST IN RED DRESS

"The sacred earth, where our ancestors' blood flowed, our fathers soiled it forever!"

THE THREE WOMEN TOGETHER

"Hee! Hee! Hee! HeeHee! Hee! Hee! Hee! HeeHee! Hee! Hee! Hee! HeeHee!"

WOMAN ECOLOGIST IN BLACK DRESS

"Woe unto us that give birth to woe.

For our country's future runs black from our sex organs ..."

WOMAN ECOLOGIST IN BLUE DRESS

"Our sex organs are our pain. Fear has replaced pleasure.

On whom will our spit land, that will mark our child?"

WOMAN ECOLOGIST IN RED DRESS

"This wine stain on our brow or on our ass, on whom?"

WOMAN ECOLOGIST IN BLACK DRESS

"We thought we controlled the Earth, but it is she that holds us in its grip.

The more we pollute it, the more it tightens its grip on us.

Pillaged earth, dishonored earth, humiliated earth ..."

WOMAN ECOLOGIST IN BLUE DRESS

"Yes, pillaged, dishonored, humiliated ..."

WOMAN ECOLOGIST IN RED DRESS

"Pillaged, dishonored, humiliated... yes."

WOMAN ECOLOGIST IN BLUE DRESS

"The earth was our sister, and we assassinated her ..."

WOMAN ECOLOGIST IN BLACK AND RED DRESSES

"Yes, assassinated ..."

WOMAN ECOLOGIST IN BLUE DRESS

"And we're the ones who are dying ...

Suicide. Suicide. Suicide."

WOMAN ECOLOGISTS IN BLACK AND RED DRESSES

"And Lusineh who lives below has brought a deformed child into the world.

This very week.

Whose turn will it be next week? And the week after?"

WOMEN ECOLOGIST IN RED DRESS

"And my neighbor Garineh's yellow dog who died last week.

Whose turn will it be next week? And the week after?"

WOMAN ECOLOGIST IN BLUE DRESS

"For we are a part of this earth as much as it is a part of us."

WOMAN ECOLOGIST IN RED DRESS

"Yes we are, plainly and fully.

Everything that happens to us, happens to it as well.

Everything that we take away from it is taken away from us as well.

WOMAN ECOLOGIST IN BLACK DRESS

"Our father's ashes are sacred. Their grave is a sacred land.

But in throwing death into this pit, they've soiled their own death.

And the hills born before them, and the trees born after them...

They've also soiled them ..."

WOMAN ECOLOGIST IN BLUE DRESS

"They spoke into the stream's gurgling, into the river's shimmering,

Now our streams and rivers are dying,

And flow underground."

WOMAN ECOLOGIST IN RED DRESS

"And our apricots taste like apricots, but their meat eats at us from within.

Otherwise, why would our elderly die like flies after eating so many of them?

And Gabo who died suddenly.

And his wife Hasmig, as well.

And even Louisa, right after them, as she was making some of her jam,

They all loved juicy apricots."

THE THREE WOMEN TOGETHER

"Hee! Hee! Hee! HeeHee! Hee! Hee! Hee! HeeHee! Hee! Hee! Hee! HeeHee!"

WOMAN ECOLOGIST IN BLACK DRESS

"Our fathers' tombs are sacred.

But the poison that they threw in this pit is invading them.

They're choking.

Every night they go out and spread death on the city.

Onto our trees, in our fountains, and our stray dogs, statues and sidewalks.

And we bring this poison into our homes with our hands and feet."

WOMAN ECOLOGIST IN BLUE DRESS

"And on the flowers that we offer to our newlyweds and on their wedding dresses."

WOMAN ECOLOGIST IN RED DRESS

"And on our *khorovadz*, our *manti*, our *lahmajoun* ...

And even on our *tân*.[16]

THE THREE WOMEN TOGETHER

"Hee! Hee! Hee! HeeHee! Hee! Hee! Hee! HeeHee! Hee! Hee! Hee! HeeHee!"

WOMAN ECOLOGIST IN BLACK DRESS

"It is the beginning of the end for us?"

While the city is having fun,

Invisible forces march against it.

While its inhabitants get drunk from sounds and happiness,

They are besieged,

Having no one to combat,

And nowhere to run."

WOMAN ECOLOGIST IN BLUE DRESS

"Nowhere."

WOMAN ECOLOGIST IN RED DRESS

"Yes, no mountain to take refuge on.

No redemption to obtain."

WOMAN ECOLOGIST IN BLACK DRESS

"Days of confusion, annihilation, and consternation.

---

16   Khorovadz: shish kebab. Manti: meat dumplings. Lahmajoun: ground meat pizza. Tân: Yoghurt-based drink.

The walls are intact. The avenues have remained avenues.

No army to combat."

WOMAN ECOLOGIST IN BLUE DRESS

"Tomorrow the sky will conserve its glory, its eye on our nation's mourning."

WOMEN ECOLOGIST IN RED DRESS

"Unavoidable mourning. And the earth will return to earth."

THE THREE WOMEN TOGETHER

"*Hee! Hee! Hee! HeeHee! Hee! Hee! Hee! HeeHee! Hee! Hee! Hee! HeeHee!*"

WOMAN ECOLOGIST IN BLACK DRESS

"Our sexual organ is a hideous wound. Why?"

THE THREE WOMEN TOGETHER

"Why? Why? Why?"

Hidden behind his tombstone, his feet still on Araïk's grave, Gam peeked at the whining women. They were throwing fistfuls of earth into the pit. Sometimes they even used their feet, out of spite and rage. Excited by the liveliness of their words, they were filling in the pit. And since they rubbed their eyes from time to time, some of the earth entered their tears, leaving brown traces on their cheeks. Then suddenly they stopped. Emptied out, despite their vehemence. Irina hid the saucer in the grass, pulled on her dress to hide her round spots, and suddenly rejoined the road. The other two women imitated and followed her, like belligerent geese waddling forth. They crossed the field of light, which once again put their nakedness on display. Roubo was sharpening his words already with the idea in mind of latching onto the graces.

"Next time, we'll let go of our anger at the garbage dump," said Irina, even before he could begin to let loose of his gibberish.

"*Asdvadz kéz héd, kouyrik djan*" [17], he called. If you could only teach that little *khelkits tôpal*[18] of a Dro a lesson...

---

17   God be with you, little sister.

18   Limp spirit.

12.

Gam had to walk a hundred paces before reaching the gate. Beyond him the three dresses and their corresponding butt cheeks cheerfully collided an instant before disappearing once again behind the wall. Roubo, who was about put his ass down on his stool again, crossed his legs and began to pull on his cigarette butt. A hundred paces from rejoining the road to Nubarashen and crossing it, to finally find himself in the courtyard of the garbage dump. Amidst the fragrance of its somber poison, its squawking albatrosses, its trails of sparrows, its endless smoke, not to mention the puff-puffery of Dro's digger. His life on the other side of the road. His life according to the garbage dump. Hell for some, mother and giver of life for others. Roubo thought these things over before arriving at his side. Occasionally, he turned his head to make sure that he was the right distance away to unleash his verbal farts at him. But Gam cut him off at the post. At twenty steps away he intoned:

"Tell me Roubo djan, Djilo's tomb is one of the barest in the cemetery. Someone could at least have added a slab by now. For a poet whose statue is located exactly where he was struck down drinking his *oghi,* it's pitiful. At the very least a simple plaque. As if it were for some plain old country bumpkin. And that thing in the middle that rises out of the ground. It looks like Djilo's still got a hard on, even after he's passed away. Djilo? What harm could a slab do? Where would the glass of *oghi* that we'd pour him go? With earth on the other hand, it can go all the way down to his mug. And believe me, he must be thirsty by now. He liked it so much while he was alive that it broke him in two. It killed him in the end, and it will forever be part of him. As for his thing, that's another story altogether. But women. What! Open up! My fatty ones, their bodies polished by all that rubbing, like a stone in a river. You must have lusted after their curves as they passed under the sun. I'd bet my *klir*[19] on it. And their joyous rhythm, like a heartbeat. Chests forward, free, a delectable drink for the eyes... that's why they go about naked underneath. It's an act of defiance, but also to put their bodies in unison with the world around them. If they could, they'd take everything off. But in this country going naked whether you're male or female is considered an intimate act. An intimate act for two people. You saw them lean over their pit and vomit forth everything that's on their minds? Not your everyday complaints huh? Our *dôlma patatôgh*[20] have a real hurricane under their dresses! They would have bitten anyone who opposed them in a nanosecond. The rage that's pent up inside them! The rage! On her way out, Irina promised me that their next visit would be for Dro. And believe you me, it'll be tailored made. Dro can make those explosions from his machine go up a notch, they won't let go of their bitterness. But tell me Gam, what do you find in these piles of trash? A mere pittance! Come on now! As if you couldn't find a better place to thrash around. What about your work? Given how things are today, I can understand, *tsavet danem!* [21] But then why not just work on construction sites? They're building everywhere the eye can see in the City. And to build the new they're destroying the old. You know it. I know it. But I'm not one to work in the City. Or to put myself at the mercy of speculators. Imagine: they pulled people into the streets, and one woman even died from it. Better Dro's shithole than the President's. But *ésh nahatak,*[22] what can a sane man, an honest man, find in all this refuse, will you tell me? You're absorbing poison after poison. This repugnant place, where the ragmen slave away, it's like a refuge... No sane, honest, or straight man can walk five hundred meters from the road to the center of all that rot. That much I know. Unless he's under specific orders ..."

Roubo had a lot against the garbage dump, but he didn't hold anything against Gam *per se*. Gam had some elegance about him, all he was doing was

---

19   Penis.

20   A woman who knows how to prepare stuffed grape leaves is more likely to be substantive than frivolous.

21   Literally: *Let me take your pain from you,* a term of endearment.

22   Literally martyr of a donkey, or buggered ass.

adjusting his secrets to his own physiology. Every morning before entering the garbage dump, he'd stop for a little chat with him. Roubo would pour out all his thoughts to him, both diurnal and nocturnal. Sometimes the two would share a glass of *oghi*. "This is good stuff," Roubo would say, "Made from my own prunes. Trees that I planted upon my arrival at the cemetery. Today, they're really bearing fruit. Dead people make for good fertilizer, no?" Gam would bring him the City and Roubo would pay him back with brilliant folk wisdom, transformed from his usual taciturn state into someone full of his own brand of nonsense. As if he knew everything and had access to everything that was going on. You had to wonder where he got all his information from, since he never left his stool, even when the sun was blazing above him. "What's the point of going into the City? She comes to me," he'd say. "The entire City passes before my eyes. One day or another. The big shots like the fallen. One by one, I observe them, down to the smallest detail. In one move they make, I can guess if they're kind or mean, someone who takes pleasure in life or a whiner. An article of clothing, a color and I recognize a way of life. In my eyes, the people taking their small steps between the City and the cemetery become epic." Sometimes Gam would bring him a newspaper that he had found in the dump. First Roubo would act disdainful. He would ask him to leave the newspaper next to him, so it would get some air and lose its sewer odor. If he did pick it up, it would be by the tips of his fingers as he perused the national news. Like when an article took to task one of the three Presidents: the Scholar, the Cobra or the Samurai. The pointed humor of *Vôzni*[23]: he farted from joy. Especially when they ripped Bella a new one, Bella the wife of the nation's second pastor. He knew that Dro had named some of his pigs after them and that his sow with the largest teats was named after Bella.

Dro is a sensual bumpkin. In his wild moments he'll even recite some Koutchak for you. His father must have educated him well in that respect. He cites lines from the salivating priest whenever any woman walked by. And of course, that stays imprinted in your brain. If he'd seen our ecologists, Dro would certainly have spewed out some lewd poetry. I'm not like him in that way. I'm

---

23   Or *The Hedgehog*, an opinionated humor magazine.

more of a Narek[24] type of guy, obsessed with the last judgment. And anyway, you noticed the same thing. Except sometimes that pleasure seeker of a Koutchak rubs off on my more mystical feelings. Then without even noticing it, I quote my monk and finish by reciting the other guy and going even deeper into nature. I can't help it. Dro and I have our itches, but even when we don't have food, we have a whole stew of words, some of the spiciest in our language.

Yet Roubo wasn't going to wax tender too long about his rival. If he continued, it was because the other one forced him to smell the garbage dump. It ruined everything for him: his view, the sky, the entire horizon. Since it went beyond its technical limits by crossing the road, he accused Dro of overdoing it. And from time to time, he lost it.

"I kept telling Dro that eventually someone would get his old bear carcass. That his garbage dump was an apocalypse in reprieve. If you keep shitting in your own bed, you eventually die in it. He can do all he wants to burn all this filth in place, he can't get rid of it all. And what about the rest? What happens to the rest? It piles up and piles up. It rolls underneath, it smokes underneath, and it extends in all directions. My dead are already suffocating. And soon people will refuse to be buried here. Believe me Gam, those enraged women ecologists will never let go. They hassle all the ministries, and they stick their noses anywhere that the future begins to stink. Nasty, that's what they are. But they know in their skin how much a life costs. They won't let this octopus menace the city. Irina told me in confidence that there are rumors going around the ministries. All the people who are screaming about our dump are letting the pachyderms who run our country know how they feel. They're seeing red. A couple of pages of a novel being written about this shithole appeared in *Zhamanak*. Imagine. A novel all about Dro's crap! And what about my cemetery? Does it matter? Does it even exist? My field doesn't deserve to be turned into a novel, perhaps? The author doesn't dare appear in public. Afraid of reprisals, of course. That *Sovétachénits pakhats*,[25] who knows if he isn't hiding among us, digging

---

24 10th century mystic monk, author of *Lamentations*.

25 A crazy person escaped from the *Sovietashen* asylum (the old name for the

up things behind the scenes, only to scribble it all down on paper when he goes home at night. A taciturn guy, one sly dude. Oh yes, absolutely. And someone who's waging his war in secret. Well, it's true that the pachyderms who are ruling us have a lot of power. Little pokes coming from one person or another don't even reach them. Except in this case things something tricky. A real *coup de grace* threatens their interests. They're anticipating the worst. The whole country in one giant lawsuit. Everything turned upside down. And our artist, another one who's going to destroy our paradise with this smoking gun which is giving our moral sense gangrene. Already the Samurai President is seeing red. He thinks the garbage dump is his regime. As militaristic as he is, he can still recognize mockery when he hears it. As soon as they brought him the piece in *Zhamanak,* he sent his henchmen out with orders to kill the author. They're still searching the country. Scouring it. Except places where there's actually something going on, of course. Nice camouflage, no? They surround themselves with what's most repugnant to keep the nosy at bay. As you can imagine his henchmen won't exactly volunteer to shit up their boots by walking around here or smell this pestilence with their own nostrils. That, certainly not! Meanwhile Irina is digging in. The idea would be to convert the dump into a park. Ideal for my Sunday visitors or our days of the dead. You drink a glass of *oghi* on a dead relative's tomb, to warm yourself up or jog your memory. You speak to him, you recall all his good qualities while caressing his features, which have been turned to stone. Then you have to go by the road to look at Ararat and the City, sitting on a bench, in the middle of a nice, civilized lawn which goes on forever. Except the authorities don't seem to see things from my point of view. A lawn doesn't bring in any money. They'd have considered building some condos, but the ground below doesn't inspire much confidence: it's too soft, too elastic. And that's not even considering that you'd have to dig into layers of junk to build underground parking lots. So, they thought of the Japanese. The Japanese are meticulous. They calculate everything down to the last millimeter. We push. We sew things up. It's our most charming quality but also our most catastrophic.

Noubarashen asylum) is easily recognized by any normal person.

But anyway, no matter how good you are at patching things up, nothing resists an earthquake. So what's the point? When it comes to the garbage dump, the Japanese would have recommended installing an incinerator. And what's more, they'd supply gas to the entire city. Irina's the one who let me in on this. Well, if they're smarter than we are, let them come already! Thankfully, our men answered that it wouldn't come free for them to help us, the Japanese. We're brilliant as well! Let them kiss our ass, those *brindz oudôgh!*[26] Not to mention the fact that they'd kill two birds with one stone and add a crematorium to the incinerator. A crematorium! Imagine the smoke from dead people on top of my dead friends! And then you can say goodbye to all the cortèges and processions on the road, the dead person in his casket of flowers watching the sky float by him... The end of traditions... The beginning of the end of what we are. I protested with Irina. She pinched her cheeks while making her chicken ass and didn't answer."

A truck waited to enter the garbage dump. The chauffeur put out his left arm and drove around in Gam and Roubo's direction. His fingers made some undecipherable shapes in the air. Was he letting Dro know that his attacks on Roubo were old news? Or telling Gam to go back to where he came from?

---

26   Rice eaters.

13.

(Anyone busy walking in a certain direction could ignore that fact that his steps were obeying some blind fatality and persuade himself that they were paying attention to his own volition. Was it willpower or fate, this frenetic search for a urinal? Or perhaps a coïtus rapidus? Or the desire to sit down at a table and eat? For months now Gam had been walking under the portico to the garbage dump. Willpower or fate? But even if he went along with an open eye and spirit, he couldn't help it if, from the panel that held up this portico, the inscription in red letters fell on top of him—on his head, intellect, ego, imagination, noggin', you pick—the emerging red[27] of an inscription that would have otherwise been lost in a sea of troubled blue. In the middle of this same panel and above it, the image of the ironic crowned lion triumphed, scepter in paw, above the name of the city, Երևան.)[28]

This portico... My Brandenburg Gate. My Arc de Triomphe. Canto III of the Inferno. My annus horribilis. And sometimes, my Ali Baba's cave. All in one. And that capital letter. It annoyed me every time I walked by. A lone tooth left amidst a devastated jaw. Why that one, lone letter selected from the others that it started off with, by the grace of the heavens on high. And who, like a grownup, has overcome a thousand storms. Climactic as well as political. Rain, communism, wind, pogroms, snows, quakes, deportations, arrests, genocides, cold, fires, mists, sun. The victor emerged from a process of natural selection. Here, the lost word transformed the panel into a hanélouk, an enigma or

---

27   The sound é or yé.

28   Erevan or Yerevan.

a riddle. Every morning. A thousand and one times, I forced this letter to enter some logical inscription. Always respecting, of course, the position it had taken among its sisters, shipwrecked amidst all that blue. But my hypotheses never corresponded exactly to the stink from the garden of horrors, and I was forced to go to work. And every morning my spirit took on the rhythm of my steps, as I walked from my shack to the dump. I let words rise within me that included the sound é. I dug into my language and into obsessive refrains, ancient or new ones. Hence:

Ինչպեսորհներիցմեկն ասելէ. «Մահ ոչիմացիալ մահ է, մահ իմացիալ՝ անմահություն»[29]

Ma che sciagura d'essere senza coglioni![30]

You don't read the bible over fighting dogs.

Ηλι ηλι λαμ σαβαχθανι[31]

Մեկ ազգ: Մեկ հայրենիք: Մեկ ժողովուրդ:[32]

Éden! Éden! Éden!

But these excerpts that I had stored away in my memory were like twisted keys. I couldn't quite understand what they meant. Until the day when I finally read something written long ago, something even more heinous that filled me with exactly what I was looking for:

ARBEIT MACHT FREI

I had finally finished my panel. And despite my poor knowledge of German and nasal accent, in my mind my orphaned letter had found its family again. Even if I had tortured her a bit, the *é* became more of an actual *a*. And today, I rush out my door like a firefighter ready to take on a smoldering blaze. Work makes you free.

(Let's not exaggerate. Other have been told this before, even the most

---

29   As an ancient man once said: "Death that you don't understand is simply death, death that you understand, immortality."

30   *Oh, what tragedy to be without balls!* From *Candide,* by Voltaire.

31   *Éli, Éli, lama sabachthani?* (My God! My God! Why have you forsaken me?)

32   One nation. One homeland. One people.

humiliated of men, without leaving them the time to work or to be free. But who knows? Gam, his meshog on his back and his hook in hand, wasn't exactly smiling. He entered a dying landscape. Everything took on a feverishly rusty color. Pain that left everything forever tortured and strange, like bastardized forms. Twisted, hollowed out shapes that moaned in silence. Every object that's been disposed of that took the form of some construction and its beginning, has been recuperated in its last, terminal phase. Pieces of walls, poles, wire fences, water tanks. Without mentioning the fetid smell that, uninterrupted, poisoned the air that one absorbed. The earth inhales and exhales the odor of permanently burning skin. It never stops to burn. Pity the man who enters here.)

A toilet set apart from the rest of the world. All the frenzied stages of deterioration—visible or invisible, slow or violent—merged here, bordered at one edge by a tall cliff that sheltered those curious enough to visit. But each time as you walked towards it, even when the sky is clear, your gaze met those snowcapped mountains that made you smile no matter what, high up in the sky above the smoke, beyond the hilltops. It perked you up, this purity that floated above everything else and which never disappeared. You learned to look at the bottom of the pit without ever losing sight of this celestial light that no one could ever conquer. In the dump's grittiest place, you felt as if the apocalypse were at hand. Chaos held you in its grip. But all you had to do was look up at the mountain to relax. Others, suffocating, beaten down by the inner workings of contempt, weren't so lucky. Their bodies harassed by hatred and losing all hope. A glacial wind blew over the plains where they'd been left out in the cold. But here the weight didn't bury you.

(An ogre, this garbage dump. Every day it swallowed up countless tons of refuse. The trucks never stopped feeding it its daily rations of waste. A human need. It swallowed up everything that people threw away and stuffed itself with it. It digested the waste in different ways: by fire, air, water, and organic gluttony. An insatiable place where men forced nature to eliminate that which could no longer be made human. But the

monster ended up taking on a life of its own. Like those who created it. Not content to simply let the things it has been given rot away, it became a murderer. Swallows fell to their death. Piglets simply laid down forever, where before they had been munching on waste. Or that Russian guy, who died in a corner, forgotten by all. The garbage pickers' greatest fear was to stray far from the others and to die from cardiac arrest. Because the monster released gases that blackened your blood. It let its urine run loose like underground tentacles that surrounded the City.)

One winter, they found the Russian man frozen in the snow. That same day, out of loneliness, he'd started to drink. A well-built guy, but fragile on the inside. Going crazy because people disliked him because he was Russian. "And you think those of us who are from here even like each other?" I had answered him. But he wouldn't let go of it. He drank more than was reasonable. And the cold took him one day while he slept. *Khmoug, kskzou méroug,*[33] Tsknors said when he saw him lying in the snow. Whoever drinks will die of it eventually. He wasn't even fifty years old. He had disappeared for a while before he reappeared with the first snows. I fit his body inside his two *meshogs,* headfirst in one, feet first in the other. And since he was tall, his stomach wasn't even covered. I threw him like that into one of the pits and observed a moment of silence. That dead body, no more than an anecdote now. And tomorrow... I pushed some ashes and dirt into the pit. And he disappeared. Completely disappeared. And I thought that the pit might do him some good. As warm as a cave, but not warm enough that the body would begin to putrefy. Hence the Russian's body would stay intact until the first spring heat.

(The smell is the smell of death: like in a cage, a prison, a camp. Anyone who enters knows that you can't mention God's good name here, except perhaps to ask him where he's disappeared to. But where can he be? What would he even be saving amidst this stench that chases him from people's thoughts? The sky may be the deepest blue in the universe, but the garbage pickers barely notice it. They're so used to looking down, to

---

33   He who drinks his troubles away, dies away.

poking, sorting, and picking things up, to breathing in the putrid vapors that their souls have frittered away. What else can they be concerned with, apart from simple survival? Their only hope is to find some hidden treasure. Thanks to these national latrines that have disposed of all of them and forever hidden them down below. In the Gyumri dump, at least Tsknors was able to look up at Mount Arakadz. The view was so perfect that you saw it every time you looked up even the slightest bit. In winter, under a blue sky that hovered over the walls of an abandoned factory, its snows were like a gift of unending beauty, he'd say. But the trucks that kept dumping their waste higher and higher in the air eventually blocked your view. Here, the daily chaos had ruined people's ability to see. And when the beauty of Mount Massis shone above the eternally bent-over bodies, it was like some obscure, ironic smile which imprinted itself on this petty humanity imprisoned in its bucket of waste. Gam had one foot in the courtyard now. A group of garbage pickers was coming down from Nubarashen. He heard their joyous conversation, but Artemis captured his gaze. Sitting on a large stone, she was breast feeding her three-year-old son Artem. Gam stopped in front of her and whispered to himself: "Your breasts are grapes in my palms/Your skin is like a vibrating, blushing velvet.")

14.

*A*rtemis! Artemis! Artemis of the thousand titties! White udders. Skin creamy like *Oshagan madzoun*.[34] All hanging loose so that Artem doesn't know where to put his mouth anymore. You overflow. Your throat expands, you spread out endlessly, your little man hungers. Point your udders, my beauty! With such large breasts, you have quite a reputation. Your mating dance is a field of lilies, and you stand tall, the most bounteous of all! There's enough to teat for all tastes and ages! You get drunk just staring at them. You never get enough of them! The best around, the youngest, the fattest, the most ecstatic. Oh, naked breasts, twin sisters, my islands playing next to each other. Each one with its own tropism. Full of memories buried long ago, obscure sensations, which suddenly make you drunk with pleasure.

> *New breast... Onward... for life! Secret breast and breast that wakes up... Jacqueline.*
> *Muscled dancer's breast, dancing jello breast, emptied of all strength.*
> *Or else as soft as silk, like Julianne's.*
> *Frivolous breast, like Lusiné's or sincere like Anaïs.*
> *Tired breast, from having been manhandled so many times.*
> *Chewing gum breast.*
> *Rubber breast, that automatically returns to its original shape after you've kneaded it.*
> *Or erased, like an air bubble under your skin.*
> *Breast in your palm, sun which rises round on the infinite sand.*

---

34   Yogurt.

Untouched nipple. A long-distance virgin's. Like Nouné's néné, most probably.

Old maid's breast, which smells locked in, flesh that gets bored and fades.

Or that has done its time and hangs down like an old rag.

Vast living pillow, like Vivian who accepted me onto hers.

Or tiny rose bud. Or short phallus, pointed downward.

Puffed up knockers. Pickle breast.

Melon breast or pear breast. Pea breast or pumpkin breast.

Breast with blue veins like fine Italian marble.

Black eyed breast.

Cumbersome, flabby, greasy, watery breast, breast with a heavy destiny, breast that you grip from the front.

Hated breast.

Breast in paradise.

Excrescence that brings both happiness and sorrow. Mischievous bag of a breast.

Crumpled belly button.

Round: a hard-boiled egg, a perfect sphere. Arrogant like a pointed shoe.

Or so turned in on itself so that you'd think it were sick, the sheets pulled up on it and only showing off its nose.

Timid, politely ashamed, a frugal puritan breast that fasts. A man wouldn't make his home there anymore.

Breast of Mary, perfect in its grace, giving its milk to Man's Son.

Artemis, you possess all these breasts. A multitude of many-shaped protrusions growing on your chest. From your belly button to your neck how many bags, balconies, and bra cups. Not that you entered adult life equipped with such an armada! But looking at you... looking at you brings so many pictures to mind!

And you keep giving and giving and giving! And how he pumps your breasts, your son! As hard as he can, moving from one nipple to another, a famished animal. His body sucks yours up, his life devours yours... But that's what you were made for, to serve as food! Little Artem has his eyes closed. He swims in a bath of nipples. He drinks his pleasure. Nothing but his own pleasure. And you've also closed your lids. A river flows through you, you can feel it, a river that comes from deep within your organs. And this river flows all the way up to the breast that your son has chosen. Liters of blood to produce the milk that reaches his mouth. From him to myself, in my soul. My eyes close. They keep you in sight, even if I begin to bend under the nauseating corruption. Your movements are heavy, your hands are sainted, while mine are called upon to tear open trash cans. Always those same trash bags with their pathetic prizes. Seeker of glass, iron or cardboard but always hoping to find something rare, a miracle that will save you. Hopefully he'll keep pumping until you're at peace, that Artemis! And let his heart beat to the rhythm of life! *Boumboum! Boumboum! Boumboum!* He holds one of your thousand breasts within his little hands, and you enjoy that. He feels it. Presses it. Or pinches it. He gnaws on it and has fun doing it. And you enjoy it. Which hole within you does he live in? You have no idea. You give it to the little man as much as he gives it to you. Nothing exists for you anymore, apart from this contact which sets your flesh on fire. You don't even feel the hard the stone that you sit on. The acrid odor doesn't bother you. The dump unleashes its pestilence on you, but the little one's fangs don't bite you. You're as calm as an island, and around you life stinks and is trampled. And the cemetery tombs, from the entrance up until the top of the hill, are all turned towards you. They look at you, bent over you like the child that you hold in your arms. The seagulls have stopped rowing through the air above the trash. Grouped on the roofs, they stand guard on one leg, their beaks in the air. The smell of your milk has attracted a small yellow dog and a piglet. They want their share. They bother you by playing with your legs. They whine and gripe. They jump on your knees. They search out a nipple that they smell at the lower end of your stomach. They'd latch on with delight if Artem didn't kick them both nervously. And we think that our hands secretly extend to find something pleasurable, that they plunge into a dark nostalgia when our own mothers gave us their entire bodies to drink. *Your breasts are grapes in my palms/Your skin is like vibrating, blushing velvet.* Artemis! And at that moment you forget the headaches that afflict you. Holding it violently in their fists, they squeezed. Something breaks and all hell breaks loose. Pain beyond belief. It ravages your spirit. Paralyzes your will. As for myself, Gam, I told you so. You have no business being in the garbage dump. It seeps into you through its gases. Its roots grow inside its own organism. And so, from time to time, your blood puts you in a foul mood. Then suddenly, your enemy disrobes.

Unless... This hole left by your husband is impossible to fill. The wound rips at your insides. Without him now and until the end. Without him during the day and without him at night. The two of you stayed together just so long as it took to bring a child to life. Then you lost your husband. Dead from a flu that he didn't take care of in Leningrad. At least there, he'd found some work. Any work, work that his own country couldn't offer him. Like so many other fathers who left their families to sell themselves abroad. Like so many others who sell one thing or another. In his case, it was pizzas that he was going to go sell in the middle of a winter whose chill you felt all the way down to your marrow. He began to cough more and more. But that was nothing. Ruined his lungs. And still he claimed it was nothing. He'd be okay. He had his household to provide for. They all have a household to provide for. And so, they push their bodies beyond their limits. Until he spat out blood on the hospital sheets. His last blood.

Thus, widowed by fate, Artemis. And without a man ever since. Who'd want a vagina that's already been used? You begin to attract pity. The poor girl! She really has no luck, that one. Mothers keep you away from their sons. You're considered dangerous. Women who aren't innocent anymore. Women who prey on and want to harpoon a virgin or a naïve boy. You're like a stain. What family would accept to have a used vagina for a daughter-in-law? You have no more future, you become fatalistic.

You hung your husband's portrait up on your living room wall. His look of old haunts the air. You breathe in his ghost. Like you, Artem also breathes in his ghost. The quietly distilled look of a man who's never smiled. An unchangeable mask through which he sees the world. The thought that this country mutilated his life.

Luckily, he left you this apartment. A studio at the top of a skyscraper. The elevator never works, so you go up and down, counting the floors each time. Your burden is to always be counting, ascending, and descending. Artem becomes heavier and heavier in your arms.

What are you doing amongst us, Artemis? You're a reject as well. Something no one wants anymore. Yes, you come here now because it's the only way you know how to feed yourself.

For now, you're calm. You're hiding from the world. A calm that makes you want to cry. But voices are coming on down from Nubarashen. They flow down the road. Familiar voices, our people. Shousho, a few kids. Haïk and Edik, who speak loudly of recent developments.

15.

Hey Shousho, people say that you're rich although you run to the garbage dump every day."

"That supposedly you have some treasures hidden in that hovel of yours."

"And that you wear those old rags to make people believe you're poor."

"A really poor old lady!"

"But poor you aren't, old Shousho. No, you're not, that's for sure. Ah, you come here without your dentures, but you put them back in when you're at home."

Back bent, she walks almost at right angles, that old Shousho. (As if after looking down at the ground so much, the curvature in her back had remained. As if with age, her name had contracted as well, from Shoushanik to Shoushik and then Shousho.) She walked with her *meshog* hanging from her shoulder and pressing on her stick, always the same one, which helped her to search the trash. The children of Nubarashen made fun of her every time. She would chase them away with one swipe of her stick, but that only excited them more, and they'd hop all around her to avoid being hit by her stick.

Shousho!

Vaï, you misfits, the whole bunch of you! Bunch of *shan' lakots!*[35]

They answered her with peevish, teasing laughs. "Shousho! Shouuuusho! Shoushooooo!" the brats repeated to provoke her. Once they arrived at the parking lot, they latched on to a garbage truck that had already begun to empty itself. And Shousho began to trot behind them.

---

35   Sons-of-bitches.

As was often the case, Edik and Haïk found themselves on a road leading down from Nubarashen. They walked and then stopped. Edik's age made it difficult for him to continue, even downhill. His knees felt like jelly, but he didn't need a walking stick to keep walking, as his neighbor Shousho did. He only used his stick to poke open the bags. If his body had already begun to fail him, he still had a keen eye, and his spirit could strike down his enemies in one fell swoop. The two men were advancing, absorbed, side-by-side, like twins attached to their mother's nipples. The first listened to his friend as he read an article from *Zhamanak* out loud. From time to time, they roared with happiness. Haïk played with the tone of his voice and took fun in exaggerating his ironies to make their guillotine-like jokes even sharper as they dropped. Then catching his breath again, he started anew. You'd think that he was the one who had tossed the newspaper away. But that wasn't the case.

... it's just that you can divide our people into two camps: the saviors of the nation and those that have been shipwrecked by this same nation. Unrepentant saviors on one side and on the other, the shipwrecked caught in the process of being shipwrecked. Of course, the former are much rarer than the latter. But don't think for one minute that there aren't saviors as well among the shipwrecked. In fact, that's all there is! In their case, the savior part is just slumbering. From time to time, a fever overtakes him, and his salvaging spirit pierces through their shipwrecked boredom and comes to the surface. Then, after a while, his fever goes down again, and the savior returns to his shipwreck. Which doesn't stop him from living elsewhere. He even lives elsewhere quite happily. But everywhere he goes, he takes along with him that ambiguous feeling of loss and humiliation. Especially when he listens to the saviors speak, the real ones, the active saviors, the ones who want to save our language, our lands, our children, our schools, our genocide, our ruins. (Ah!) Our Book which no one reads anymore, our dances which people dance too much, and our entire country in fact, preferably with Ararat within its borders. I know what I'm talking about since I'm a part of it. When I write, I write to save someone. When I eat, I also eat to save someone. And when I fart, it's also to save someone. (Ah! Ah!) I dream of saving ourselves from each other. I dream of freeing each citizen

from the cage that his own people have built for him. But unfortunately, I have my limits. In the end it gets tiring. Yes, wanting to save everyone is exhausting. I just sink on the spot. That's why I have such admiration for people who want to save others 24/7. Their brains are saving machines. In fact, they get off on other people seeing them as saviors. This pleasure they derive from being a messianic savior, constitutes their very essence: it's their nature and what fuels them. You find them at the top and at the bottom of the sociological ladder, from the self-made ones to the ones that have been elected to save us. The three presidents of our third republic are a good example. They were all able to rescue the country from national catastrophes. (Ah! Ah! Ah!) In fact, the only thing that they were able to save was a widespread attitude of everyman for himself. And our citizens prefer to be saved elsewhere than at home. Being saved here at home means forever swimming amid a permanent shipwreck. As for the third president's Prime Minister, he wants to save a corrupt nation from corruption. (Ah! Ah! Ah!) At least he didn't declare that he also intended to save Ararat from its eternal snow caps. He's too smart for that. Or Idi Gago from his megalithic fat. Nor his president from his militaristic past. All our presidential saviors were at least able to save themselves, even if they couldn't save their people. For example, the Cobra president saved himself in a sumptuous villa after having added a moral shipwreck to our physical one, while Arpineh still lives underground in Ashtarak. (Ah! Ah! Ah! Ah!) The three presidents managed to live in luxurious European accommodations, while they couldn't lodge the survivors of the 1988 earthquake in the most basic human housing. Recently, the last of these three presidents, while he was visiting newly built houses, transformed himself into a Minister of Unfinished Housing, noting that there always seemed to be something missing from these constructions: a faucet, a gas pipe... (Ah! Ah! Ah!) That still doesn't stop us from building more and more churches. (Ah!) But no one ever blames our officials, so that our own people aren't forced to go work as slaves in Europe or as pariahs in Turkey. (Ah!) Isn't it in our own country after all, that they should escape the fate of being slaves or pariahs? (Ah!) Such that it would be indecent to confuse our presidents with those lucky saviors who made our history by undoing our nation. One day, we counted six of them, who became nineteen all at once. But since they couldn't save us, they saved themselves instead. After which a real collapse occurred: seven thousand dead. A bloody collapse. Besides, you'll tell me that all our political parties are geared towards saving the people. That's normal, you'll say. But our so-called saviors are so focused on saving us no matter what the cost, that they've developed a chronic ideological constipation. Try to think clearly when your ass is all stuffed up. (Ah! Ah! Ah!) Still, we shouldn't think that the moon is made of cheese. Our saviors really brighten our nation's path, the one which lets anyone do as they please while forgetting the rest of us. But how, you'll ask me, can you forget all this? Well, because someone who is shipwrecked 24/7 gets tired of waiting for someone else to save him. He needs to have fun, to get lost occasionally, to go to the country and, who knows, sometimes even to dilute himself in the world's ambient air. But the saviors begin to scream and to jump up and down. Come home already! they say. But what on earth can they have against the surrounding world? Nothing. That's why our saviors are to be commended. The more the surrounding world grows, the more they feel the need to save us. From time to time, they make great patriotic speeches, they paddle and paddle against the current, fighting like devils. But the surrounding world, which is as attractive as a cheap whore, acts with as much malice as an octopus that attaches its suckers to anyone who gets lost along the way. And then, you try and pull your shipwrecked friend away! But faith is faith. False faith or real faith, what's the difference? The main point is to remind those who are shipwrecked that they should save themselves. I can already tell that some people hold it against me and think that I'm a pseudo-savior whose only credo is catastrophe itself. They must be right. Everything falls apart. It's my shipwrecked side that's talking. It's true that if we weren't already shipwrecked, we wouldn't need any saviors. And one would think that any country that produces so many saviors, amateur or professional, is a nation that already feels the shipwreck coming. We can fart or complain as much as we want, oil-covered sea or windy ocean, isn't the main point simply to row away from here? (Ah! Ah! Ah! and Ah!)

Edik and Haïk were laughing their heads off as if they'd just finished a good meal. They were rubbing their eyes after laughing so hard at their own jokes!. Then suddenly, silence. A quieting down during which you start to breathe normally again. In the sky, one even noticed downy waves of seagulls flying by, when suddenly the earth started to tremble with the same turbulence as a garbage truck arriving from the City. Dust rose and plastic bags danced along with old papers. They began to glide a moment, embraced each other, and then took off in different directions.

The article was signed: *The Hedgehog*. Only a few months old, it went from reader to reader without losing any of its freshness. Some read it without rancor: alone, at home or in public. If you heard guffaws at a restaurant table one day, you just assumed that extracts of the article were being passed around like a saltshaker. Students with their heads bowed at outdoor cafés awoke the same suspicions. As did a random guy at the foot of Toumanian's[36] statue who was engrossed in reading a newspaper. Retirees kept it lodged under their elbows or by their nightstand and read a few lines every night before falling asleep. It made couples happy and functioned like catnip. University professors commented on it to each other. But when a student had the temerity to ask whether he could use the article as the subject for an essay, they became embarrassed and declined, stating that the piece was anonymous and too young to be considered a classic. Which didn't stop it from being found in almost every toilet in town—the most popular reading spot known to man. It likely worked as a laxative of sorts. In any case, one let go of a certain weight while taking in its main points. The mudslingers were sure to point out what was libelous in the piece. They could tell by people's reactions whether they'd read the piece or not. They'd barely finished slinging their arrows that they'd ask: "Have you read *Pravda*?" (That publication which was supposed to tell the truth, the whole truth and nothing but the truth, that existed under the old regime and was now used as toilet paper.) The allusion was to the pamphlet, of course. "It lubes up your moral sense," commented some. Or better yet "It's our story. But with a universal slant, on top of it all."

---

36   Popular poet, from the Lori region.

People photocopied it in secret. Others memorized it. Parents made their children read parts of it in the morning before going to school. At the Arabkir market, four seasons a year, merchants would wrap your carrots or strawberries in printed paper. You go figure what was inside them.

People said that the authorities were tailing the Hedgehog. The Hedgehog? Where on Earth was he hiding? Under whose skirt? Under what name? And in what disguise? Had he defaced himself perhaps to avoid detection? Did he have a mistress, so that he could be blackmailed? That piece of trash! Crybaby! Traitor! He should be hanging from a butcher's hook! Rumors had it that he was working as a shepherd way up in Siunik region, in bear country. The bears protected him from trespassers. Others suspected that he was hiding inside the American Embassy waiting to get his green card. Or that he was by himself in a rowboat all day on Lake Sevan reading Dante, 'Yeghitsi louys'[37] or cultivating other hedgehog quills to stick people with. Yet others thought that he might be working in the garbage dump. But that was unlikely: the stench wasn't for everyone. Had the Hedgehog secretly slipped the article in question on his editor's desk to get it published? After an investigation and a requisition which led to nothing, the publishers were subjected to several new investigations by the national tax commission. It was easy to find fraud anywhere one wanted to, like illnesses on a healthy body, just to punish someone who was a real thorn in one's side. The publisher, Pasha Nikolian, was put in chains and locked up in Nubarashen over the matter, a place where every day you fight for your life like an insect. And yet. And yet. The henchmen who had been sent on the Hedgehog's traces went crazy over their own impotence. Their eyes were everywhere in the City. They randomly bugged telephones. They hung out in bars and drank endless glasses of *oghi* until they forgot why they were there in the first place. Or they spent entire days in libraries, surveying everything with telescopes for eyes, while pretending to be pouring over an illuminated manuscript. Their spies searched as much as they could, on tiptoe and on all fours. They had nothing else to do, it seemed, apart from trying to nail that damn Hedgehog

---

37   *Let there be light!* Pariour Sevak's final, luminous book of poetry, written
      before he and his wife died in a car accident under mysterious circumstances.

to a cross. Despite all these different searches, beatings, inquisitions and impositions of all sorts, the City grew more and more sarcastic by the day.

Gam had joined the two men and laughed along with them. He would remove his glasses to look down at the newspaper from time to time.

EDIK

And to think that they were trying to trap him.

HAÏK

When for all we know he could be one of us, that Hedgehog. Right here in the dump. Right Gam? That's what I'd do if I were him. To hide, I'd come lose myself in all this zibil.[38] There's no better ally that this stink.

GAM

Our saviors may be corrupt, but they'd never dare put their feet in this rot. That's for sure.

EDIK

Indeed. That's for sure. You can bet Mount Ararat on it.

Suddenly, the insane asylum manager's four by four stopped right in front of their noses. The dust made the three of them cough. It was as if a meteorite had fallen into their parking lot, as black as the Kaaba in Mecca, which the Archangel Gabriel offered to Abraham. *Halleluiah!* But none of the doors opened. Whoever was inside the truck was obviously waiting on purpose. And also waiting for the air to become more breathable so that he could get out of the car. When he finally appeared, he wore a pitch-black suit which clung to his round front and backside, a pink shirt, along with an orange tie and a color-coordinated hankie. Bald and wearing a mustache, he immediately pulled out his hankie and covered his huge nose, which looked like a sign over a sex shop. Edik, Haïk and Gam paused for a moment. After all that laughter, this frightening director had appeared. From the beginning, this master of pathologies could sense that he'd have a hard time making these three laughing hyenas enter his cage.

––––––––––––––––––––

38   Trash.

DIRECTOR *(Looking at the ruby on his pinky ring.)*

One of my crazies has escaped. I'm looking for him and I'll find him. The republic made me let go of half of them in the middle of the City because of budget cuts. Lunatics that their families agreed to take in. Maniacs, the chronically depressed, unrepentant fascists, nostalgic communists, all sorts of nuts that Independence had suddenly unhinged. The shallowest, in a word. I should have fifty left. But I'm missing one. The son of a bitch took advantage of things to steal the keys to the front door. And I think that he's hiding among you.

HAÏK

Are you looking for anyone in particular or will just anybody do? Those are two different things. And I suppose that you want to save him, right Herr Mister Director?

THE DIRECTOR

Yes—whoever it is. It's my job to save crazy people from their own craziness. I could even grab one of your flea-ridden buddies to make my job easier.

HAÏK *(Turning towards the others)*

It's every man for himself! A savior of crazy people! A messiah! A Stalin!

EDIK

A presidential candidate! It looks like the country's father has taken aim again! This time they won't send us to Siberia, but to the loony bin instead. (The three laugh hysterically. The director looks on, stunned) Excuse me, Mister Director of the Nubarashen lunatic asylum. But I'm also from Nubarashen. Like old Shousho, who you can see from the back on the road. Please do us a favor and leave her alone. Leave us all alone. And anyway, there aren't any crazy people among us, even if we do yuck it up like a bunch of whackos. You and me we're part of a twisted race. The Giants of Sassoun, you've heard of them, haven't you? Those legendary giants that are our national heroes and models. We scream more than any other people on earth. But the craziest people in this country are running around free. That's why everything's going badly. That everything is upside down. That there's chaos everywhere. That the streets and people's spirits are both so crazed. The entire country is one big *guijanots*[39] Your missing crazy person, you can find him among the nabobs

---

39   Lunatic asylum.

and the Cresuses. Like the one who fed a donkey to his pet lions. Or the one in the suburbs of Bangladesh[40] who thinks he's a Roman emperor. Take them with you! They're all yours

THE DIRECTOR

If I don't find my fiftieth crazy person, I'll be accused of falsifying records and getting rich off the money of the Public Health Department.

EDIK

Who cares? All they'll do is put you in jail in Nubarashen. You'll just move from one neighborhood to another.

HAÏK

If you can't find a crazy person, just make one up! A recipe for a crazy person? Hmm, let's see, Mr. Director of the Nubarashen Lunatic Asylum. It's quite easy. First, select a political opponent. Any one you want. They're literally thousands of them, multiplying like rabbits. If you can't find one, just fill out a form at the police station. There's one for every taste.

EDIK

Opponents who participated in opposition rallies.

GAM

Opponents who've made opposing speeches.

EDIK

Opponents who fought during the war of independence.

GAM

Opponents who frequent the heads of opposition parties with fervor, like the Scholar.

HAÏK

Opponents who write for opposition papers. Editors-in-Chief of these same publications.

EDIK

Preferably, opponents with subversive intentions, even if they used to tell their supporters to remain calm during their opposition. If they happen to have such intentions, the police will easily prove the opposite. Or they'll just

---

40   Derogatory name given to a poor neighborhood of Yerevan.

take out a weapon in secret from their glove compartment or trunk.

GAM

And in case the police don't have any opposition members handy, just stop any passerby in the street. Any which one. Just a passer-by passing by. Someone going to buy bread or picking up their kid from school. A passer-by is never as innocent as he looks. The judge will easily turn him into an opposition member. A signature here and there and you'll be done.

HAÏK

And since an opposition member is just a crazy person who doesn't recognize the virtues of the party in power, you'll have found your man. Negotiate with the police who've decided to put him in a cell in Nubarashen. Make them see that the distance between a jail cell and a loony bin is short—so they might as well just drop him off at your place.

EDIK

I told you, already. All you have to do is drive from one neighborhood to another.

THE DIRECTOR

Oh my, my, my! It's a triumvirate of *parap klir*.[41] Little paper Hedgehogs. Keep your political epilepsy to yourselves and stop being such wise guys, OK? I could lock you up just for making statements harmful to the republic. What's suddenly gotten into the three of you? Haven't had an orgasm in a while? Is that it? Looking for someone to bite into huh? Bunch of wild dogs! Beware! Soon you won't have any more trash dump to fill your plate with. The Japanese are going to change all that for you and you'll end up in the street. In the gutter, like a bunch of rats! An incinerator would be preferable to this godawful nightmare that stinks up my way and makes the view so ugly. In its place, an English lawn. And why not a golf course with a view overlooking the City? Or an amusement park. That's a great idea now, isn't it? I already discussed it with the guy at the cemetery. People visiting their dead would simply have to cross the road. After lighting some *khoung*[42] they could make

---

41   Literally, empty penis. Someone without balls.

42   Incense.

a fire for their *khorovadz*.[43] And you my dears, if you play nice and listen up, maybe we'll offer you posts as guards. With a whistle around your neck to catch the bad guys. What do you think about that?

HAÏK (combative)

What do we think? That you're nothing but an ass wipe.

THE DIRECTOR (pointing his index finger at Haïk)

Voress patchi, kekhtot! Vôtchi[44] (Then turning towards the others) And anyway, what do any of you really understand? You live here without even realizing what a special place it is. Take myself for example: after driving up this road so many times, I finished by seeing the City in a totally different way. Once, I even thought that it looked like a woman lying on her back. With her legs open.

GAM (like a Jesuit)

How so, open? Like a holy book? With a burning bush?

THE DIRECTOR (electric, then parabolic)

Do I have to draw it for you? Or breasts like Greater and Lesser Massis, sucked by the sky?

Another time I saw the City full of tiny animals running around in all different directions. A bunch of perverts who wanted to impregnate everything in life. And I realized that a woman lying on her back was a living organism. In the end it feeds itself, produces its own energy, and evacuates its waste. And I was

---

43 Barbecue.

44 Kiss my ass, you dirty piece of shit!

right in the middle of this waste that people bring all the way here every day.

HAÏK *(critical)*

Well, that's a dump, Mr. Director. Like your asylum. A dump...

THE DIRECTOR *(dogmatic, then apocalyptic)*

Well at least I stay clean, and I don't stink. I'll keep going. The capital was overflowing with excrement all the way up to my feet. IT was getting rid of it as best it could, pushing it as far away as it could manage. To your dump, in other words. *(Talking to Haïk) Are you happy now? But since we were burning it to reduce it to ashes, it returned to the City in the shape of stinking smoke blowing in every possible direction. After this* kâkot [45] *image, it was Erebuni[46] hill that began to haunt me. I couldn't sleep anymore. I had nightmares. I was sinking in all sorts of hideous vomit. Well, I ended up thinking that the hill pointing downwards was that woman's clitoris.*

EDIK *(comic)*

A clit as high as a hilltop! Oh, I would have loved to climb up a hill like that one, when I was young.

THE DIRECTOR *(ecstatic, then didactic)*

It had taken on the form of ecstasy itself. An entire people that became excited upon encountering its own history. Visited from top down and bottom up, petted at length, everyone could climb on top of it. Women, men, the old and the young, everyone laid on top it, rubbed themselves on it and then rubbed their stomachs and lower parts on it in a type of patriotic orgy of sorts.

EDIK *(enigmatic)*

That's for sure sir, people like to play on roller coasters!

THE DIRECTOR *(dramatic)*

I know. All those visions literally dance in your head. You think my words make no sense. And that I say crazy things. Just be patient. You haven't heard everything yet. Another time.

HAÏK *(rustic)*

There's more? That didn't seem to ruin your visions! It looks like frequent-

---

45   Shitty.

46   Ruins of the Urartian fortress that lent its name to Yerevan.

ing crazy people turned you into a mystic instead!

THE DIRECTOR *(spermatic)*

Let me finish. I've seen Greater Massis, our Ararat, which lies on the other side of our border. I've seen it like some great erect penis, burning like white iron thanks to some luminosity that licked it at one end. That's it, that's him, I told myself. It was our people's penis sapped by the nostalgia of its own power. And that's how he sees it. As the symbolic expression of his lost virility.

HAÏK *(skeptic)*

As the symbolic expression of his lost virility.

EDIK *(skeptic)*

As the symbolic expression of...

GAM *(skeptic)*

... his lost virility.

For a while, Haïk, Edik and Gam wondered if they were dealing with a director or a lunatic.

THE DIRECTOR *(Eschatological, prophetic, analytic, or pragmatic?)*

And so, when all is said and done, when there's no more energy left at the heart of the collective orgy, everyone comes and deposits his body in the earth, in the cemetery that is there, on the other side of that road that serves as a boundary between the City's waste and humanity's. For everything that is earth returns to earth and everything that is dust returns to dust. In fact, I'm not sure if our authorities did it on purpose or not. But they mixed up the organic and the erotic. That's as good a reason as any to put an amusement park or a golf course in place of that cesspit. It's a great idea, isn't it? I've already submitted the plan to the department of urban development. I know from a close source that they've given up on constructing any buildings there, due to the layers of trash that have been deposited there for decades. There's no way any house would stay up when it rained, and water seeped through the ground. And that's not even considering that it sits on a huge seismic fault. But officials would be favorably disposed towards a golf course. Just a golf course. At least I wouldn't have to close my window because of the smoke that pours over the road every time the wind changes direction. (The three men who were listening to him felt caught between a hammer and sickle. Should they laugh or cry? They were hesitating in the inside without really knowing what to do, when suddenly Haïk threw the first salvo.)

HAÏK *(Taking a carrot out of his bag and munching on it.)*
When a lunatic speaks, a wise man eats his vegetables.

EDIK

You don't read the New Testament over the head of a wolf who's chasing a virgin.

GAM *(Addressing the Director)*
A man dressed in black doesn't necessarily have white teeth. Hey, mill without water, lunatic with a full stomach who thinks he's lighting the way for others, don't you know, you who improve with age like a fine wine, that man is man's own worst enemy? Don't you know that youth is wasted on the young? That he who feeds you today will betray you tomorrow? Don't you realize that? Little man! Hey you, little man! Little man with a big mouth! Little man with crazy dreams! (Tapping him on the head.) Is anybody home? You have the least power but talk the loudest. Your beard's on fire and the other guy is telling you to wait until he lights your cigarette. He who flies at night says *Dèr voghormia!* during the day. The mighty cannot be judged, the mighty...

HAÏK

Mister the Director of All Lunatics, the world is crazy and you're crazy enough to see just how crazy it really is. But I'm convinced that the main reason for our craziness is corruption, which exists in every part of our lives.

EDIK AND GAM *(Singing to the tune of* West Side Story*)*
Corrupzia! Corrupzia! Corruuuupziaa!

HAÏK

Here's an absolute truth: *la corrupzia* is power and power is *la corrupzia*. But the more power becomes lost in *la corrupzia*, the more it drives the whole country crazy.

EDIK

Corrupzia! Corrupzia!

GAM

Corruuupzia!

HAÏK

Today, the average citizen is unhappy with those in power. Because they have violated him. Worse than that, those in power have castrated him. What a hard on! And what a symbolic expression of lost virility. Castrated, I tell you, Director General. We've been castrated.

GAM

Ma che sciagura d'essere senza coglioni!"

HAÏK

Yep. Impotents, eunuchs, castrati, limp dicks: that's what we've become. And our homeland is nothing but a dumping ground that its children want to abandon as fast as they can. Parties and individuals have insinuated themselves into the power pyramid. And now they claim to be above the law and to impose their will on the people.

EDIK AND GAM

Corrupzia! Corrupzia! Corrupzia! Corrupzia! Corrupzia! Corrupzia! Corrupzia!

HAÏK

Our elections always end up consolidating the crushing power of corruption. Everyone knows that the results have nothing to do with reality.

EDIK

Corrupzia! Corrupzia! And if you want to go into politics, it doesn't help to be wise.

GAM

But to have any opportunity to become wise, it's better to avoid going into politics. *Corrupzia!*

HAÏK

Whether they're wise or ignorant, Mister Director General of All Lunatics, most of our deputies regularly violate Law Number 65 of our Constitution.

What does this article say? *(Haïk takes an old pad out of his pocket and reads).*
"A deputy cannot run a corporation and occupy a political posi-
tion in the State or in commercial organizations and receive a
paid salary unless they work in scientific, educational or medical
posts. A Russian agency investigated our saviors' personal wealth.
The Cobra and Samourai presidents seem to be sleeping on a mat-
tress in which they've stored a few billion dollars each. Luckily,
to take a break from visiting all his factories and his thousands
of acres of personal land, the President of the National Assembly
also owns a hotel worth seven million dollars and a Dutch Gazelle
woman's bicycle. And while the Prime Minister regularly asks his
compatriots to go on vacation in Armenia, it's only so that he can
take their place and spend his own vacations in his luxurious villa
in Spain. He's a stockholder in three of our banks, but do you
think that he can find the time to manage his personal fortune of
about 30 million dollars?"

EDIK

Corrupziacorrupziacorrupzia. Corrupzia...

GAM *(singing)*

... rupziapziapziapziaaa.

HAÏK *(still reading from his notebook)*
"Our president is like Napoleon the Lesser. A Cesarion who
controls our money, our banks, our safes, our urinals, and all the
people who go back and forth without ever feeling the slightest
shame. I am citing Victor Hugo, or something close to it."

EDIK AND GAM *(As they crush insects under their shoes)*
Pzia! Pzia! Pzia! Pzia!

THE DIRECTOR

You'll pay for this! Trust me, you'll pay very dearly for this! *(He opens the*
door of his 4 by 4 and disappears into its entrails. The car U-turns to head
out the gate and turns right towards the Nubarashen heights.)

EDIK

Go back to where you came from, you retarded dog! Go!

"I was born in Nubarashen. It's where all the losers come from. It's where everyone in the Republic that you leave behind is from," Haïk stated.

"Under the old regime, Edik, the Nubarashen that came before *our* Nubarashen must have been like a Swiss village looking out on the country's sacred mountains.

"Sacred mountains!" Gam sighed.

"You can say that again," Edik stated. "And then the dollars from our brothers abroad started to flow in. They wanted to finance a pioneer colony. But you couldn't find any water on this blasted flatbed. No water. Hard to believe that our directors who were directing things couldn't find a better place to settle than this hole in the wall.

"Not to mention that it's the coldest wind tunnel in the country," Haïk added.

"They diverted the money flow and the irrigation system ended up not irrigating anything whatsoever."

"And the mythical Ideal Village died of thirst under the sunlight of socialist idealism. First, they baptized us Nubarashen after our main benefactor, Nubar. Then we quickly became Sovietashen. So, we wouldn't forget who our real guardian angels were. I even worked there for a while as an engineer. I used to tell myself, what difference does it make which regime is in power, since another one will replace it? But what you build will always be a part of this nation. Right. Gas is so expensive in winter that you have to sell your house to heat it. And you can't just sit around all day complaining repeatedly about the vultures who have stolen everything. They've even run out of excuses to take away the tiny pensions they've allocated to retired people.

"Yesterday it was our idealists and ideologues who cheated us, today it's *the independistas* who are wiping us clean."

"They weren't content to give us back the name Nubarashen, they left us a miserable old lunatic asylum which doubles as a detention center for political prisoners, and which is flourishing, as you well know...”

“Where we’ll all end up anyway,” Haïk prophesied.

“It’s such a sordid institution,” Edik added, “full of mentally handicapped orphans. One of my sons works with the loonies. When the country fell into Independence, a lot of people fell along with it. There was a certain comfort level under the old regime. There were jobs for everyone and free education. I took night classes, for example. But I know why the caged bird sings. And liberty is irresistible. After then everything went completely awry. Men had nothing holding them up anymore, they were birds without wings. People’s natural rapaciousness overtook communist “brotherhood,” which was only ideological anyway. The ones who fell lost all hope. The ones who ended up exiled became rootless nomads. Democracy made some people into savages, others into exiles, and turned everyone else into lunatics. What else is there to say when the special children’s hospital becomes a dirty, outdated beehive of sexual abuse? The administration uses those poor kids as slaves to do any old job they can find.

“We read about that,” Gam said. “It’s horrible.”

“The country has no future,” added Haïk. “It’s lost all compassion.”

“Today,” Edik continued, “when I think of Nubarashen and its political prisoners, its unemployed and its old people, I think of a stockpile of trash. I made sure my two other sons got out of here while they still could. They keep telling me to come join them. But Los Angeles isn’t for me. To stay holed up all day and watch the city from a skylight? No thank you. People older than I am scratch their bow on a violin in the street and others put their scales out on the sidewalk and offer to weigh you to make some money. And I spend my time in the garbage dump. My sons have no idea. *Kouném’ yéresset, President!*”[47]

“But we created this country, didn’t we? There used to be a knitting factory. And another one that made shoes,” added Haïk.

---

47   Literally: *I fuck your face, President!*

"When they were new, your shoes only lasted three days on your feet. A record in the Soviet empire."

"An entire village lived off that one factory," added Edik. "Well, it's been abandoned like all the other factories. National sovereignty gave birth to a republic of monsters. Someone schemed to take our factory away from us. A public good, to be precise. Took it apart, piece by piece. Anything that could be stripped, including machines and metal. And also the doors, windows, shades, toilets. All that's left of that carcass are the walls and the roof. During the grey decades of lies, we wanted to be free. Well now they threw it all up in our faces. The villagers still don't know what hit them. The minute you go out in the street, it jumps out at you. It's still there. A ghost. Humiliation has seeped into our bones. You can hear it in my words, *meret kounem!* And against our witchdoctors, there's nothing you can do, there's no medicine you can take."

Farther along, on the other side of the shacks where the dump opened, some barking attracted the three men's attention.

"Dro's pigs are fighting the stray dogs," said Haïk. "It's always the same thing."

Gam observed Haïk. Haïk is the country unto himself, he thought.

16.

*H*aïk and your disheveled, bedeviled look. As if you'd just emerged from some pit. You look like one of the convicts working on the Arpa-Sevan tunnel.[48] That's how much the smoky earth clings to your skin. You stink of the city's excrement. Because you're one of the diggers, one must ask oneself if your lungs don't spit out all that stench into the open air. Others simply pop plastic bags open. You've been alive forty-six years, of which you've spent six in the garbage dump, come winter, spring, summer, or fall. Now you know it by heart, like a map. You know where to find the juiciest layers. During the old regime, they used to throw out metal parts that people sell for a lot of money today. You can cover your mane of hair all you want under your hat; your crazy eyebrows tell the whole story. Your anger comes rising out of the stone. Your Lori accent. As if you were chewing on some Tumanyan with your mouth full. Fifteen years spent in Russia haven't change a thing about your language. Except you had three rug rats when you came back. All unemployed today. And anyway, who can find work? You certainly wouldn't encourage them to muck about in our trash. If they only knew where you spend your time. You never mention it to anyone. When anybody asks you, you say that you work on the construction sites. And why not as the Samurai's chauffeur? Or a toilet attendant at The Metropol? Everyone knows that wages often arrive months late. When I first started, you told me: "At least here you get paid daily. Bad days, good days. A metal searcher looks for the right piece of scrap. He collects bars, sheet metal. He takes apart old motors or out-of-use machines. A week or two of this type of thing? It costs about 4000 drams to rent a OUAZ to transport the stuff. But you get about 15, 000 when you

---

48   Dug to divert the water from the Arpa river into Lake Sevan.

sell it. Without mentioning the copper and aluminum. For that you don't need a truck. You are your own truck. You end up with 3,000-4,000 drams." You make about 200 dollars a month. But to earn that much you pop open all the filth and enter its entrails. Those who aren't as aggressive as you make less. Some days, they only make 400 or 500 drams. But what do you do with all this money that you make from these metal works? You don't play Lotto with it. You don't enjoy Ararat cognac. And you don't go on vacation in Antalya. So, what then?"

"What other hope do I have but to get the hell out of here and go back to Russia. And in any case, the government's perfectly happy to have its citizens living abroad. People who are exiled abroad become whores for foreigners and send money back to the old country, obviously. Otherwise, how would our elderly survive? They survive yes, but in their souls they're dead. The country gets rich by tearing itself apart. In any case, the government takes advantage of the situation to the max, so they don't have to pay their veterans as much. Edik will tell you. How many houses in Nubarashen have been emptied out by people who left to go work in Russia? Entire streets. Democracies are dirty. That's just human. It's going to take decades before our republic reaches a respectable stage. Certainly not during my lifetime! Here your future is just a dream that constantly gets aborted. Some people find work in the land of our historic enemies, but here there's nothing you can do. You won't see me, over there. Yet our governments are supposed to provide us with enough to survive, no? The truth is they don't give a damn. They couldn't care less if people suffer, and their lives permanently fade away. And when, in order to bother you, people claim that things have changed recently, you become incensed."

"Our leaders change places but nothing changes. They change underwear, not their mentality. Each one takes his place, picks thing up, piles them up and returns home feeling it's mission accomplished. One day I was standing next to the hole where I was digging, and I asked you what on earth you went to Russia for."

"For work! First I was an electrician, then a cook, and then a mechanic. I learned three professions one after the other. So why did I get stuck in this fucking pit? Before getting to this point, I applied for work everywhere. But instead of offering me a job, some henchman would ask me for three hundred dollars, sometimes a thousand. As if a job were some type of privilege that you had to buy! Three hundred dollars. To shell out that much money just to have the right to work, no thank you, that's not for me. Not like the ones who sold themselves to those in power. My friend Serdjik, for example. At the beginning he just went from one petty job to another, then he started repairing body parts in auto shops. He could never make ends meet. And one day the elections were just around the corner. In the meantime Samurai, the Prime Minister, woke up one morning and ran for President. Since Serdjik had fought on the front during the country's worst moments, the candidate's little clique fixed things for him. *Here you go, something to renovate your apartments with!* To thank him, Serdjik offered the Samourai his big mouth and strong arm. That helps during meetings. Serdjik glued posters, made a big stink and went around supporting him. Samourai became President. And now our Serdjik has become one of the chosen few. They didn't just give him one job; they gave him two. Necessity is the mother of all convictions. They say that today he even helps prison guards put people in their place. Like in Nubarashen. And to do their dirty work they make people wear hoods. *Prudence oblige.*"

"Here you feel free. There's no foreman tracking you all the time. And with the money you make, you can keep your family above water. But there are also days where you jump for joy because of something you find. Like that bag that you removed from its dirt packing. While you were peeling away the oily papers from around that baby, you screamed to me: *Get down here! Get down here! I think I've got one!* I was already by your side when you removed the handgun from its covering. It was still clean. Its oily paper had protected it, not to mention the oil that it was bathing in. A Tokarev. A TT 33 to be exact., like the ones that Moscow distributed to all its brother republics in the sixties. Our police used them. Some agent had probably tried to get rid of it when Independence came around. There were no bullets inside, but you knew where to find some. And how many times did you stumble on envelopes, old correspondence, or ancient newspapers that had remained protected inside of boxes. And also, cheap medals.

Part of those baubles that they rewarded you with it the old days—they left nothing to the imagination as to what the guy had done or endured to receive them in the first place. Secret archives, black suffering hidden beneath our feet. Documents that had been improperly shredded, with the name still intact on them. The names of victims and collaborators. You even found old school notebooks. Lost at the bottom of a drawer or in a desk that had been improperly emptied, or carefully wrapped inside a newspaper inside a mattress. Everyone was wary at the time. If you complained about anything, you'd end up in Siberia. The author of one of these notebooks had written everything down, in maniacal detail: the price of bread, the artificial conversations he'd had, as well as all the low blows and nasty things that escaped from colleagues' mouths. But also the lies that his children were learning at school, and the words belonging to the Russian occupier that were raping our tongue. Our language which had been developed to translate the Bible and had been perfected by our wandering poets: the guy used it to describe his petty, everyday battles for survival. Once he was dead, his notebooks ended up in our gluttonous dump. One day you picked up someone's black notebook, which had been miraculously saved. A cheap leather cover, a dozen lines on each page, the pages dirty at their edges. The man was addressing his notes to his grandchildren. They were written with a fountain pen, in red ink that was fading to mauve. A story that came and went according to the vagaries of his memory. A water salesman from Smyrna. Three children. They lived so close to the French consulate that they didn't dare treat them too badly in public. And so, to starve them to death, they weren't allowed to leave their house. It was a particularly scorching summer. One day they heard somebody knocking at their door. A neighbor was bringing them food at her own peril. She saved them all. Later, pushed towards the sea when they burned the city down, they made it to Athens on French ships. He enlisted in the Greek army, was taken prisoner, and then was released to the care of his own people again. Twenty-five years spent in Athens. And then the family decided to move to Armenia. The homeland... Another time, someone brought you a package tied with a string. Letters written by a certain Hovig, a soldier posted at some god- forsaken front. He was writing to his lover Lusiné, narrating what he saw to her. A mountainous place where only the seasons changed. But Lusiné never answered his missives. At the end, he was begging her to write back, in order to avoid going crazy. He could feel that the distance between them was only making things worse. But lost boxes are your favorite discovery. You open them and find old photographs inside. One day you even said to me: *Come have a look, you miserable man, you have no idea how thrilling this is.* The pictures had been taken during someone's youth. Dreams, dancing on the deck of a snow-white ship. Compatriots, snatched up like our French friends at the end of the forties that were coming home to the motherland, enticed by Stalinian promises of a glorious future. At the time, the indigenous people were sharing a lone, rare piece of dry black bread for dinner. These Utopian patriots who had left their lives of revelry to come here and nibble on a few crumbs were welcomed by the native Armenians with the lovely name of *aghbar.*[49] Which technically means *brother.* A nickname which the native made venomous by accentuating the syllable *aghb.* In other words: trash. In other pictures, one of those cuckolds of the Promised Land was chopping wood in a snowy countryside that resembled Switzerland. You even found piled up rolls of bank notes sometimes. They weren't worth the paper they were printed on. But the boxes ...

At night, you sell your scrap metal, eat well, and then start to sort out these remains that you stuffed into your pockets: letters, photos, books, notepads. And you think: this is part of our culture too, isn't it?

---

49   Pronounced *arbar.*

17.

*D*ro djan', keep your pigs in check! Otherwise, they're going to feast on a stray dog." Haïk didn't like the idea of Dro letting his pigs loose on the garbage dump, as they shamelessly rummaged through everything in sight.

"We're always tripping over them, and they scare the women away," added Edik."

"They're aggressive, they are," said Gam. And like our Oligarchs nothing makes them sick, although they make everyone around them ill." They laughed.

"Our saviors, you mean, right Gam?" said Edik.

Dro stood in front of his shack looking worried. He was cursing the garbage trucks which were streaming by one after the other. This wasn't the usual procession. Something abnormal was preventing them from going home.

"Why don't you leave my pigs alone, Haïk. They're not about to give up today. And I don't have the time to read them the Bible."

The pig vs dog war had escalated. Screaming bitches, squealing piglets— hate against hate. Knocked over as they made their way, the dogs had regrouped in front of a large rusty cistern. Hairy, black, with razor sharp vision, their snouts on fire, the pigs charged with their heads lowered. The dogs showed their fangs.

While Dro kept his eyes on the road, the three men watched the spectacle unfold in front of them. They had learned to tell certain boars apart: the fiercest ones, the leaders. One day, Gam heard Dro calling them by their names. The same familiar names that one could find anywhere in the City. But here, in the dump instead... On the day in question, he was admonishing Idi Gago, the Botero of his boars, who was as round as a water tank. A fat one who never lost weight, like a big barrel of lard. Bella was Dro's favorite sow, low to the ground, made up of pink and sensual fat, and as titted up as Artemis. As for his black sheep, he'd given them nicknames to match their individual temperaments. He'd call them without ever raising his voice, in order not to divulge his political hatreds. Cobra was the most supercilious of his mating pigs. A hostile short-haired Panzer, he dominated the rest of Dro's most aggressive males. When it came to eating his share of fat, he'd squash a rival without bargaining. Another way of recognizing them: Cobra followed Bella by smelling her ass. And Samourai was right behind him. Samourai, whose eyes were so small that they looked like two tiny knife gashes. That's normal, Dro thought to himself, a Prime Minister is always trailing his President. (This was when the Samourai was still waiting to take his place at the head of the country). Since then, all the rag pickers were playing the surname game. It relaxed them. "Watch out guys! Idi Gago is coming to poke around our legs." Women got out of his way, afraid that they would get knocked over. When it was Cobra's turn, a jealous Bella would grunt menacingly in the air. The Scholar on the other hand had lent his name to one of the stray dogs, because he was in the habit of standing still with his left paw always up in the air, his eyes looking away, drooling after the future.

The boars grouped together and formed a semi-circular wall of muscle, backing the dogs up against the water tank. Occasionally you'd hear some *houas*! turn into plaintive whines. Some thought they would escape by leaping over the porcine wall. But the ones who failed to clear the wall fell into a chaos of vices, hammers, and anvils. Trampled, torn to pieces, all shriveled up *allegro con fuoco furioso*.

The three spectators had their eyes fixed on the fight between the leaders. Idi Gago had Cobra's back. Samourai was right behind his master, but Cobra was afraid of the Scholar's and his vassal's kicks. The Scholar was aiming for his eyes and snout, his most sensitive parts.

"Get him, Scholar! Get him!" the men were screaming. "Scratch him up big time, that Cobra!"

The Scholar was barking, haranguing his troops who now operated in unison with him. Every bark that he belched forth was like a critical salvo. And although they weren't dogs, the three men knew how to interpret these vociferations. They let their rancor interpret the proceedings at will: "Bunch of steam rollers! Squashers of democracy! Bunch of rapists! You've eaten away at the people's souls! You're sucking their blood. Get outta here! You've transformed the country into a dump, and you won't even let anyone have enough to eat."

The boars, their tails corkscrewed from rage, were advancing on the mutts. Suddenly, Cobra felt something stick him in the ass. It was Samurai who was shoving his master into his foe's teeth. He kept pushing and pushing until Cobra turned against him. A battle for dominance ensued. A general confusion now reigned in the pigsty, the pigs being particularly pig-like and thus screaming as if they were being led to the slaughterhouse. Bella came to Cobra's rescue, while Idi Gago kept his aggressiveness in check, to the great joy of the three men who were doing the play-by-play on their way to the heart of the trash dump.

All the while, on the roofs and in the poplar trees, the crows were astounded by the fight that they were witnessing. On the mounds of trash, blasé seagulls took in the sun, one leg lifted in the air. They weren't waiting for the fight to stop or to continue. They weren't waiting for anything, in fact. Swallows flew around in a cloud of air. Smoke rose lazily into the sky. Sensing that there was trouble on the ground, the rats fled to more peaceful parts. The field mice fled into the smallest holes that they could find, and the dung beetles returned to their nests. These fights ended up annoying Dro who clubbed the belligerents until they dispersed."

"Traffic in midtown, supposedly. Really clogged up."

18.

Dro to Khatcho: "Khatcho! Allo Khatcho!"

Khatcho to Dro: "Dro *djan'*, is that you? I can't hear well."

Dro to Khatcho: "Yes, it's me Dro! God, what *nanar*[50] did you go stick your *koukourouz*[51] inside again? Come home, will you, prodigal son? You should already be here. The trucks aren't arriving anymore. The midtown ones, I mean. From the Opera, Abovian, Sayat Nova, Groucho Marx and Baghramian avenues."

Khatcho to Dro: "But it's the crowd, Dro. The crowd is stopping us from getting through. And not just any crowd. An *up your ass* crowd. What else do you want to do? Maybe you know why people are in the street like that? If you could see, it's like our Hraztan when its waters are on the rise."

Dro to Khatcho: "How on earth would I know? I'm not a journalist. I'm stuck to my garbage dump. But I've been waiting for you here for more than an hour! Go through Bangladesh or Etchmiadzin[52], whichever way you want, just come home now."

Khatcho to Dro: "Dro! Dro! Just imagine! Despite the truck I was driving, the police asked to see my papers. As if they couldn't tell that I'm transporting household trash! Just think, I couldn't even remember where I'd stuffed those damn papers! I finally found the bloody documents! You know where they were? Inside the foam on my seat. Who on

---

50   Girl.

51   Corn cob.

52   The seat of the Armenian National Apostolic Church.

earth had the idea of sticking my identification papers inside the rip in my seat?"

Dro to Khatcho: "And what did they want exactly?"

Khatcho to Dro: "How the hell do I know? They were just doing their job. They were checking documents, car by car. I thought they were looking for *Tadjiks.*[53] Is there another war? I asked. Did they invade again? And you, did you learn anything on the radio?"

Dro to Khatcho: "It took them that much time just to check your papers?"

Khatcho to Dro: "On the contrary, I'd already started my pick-ups. My truck was half full, they requisitioned me."

Dro to Khatcho: "Requisitioned? What equipment did they requisition?"

Khatcho to Dro: "First they ordered me to dump my load in front of the Scholar's office, on Guriun Avenue, then they made me go in behind the Opera, on Liberty Place. There were tents, signs, scaffolding, kitchen utensils, pieces of wood, iron rods, clothing pins, knitting needles, mattresses, blankets and lots of flags, piles of torn flags, torn as if a storm had passed over them. It made me cry. Everything was on the ground, piled up like at the garbage dump. Some posters were even stained with blood. Yep, I saw that. Some police officers filled my truck. They were still equipped for street fighting, their billy clubs hitched to their belts, but without their shields. After that, they ordered me to leave. But the roads were slow because of all the people. Especially Tigran Medz Avenue. People were coming down Northern Boulevard carrying all sorts of banners and flags. Other groups were cutting across Central Square through Sargsian Street. I got stopped on Krikor Loussavoritch by the protesters."

Dro to Khatcho: "You were stopped?"

---

53   Turks.

Khatcho to Dro: "They recognized my load. I was carrying *their* tents, *their* mattresses, *their* flags, *their* signs, and *their* clothing pins."

Dro to Khatcho: "And it was also their blood, no doubt."

Khatcho to Dro: "Yes, their blood. They saw red right away. They wanted to lynch us. They started to throw everything on the ground. Suddenly, we were surrounded like a herd of sheep. But the truck stank so much that they started to make room for us to go by."

Dro to Khatcho: "Did you see any of our friends?"

Khatcho to Dro: "Not one. Someone may have stopped them as well. Unless they thought they were circumventing the protests by taking Avan."

Dro to Khatcho: "Why Avan? If I understand correctly, you're going to have to redo your sector."

Khatcho to Dro: "I couldn't go all the way back up Sayat Nova Avenue. I'll have to return tomorrow. But today, I wouldn't count on it too much."

Dro to Khatcho: "I'll wait for you to come home. You figure it the easiest way. Just come home."

Dro to Levontchik: "Allo Levontchik! Which sector are you in now?"

Levontchik to Dro: "Baghramian Avenue was completely blocked up. I wanted to take the stadium road, but they closed that one as well. Now I'm parked in front of the restaurant at the entrance of Kiev Bridge. I'm with Ardo. We're waiting for it to open so we can eat *lahmajoun* with some Kilikia.[54] What else can we do?"

Dro to Levontchik: "What else can you do? But I'm waiting for you. This is what I'd do. The minute you can, speed up Goriun Avenue. They forced Khatcho to dump his load of trash in front of the Scholar's offices. Pick it all up and come home. Take whichever way you want but I want to see you here as quickly as possible."

Levontchik to Dro: "Okay, I'll take Goriun. Understood. I'll go by

---

54   A brand of beer.

Komitas, Monument Road and then Terian. *Prablem tchka.*[55] That's what I'll do."

Dro to Levontchik: "No problem. I'll be waiting for you."

Levontchik to Dro: "You can count on me."

Levontchik: "*Ara!*[56] Make sure to roll that *r*, like in Italian, that *lahmajoun*," he chewed on some of the pizza "has just enough spice and with a lot of oil, it turns your mouth into a symphony."

Ardo: "The best I've ever eaten is still my mother's. And you know why?"

Levontchik: "No! Do tell!"

Ardo: "It's a question of magic. I used to watch my mother make it."

Levontchik: "And how did she do that, your mother?"

Ardo: *(ripping off a piece)* "She'd pinch her lips."

Levontchik: "And that was her magic?"

Ardo: "No, but when I saw her pinching her lips, I knew that she was putting all her heart in it. As if she was back in the old country..."

Levontchik: "Is that all?"

Ardo: "First she would dilute the yeast and mix it in with the flour. Two soup spoons of sugar and two coffee spoons of salt and four cups of water. Then she would knead the whole thing with oily hands. You have to oil up your hands if you want a soft dough that you can work with easily. Here, take this napkin, you're getting oil on your mustache."

Levontchik: "Thanks, *djanikess.*"[57]

Ardo: "She would knead the dough like that for fifteen minutes. At the end she would use her fists. Then leave the dough for at least three hours. Then you make some balls out of it. As many balls as slices of lahmajoun

---

55   No problem.

56   Slang: *Yo!*

57   My dear.

that you want to make."

Levontchik: "Should we order some more?

Ardo: "Good idea!"

Levontchik (to the server): "Two more. *(Turning to Ardo)* And the stuffing? It's the stuffing that makes the *lahmajoun,* no?"

Ardo: "I'm getting to that part! For the stuffing, use finely chopped shoulder of lamb. Two types of ground peppers. Ground parsley. Lots of onions, ground as well. And some dried mint. My mother would add garlic and small red peppers. That spices it up real well. Then tomato juice. Salt. Pepper."

A passageway lay between the bridge's parapet and the restaurant wall. The first few meters were paved and gave way to a dozen or so steps. Then a dizzying, stony slope, and a valley with only a few lone trees spread out haphazardly. At the end, a river. The Hraztan. Scintillating, flowing along an asphalt road.

A man emerged from this passageway wearing a black cap. Two pieces of anthracite as a uniform. Black glasses. A pointy pair of shoes. A matching sweater hugged his neck. And a shaved head. Latex gloves, carrying something he'd wrapped up under one arm. Something long, heavy, horizontal. What was it? You go figure.

Ardo: "Well, that's the best *lahmajoun* I've ever eaten. Better than the one at *Mer Tâghuh.*"

Levontchik: "*Mer Tâghuh!* [58] Their dough is too dry. As for their meat, I won't even tell you. Just enough spice. Tân is good for washing it all down. When it passes over your tongue, it helps with the burning sensation."

Behind him, the first man's twin carried the other part of the package. Human sized, covered in a blanket. A black mane of hair escaped from beneath it. The two men found themselves with their noses poking into the garbage truck's backside in the parking lot. The first one didn't hesitate. He lifted the

---

58 Our neighborhood. (You roll the *r* in *Mer* but the *ghuh* in *Taghuh* is prounounced like *Paris* in French.)

package. The other did the same from his end, and together they threw it in the truck. It made a dull sound on the metal. The first guy went up to Levontchik and Ardo, who hadn't heard or seen any of what just transpired.

"All good?" He said to them.

"Yes. Come sit down," Levontchik answered.

"Thanks," answered the other. "We have work to do." They went back to their car and exited the parking lot. A black four by four with tinted windows.

Ardo: "So you must love the *lahmajoun* that the Jehovah's Witnesses make? You know, the place at the far corner of the dead end, with a vine growing in the middle of the room that goes up through the ceiling."

Levontchik: "And how. We used to go there all the time. But now management has changed. And even their *lahmajoun* has changed. It's not as soft as it used to be."

Ardo: "The waitress was Russian. She had a tiny voice. She claimed that they made their *lahmajoun* only with natural ingredients."

Levontchik: "We'd order a pitcher of *tân*. Now they serve it by the glass."

Ardo: "And they were always busy. Only men hung out there, except for once when there was a couple. No out-of-towners. The guy was older, the girl much younger, in her thirties. You kept telling me: 'Look at her look at her, that's the type of girl I like. A nice specimen.' And she kept looking at the guys the way you wanted her to look only at you. She would bite into her *lahmajoun* as if she were devouring her lover. Sighing *akh!* with each mouthful. She was wearing a red flowered dress that day."

Levontchik: "She was European and had fiery eyes. She never stopped staring at the old guy."

Ardo: "It might have been her father, for all you know. Or a friend. A guy. Nah. I saw her put her hand on top of his."

Levontchik: "Then she was his lover. Now we must go and fly up Charents, otherwise Dro is going to be in a foul mood."

They asked for the check and lit a cigarette. Then they tilted their heads way back into the air, blew out a huge drag and paid: 1, 400 drams. While he opened the door to his truck, Levontchik heard some women's voices. Vociferations. Lamentations. Angry hysterical screams coming from the bridge. Some thirty meters away, he saw some women facing the empty space below and crying out while hitting the large metalwork ramp that dated from the old regime with their fists.

A small old man with an uncertain gate walked by. He held himself up with a cane, his look buried in old age, and approached Levontchik. He had just crossed the bridge.

"You don't have a *papyros*,[59] my son?" Levontchik took his pack out of the pocket of his jacket. The old man removed two cigarettes, questioning Levontchik with his eyes.

"That's fine, old man!" The old man put one cigarette in his mouth and placed the other in his jacket pocket. Then Levontchik gave him a light and the old man took a puff.

"Those *lâtchâr* feminists, *they gave me a splitting headache by squawking like a bunch of geese.* But there you go. I was still able to pass by." He took a second drag. "I walked across this bridge; I walked across my life. Not like you, you've still got some way to go, don't you?

"Who knows, I tell you. Who knows how long I still have to live," Levontchik answered.

"That's what I said," answered the old man. "You're still in the middle of things. Me, this Kiev bridge, well I saw it when there was nothing left. The bridge is cursed. It collapsed once, during construction. That was in the middle of the nineteen fifties. Lots of dead among the Romanian prisoners of war. They'd all been dragged back from Hitler's jails to work on it. The architect, a certain Nersessian, was accused of sabotage. They exiled him. You know where, of course."

"*Sibir,*" Levontchik let loose.

---

59 Cigarette.

"That's right, Siberia, the little old man continued. But ever since it was completed, it's held up well on its own two legs."

"Yep, it looks like it's taking a piss and creating the Hraztan River all by itself," Ardo interrupted.

"I guess so," the old man continued, "but ever since it was built the Kiev Bridge has been able to help a lot of desperate people of all types. They used to drop like flies. You must remember that from our long, cold nights of independence? Yeah well, this bridge has seen more than its fair share. People would jump into the abyss—in secret of course. Eighty meters high. That way you're sure of waking up in Paradise. But the newspapers were banned from talking about it. In case others should get the same idea. Then in time the bridge calmed down. Now we're desperate again, but it's a different type of desperation. One that stops you from breathing. The desperation that comes from being without hope. They cut the wings off our dreams."

"The Cobra's henchmen," said Levontchik.

"That's right," added the old man. "The Cobra's killers. He spent his time hunting down his opponents. Occasionally you'd find people all the way at the bottom. Crushed they were. Try to find out who they were or how they ended up there. A lot of men ended up that way. Some are still falling that way today, from time to time. Men who like men and who aren't liked because of it. So they throw themselves from the bridge. But women also jump. And for other reasons. You go figure it out. Go figure." The old man kept repeating himself as he walked away, his hand gripping his cane. "And thanks for the *papyros!*"

FIRST FEMINIST

One more! One more! One more that they've thrown out like trash into the void.

SECOND FEMINIST

Like a raw egg on a rock. Like a baby against a wall.

THIRD FEMINIST

Like a fruit ripped from a tree during a tornado.

THE THREE FEMINISTS TOGETHER

That's how the women fall. They fall. The women fall.

FIRST FEMINIST

In the swirling tempest-filled night, the woman falls.

SECOND FEMINIST

The Kiev Bridge: a tomb. An accursed bridge.

THIRD FEMINIST

Because men unleash the tempest and, uprooted, women simply fall.

FIRST FEMINIST

They fall, they fall. Under the man-made tempest.

SECOND FEMINIST

Who knows why?

THE THREE FEMINISTS TOGETHER

No one.

SECOND FEMINIST

Who defends them?

THE THREE FEMINISTS TOGETHER

No one.

THIRD FEMINIST

Oh, Mount Arakadz, look how they fall the women, between this bridge's legs!

THE THREE FEMINISTS TOGETHER

Kiev bridge. Accursed bridge.

FIRST FEMINIST

Thrown by whom? And for what reason?

THE THREE FEMINISTS TOGETHER

No one knows. No one wants to know.

SECOND FEMINIST

Thrown down by those who are drunk from taking justice into their own hands.

THIRD FEMINIST

Thrown down by those guardians of the national soul.

FIRST FEMINIST

The drunkards of history. Heinous defenders of honor.

SECOND FEMINIST

Oh, Mount Arakadz, look and see what they do to our women who cross the border!

THIRD WOMAN

Because they're hungry.

FIRST FEMINIST

Women who go feed themselves in our former enemy's lands.

SECOND FEMINIST

Because they're hungry.

THIRD FEMINIST

They violate their dignity. They prostitute their innocence.

THE THREE FEMINISTS TOGETHER

Because they're hungry. Because they're hungry.

FIRST FEMINIST

Because their children are hungry.

SECOND FEMINIST

Because their husbands have left them.

THIRD FEMINIST

And why have they left them?

THE THREE FEMINISTS TOGETHER

Who knows? Who dares to say?

FIRST FEMINIST

That's how Amalia Amalian met her end. She'd left by bus for the enemy's country. She had the nerve to cross the border to the other side. She had the nerve to go looking for work when her own country wouldn't offer her any.

She'd barely returned home when they found her at the bottom of the gorge.

SECOND AND THIRD FEMINISTS

The Kiev Bridge. The accursed bridge.

FIRST FEMINIST

God in Heaven may your Glory give succor to this poor woman!

SECOND FEMINIST

Let your goodness erase her stain.

THIRD FEMINIST

Let your light warm her soul!

THE THREE FEMINISTS TOGETHER

Halleluia! Halleluia! Halleluia!

Their bodies stooped over, trembling. Their hands stopped hitting the ramp. The cars roared behind them. The valley waited at their feet, a black monster with its maw held wide open. Hoping they would also fall? Who knows? While in the distance, covered in quartz, Mount Arakatz sat imposingly. Suddenly the first feminist let out a word. At first it sounded like a painful murmur that the wind periodically blew all the way to Levontchik's ears. Then a song that rose into the air. A rage that slowly matured. A supplication which sounded like: *Let there be life! Let there be life!* Her body swayed and slowly these vibrations rose in a spiral towards the sky like a heartfelt breeze, a hunger looking to draw from the light until its movement infected the two other women, all despairing and searching for answers, and swaying from side to side as well: *Let there be life! Let there be life!*

19.

O ld and lumbering, Bus Number 13 crossed the Kiev bridge for the millionth time in its forty years of service. Accursed bridge. The sound of a loud clink from the token machine and a sputtering its decrepit motor. Levontchik didn't hear *the spirit of man.*

Or the first woman who said: "How much are lamb's feet? My husband wants to eat a *khâsh*[60] with his friends." The three women had fixed their dresses and were now walking in Levontchik's direction.

Second feminist: "I don't know. I'll find some at the Arabkir market. It's easy to recognize the butcher there. He puts their whitened feet in a pail like a bouquet of flowers."

Third feminist: "Khâsh is poor man's food. I think it's disgusting. A man's dish that they eat all winter. The garlic in that soup burns your mouth all day. Without even mentioning the *oghi* that's like fire in your stomach."

Second Feminist: "To wake up as a group at dawn and to start lapping that up."

First Feminist: "Not to mention all the grotesque burps that your body makes afterwards."

Levontchik had already slammed his door shut and revved up his motor when:

First Feminist: "That package there in the truck ..."

The truck had just turned onto the avenue, spewing black fumes onto the

---

60   Marinated pigs' feet with kasha and garlic that Armenians eat with lavash bread and copious amounts of vodka.

three stupefied women who were instantly transformed into soot-covered statues. Six dumbstruck eyes staring at the back of the truck. Six open wounds. Six imploring mouths. Is this how you're supposed to end up, woman? Like a piece of trash? Like some garbage destined to be forgotten and burned? Once he arrived at the end of the avenue, Levontchik drove into the crossway and turned left. That's how the three stunned women saw the truck disappear.

The two garbage collectors drove on, up Komitas Avenue, now reconstructed to be long, wide, and smooth, but clogged up at this hour by a horde of frenetic automobiles. Then they plunged towards the Monument, a tall grey tower crowned with a golden spike.

"Look! Look!" Ardo cried. "It looks like Idi Gago dressed up as a Roman warrior. A naked bronze Botero wearing a huge helmet, and a ridiculous shield, short and with fat coming out at all sides. Have you seen his *bouboulik?*[61] It's as if someone had planted a small carrot there. So small that nobody would want it. They could have given him a *koukourouz* at least, no?"

"That's true," answered Levontchik. "But at least he's got someone officially guarding him, day, and night."

"God save me, I don't ever want a guardian who looks like that!"

"*Vaï dm'bo!* You're worth less than that thing!" Levontchik exclaimed, annoyed. "That's why they let you come and go as you please. You're more of a third-tier citizen than a Roman soldier. Your corpse will barely be worth throwing into the garbage dump!"

"And why would I even care," concluded Ardo, "once I'm dead?"

They turned on Guriun Avenue and parked on the street, in front of the entranceway to the old regime building where the opposition now had its offices. The trash formed a huge nauseating pile of stuffed bags, bric-à-brac, food and kitchen leftovers that were slowly decomposing. Flies already buzzed in all directions and bees zoomed around it. Acknowledged pros at their job, Ardo and Levontchik got to work immediately, starting with the bags. They threw them

---

61   Foreskin.

onto the truck without looking where or on top of what they landed. Two policemen on duty—the dutiful, petty civil servant types—potbellied like devourers of *khâsh*, approached the truck, their mouths ready to unleash cannon balls of invective.

First Police Officer: "Put those bags back on their piles where you found them! We're watching them, so that no one touches them!"

Levontchik: "Come again? I'm a garbage collector, Mister Law and Order. I don't take sides. My job is to take the city's trash all the way to Dro's garbage dump."

First Police Officer: "Well then take the trash that belongs to the people who come to this building. For now, this trash doesn't move."

Levontchik: "In that case, show us the court order that says we can't touch it."

First Police Officer: "*Pitoukh!*[62] I'm the court order, standing right here!

Levontchik: "And I, barracuda *djan!* I'm a garbage collector. I'd like to point out that this trash can bring disease. The bubonic plague, vaginal infections, cholera, AIDS, typhus, rabies or scabies, epilepsy, Abaran syndrome, memory loss, alopecia, eczema, psoriasis, yellowed teeth, incontinence, obesity, follicular lymphoma, and especially impotence, mister the barracuda agent. There are no more Marshall with big *gavazans*[63] like Baghramian. Only soft, shrunken, mini carrots. And the longer that trash stays there, the more dangerous it becomes. Dogs and cats will rummage through it to find their sustenance. They come and go carrying disease with them."

First Police Officer: "Sorry, no dice! You're even going to empty your truck completely on top of this trash. Then we'll see what you take with you. Do it now!"

---

62   Rooster.

63   Stick.

---

1   *[n. b.: translation of sheet music: Now that my body's in danger. Let there be life! Let there be life! God of mercy and God of terror. Spare us the sharks and narks. Spare me! Spare us! We are our doctors' dead who think they know the truth. We are the dead. We are... We are the dishonored who belong to the animals who control our bodies. The dishonored. We fall prey to thoughtless beasts. We fall prey. We are the beasts' prey. Father oh heavenly father make room next to you for the woman who falls. Next to the women whom this misery has destroyed. Misery. Such misery. Their souls are exiled in solitude. Exiled. Exiled in solitude. Voiceless creatures, suffering and near death. Voiceless creatures. Voiceless creatures suffering. Let your pity lift them up*

because they have not sinned. No, they haven't sinned. Let your goodness pull them out of the abyss for they have not sinned. No, they haven't sinned. Thrown from the top of this bridge by lunatics and beasts. The Kiev Bridge. Accursed bridge. Creator of life, have mercy and recognize your creature who is in the dark. Creator of life. Creator of life. For her pain is a stain on man's soul. A stain. A stain on man's soul.

Levontchik: "Sorry, that's out of the question. First, I must call my boss and let him know."

First Police Officer: "Call whomever you like!

Levontchik calls Dro on his phone: "Dro, it's Levontchik. I'm on Guri-un. There's a cop here who wants to keep all the trash for himself and who'd like us to dump all our garbage out for him."

Dro: "What the hell is he doing poking his nose around in our business? That trash is ours! That's theft! Do I steal his police cap, *huh*, do I?"

A group of onlookers had formed and was gawking at them. Suddenly they started to put in their own two cents about the situation at hand: "Can't you smell how much it stinks?" A lady addressed the police officer. "It's a disgrace to pile up our sidewalks with this trash. If things keep going in this direction, we're all going to be wading about in an actual pigsty! The trash belongs at the garbage dump, not here," another woman added. "You want to make us catch all the viruses inside it, is that it? He knows what he's doing, it's his job. Maybe you want to genocide us, is that it? Get rid of the opposition by contaminating us?"

"And what if we dumped this in front of your door? Would you be happy then?" A young man added. Here and there, some barbs still flew, directed against the Samourai's henchmen.

"Why here, in front of the opposition offices? Nothing happens by accident. You can see right through this ploy."

A small crowd was beginning to form. The two police officers were starting to feel threatened by the anger of the people surrounding them. They became anxious. What if people decided to lynch them or run them over, with all the crazed power of their bitter hostility? They began to sweat profusely. The first policeman spoke into his walkie talkie. Then he turned towards Levontchik: "It's all good. You can take all this with you. But hurry up!"

The two were already using their brooms and shovels when Ardo asked Levontchik:

"How do you know about all those illnesses?"

"How do I know about them?" answered Levontchik. "I used to make my brother recite all his medical classes out loud. I could have listed others. But I was afraid of scaring people."

"And what is this so-called Abaran syndrome?" asked Ardo. "Because I come from Abaran."

"I invented it, Ardo *djan*," answered Levontchik. "But I'm sure it exists. If you look hard enough."

They made it back onto the road. To reach the dump as quickly as possible, there was no other way, apart from taking Archakouniats Avenue. But to do so, they had to cross midtown. Some roadblocks had just been lifted. The truck penetrated into a mayhem of annoyed crowds with frayed nerves. The motor was purring away on its pistons but was close to puttering out and dying right in the middle of that beehive of activity. Ardo watched silently, paralyzed like a bird, unable to say anything, conscious of his prey-like status. As for Levontchik, he kept pushing on the accelerator whenever the slightest opportunity opened up for him to squeeze by. Finally, they drove onto Archakouniats Avenue relieved. After that, the road became easy going.

"Dro! Dro!" Levontchik spoke into the telephone. "We're arriving with the load. Where should we dump it?"

"Where should you dump it?" answered Dro. "All the way South, like yesterday, but more to the right. And hurry up otherwise you're going to block the way for the others who are on their way back."

The truck unloaded all the way South, a bit to the right side. As usual, this godsend of trash attracted a colony of seagulls. A dog lifted his snout into the air when they unloaded the trash. Gam saw him flair the new odors to distinguish them from the ones that usually reigned in the garbage dump. The dog left what he was doing behind him and rushed to the location where the truck had unloaded its pile. Quick on the uptake, the other dogs followed suit. Dro was too busy maneuvering his digger to notice the plot that was being hatched behind his back. Gam asked him to turn off his machine. He needed to talk to him.

20.

*D*ro stopped the motor. "What is it?" He asked, annoyed. "Why are you messing with my routine? You know I'm late! And that the trucks are late because all those street protests are preventing them from picking up!"

"Those dogs over there," said Gam pointing to the corner where Levontchik had emptied his load. "They're fighting over something that's wrapped up. It looks like something stiff that doesn't belong here."

"They're scrambling for the spoils," answered Dro. "You've never seen starving people? Even humans would do the same thing. They must have smelled some new blood and now they've gone nuts. They'd eat anything they can get their teeth on."

"That's just it," said Gam, "it doesn't look like just any old thing."

Grumbling and cursing, Dro hung his leg outside the narrow driver's seat to help propel himself completely out of the truck. *Look at him get out of that box of his! If he'd been cast in bronze atop his horse Djalali at the main train station, he would have made a great living replica of the Sassuntsi Tavit statue, thought Gam. Powerful nose, stubborn forehead, a full head of hair, a head as big as two others. He was a real colossus, Dro. But what type of a man was he, in comparison?*

He kept repeating his story. How many years had passed since he'd first been appointed to the city's sanitation department, administrator of the city's crap? No one knew. No one dared to ask! He walked around with his blood-speckled black eye. *This garbage dump was here long before I was. And I won't go fill my own grave at Roubo's without having first buried him in dirt myself with my own two hands. The dump is like an open pile of entrails. I've been taking care of people's disappointments forever now, just as Roubo takes care of people when they pass into their eternal sleep. Roubo deals with death. In my case, the stuff I take care of is still living matter after all, even if it is half dead. I'm the only person who knows all the endless swells that occur in this chaos. I'm the only person who can take care of the pressures caused by these daily arrivals. An ocean that grows ever more violent. But what can a man, one lone man do, to combat these intestinal monstrosities, I ask you? The city looks like a continually expanding body. It grows and grows! They make it hunger so that it so that it guzzles four times more than it needs to. I understand that the heat makes you thirsty. Without mentioning the nights of pouring rain. Boxes, bottles, cans, papers, cardboard, and every imaginable type of wrapping material.* Gam had always known Dro to be the person in charge of this underhanded skulduggery. He had discovered his exceptional ability to tolerate the most abject situations from others. That's how Dro had survived the purges and managed to survive the most corrupt regimes. Admitting with the smile of a fallen angel that the garbage dump was his own creation and dominion. He drew the pathways with his digger so that the garbage trucks could get through. He remembered the age of each different layer of trash simply by its relative position. But Dro wouldn't share his knowledge with anyone else, even when you forced him to drink. He would never reveal where the most valuable stuff was buried. At most he would point in a general direction and hint at where something might lay. But how could one possibly find one's bearings in this obscene bazaar, as large as an airport runway? Only Haïk could read on his face whether he had any chance of finding a lead. It was a good sign if Dro became agitated and shivered like so many tintinnabulations. On the contrary, a smile at the corner of his mouth, meant: *Keep digging, sonny boy, keep digging!* That deep cesspit belonged to him and to him alone. Some people, like the garbage pickers, were simply tolerated. Tolerated out of a sense of humanity, he would grumble. Dirty parasites! But what could one man do against forty or so poor wretches? He disregarded dumpster science and confined them to this space so they would survive. He had been refining his theories since birth, it seemed, forever marinating in putrefaction. His body had become intoxicated by the toxic farts it produced. The malodorous smoke had ruined his lungs. His voice was hoarse. And his skin had been transformed into dark and crumpled leather. He would spit his innards out in coughing fits, hunched over or bracing himself against his digger, his eyes reddening and his veins dilated.

"Dro djan', have you ever thought of leaving this cursed place?" Haïk asked him one day after one of his attacks.

"It's a place all to ourselves. Can you imagine me abandoning my digger and my pigs?" Dro answered. "I'll end up over there when it's all over," he said, pointing to the cemetery. "All I have to do is cross the street, if there's still someone nice enough to walk me to my grave. And I want is for my pigs to be part of the funeral procession!"

Dro was part and parcel of the dump. "If I can make it till the end," he would say, "scientists will fall all over each other to study my body. The thing is that I'm something completely novel for them. What happens to someone after he's exposed unabated for years on end to the completely polluted air that develops from organic decomposition? My body is the only one that can provide answers for them. And don't even try to match me when it comes to length of exposure, because I'll always have you beat by a few years. But today these scientists are pretending not to understand. I bet you they're planning to steal my corpse. They wouldn't even let me cross the road if they had their way. And it would all be free of charge. I'll have worked my ass off my entire life in this dump, poisoned myself in a regular and systematic way, and all for nothing."

The dump had turned his body into a human expression of itself as surely as an ideology can petrify a face and become personified in that face's expression. This was the case when an idea occurred to him. He would exude smoke as much as his field of burning garbage. An animal, this Dro. As much of an animal as the rats or pigs who stuck their snouts everywhere. A good forty people daily joined the creatures in this daily to scrounge for something to keep them alive. To suffer the fetid air that the City's privileged breathed on a regular basis. In the end, Dro and this little group of starving obstinates had chosen this daily regime of grease and its fetid odor. Like others in this world or any other. And if this cesspool should ever be covered in dirt one day, they would scatter like crazed ants chased from their homes by a solid kick. Dro threatened them on a regular basis.

"I'm going to submerge this dumping ground with the earth from the surrounding hills," he would warn. "In a week or two, I will have made everything disappear with my digger. And then there will no more rats, no more seagulls, no more crows, no more men, no more you!"

But the rest of the time, Dro would show off his strength by releasing his swine into the trash to induce panic among the weakest. The others were chased away with the needles of their *lapatka*[64] the same way they pushed back their dogs. But Dro's black woolen hogs advanced in groups. They searched the contents of opened bags with their snouts, and slashed open boxes, pulling, tearing, and sucking wherever they found an odor stronger than theirs along the way. Everyone stayed away from these four-legged octopuses because they laid waste to everything and would do the same to human flesh as well. This competition was looked down upon, but Dro liked to take vengeance on any insult or setback by exploiting it. When they were particularly hungry, the coprophagous pigs and errant dogs would sometimes knock into each other with their ribs or heads. When one group squealed, the other showed its fangs. These beasts would draw blood for a piece of bone with a bit of meat on it. Scuffles that frightened young girls. Dro wasn't always able to stop them. But if he chased the dogs away, it was to defend his pigs. The two men would disperse the swarm by kicking them with their boots, producing plaintive cries from the angered dogs.

They uncovered the object at hand. It was without a doubt a human corpse that had been carefully hidden inside a blanket. Long black hair to one side. It was a woman. From that point on, they delicately unveiled the body, starting with its feet. Gam wondered why they began with the feet. A leg appeared covered to mid-thigh in leggings. White skin that Dro brushed against with his big grease-stained fingers, ecstatic from the unreachable innocence that lay dead

---

64   Pail also used to dig.

in front of him. He stood up, his hands joined, his eyes fixed on the woman's leg that awakened long hidden dreams within him. He mumbled in an erotic, psalmodic mode:

> *Oh, cherished native girl*
> *Your skin is soft and like milk*
> *Your taste sugary, your hair silken*
> *Oh cherished native girl*
> *I ask of you one favor:*
> *Come dance a devilish Sarabande*
> *In my arms.*

Then overcome with pain, in a voice that alternated between the grave tone of religious chants and the plaintive one of criers, the anger of indignation and that of a murmured secret, he launched into an incantation worthy of the prophets themselves.

> *I am only a picture of death.*
> *A form delivered of its soul*
> *Tortured to death,*
> *Here I am, a broken jar.*
> *I have undergone the hell of condemnation,.*
> *They murdered me like a dog,*
> *Crushed me like a flea.*
> *I am like an ash that one discards,*
> *Dust that one disperses,*
> *A horrific stench.*
> *Even as I speak in this life*
> *I am dead in the eyes of eternity.*

Then silence.

Religious, ironic, beautiful. From a living man trying to decipher the mystery of death. The phenomena of appearance and disappearance that transform life into theater. Called upon, he who has asked for nothing, denied, he who has understood nothing—man. But what did Dro think? What had he not implored God to do? *Because you are an unknowable God. You alone are omnipotent and forever blessed.* The torpor was silent and deep. But when Dro found the completely dislocated head, chest and body and pushed aside the dirt-filled hair mixed in with black blood to uncover her neck, Gam became dizzy. Her face was unrecognizable, Dro said. Crushed and bloated, most probably due to a shock or a long fall from somewhere else. He rummaged through her clothes but found no identification papers.

"They threw the body onto the truck in secret," he added. "Levontchik and Ardo were probably busy doing something and never noticed. What I do know, is that they stopped in a pub near the Kiev Bridge. That explains everything."

What other choice did he have? He asked Gam. Tell the police before putting it in a pit? Of course not. Instead, he would pretend to be blind and not see anything. In the end, he was afraid for himself, but also for his pigs. Dro was already frightened at the idea that his disappearance would turn them into orphans. Hunger would drive them to rip each other apart in the sty where he used to leave them. And their pink skin would be sullied by their own excrement.

As for Gam, death haunted him already. It grabbed onto his body. It ripped his spirit apart. The circumstances and its causes confused him. That dirt in her one ear and eye located on the same side of her face. The one that had undergone the shock? And that hair—that hair that flowed black onto her shoulders. And what about that wound on her face? Dro was right. It had most probably been one long, uninterrupted fall. Like the ones that his friend Zara had witnessed when she investigated the deaths of those women that one found at the bottom of the bridge eighty meters from the parapet. They all had same type of wounds, she said. And now Dro covered the body again and left it the way he had found it.

"I'll tell Levontchik to pour gravel over it. In the meantime, not a word to anyone."

"No," said Gam. "I won't let this woman's body rot along with the trash."

"Roubo won't be able to help you" Dro said. "One of his graves is expensive.

And you know very well who you have to pay."

"Let's carry her a bit higher up," Gam suggested. "In the abandoned zone, eventually we'll find her a grave."

They carried the body in the direction of the road, crossed it and climbed onto the embankment. Then they placed the body, wrapped in its blanket, inside a hole in the burnt zone. Just then Dro noticed a large four by four in the parking lot.

"Look!" he said, "That *chan' lakot* haven't lost any time in getting here. They came to eat me for dinner."

21.

*C*ome along, let's find out what these toilet-cleaning Gestapo agents want from me," proposed Dro. They had taken the road reserved for trucks to reach the parking lot. A garbage truck was slowly dragging its load uphill: it was Gago. He stopped without cutting the motor and stuck out his broken hair-flecked mug of a face. The dust that he was dragging behind him landed on the two men.

"Dro! The big rectangular car in the parking lot! Looks like they're here for you! Looks like they might be looking for a fight."

"Why don't you just worry about dropping off your last load," Dro said, annoyed. "If they think that they're about to write my epitaph, then they've got something coming to them."

"But it's a tank!" exclaimed Gam.

"It's basically a four by four disguised as a panzer," Dro corrected. "When a small country begins to ape the Americans, it looks gaudy and in bad taste. People who drive these things want to crush their compatriots like flies, without a second thought. And it works automatically. Look who's about to come out of there. No one sickly like you. Giants with shaved hair. Buffaloes. No need to have gone to Oxford to do what they do for a living. Their size is their diploma, their stature. Submit, obey, menace, hit. That's all."

Dro wasn't wrong in his assessment. They were twins, tailor made for each other. They had shaved heads and wore black leather caps, matching pointed shoes and matching tight black sweaters. They gave off a robotic air, like a machine that asks banal questions to put the person being questioned on the right path. It was obvious who these guys they worked for.

The men didn't exchange a single word. Dro pushed the door to his office open. They followed him without taking off their sunglasses. The anteroom stank like a pigsty. They quickly lit American cigarettes to do battle with the infection and overpower the smell. Dro got out his French cognac, a bottle that he'd found inside the dump.

"It's the real thing," he told them.

They turned down the invitation with a scornful gesture. Dro quickly understood that they weren't here to get some fresh air.

"Is everything okay Dro?" one of the shaved heads asked in a low voice. "You like your job? You're well paid?"

"Nothing to complain about," Dro answered. "The air is pure. So is the water. I have as much to eat as I want. And I even have work. Yep. I have work. The work is dirty, but I manage to stay clean. I wash myself with soap."

He kept smiling despite the boring conversation. The other one took the hint: "Well then, let it rot!" he said, moving in towards Dro. "That's our only advice, Dro *djan*. Let it rot. You never saw anything."

"I didn't see anything," added Dro. The threat had been made. His life wouldn't be worth much if he decided to alert the press. Dro concluded that his only choice was to let the body macerate in a bath full of trash.

Gam saw the twins run out of the shed while they breathed in the dump's rotten air. *Pouah!* one of them cried. *Ouf!* added the other, as they both breathed in a heavy dose of the fetid air that stagnated in the dump. The comings and goings of the cars, trucks, buses, military jeeps, and dump trucks were unable to create any proper ventilation. It stank like sheep's cheese mixed in with cadaver meat and burning greasy paper.

They rejoined their vehicle relieved, joy etched on their faces. An impassive and magnificent vehicle. An island of green amidst a sea of excrement.

"*Ara!* you smell. I think you stepped in a *kâk*[65] maybe?" Asked one of the guys.

---

65   Excrement.

"You've got nerve! You're the one who smells like a toilet!"

"You're not going to smell up my car, are you?"

"Go have mom clean your ass before you accuse me! *Vai!*"

"Leave my mother alone! Leave her alone, I tell you! *Bôzi tegha!*"

"Hey! Why don't you ask Dro to hire you? You wouldn't have to pass your stink exam. You're wearing it."

"Is that so?"

Then one of them took off his shoe and threw it at the other. Then the other took off his leather hat and hit his brother with it.

"Go for it, guys!" said Gam. "Harder! Come on, harder! You're creating some ventilation for the bad air and bringing a bit of life to this boring old place!"

They fought with as much rage as they could muster. Each one used the car as a protective wall or shield. They continued to trade punches and make noises like thunder or crazy-sounding fireworks: *Wham Bam Pow Pow.* They exhaled loudly and screamed at each other, and things heated up, as if the entire world were in revolt. The cap, lost in the hurly burly, was replaced by a vest as a weapon. The other one pulled on the vest, forcing his adversary to let go of it, enraging them both. They took off their shirts, revealing two wrestlers as hairy as bears. Then they removed their pants to use as whips. Both were in their underwear now, white with black polka dots. But the pants didn't hurt enough, so they took off their belts and dragged each other to the ground. Grabbing fistfuls of dirt, they flung this sacred earth at each other. It flew in all directions and onto the road, sometimes hitting cars, trucks, taxis, and military vans as they passed by. Even Roubo wasn't spared as some landed on his face. Suddenly he leaped up like a tiger ready to tear apart some ill-advised intruder. But he quickly rejoined his stool, realizing that he wasn't up to the task. He was content to yell out, patriotically:

"Lakotner![66] Aren't you ashamed to waste earth like that? We have so little of

---

66   Thugs, louts.

it left and you're throwing it to the four corners of the world!"

There was so much noise that no one even heard him so, resigned, he placed his stool on the sidewalk to get a front row seat. The more action at Dro's place, the better! And he began to calmly roll a cigarette, as usual.

"If you hadn't thrown it out of the truck, we wouldn't be here stinking like pigs!"

"You still grabbed it by the feet, didn't you? Someone had to say something!"

"I held it! Yeah, I held it! And why wouldn't I hold it? It wasn't to keep her feet from getting dirty! It was to help you! To help you! You weren't going to climb all the way up carrying her all by yourself! *Kekhtot vôtchil!* And it was your idea after all, right!"

"My idea? My idea? We had to get rid of her, didn't we!"

"And how did she end up at the bottom of the bridge?

"*Kâki ktôr!* [67] You know perfectly well why we do certain things!"

"Sometimes I can't remember anymore ..."

"But you know why you named yours after the Scholar!"

"And you named yours after the Samourai!"

They ripped the metalworks off the palisade and flew in all directions. The seagulls jumped up on the rooftops each time they hit the ground. The ground trembled. The entrance gate lurched forward with each hit. Gam screamed for this fratricidal war to end. But the air began to boil. Armed with stakes, they were now fighting to the death.

"You're spitting in the soup now, *tarakan*"[68]

"And you, you make me vomit that soup! Vomit, you hear? Your soul is doing a wolf's bidding."

"Go work for someone else then if you dare!"

---

67 Little shit.

68 Cockroach.

"To end up at the bottom of a bridge and most likely thrown there by you. Go eat out of Gago's hand! Goon! The hand that feeds you is the hand that'll smack you as well."

Emerging from his shack, Dro joined this epic battle. He immediately made his way towards the car, gait steady and eyes enraged. What would he do? What would he scream at them? He punched the van's innocent hood. The punches made the van and the two men inside it shake.

"No boxing allowed here!" He screamed. "Go settle your issues elsewhere! I'm the only orchestra leader here! Stop this right away!"

His words worked like electroshock therapy. Switching from their status as enemies, the two brothers went back to being best friends. They picked up the torn threads that they had spread all around the parking lot. Their clothing was so similar that one took what belonged to the other. They disappeared into their van for a minute before they reappeared and lowered the four windows. They looked like two nitwit nudists caught having some fun. The car was barely back on the road when the gateway, relieved of the stress weighing on it, reverted to its old shape. Roubo was upset.

Gam approached Dro, furious.

22.

*D*ro! Now I know who the dead woman is," said Gam. "I knew it when I saw her hair. My eyes remembered. And yet it's been years. From the minute I entered the dump. It's been years since I last saw her, but her eyes, her eyes. How could I forget them? I think we must tell the police. Those two are involved in the crime. I'm sure they're involved. I'd bet my life on it. They knew exactly where to find her. Can you imagine? I mean, you can just throw someone over a bridge and everyone looks the other way?"

"The police! The police!" said Dro. "Can you imagine them even coming in here? With them you know where you start off, but you can never be sure where you end up! We've seen people go in who never came out. Or feet first. Now believe you me. Better to let her rot, and I'll put some gravel over her corpse. That way the dogs might smell her, but they won't be able to touch her."

"But it's a crime! A major crime!" Gam yelled. Gam had taken off his bonnet and was fiddling with it nervously. Then, solemnly, he intoned:

"One crime, Dro djan, just one crime where we don't try to find the perpetrator and we're abandoning all of humanity. You understand. Because one day they'll kill another one, and another one, and another. And who knows, why not you and me? Because we'll be abandoned. What will become of us if we're abandoned? Because we'll have been abandoned. And what becomes of an amnesic nation? It puts all a people at the mercy of others' bidding."

"And what will happen to my pigs if they detain me in a police station? *(Dro had stopped walking and was looking at Gam straight in the eyes).* Orphans. Because they'll detain me, mark my words. Not for an hour. Not for a day, but for entire months. And what will happen to the garbage dump without me? Did you think of that for even a split second? You jabber on and on. It's a crime and *yadda, yadda, yadda.* But we're drowning in crime. Every day is a crime here. There are as many crimes in this country as there are people. Every instant of the day they kill something inside each citizen. Our executioners produce victims and the victims in turn become executioners. There! You tell me! Haven't you died a bit every day slaving away in this dump? Yes. You have. You're trash yourself Gam and you're dead! Buried almost. Barely anybody even knows where you are. That's the way you wanted it, isn't it? You wanted to bury yourself alive. Even your mom didn't know that you were here, in the garbage dump. But that's exactly why we must report this crime. To do otherwise is to already be dead. Like dying under duress."

"Well, my friend! I don't feel like croaking. You can report your two donkeys with shaved heads, if you want, but don't count on me. Tomorrow, four more will pop up, all identical. Then eight. And they'll play football with your head. Or with mine, more likely. And as for all you bumpkins, what would you do without me? You'd all end up badly. You'd end up on the outside. They'd chase you out. And how would you survive in the City? You'd be no better than stray dogs. You'd see what evil would befall you. Trust me on this one!"

"Whatever you say, Dro! But let me tell you! The dead woman's name is Zara Zaraian. She was a journalist at *Zhamanak.* For a few months she was researching women who take a car once a month to go prostitute themselves with the *Tadjiks.* Anywhere else, I might understand. But in Turkey? What we do to survive in this shithole is bad, but what they do is much worse. What pleasure can you take in being fucked by your own executioner's sons? They told Zara that. It's to get revenge on our leaders. And so that we realize what our mothers, our heads of families, have been reduced to. The shame isn't theirs. It belongs to our three presidents. Scholar, Cobra and Samouraï. But which president can accept that a bunch of scatterbrains ruin their mandate? They still find women's bodies under the Kiev Bridge on a regular basis. Zara was looking into the why of it all. But also, how it happened. She had a few answers. Suicide. Like in the darkest times of our young republic. Or else thrown over the railing. But by whom? Pimps?

Unlikely. These women left without any protection. And on their own. No: they were undoubtedly thrown over the bridge as a warning. And whose mission was it do so? The President's shaved heads. It doesn't matter which one. These three are all equally responsible for throwing the country into its present state of despair. Who else had any interest in throwing these women from the bridge? Nationalist henchmen who don't respect the country's good name, that's who."

Zara. Not a woman who gives up easily. Especially since she was convinced that she had found the thread that held the entire scandal together. The type who keeps digging. Tireless in her attempt to get to the bottom of things. Like an archaeologist who clears some sand or mud and screams *hoorah!* at the smallest new find. One day she had spoken to him.

"We aren't any better or any worse than other nations, but we are who we are, she said to me one day. And this country doesn't deserve to silently waste away under the mysterious goings on of the rich and powerful. When I was young, I was blinded by my patriotism. I wouldn't allow anyone to say anything bad about our country. Or that we air our dirty laundry in front of foreigners. I thought that we could only criticize our country away from the gaze of others, in private. But I always found excuses to exonerate ourselves of our national illnesses. Other nations, I reasoned, suffered from the same foibles. Sometimes in even greater proportion than we did. Until the day when I realized that this type of thinking was blocking our way towards democracy. When you don't discuss your own scandals, you encourage criminals to continue in their ways. You encourage crime. Until then, I lingered on the country's beauty, its churches and landscapes. But everyday people were undergoing so much hardship that they didn't notice any of these things anymore. I had undergone my very own journalistic conversion. Since then, I don't hesitate to be a muckraker. Even if it bothers our more idealistic souls. Suffering is the symptom of a pathological culture. A country's destiny matters little. My role is to denounce those who, directly or indirectly, take it out on the least privileged in society. The ones who lie openly for the profit of their business or political careers. Today, I even publish abroad sometimes. I always end my pieces by accusing politicians that I identify by name, for their deliberate obstruction of law and justice."

And she'd paid for her obstinate work, as she recounted:

"It was late one night, very late in that greasy spoon near the entrance of the Kiev Bridge. I was interviewing a witness there. He claimed that he knew who was throwing everyone over the balustrade and why they were doing it. Once he'd left, a man accosted me. He suggested that we go for a walk on the bridge. He remained silent. I was walking over an abyss. And what if he suddenly felt like chucking me overboard as well? He squeezed my arm and forced me to look at the emptiness below. Now scream if you want to join the others. He wasn't kidding either. Keep questioning people like you've been doing, and you'll go straight into the hole that you're staring at right now. From time to time, he'd throw a furtive look at both ends of the bridge. As the cars disappeared in the distance, he picked me up by my elbows. The Hraztan's water was shimmering at the bottom, reflected in the light of the streetlamp.. I could feel my last seconds on Earth ticking away. I thought of the dazed women, as they fell into the abyss. I was crying. Tears of rage against myself. But out of fear as well. I was two steps away from peeing in my pants. He put me back on the sidewalk. I breathed in. He would have thrown me into the river in a heartbeat. I was like a rag doll at this mercy. That's okay, I thought, I've had enough of all this! Enough of this insanity. I'm stopping everything. My inquiry into these women and who throws them over the bridge. Enough already. I don't want to hear about any of it anymore. I may even move abroad. I see that you understand very quickly, he said. You get stubborn, even if you know where this type of curiosity ultimately leads you. But now let's walk, OK? His hand was still grasping my arm tightly. A hand like a vice. We walked to the other side of the bridge. Then we crossed the road. He drove me towards Tsitsernakaberd. We must have reminded people of lovers in search of a dark, quiet corner. Two police officers lost in conversation ignored us as we went by. We continued to walk up the hill and I was having a hard time in my high heels. Where are you taking me? Walk, you'll see. I'm going to make you hear the memory of our dead. Those that your girls defile while they're getting plowed by Turkish guys. I was dragging my feet. But he was pulling me forward. His hand was crushing the bones in my arm. You're hurting me. Ouch. You're hurting me! And why not? The more we went up the hill, the fewer lights there were. On the benches, you could make out the silhouettes of lovers. We

reached the esplanade, which was deserted at that hour. The lighting gave the monument the appearance of giants sitting in a circle around a flame. My heels were making incongruous sounds. I had the impression that I was being pushed towards a pyre. He stayed rugged and steady. The more I resisted, the harder he pulled me. A chant on the inside rose plaintively into the dark. And men and women's voices alternated telling their sad tales to the night.

The horrors that took place there, in Kemakh, to hundreds of thousands of men, are the very picture of unimagined barbarity. One might think that the insanity of thousands of years piled onto itself and was concentrated into this one corner of accursed earth, like a monster screaming under a hot June sun.

A policeman recounted in a vivid manner how, little by little, the men had been massacred and thrown to the bottom of the gorge. Kill! Kill! Throw them in! How at every village, the women had been raped, how they had split open the heads of children when they cried or slowed down the convoys.

He pushed me down on the stairs in between two of the columns overlooking the eternal flame. He twisted my arm and forced me to bend down. I was lying down on the stairs. He let my thighs go. I was in such pain that I couldn't scream. The flame distorted his face without consuming it. He covered me with his cold, cruel air. I was panting and tried to stay still to avoid the torture growing worse. A hard knife, penetrated into my flesh once, then again and again more and more frenetically, nailing me to the spot. I couldn't withhold my tears. Then he disappeared into the night. I was bleeding."

Zara lay prostrate in her apartment for an entire month. Without knowing if she should continue her investigation or renounce truth and have people forget about her by leaving the country. She persevered.

"If I call the cops, like you're asking me to, who will get in trouble? You will!" (Dro had abruptly stopped and was pointing his index finger at Gam's face) "I know perfectly well why you decided to spend your life in the garbage dump. To hide. If the Samourai's truants stuck their noses in here, they'd have no trouble making the Hedgehog come out of hiding, don't you think? And anyway, rumors have it that this Hedgehog is writing a book about the entire shithole surrounding us. No one's sure exactly what form it's taking. A novel, some people are saying. A shit-stirring novel. Or one that peers into the darkest corners. That's what they're saying. Because I haven't read anything at all. (Once he'd reached his digger, Dro dove into the cabin and turned the motor on.) Not a word. Not a single page. Nothing at all.

Your breasts are... Gam put a *lapatka* on his digger and drove to the heights where Zara lay, her body wrapped in a blanket, in her hole. The ground was black in every direction surrounding him and in front of the smoldering dump beyond the smoke, far beyond the hilly slopes lay the City. Gam stood above the pit, sheepish and poor, with Mount Ararat at his side, vibrant and pure. *Dèr voghormia.* Gam said to himself. *Dèr voghormia,* Ararat echoed back. Then nothing else came to him. His soul was empty. And Zara spoke to him. Zara wrapped in her blanket. Continue. Continue. She had returned to the City for that. But him? He didn't want to hear it. Because to continue one had to stay alive. And to stay alive, you had to shelter oneself from the people hunting you down. *Your breasts are like grapes in the palms of my hand/Your skin...* Those were the words that came to Gam. One day he'd let go of these words while they were walking up the Memorial Hill. As if he wanted to nail them to her soul and illuminate them. Words that slept within him. Words... And here he was reciting them to her, as he had just done yesterday. *Your breasts are like grapes in the palms of my hand.*

The smoke burnt his eyes. Tears welled up inside them. Mechanically, he threw the first fistful of burnt earth on the body below. It made a hollow sound on the blanket. Then another. *Your skin is a vibrant velvet of confusion...* Another fistful. *Your forehead a graceful tabernacle. A fourth. Your laughter a deliverance.* And a fifth. *And your silences immaculate...* He stopped, then wiped his brow with the back of his hand and started to scratch again. *I spread your legs like a book in a canticle.* He pushed the earth with his foot. *Under your burning bush there lives...* He threw another fistful down as he became increasingly enraged. *Water thirsty to be drunk...* He scratched, dug the ground, scratched again, and dug some more.

My tongue searches out/The juice that will revive/Man in his bitter agony. And then he threw her into the pit. *Man in his bitter agony.*

Then he started to fill the pit. Filled it and kept filling it. He wiped his brow again. Continue, he said aloud, in a voice that didn't sound like his anymore. He raised his eyes. And Ararat echoed back its approval from its snowy mount.

23.

*G*am climbed onto the pile that was made up of old layers of trash, some burnt, others spared by the flames and which emerged from the rusty earth. But as one penetrated into this abandoned zone, the ground became black, like after a bombing that has scorched everything below. Far from being uniform, the dump extended into the distance in a series of hillocks and small slopes dotted with dark crevices. Gam was used to keeping an extra supply of scrap metal at the border of this abandoned desert. For a moment, he stood and stared at the living part of the dump. Like a fishing troll laboring against the sea and lost in waves of smog, Dro's digger maneuvered among the swells of trash, surrounded by white fluttering. He would make his caterpillar wheels creak and the smoke spew forth with the convulsive noise of the motor, concentrating them around the clouds of seagulls and the dozens of garbage pickers who labored, their heads lowered amidst the pigs and dogs. Their silhouettes lurched back and forth above a vaporous and colorful mass of trash. And Dro continued to drive back and forth over the piles that had been recently dumped, to push them back and flatten them out. As the day went on the newly deposited trash covered the old. A thick layer several meters high had formed. Dro slowly pushed it towards the cliff, where the trash burned in perpetuity while giving off a ring of vapor that ran along the ground towards the middle of the dump. To the North, the City extended under unending plumes of heat, as cranes and skyscrapers pointed upwards.

Dro was fuming as much as his truck. He played with the levers, his eyes clouded over, and looked straight in front of him. The motor penetrated the trash's greasy flesh, which offered itself up bodily to his complete joy. His digger extended outward like a servile instrument, like some mechanical organism of his macho power. It was at times like these that he huffed and puffed along with his motor to force the bitch of a truck forward and let loose with his lips a litany of *Kounem ko puzets yev kohayrenikuh!*[69] Insults whose only function was to increase his hatred.

He was so afraid of his power being usurped that he forbade anyone else from driving his truck. And once he was inside comfortably seated and had filled the medium-sized cabin with his large-sized body, he felt as mighty as a King sitting on his throne. He thought of himself as being at an observation post from where he took in a large part of the garbage dump, from the cliff all the way to the Nubarashen road. A panoramic view that gave him a feeling of domination. On the side of the burning parts, just about anyone could enter his domain, while to the west, the open hill was difficult to climb.

The trucks had barely finished their rotation and the trash pickers had just left to sell their bounty when he abandoned the digger, and it turned into a perch for the seagulls to spend the night. Dro was worried that someone with bad intentions would come destroy his machine in the dark one night, as there was direct access to the burning zone from the road itself.

The dense smoke didn't stop Gam from recognizing the rag pickers who were popping open the plastic bags: little Lala, Mariné standing next to Vatchik, Anoush, Lousso, Arsen and Ardak, Artemis and her baby Artem who kept her company, Hovan, Donatello, Nina, Lisa et Sara, Larissa, Maya—the most beautiful woman in the whole dump—Lili, Nara, Ano and Bertha, Tsknors and his brother, Sako the singer. Haïk was digging somewhere. Mouk was invisible.

---

69   I fuck your pussy and screw your homeland!

24.

LALA according to **GAM**

You're fifteen years old, Lala. And already like a cat. A little girl edging her way towards adolescence. And seeing you, speaking to you, I fall back into my own teenage years. Crazy guy that I am! As if I were forever seventeen! *Dèr voghormia!* You're like a gazelle, lost in this desert of trash. What are you doing among us? They are murdering you by throwing you in here! Even your dirty clothes fail to make you ugly. Not in my eyes in any case. I see your body underneath. Your budding breasts. It's... pure delirium. And your sex... just like an apricot... You plunge your hands into the plastic bags along with the rest of us. But why? They're so beautiful... They should be playing the piano, your hands and your black eyes with their long lashes that radiate out from them. Simply amazing! Except for that day when you received your treasure. That dictionary that I found and offered you. A dictionary from elsewhere. In a foreign language that you didn't know, but what difference did that make? A real dictionary with pictures instead of certain words. And you read those images. Lives. Objects. You guessed at its mysteries. I taught you the letters. And now, you plunge into it when you are done sorting. What are you reading, I wonder, that's so interesting, Lala? Your eyes wide open. Your mouth in the shape of a surprise. Sitting next to me during the break, you ask me. Me. But what can a man tell you about these female mysteries? Especially me, to an adolescent caught up in our pain. You ask and ask away. And I am the one who turns red. I have a hard time saying these words to you. We are seated apart. The sun warms me up, the smoke browns my spirit. And how does a man do this with a woman? And why do some women do it to each other and why do some men do it to each other? I hold my tongue. Later. Later, you'll understand, I tell you. And I sing inside my head.

> *Chinar ess, geranal mi,*
>
> *Yar, yar, yar.*
>
> *Mer trnen heranal mi,*
>
> *Yar, yar, yar...* [70]

LALA according to LALA

Gam found the dictionary as he was tearing apart a plastic bag. He cleaned it and gave it to me. But I can't speak this language, I pointed out. Gam told me it was French. He told me that I should keep it just for the pictures. I looked at them all. One by one. During the breaks, Gam explained some of them to me. I didn't understand them. Especially the ones that show a body and all its organs. A woman and a man, and what they look like on the inside. He tells me the names of things as I point to them with my fingers. I repeat them. It makes me laugh. I like to sit next to him while he explains the words. Gam is big. Mysterious but strong. And yet some of my questions bother him. Once he even stuttered. Gam lives all alone. That's what he said. In truth, I have no idea. Once, I asked him if I was going to spend my entire life in the dump. He answered that I should do anything I could not to remain there. Anything? But what? He said that I would find a boy one day to take me away from here. But in the meantime, I haven't seen any boys. Gam is the only man with whom I discuss these things, thanks to the dictionary. Even if other people make fun and curse at me. Sometimes I hold his hand and lean my head on his shoulder. As if he were the father that I've never met. I feel his strength, his muscles. And even his smell when he's been sweating. And Gam doesn't protest. He seems to like it when you hold him like that. And I do as well.

VATCHIK according to MARINEH

---

70   Beautiful like a plane tree, do not bend/My loved one... /Do not leave our doorstep/My beloved one...

Vatchik sidled up to me to pop some bags. Truth be told, I had been calling to him in secret. I used to look at him while I was hunched over. Maybe he knows that I did that. Who knows? I called him secretly so that he'd come, and he came. As if he'd heard me calling him. Once, twice, and then every day. But Anush was always sorting things along with me. Until she finally understood. Vatchik has thick black hair and dark, deep eyes. He worked for a while at my side before even talking to me. But one day, he grabbed her *meshog* to put it in the truck. He placed his there as well. And we all got in for the sale. I was afraid of getting too close to him. Because my work clothes smelled so much. Even if I keep my hair away from the fumes by wrapping them in a scarf, some of the odors still come through. And then one day we didn't come to the dump. Neither of us. One single day without wearing our stinking rags. I had gone back to being myself and he had gone back to being himself. We walked along the Tzitzernakaberd hillside from which you can see the entire city. And even some of our smoke rising in the distance. People told me that our absence made the others gossip. Especially the women. They said that we had forgotten to wake up. Or that we had gone to Etchmiadzin to light a candle. That the night had tired us out. All sorts of nasty things. When Vatchik went to guard the border, I was already pregnant. At least over there he had enough to eat. But he had forbidden me to work in the dump because of the smoke. When I got back, he kept working there. Alone...

ANUSH according to MARINEH

Your father Sero put you to work sorting trash when you were just seventeen. Right after your mother passed away. You've always had that sad face, for as long as I've known you. It wasn't the sadness that one notices in orphans, for example. Instead, it was the face of someone resigned to working in the dirt all day. Sero never saw your face the way it really was. Or the disgust that you felt at having to stick your hands inside trash bags. You were always nauseated when you leaned over the City's innards. You weren't like me or the others. You gave the impression that the stench was flattening out your chest. That it bored into you. At times you even vomited. Thank God you had Adom, your first cousin. But Adom didn't know. You and your father hid what you did to survive from those who were closest to you. Adom didn't ask any questions. You always smiled at him. I even saw you looking enraptured at times. And then you would take long showers. Wash your hair out, then your body. You used up so much water that your father upbraided you for using up your family's emergency reserves. Yet it was only after performing these ablutions that you could forget how dirty you'd become during the day. Then one day you and Adom suddenly realized that you were like any other man and woman. The doctor that you went to see explained that you had done it unconsciously. *Your relationship is taboo biologically. Think of the calumnies that will fall upon both of you. Especially on Anush.* The entire country would have stoned you, under the pretext that you had seduced a young man. But especially because your union was condemnable and hateful and against nature. But Adom and you were ready to take on the world. One morning Adom surprised you while were walking towards the cemetery with Sero. He hid from the two of you. For a moment he thought that you were going to go spend time at your mother's grave. You were walking in silence behind Sero while he quickly advanced. Adom saw you pass under the garbage dump gate. He was hurt by what he discovered. He could barely believe his eyes. After that, he told you that he couldn't see himself tied down to a woman who was cursed like you were. He even believed that the putrescence of the dump followed you to bed and into your pregnancies. From that day on, he no longer cared for you. Adom locked himself inside his own confusion. Night and day he dreamt of coupling with you while fearing that you would give birth to deformed children. For a while he thought of freeing you from this swamp. As if you were a prostitute at the hands of some powerful master. But how could he forget that your blood would come back to haunt you? Or that the dump would do the same when the time came because of the poison that your body had undoubtedly absorbed? And now you've become like a ghost.

LOUSSO according to TSKNORS

You don't have a door on your house any more than a naked man has clothes. *Aï*

Lousso! Andouni Lousso![71] More dead people in your life than feathers in your cap. *Aï Lousso! Errant Lousso! Orphan! Orphan! Orphan!* As if you had to cut off your own umbilical cord. By yourself. Your cradle was doomed in advance. We left, you stayed. You went back to your shack. Refrigerator carcasses stacked up against an old Jigouli with no wheels or doors. Lousso *djan!* You live on the moon. In the world's forgotten zone, safe from robbers. The ground you sleep on is dead. Scorched earth where no one else dares to tread. You live surrounded by the smell of old ash. And you breathe it in all night. Darkness that lunges deep into layers of trash that date back to the Second Republic. Right where Haïk and Gam dig deep into the depths. You've collected some old red sofas with broken feet. And a bathtub where you cook food that you've found on the spot. Sometimes with Arsen, you attack sparrows who've been shocked by the sun's rays. And you grill a few of them. Lousso! Lousso! This is your home. He sleeps there, eats there, defecates there, and sometimes he jogs around his Jigouli to forget about the day's events. As if he were imitating a seagull. You said it Haïk. Your story is the same as ours. Your grandparents' house collapsed during the earthquake. I know that happened. From one day to the next, you found yourself in the street with the other survivors from Spitak! The walls of the houses? Torn up like paper. Just walking along, you were afraid that everything would collapse. I was also tired of watching this. And like you, I left for Yerevan. The garbage dump was our last refuge. One day you got the idea to build your refuge against the carcass of that old abandoned Jigouli. Luckily, you're here. People trust you. So, we fill our *meshog*s with scrap metal and wait to rent a truck and take it to auction. But Lousso, why have you always operated in the shadow of those two brothers, Arsen and Artak?

GARO according to GAM

Nothing is more valuable than shoes. If you find a good pair of shoes, you can walk around anywhere you want in the trash. Freely and easily. Without being afraid of hurting yourself. If water starts to leak through your soles, let me know.

---

71   *Oh Lousso! Homeless Lousso!*

We walked by the office. Who knows if someone won't stumble upon your happiness by accident? Blind hearts can't see anything. They'll stuff the shoes in their *meshog*. To keep them or to sell them. They glue the soles onto new material. And it's done. Good as new. It hurts just to look at old Garo. His worn-out shoes refused to go on. Worn out by age and open in the front. Not to mention his sad gate. It made you want to cry. I've gotten to the point where I'm going to cut myself on some glass or scrap metal, he'd say. By pure luck, I chanced on a pair of sneakers. We could have sold them, but we gave them to Garo instead. He was as happy as if we'd given him a newborn babe. He was trembling with joy and tears of gratitude. He was finally going to throw his old shoes in the dump. He removed them with care. Sometimes his feet remained stuck to his soles. He had laid them out on a torn newspaper. They were breathing with relief. Happy was the man who was about to put on his new sneakers. Their owner, probably a fashion-conscious runner of some type, had worn the once or twice at most. He must have preferred a better-known brand. And so, he trashed these! Garo put them on hastily, without any socks. He'd wear socks against the winter weather later. Then he looked up at me. Smiling with gratitude. He was grinning like a child. Because the garbage dump is more than a mere cafeteria. It also clothes you. Garo, this same Garo, lived in a coat whose elbows had been worn away. He slept in it, even in the middle of summer. Better to sweat in one's coat than to do without. They were inseparable, like a chicken and its feathers. But once winter came, the coat was like a sieve. Icy winds would blow through its holes. Haïk suggested that he just burn it once and for all! *You can see that it's too used to stop the cold*, he told him. *I'll find you one that you can at least cover your chest with. What are you talking about?* Garo had answered. *I'd cry if I had to burn it.* Garo was attached to his coat like a lover. He carried it down the street and the coat protected him from the outside world. That's how we recognized our Garo, with his long silhouette, hunched at the top. As Garo grew skinnier with age, he'd begun to float inside of it. In the most oppressive August heat, the air circulated and cooled down his body. One winter day, he was standing too close to a fire and the flames reached his coat. Burnt at the bottom, the coat reeked of years' worth of grime. He cried with rage, Garo. Then in an act of complete rashness, he threw it in the furnace one day, and remained in the cold, his arms crossed, watching the fire do its work. Finally, Haïk gave him a jacket. The one that he wore on top of another whose sleeves had been torn. Perturbed by his coat's sudden disappearance, Garo fit into his new jacket like a baby. A pink jacket with white horizontal stripes over the chest area. And everyone behind the curtain of flames was laughing.

HAÏK'S Jacket

There's a story behind Haïk's sleeveless jacket. A dumpster story. One day, the last dump truck had dropped off an old mattress in some god forsaken corner of the dump. There was a bag hidden underneath it. The driver was in a hurry to get home and the rag pickers had already departed for the night. At the crack of dawn, Haïk found the jacket and picked it up. A military jacket with a hood. News of the find reached Mouk's ears. He went to see Haïk to tell him that he was the one who had hidden it under the mattress, and hence the jacket was really his. Haïk shrugged. It's hard to believe that you'd leave such a nice jacket here. Mouk claimed that he wanted to pick up the jacket early in the morning, but Haïk had beaten him to it. The nasty look that Haïk gave him made his blood boil. He jumped on the object in question, grabbed it by the sleeve and pulled. The two men flexed their muscles, neither of them wanting to lose their prize. Mouk was cursing a mile a minute while Haïk remained silent. The outcome of this tug-of-war was uncertain. The rag pickers were grouped together like idiots and were exhorting Haïk to stay calm. They were pulling the jacket in opposite directions, so the two men couldn't get into a fist fight. Suddenly Haïk took out his pocketknife. You needed more than that to scare Mouk. Suddenly the blade opened. Leaping forward, Haïk plunged his knife into the sleeve that his rival was holding and Mouk fell backwards like a circus clown. The small crowd that had gathered was still laughing when Haïk cut off the second sleeve from the jacket. He threw it over his vanquished foe and wore what remained of it. On that day, Mouk's hatred of Haïk was so great that he would undoubtedly have killed him. Since then, they stare each other down like enemies out to destroy each other, getting into alpha male arguments over disputed finds, even when it puts the other rag pickers' lives at risk. But Haïk wasn't the type of man who'd sacrifice his friend's daily bread because he had a score to settle.

ARSEN and ARTAK According to LOUSSO

Summer. Sun. Always that same sun over the dumpster. Its light beats down on us. The trash heats up and you absorb these rotting vapors all day through your skin, your lungs and even your eyes until they sting. Thankfully Arsen and Artak are back for three months. Brothers, those two, closer to each other than blood brothers. Artak scours the trash like a crazy person. Calm down! I tell him. But no! He stuffs everything in his *meshog* that he can, to finance his university studies. If his friends only knew. They can never find out! Artak screams. He's afraid that someone will discover him in the act and that afterwards people will look at him like a rubbish eater. A camera in some random person's hands and he's had it. As for Arsen, he's planning to go far away when he's finished. He's aiming for Europe, saving his money with this idea in mind. Since he must spend money to live, his departure keeps getting delayed. Every year in July he comes back to us. The dumpster holds him captive. But it holds us all captive as well! What's he thinking? When the two brothers are there, we pick up plastic bottles together and re-sell them to the sand factory in Massis. On a normal day, we're talking a minimum of 30, 000 drams. That's more than the City can ever offer. Arsen is one hell of a storyteller. He knows how to lead us on. Last summer, he found the most amazing thing you can imagine. A fairy tale in the middle of the void. Ever since that day, we've become like kids. We believe in the dream. And I believe in it more than the others. Crazy, isn't it? Arsen explained that one day one of the rag pickers ...

The day when HAMLET... as told by ARSEN

His name was Hamlet. That day, he was working off to the side on some newly arrived trash. Then suddenly he chanced on a huge wad of 20,000- dram bills. He counted them, again and again. So much money that he started to drool. There was about two million drams. Soon, after he came down from his high, the lucky guy stuffed the wad of bills into his jacket. He abandoned his hook and his *meshog* on the spot and disappeared before the others grabbed him. They might have forced him to share his treasure. He took off so quickly that no one knew what was happening. But I saw everything. And I started to tell everyone I could, as quickly as I could. The rag pickers were feeding off what I was telling them. I was reciting an operatic plot to them. Some spat up from rage, others cried from joy. All they could make out was Hamlet's back as he walked off. A robber's backside. The news spread like wildfire, beyond the dumpster, as far as police headquarters. Two days later, the two policemen were driving around the City like hawks on the lookout with some plan in mind to get their hands on the cash. They were followed by a representative of the Papolikos,[72] encased all the way from his varnished moccasins up to his pointy hat. An impeccably trimmed beard, black like his cassock. It was the church, mother of the poor and of drams, getting out of a large car, as shiny as obsidian. The priest asked to see the director, in this case Dro, everyone's shepherd. He let Dro know his Sainthood's wishes. And immediately added that the chosen one should share this gift from God with the less fortunate. His fate hung in the balance. Because there is always someone less fortunate than the less fortunate of men. This is a known fact. As surely as the wads of bills that he had found had a true owner. An owner who was desperate about having lost the fruit of his labors. The goods might even appear to have been stolen. Also, in order not to ruin his capital with the man on high, stiff Hamlet might consider donating the whole sum to a goodwill organization such as our patriotic and national church. Dro listened to the religious man's speech and paused for a long time. Into his soot-encrusted ears, someone had just poured unctuous and sainted oil. At the time, his eyes weren't hiding any mockery or sarcasm. But once the pause was over, he spat out his brown tobacco juice. He stared at the priest with fiery rage and burped like a wild pig whose throat was being slit open. How's that, a robbery? Some well-fed guy covered in gold and dripping in incense–that's what he said, after all I was close by, and he had stopped his machine and here was this guy with the gall to dole out lessons about sharing to someone who was starving and poisoning

---

72   The Armenian Pope.

his body with noxious gases all day. Just imagine! When you inhale your soup in your fine porcelain plates, when you sip your wine in gold cups during mass, tell me if you've ever once given so much as a thought to people who go through trash dumps to find their dinner! Let our Hamlet enjoy his victory! Stay out of it! Actually, he's not in this world anymore. And don't go looking for him in yours either! In fact, our man Hamlet, pursued by this ecclesiastical hyena, had killed himself out of sheer happiness. Disappeared without a trace. They didn't know his last name or the name of his village. And the police had missed its chance. And the church had gone back empty-handed to its palaces. Lucky Hamlet.

SHOUSHIK according to LOUSSO

Arsen doesn't believe that we're both flea ridden. And that some of us are pretend poor, supposedly hiding jewelry by the fistful. While others drive around in fancy cars. So, what about all this? Pure pretense? And what about my jigouli, fake as well? I ask him: and little old Shushik? Also invented? She's so deaf that she always answers the same thing whenever anyone speaks to her: have you seen what has become of me, a *zibil* collector? And you think that's a life at my age? I am living proof that this country is sick, am I not?

MARO according to ARDAK

Maro is a twenty-nine-year-old widow. I liked her husband Vano a lot. I would see him every summer. He started sorting a long time before I began. One day, he suddenly keeled over in the trash, went home and lay down. And then he died. Just like that. We never knew what disease he had contracted exactly. Maro's parents had always swept the city streets with brooms. But they didn't want her anymore. You can't marry off a widow again. So Aroussiak, Maro's godmother, took her in. It was as if Maro had come to take her husband's place at the garbage dump. Now the two women are a team. By selling the scrap metal and the bottles that they find, they make as much as 10, 000 drams per week. The buyer doesn't come pick them up, so they have to carry their *meshogs* on their backs all the way to a truck that they rent together with others. Meko the truck driver is one of their neighbors. A friend of Vano from elsewhere. He's the only one who knows that they work with the trash, apart from their close friends. Vano told me that it's honest labor and that the economy forced them into this line of work. For Maro and Aroussiak, it's a job like any other. They go home, clean up, get changed and buy decent food just like everyone else. At the beginning they dressed in clean clothes and walked upright to pretend that they were coming from home, the office, or the factory. Once they arrived, you could see them enter the shack across from Dro's house. They came out in boots and clothing that was more suited to the garbage dump. The neighbors couldn't gossip and make up strange stories. They left home every morning and came home at night like normal people. But one day they grew tired of this charade. They just left dressed appropriately for their dirty work. Thick tights, a pair of heavy jeans underneath an old dress, a hat, and a thick pair of gloves. From that day on the other diggers forgot all about their femininity. They dressed like men. And like them, they started to pop open bags that had fallen from trucks and carried their *meshogs* all the way to the truck.

MOUK according to HAÏK

Mouk, obscure Mouk, predatory Mouk. Hungry like a wolf. He lives only to devour. Dreams of taking over the whole sorting operation. Not by force, but by cunning or blackmail. It's in his blood. For now, he's just trying to create despair among us. A return to nature cruel and unfair: each man for himself, even if this made no sense. But I think he must be working for someone. On Samurai's team, of course. And suppose he'd been ordered to wreck our workplace? To pit each one of us against the other? The police would intervene. And the garbage dump would become off limits. After that, we'd have a choice between going abroad or ending up in the cemetery rather than returning to the City. One morning, everyone was following a particular truck. Meko was driving. Suddenly Mouk detached himself from the group. He grabbed onto the small blinds. You would have thought that he was imitating a clown. Well no. He beat us all to the chase that way. When we got to the truck, all the bags had already been popped. He'd cleaned up—all the best items had been grabbed already.

That day, Mouk didn't understand the silence surrounding his discovery. All on his own, he was sweating to grab what was left. The others refused to join in. An unforgettable injury, because of that enraged animal. But he started all over again. Last-minute victories. He'd chosen sides against all of us. Resignation wasn't enough anymore to put up with his insolence. He was taking us for stool pigeons. Let's chase him away! Tsknors fumed. We have our own laws here. If he doesn't obey the laws of the trash dump, then we'll take things into our own hands. We'll gang up on him, another one added, give him a good beating to make him understand and after that he'll know his rightful place. Mistrust and disgust, that's what he inspired. But also, a menacing feeling of danger. Who knows if he wouldn't wake up hidden aggressions that had been waiting forever to emerge.

MOUK according to GAM

I used to watch him popping his trash bags. As if he were bashing in heads, trying to make them explode. I used to watch him. He hooked things like an animal. I also saw his whole circus act when he tried to win over Lousso. He also tried to win over Asen and Artak in the process. But Lousso saw him coming. So, he went after Maro. To make her his ally. Easy bait, that Maro. You could tell from the look in her eyes that she consented to his advances. So young Bego put himself at his service. With some *aghber djans*[73] over here, and some *my brothers* over there. Two foxes who split their money. At the end of each day, they would put all the scrap metal together and split the profits. Those two, when they smelled a hit, they went after it. And they didn't mind using their fists if anyone tried to stop them. I saw them propose deals to the most idiotic among us, badger them until they gave in, using some secret elaborate strategy. Mouk had transformed the sorting into a competition, just like the rats, pigs, and stray dogs, or the thieving crows, who also took part in the daily feeding. One day Mouk and Bego didn't show up. Tsknors was convinced that they were taking part in the Samourai's meetings. That they had bet on him. And that Mouk was one of their henchmen. For Haïk, the Scholar's partisans

---

73   *My brother!* A familiar way of addressing someone.

had nothing to envy him. Complain about anything, and they'll just spit in your face, he'd say. He'd even tried once. They almost disemboweled him on the spot. They also claimed that their Scholar was the new Messiah. During meetings, every word that came out of his mouth served to demonize the Samourai. Hard to build a country with such hatred everywhere. Others wondered if Mouk and Bego hadn't fallen ill. They had so much loot that they could easily afford the trip. Personally, I had a hard time imagining those rascals having left together to spend their money somewhere outside the country. Independence had opened options to engage in all sorts of trafficking. Who knows if he wasn't the eyes and ears for these men in black with shaved heads, that Mouk? Otherwise, how could you explain that they'd shown up so quickly after Zara's body had been discovered? He's almost certainly concentrating on me, though. On me.

GAM to SAKO

Sako *djan*, your *Dèr voghormia!* haunts me. It's gotten into my bones so deeply, that even at night... It's like a song asking heaven forgiveness for all the hatred and injuries that man causes during the day. When you sing it on top of our trash, your *Dèr voghormia!* it feels as if God were passing above us. That he conquers his nausea and settles softly into our flesh. It's a no-nonsense mass without all the fuss of our bearded priests, or their golden frills. The same priests who call upon a God of mercy with such mastery. But what does God have to do with all that tomfoolery? With their awful singing and their deep, cavernous voices? With their walls carpeted over with images of the dead? And their stinking, musty incense? Their nasal liturgy and their ceilings so black that you'd think you were inside a tomb. While your *Der voghormia!* will stay with me until the day I die. Light and human. A sky that rains its joy down upon us. A silent enthusiasm. Let it be my last word and let it accompany me into the ground in my hole. My last word, let it follow me!

SAKO to GAM

I'm singing. I'm singing.

...

I ask God, I implore him. I torture my voice, I soften it, I make it rise like cream, white, unctuous, sweet to the palate, my tongue quivers and my cords vibrate. Ah! But all this is—it's only singing. Something beautiful. Something beautiful made with one's body. Only a song, I tell you, Gam. And do you think that I rise far enough with this beauty? No! All I'm doing is repeating the national hymn. I'm nothing but a parrot. People in this country find their souls in it. The taste of centuries past, they grab on to it. But I'm unable to pull them outside of the temporal. Outside of themselves. When I started singing at the Church of the Holy Sign, it was to survive. I did it for money. And now today it still weighs on my voice. This voice won't forget the times when it resonated inside a church in ruins, and one had to feed one's body. Occasionally I forget about our repulsive trash. Yes, that happens. Occasionally. Then you're right. A perfume overcomes me. In the space of a few seconds, I'm carried above the smoke. I don't hear the noise from the City or its rough caress. Or the wandering bodies in the turbulent chaos, here or farther down where the cemetery lies. I become one with the music that intercedes between myself and the heavens. And if a seagull passes by, its wings quivering on the crest of the vapors that rise from the rot, slow and white, I tell myself that it's my voice that is cradling it and the Holy Spirit is thanking me as it passes by. Komitas went to gather his songs in the countryside and crafted a human voice using the whispers of the divine. Unfortunately, life is so difficult that we've forgotten these mysteries. And soon, who knows if we won't forget how to sing as well.

25.

*O*k, and what about Sero? Maybe he remarried?"

"Who knows? Must be to someone who 'sees nothing and says nothing.' Because he's not the type of guy to put up with a gossip."

"You can tell by the way he brought up his daughter Anoush. Can't be the most scintillating conversation between the two of them at home."

It doesn't really matter why, but the fact remains that on that day, neither Sero nor Anoush showed up to pop any bags at the dump site. Their silhouettes had suddenly disappeared. Their absence seemed to bother many of the rag pickers, who all began to talk about them:

"Greetings, my gossips!" Dro exclaimed. "You're cackling like a bunch of hens in need of a rooster, it seems. And to put an end to the rumors," he added, "I have some news. Sero's dead. It's definite. Definitely dead. His body has entered the ground. No one knows about his soul."

> *And now that we've heard, the truth of your words,*
> *Blessed God, spread your indulgence and your compassion on all.*

He died yesterday, a glass in each hand. One was full of blood, the other one milk. He was getting ready to drink some milk when he started to spit up blood. He let go of everything—the glasses and his own body—and collapsed onto the floor. Anoush thought that he'd had a heart attack like the last time when Haïk and Gam pulled him off the ground. He got his breath back and they gave him a glass of *oghi*, because here *oghi* even brings back someone who's dying. Someone who's already dead, I'm not so sure. Someone who's dying but still alive though, it's a proven fact."

They all remembered the incident. Anoush was going through the trash at his side when Sero just dropped. And what if he weren't alone? Others before him had experienced the same symptoms. They felt faint and suddenly lost consciousness. Some never made it back. Like Arto, the elders said, and Saribeg, Nvart, and Ludmilla. And Vano, the last one. They clung to life and did their best. Nothing to reproach them. And then the knife came down on them. Evil lurked everywhere. All you had to do was rub up against it and you ended up six feet under. People had noticed. And yet Sero was working as hard as a cotton picker. He was so discreet that you couldn't even remember what his voice sounded like. Thankfully, some people came back down to earth after their spells. The rag pickers would celebrate in such cases. You could still live even after you hit rock bottom. As for Shusho, she wasn't worried. She bent down so low that she was practically one with the ground. And anyway, she was too deaf to hear any of these superstitions:

"Sero's dead. May his soul rest in peace. Dead after having lived his life. Not much you can say to that. He'd never hurt a fly, Sero. He'd survived the only way he knew how to."

Yet Shusho raised the key question for the rag pickers. Why is it that a person who is properly nourished just collapses suddenly under the moonlight? A strange substance must have been poisoning their blood. A substance that the body was trying to reject. Your heart started to beat quicker, fever set in and then a war raged between one's natural system and the unwanted guest.

Usually while Gam was popping plastic bags, all he thought of was hitting someone. If he unfortunately succumbed to his anger, he found himself ripping things apart and unleashing pent-up forces, those belonging to this putrid place. Suddenly a stench that had been held in too long gave way to a sound that melded into that of the plastic popping. Then the hook went in, followed by a hand that pulled out a treasured object. Rather than looking inside bags, others preferred to pick up cartons, while others grabbed some glass or scrap metal. In winter, they used plastic bottles to heat themselves. They were burnt on the spot or taken home. As a result, the dump was permanently filled with fumes. Even if the rag pickers worked in open air, they inhaled toxic odors. But even worse, they inhaled gases, the ones that develop when matter decomposes. The lungs had to submit to this law of the dumpster jungle. Emanations that filled your bloodstream and went straight to your head. In the long run, it was like being drunk. You saw strange shapes appear in the smoke, and you couldn't tell if they were friends or mysterious ghosts. As material decomposed, a secret alchemy operated within you and transformed your insides. You nourished and destroyed yourself simultaneously. A race within your body ensued between two organic processes: "When he became annoyed, Haïk used to say that the only power keeping us here is political. It forces us to do what we do here. Our political leaders have no real hold over us. But their stupidity is the law."

And when the rag pickers rested a bit, to have a bite to eat or discuss the world as they saw it, their words made no sense.

"Everything that you see here," Lousso said one day pointing at the trash dump, "All this crap for as far as the eye can see. You see it because it is there. But I don't want to think that it only exists here."

"Well of course," said Tsknors, "what the eye can see is worth more than what the ear can hear. There's no smoke without fire, no trash dump.

"Control yourself Tsknors," said Lousso, "That's not what I meant! But if you could see what's invisible, I'm sure it wouldn't be any more terrifying that all this rotten trash surrounding us. In the air or under the seas."

"Much more, even." Haïk Added. "Entire continents of putrescent trash all around us." He raised his arms into the air.

"We've lost the glory of the world and we've lost ourselves along with it," Tsknors added.

Even mothers who had nothing to complain about came to the trash dump to find extra food to feed their children! Lousso couldn't stop talking about Larissa. That really made him see red. That this mother of a few weeks had to rip apart bags with one hand and pull her little girl along by the other.

"I go out of my way to point out that she shouldn't mistake the dump for a supermarket. She refuses to listen. One day her little girl was whining. Her mother was shaking her so much that she stopped making a fuss. She was probably having a hard time breathing. Her little lungs couldn't stand the stench or the smoke from the fires. That's terrible, old Shousho cried out as she made her way past us. We adults, we're marinating in the rot, we know why. But that poor *balik,*[74] you're killing her with all this stinking trash. Larissa *djan,* she said half smiling, half scowling, you should understand that this isn't a place for such a fragile child! Do whatever else you want! Beg on the streets! Go whore yourself out in Turkey but keep that poor child away from this stench! Keep her away! You're destroying the very life that you gave her."

Bread, cheese, salami, vegetables, even if they stink a bit, they were still good. Cleaned on the run, the pieces went directly from bag to mouth. A quarter apple, a piece of banana that someone had thought too ripe to the tongue. And there was more. Why be picky? Or else she sucked on cucumber rinds that were still fresh enough to provide some needed relief. They arrived starving in the morning and left their stomachs full. Larissa always stayed to the side to work in secret. From time to time, some of the rag pickers would share their lunch with her. Larissa accepted their offer despite herself, always maintaining her distance during the lunch break when they huddled together to eat:

"Today the little one has diarrhea. I know," she said concerned, "that it comes from this trash. But what choice do I have? My husband didn't leave me anything. Neither my parents nor his want anything to do with me." Her husband was lost in God knows what corner of Russia.

Lousso often kept his head down, the better to search the trash, always keeping those same eagle eyes targeted on his work. One day, he wouldn't stop pontificating about his discoveries with Arsen and Artak.

"To empty out, women have their own technique all to themselves," he said clucking. "When you see them go away hand in hand, it's that they're itching to pee. Lost behind piles of trash, they think that no one can see them. One of them

---

74   Child.

stays on the lookout while the other one, whose pants are bothering her, has to put her butt in the air to relieve herself."

"But Dro has a toilet at his place, doesn't he?" asked Arsen.

"Well, he refuses to play toilet attendant," replied Lousso.

"Who'd expect a gallant gesture form this manager of our national trash?" added Artak.

"One woman who was about to pee in her pants went to see him," confirmed Lousso. 'Why don't you get out of here!' Dro told her, annoyed. 'If I let you in now, there'll be a line around the dump from now on. Sorry, that's my final decision.'"

In fact, Dro didn't really like these female rag pickers in their boots and pants, who are as muscular as men. You would have thought that they'd lost what was distinctly feminine to him, as if he couldn't imagine them pissing standing up, just like men. In general women made controlling their bladders into a fine art. They put all their effort and modesty into holding it in while they went about working at the trash dump, and waited for the appropriate place and time to relieve themselves. Despite the scorching August heat, some even refrained from drinking too many fluids so they wouldn't have to choose between relieving themselves and continuing with their work. They also knew from experience that some of what they ate on the trash dump often gave them diarrhea. But hunger doesn't always give best counsel.

26.

A man stood to the side, safe from the smoke, taking pictures. What type of man, you ask? A curious one, Gam said to himself. Or maybe an aesthete. Perhaps even a journalist or an informer, the type who had been sent here on a special mission. Suspicious, Gam kept him under surveillance. This guy got on his nerves. He had crossed the trash dump from the top. All you had to do was leave the main road, at the place where it turned sharply and then cross the dead zones where the fires had done their work most efficiently in the past. Then if you walked straight towards the fumes, you were sure to fall on the epicenter of the cauldron where the rag pickers were huddled. The mystery man stood on a type of hillock, an ideal location from which to embrace the entire sanctuary of a trash dump. His camera locked on to a tripod that he folded with ease, he moved around and photographed things from angles.

After a while, Gam saw him changing lenses. The bigger ones for close-ups, he thought. A picture taken from far away to capture people's portraits. But why portraits? He grew increasingly worried, as it seemed that he was systematically pointing his camera at everyone in the trash dump, one after another. He didn't look like a foreigner, but like a good old native Armenian. He was shooting like a pro and would stop every so often in between shots to turn his head and look over his shoulder. What was he afraid of? That someone might ask him what he was doing?

Gam pulled his bonnet down over his forehead all the way to his eyebrows and moved closer to Haïk.

"Did you notice him?" Haïk deliberately turned his back to the photographer.

"From the very beginning," Haïk answered. "He's annoying, isn't he?"

"What's he doing on our land?"

"That's exactly what I'm trying to figure out. And find out what he's going to do with all those photos of his. Give them to someone? But to whom? I'd really like to know."

Suddenly, squeezing his hook with his right hand, Gam turned around and began walking in the intruder's direction. He walked through the trash with ease. The man stood about fifty meters away. When he realized that Gam was headed in his direction, he turned his camera on him, took a shot and suddenly folded the tripod and vanished. He walked back in the same direction that he had come from, without talking to anyone. He had already disappeared by the time Gam arrived at his previous location. When he returned to where Haïk was standing, he was sorry that he had missed him:

"I don't like this at all," he said. "That guy must not have had a clear conscience. And please don't tell me again that he must be some type of artist. He took pictures of us one-by-one. That's what seems underhanded."

"And what's next?" Haïk protested. "They'll want to come chase us into the toilet?"

"This all stinks, if you ask me. It was as if he was searching for someone. Who knows, maybe you?"

"You know me. I haven't stepped foot in the City in ages. Even to visit my mother."

"That's true. But what about your past? Which president was it that you criticized?"

A while later, Gam recognized the man who had taken the pictures, by his gait and the tripod that he was carrying on his shoulder. This time, he was walking on the crest of the cliff at the end of the garbage dump. He stood his tripod in between the only two trees that grew there, testing his position so that he'd have an open view of the whole valley. He changed lenses on several occasions. After making the proper adjustments, he planted himself next to his camera and waited for a break in between the swirls of smoke before pressing on a button located at the end of an extension cord. As he had done in the past, he stood right in front of his subject and took shots where there was manifestly no one present, so that Gam deduced that he was more interested in the topography than in any of the men. Once he even climbed onto the crest, from where you could see the entire garbage dump, all the way to the cemetery hill. The abandoned parts, a mixture of cinder and earth color, occupied a vast surface on the eastern flank. In the center, Dro's tractor stood surrounded by the rag pickers at work. They looked like silhouettes rocking back and forth, spread out along an immense mass of small, colorful smoke-covered mounds. Dro would walk over to the stacks of garbage to flatten them out one by one. There was no better vantage point than this crest for anyone who wanted to observe the entire site. Study it to change it, most probably. In fact from way up there terrain changes, the field's limits and the relative heights of the different sections were clearly visible. You could imagine the flows of underground rivers sweeping along the toxic liquids that people had thrown out, and in which direction they might continue. All you needed was a bit of imagination to begin burning the trash and fill the pits, then flatten out, displace, and make those things disappear that deserved to disappear, before turning it all into an amusement park or a golf course. Since seeing the photographer that day, the rag pickers all feared the same thing: being thrown out. Their sticky, cheesy work, object of disdain from everyone, risked being forever brought to a halt by some anonymous decision from above. During pauses, they conversed jovially. The rest of the time they worked at a frenetic pace, rummaging through the trash from every dump truck that arrived, one after the other.

"Smells burnt," said Garo.

"That's what it smells like, ever since we started cooking on top of this trash," Lousso answered, laughing.

"Be sarcastic all you want! But the day that they decide to run us out of town, you won't even be able to cry about it. They'll block the entrance to the dump, while others will come up the side entrance."

"They'll have billy clubs, but we'll have our hooks." someone protested.

"And we'll only have this one side to get away," added Tsknors pointing out the part of the dump which fell off at a right angle onto the roof of the red house.

"Let's hope that they won't be waiting for you there," added Haïk. "But there's no point in getting upset about it now. A photographer is taking pictures, of us—so what? It won't be the first time. I can imagine that seen from on high, our dump can look like some type of apocalypse worthy of one's attention. You should try climbing up the cliff one day. You'll see just how steep it is, with its smoke and its apocalyptic aspect with guys like us milling around for something to eat.

"Yep, and after all he's not the first photographer to come our way," added Gam, joining Haïk in his calls for calm and reason. "But this one didn't seem innocent. He wasn't zooming haphazardly. He knew exactly which pictures he'd come to take. "

And then work having imposed its own rhythm and effort again, their worries dissipated into the slowly rising smoke.

27.

*E*very item has its price, every hill its slope, and in the same way as a flower only gives off its one personal scent, a rooster sings loudest in its own hen house, each man must follow his own path in life, a sharp tongue belongs to a sharp spoon, out of the mouths of babes, cats don't eat vinegar, he who asks the right questions can make it to Jerusalem, there's a fighter within each one of us, we take our fist for a stone, everyone says what they think, there's no shame in being poor, we expect people to be human like we expect a rose to be embalmed, a mill without water can't make any dough, a sheep cannot escape from the mouth of wolves, what is valuable on earth is worth nothing in heaven.

From an old jalopy of a white car that stopped in the parking that day, a mature couple emerged–she pale, he male, both looking exotic for the locale. They looked lost at first, struggling under the brutal attack bad smells, then made their way up the pathway that rises to the dump's epicenter, a steep path that became dusty whenever the garbage trucks passed by. Mouk, who seemed to have been expecting their arrival, went up to greet them. They questioned him with the avid curiosity of someone asking about the road to Mecca. They were both correspondents for a one of those frosty ethno-narcissistic publications in France. Gam had read an article published by the two of them at Zara's. Mauricette, the writer and Mahari, the photographer. They were people neither from here nor from elsewhere since they had been born elsewhere but lived here now.

Mouk led them to the newest trash, as if he were an accomplice in a report that was more duty than humanist impulse. Mahari photographed Dro's pigs, dark haired, menacing and oinking in every direction, then the young people who'd come to work after school, Artem and Artemis, Shousho curved over and so forth, while the woman was taking down the comments of some, and the hopes of others. People who insisted that they were speaking to them only so they would have enough to eat, and that they didn't envy the work being offered in the capital.

Mauricette approached young Hovan, 16 years old, who'd recently started working at the dump. He was smoking a cigarette that had been crudely rolled in a piece of local newspaper.

Mauricette: "You like it here, young man?"

Hovan: "Here, everyone does what they need to do. What do you think—that I have time to play golf?"

Mauricette: "Why not? Or maybe chess? And what about school? You have no interest in attending school? The air is clean there at least. With today's disinterested teachers, I'm sure you'd get into university as soon as you applied. You could become a journalist, like me for example?"

Hovan: "And question people covered in mud? Yeah, if I had nothing else to do. My father left to be a woodcutter in the taiga. And since then, no news. He left the three kids behind with my mom. The next day, I was here. And since then, no more school. Who even cares? Here we work all day, then we come home with drams at night. And since my sister just turned 18, we don't get any more state help. She comes along occasionally. My little brother also wants to come along, but I prefer that he stay in school. To breathe in some fresh air."

Mauricette: "It's true that the air around here isn't exactly mountain fresh."

Hovan: "We're like sheep inside a wolf's mouth."

Mauricette: "Ah! Ah! Yes, that's it. Like sheep inside a wolf's mouth. But alive. Still alive right?"

Hovan: "God only knows!"

And while Mahari took pictures and tried not to breathe in to avoid choking (pictures of sarcastic seagulls, empty cartons, pigs over here and dogs over there, men and women with smoke emerging from their clothes) pale Mauricette was lightheartedly gathering up her impressions as she walked towards Dro's machine. Gam felt the lion within him awaken at the sight of these two intruders, whose silhouettes appeared nebulous through the veiled, smoky background. He walked away and gave the interrogator approaching Lala the evil eye.

Mauricette: "It's sad being here, isn't it? This isn't going to be your profession now, is it?"

Lala: "You can't ask a mill to make dough when it doesn't have water."

Mauricette: "Ah! Indeed, you can't... I'm writing this down. Got it. Make dough, mill without water."

Lala: "It's a proverb that I found in my dictionary."

Mauricette: "The last edition, most probably."

Lala: "No. An old dictionary. It's in French. Its owner threw it in the garbage. My friend Gam found it and gave it to me as a present. I love to read."

Mauricette: "And you read French?"

Lala: "My friend taught me the letters. He also knows Italian."

Mauricette: "He's your boyfriend, Gam, I assume."

Lala: "Not at all. He's one of us. But I don't see him."

Mauricette: "Let's see. What have you read?"

Lala: "I like the drawings of the human body. They show everything. Now I can name all the parts in French."

Mauricette: "For example?"

Lala: "For example? I remember everything. But for example, *veurgé, pé-nisse, couillé, mont dé Vénusssé, glitéris, betite leuvré, grandé leuvré*"

Mauricette: "That's all?"

Lala: "I even know slang words for a man's thing. I wrote them down on a piece of paper. But I don't pronounce them properly. *As-peurgé, man-nhir, sucrré d'orrgé, flûté dé pan-pan, tourloutyutyu,* a word that I like a lot, baobabé, *membré virril, zizi et zigounetté, marto pikeu, cla-ri-netté, ez-ki-mo,* and I don't know why but also *fusil* à oun' koup', ba-gété, ma-giké, chi-po-la-ta, mar-to à boulèss, mo-ri-ssette ..."

Mauricette: "How's that *mauricette*? Really? You read *mauricette*?"

Lala: "Absolutely! Mo-ri-ssetté. It's written right here!"

Mauricette: "Repulsive! Really repulsive!"

Suddenly Mauricette abandoned Lala to her nauseating words and walked towards Dro who was officiating from atop his digger, the daily *Grand Requiem* devoted to the day's trash. He was like a rooster directing his chickens towards grain. Dro was possessed by his digger like some monomaniacal soul driven by some inner genie. He turned it off reluctantly, like a child from whom one had taken back a spoon of strawberry preserves in mid-mouthful. He had to turn it off to hear anything, as his hearing had been ruined by the sound of the spasmodic fireworks of his caterpillar locomotive. Watching the young woman stick out her lower lip as she navigated among the trash, Gam thought that she had more likely been sent by someone as a spy rather than being a real journalist trying to get at the human tragedies that she was uncovering while visiting their hole. This intrusion by a series of paid voyeurs annoyed him. Someone certainly had a lot to gain from badmouthing the trash dump. And whatever they said, when it was made available in thousands of printed copies, would undoubtedly incense public opinion, and eventually condemn it ...

"How interesting!" Dro attacked. "You're finally showing up today! Up until now you were sleeping standing up, seeing the country through rose-colored glasses, I suppose. But now you're waking up to the shit that's all around you. It's about time!"

> *Like beasts without conscience*
> *We run to our death without shudder*
> *We run towards death without fear*

"Not that I don't understand you! Some angel from above must have visited you for you to finally pay attention to the lot of us. Unless you simply had more important things to report on until now. You don't ask a cat to drink vinegar. As far as I'm concerned, I have nothing to say to you. And anyway, it's all out here in the open for you to see. But anything you write will end up being used against the rag pickers, one way or another. You see them trudging through our capital's slime. Take a good look at them! They look like a monkey's biting their neck, their eyes always looking down at vile, repulsive, dead things. They're here to find something to eat! You want to let the authorities know? Show them what a shame it is? That's the quickest way of putting these people out into the street! As if you didn't have other places to go poke about, cleaner than this one. You can walk around a museum in high heels sipping Chinese tea and nibbling on French pastries."

"Ah! What you're saying is true," said Mauricette. "We visited a house like that about a month ago. It was quite a change from our apartment in Bangladesh, all grimy and sinister, open to the wind in every direction. But in this place, you would have thought you were in Ancient Rome. Friezes everywhere, statues, horses, basins, naiads. Like a museum, as you say. Or better yet a palace inhabited by fairies. Outside of time."

"Yep," said Dro. "The opposite of my playing field. A fake Rome unlike any that the Romans ever built. It's simply that here, the luxurious stands side by side the excremental and the oppressor never sees the people he humiliates. In this country, you can't expect men to be human the way you expect a rose to give off a pleasant scent. Isn't that the case? *Pas vrai?*"

"Ah!" exclaimed Mauricette. "What you are saying is so beautiful. Let me write it down if you don't mind." Then she asked: "Have you visited the house that I was talking about? I can talk to the owner. He'd be thrilled to show you its treasures. He thought it all up by himself and achieved everything thanks to his own hard work. Pretty amazing what you can achieve in this country after all, isn't it?"

"My feeling is that it's a country full of crazy people: the disparities are so enormous. I mean explain this to me if you will. How is it that a country which has experienced a devastating earthquake, war and a revolution has produced such huge fortunes in twenty years in the middle of this miserable backwater? That's your job isn't it, to explain these things? Instead of looking at surface things and pecking at some of the regime's minor monstrosities, why don't you show us what's behind these aberrations that forces men to eat the trash left behind by their fellow men. Instead of letting yourself be seduced by the gaudy and the ornamental. Instead of letting yourselves be guided by a folly for all things wealthy, to taste this sweetness, you should have the courage to write the truth! As for myself, no thank you. I have no intention of dragging my old clothes in any such heavenly palace. I'm busy enough with my pigs. And anyway, I quite like them. Sometimes more so than I do human beings."

Without saying a word and dumbfounded by Dro's outburst, Mauricette put aside pen and paper and walked away. Then walking over the mounds in front of her and putting a Kleenex bathed in Chanel N° 5 up to her nose, because femininity is eternal, she bravely trekked across the gaseous fumes towards some air and rejoined the road as quickly as possible. Mahari galloped behind her like a female camel feeling the advances of a horny male.

"Do you remember," Mauricette asked when she had reached him, "the young girl who greeted us at the door of that roman mansion?"

"The owner's daughter, a certain Lullaby," said Mahari.

"Yes, that's it. Lullaby," answered Mauricette. "Well trust me, she isn't one of these hillbillies who spends their days surrounded by a bunch of pigs and dogs. How terrible! Finally, mission accomplished. Do you think we'll be able to buy our little Adrien his bike, with what we made today?

"I hope so," said Mahari, who didn't like to contradict his wife. Both ignored the fact that this bike, which was so important to them here on earth, would be the least important thing in the long run.

As they rejoined their car their souls all revved up, they walked by Donatello, accompanied by a foreign photographer with a camera hanging from his neck and a tripod around his shoulder.

28.

*D*onatello—as Tsknors called him because it made him sound like an Italian artist—was visiting the trash dump to take his mind off things a bit. He claimed that he saw more than it intended him to see. An ocean. A woman's cadaver devoured by vermin. An octopus. A gelatinous gorgon with serpents for hair. You go figure. But the key to his art were aluminum cans. He saw more and more of them—he saw them everywhere. While people sold them by their weight in aluminum, Donatello preferred them already crushed.

"My mind always starts racing when I cross that gate." He told Gam one day. "My art is crushulating."

"Crushulating," said Gam. "Is that word in the dictionary?"

"Dictionary! Dictionary!" exclaimed Donatello. "But there's an entire world that exists outside of the dictionary, Mister Gam."

Gam had little hope of really connecting with this aluminum can fanatic. Every artist has his muse, admitted this fetishist of tin cans, objects which responded to all his curiosities. If he looked at a tin can properly, the entire world was his oyster, understandably enough perhaps.

"Your gibberish is a bit difficult to understand," Gam admitted.

"You see Gam, for me things have a soul. They speak to me. The fact of contemplating an object constitutes a pure act, devoid of all academic conventions. A primitive act perhaps, that leads one to collect abandoned objects. You interact with them, a dialogue that is rooted in the mystery of the ages. And arbitrarily you decide to transform this act into a work of art."

"A work of art? You're not holding back, are you!" said Gam.

"Of course not. What's more abandoned than a tin can? What object is more destroyed? Shiny at first, produced in gleaming metal, you pour its nectar into your mouth, then discard it like an old skin?"

"A skin that can make you a lot of money," Gam corrected.

"If you insist," said Donatello. "A tin can carries with it the stigmata of our industrial life. First an invitation for a drink. And now an invitation to look at ourselves. To examine it is like recognizing hidden symbols. Passwords that open new doors for you. Its creases indicate monstrosities, geometries, black holes that show you what your rage really resembles. Otherwise, I crush it myself with a hammer."

"A hammer? Really?" asked Gam.

"Yes," he said closing his eyes." A real massacre. So what? What could be more touching? This end for the tin can in question, it's our own end, rolling over and then death. I'm a trash artist, who practices the art of crushifying. That's why I crush things."

The *otar*[75] who was driving Donatello around that day was of the American kind. A reporter's jacket on top of a black shirt with his sleeves pulled back. Grey hair and eyes as happy as Adam's in the Garden of Eden. The young interpreter had stopped the taxi a few blocks away from Dro's house. Tissue held up to his nostrils, barely looking at the trash. What a dog of a life and work made me land in this dump, he must have been telling himself. And who knows where I'll end up tomorrow? But the stranger compensated for the place's pitifulness with his artistic fever. Donatello was waiting for them. They said their *hellos* and then they were on their way on the earthen road to the dump's interior. The young woman jumped into the car, slammed the door shot and rolled up the windows.

The two men passed by Mauricette and Mahari in a hurry. They walked by, digging deep into the deep stench which threw up all its excremental hatred against them. Suddenly the stranger stared without appearing to stare, turned his head to the side, and then to the other, his eyes zigzagging in the air. Petrified,

---

75   Foreigner or non-Armenian.

Donatello watched him turn like a mad periscope as he tried to find an image that would send him into bouts of ecstasy. Stranger yet, the American froze and fixated his gaze on a particular spot amidst the stagnant piles of detritus. Without saying a word, he spread his tripod's legs and placed it in a location that seemed to suit his needs. He set up his camera and started spreading out plastic bags without any discernible rhyme or reason. Donatello imitated him. They came and went under the piercing view of the gulls, in a half hour ballet that grew increasingly bewitched. The *otar* took a few shots, then started to walk again towards the first mounds of trash. He explained aloud that he was stripping naked the hidden face of a society that lived off such randomly discarded trash.

"Seen from afar, my pictures form a banal whole. But the eye soon becomes exasperated. It feels cheated, and even made fun of. The shock occurs when you reduce the space between the ego behind the gaze and the impartiality of the photo itself. Then things become clearer. The coming together of the two lets you understand. The effect is obtained by the accumulation of the same object. An organized piling upwards, or as it exists in the wild. A quantitative cantata that mutates into the qualitative. *Magnificata* of the manufactured object. All told."

"God. It's all very pantheistic now, isn't it?"

"I get it," Donatello said, somewhat stunned.

"For example," said the American whose eyes seemed to breathe the air of the Grand Canyon, "I was able to find 29,569 handguns to evoke the number of people killed by firearms every year in the United States. 29,569. Not one more and not one less. Our America is deadly. Firearms circulate like automobiles. And in the same way that cars spit out their exhaust, guns spit out bullet fire. *Boum! Boum!* And *halleluia* from here to the heavens on high.

"*Halleluia* to the heavens on high," Donatello echoed.

"Yes," the *otar* continued, "410,000 paper goblets to make visible ten minutes of American drinking sprees. Or still yet, 2.3 million uniforms of detained prisoners, folded and stacked, to represent the number of Americans incarcerated each year."

While Donatello was explaining his work with tin cans, the photographer revealed that he had himself used some in his portrait of George Bush Jr.

"109,637 exactly, which corresponds to thirty-four seconds of consumption in the USA. Another time, I stacked up photographs of car crashes, clocks, and those things that women stick inside their vaginas to sop up their menstrual blood. It was beautiful and terrifying, as if it had come out of some mirror which reflected one's own obscenities."

He'd made the trip to find the unknown sign, without his usual artistic arsenal. Some guy had tipped him off after a conference. It's the most poetic garbage dump, he'd told him, as if it were the holiest of places. He'd fallen in love with this country and spent his time writing something wild, obscure, and organized about the country's latrines. After taking a few steps inside the dead zones, the stranger stopped in front of a wall of rusted scrap metal mixed in with the dark grey of the burnt soil. He had just found his proof and fell into a melancholic ecstasy. As if he were subject to a coming apocalypse, mute and unflinching. Donatello wouldn't have noticed anything, if the other guy hadn't concentrated on this forgotten corner of trash. The two men said nothing, frozen on the spot by the crushulating.

"It looks like the country's entrails," Donatello dared to say. "Its history can be read though each subsequent layer of metal trash. But another type of history is hidden here. In the form of a historical prophecy."

Then two men fell silent.

"Men disappear but their objects survive," said the *otar*. Donatello felt a century of tears well up inside him. He didn't dare admit anything to the stranger. That day, a series of images came to him of naked bodies, piled up pell mell and in layers, first men's bodies, mutilated, killed by gunshots, then moving up the layers, those of emaciated men and women, tortured by something terrible that was ready to befall them, the heap exposing itself like a seismic tragedy, as dizzying as an ax wound, determined to take effect.

The *otar* and his guide soon encountered someone who was digging into the back of a newly made moat some four meters wide. Haïk was huffing and puffing with his pail and pickax loudly enough to wake up the dead. Gam stood at his side to pull up the pailfuls of dark earth. Donatello explained who the stranger was. A trompe-l'œil artist by accumulation. And one who interpreted these lands as stories, historical, geological, and post-seismic composites. From time-to-time Haïk raised his head to listen. He saw the three men like stellae holding up the infinite universe, but, who occasionally looked like they were going to unzip and take a piss on him. Their posture, legs spread, exasperated him. He took out his Tokarev TT 33 from his back pocket and aimed it at them, just to spook, humiliate them and make them pee in their pants. The stranger who had been able to align the 29, 569 guns got scared and took a step backwards.

"Whenever I hear the word culture, I wake up from my daydream," he said. "No, I undo the safety latch on my Browning," the American corrected.

"As you prefer," answered Haïk. "But I do one better," he continued: "My bullets are my paint brushes." And he started to shoot straight in front of him at the space that he'd opened with his pickax. Once, twice, three times. The bullets had torn open some holes in the painting and by clearing some of the dirt, uncovered some random forms and scrap metal. The two artists stood hypnotized.

"Ah!" said Donatello.

"Hmm!" said the American. "That's a pure artistic gesture. A rare performance. And caught live. Hence, we could attribute an artistic status to a firearm."

"And who would ever remember us, our wars, our social aggressiveness?" added Donatello

"But of course!" The stranger added. "We could even shoot at a painted canvas, at random, our eyes closed. And now what do you see after your three shots?" he asked Haïk.

"Well nothing," said Haïk, after a short wait. "There's not enough light."

"But don't you see the bodies? From here it looks like arms hanging at the sides, here to the left. Adult arms and children's. For sure, they're waiting. Waiting for a proper burial," he added.

"But I'm telling you that I don't see a thing," Haïk added, a bit annoyed. "I'll take a picture of this," the American concluded.

The shots hadn't surprised the rag pickers, as the noise from the digger overpowered everything else in the trash dump. Mouk nodded to where the holes had been made atop the smoke. Haïk didn't have time to put his gun away.

"Someone's looking for you," Mouk told Gam with a faint smile on his face." The four men over there who are walking towards Dro.

"The King's Musketeers," Gam said.

29.

*F*rom a shiny black Hummer stationed in the parking lot, four rough-hewn men emerged, built like grazing buffaloes, each one a heaving Hercules ready to break down doors and crack skulls. Tricked out in their finest interrogation wear, the colossi carried with them an air of military whorishness, ready to execute the most horrific acts at the behest of their masters. They had tied their ponytails in red ribbons, wore long blue raincoats and orange cloth tied around their waists instead of belts and finally motorcycle boots with thick soles, buckles and zippers. Sporting vicious smiles beneath black sunglasses, they moved in unison ready to trample the fire, the smoke, the shit, and its stench—and if need be, burst into the sanctuary of putrefaction that lay before them. Once more Mouk acted as a scout to learn who they were after. Gam, nimble warrior that he was, disappeared and returned to his observation post under the old refrigerator carcasses.

From atop his digger, Dro caught sight of them as they made their way down the path like predators amid jungle prey. He spat out a jet of brown saliva. That's all we needed! he thought, now they're sending their pit bulls after us. A few seconds later, the men found themselves surrounded by the nauseating smoke-saturated air. Their sturdy, erect bodies suddenly began to shake and give way. One of them started to cough. The other followed suit and bent over while rubbing his eyes underneath his shades. The third turned his head to avoid the vaporous onslaught while the fourth searched in vain for a Kleenex to cover his nose. The rag pickers panicked when they spotted the four men but fell into convulsions of laughter as they witnessed them contorting their bodies into all sorts of strange positions. Tsknors suddenly began to imitate them, dancing on the trash, his face turned upwards as if he were trying to escape being suffocated.

Then he lunged in the direction of one of the four men.

"Take this," he said. "Don't say it's bad if you want to hear it's good." And he offered up the piece of cloth that he used as a handkerchief to wipe his hands and face: "Take it, my brother, put that over your mug!" he suggested in the voice of a devil disguised as an angel of mercy. The poor colossus had removed his glasses and didn't dare look up. He grabbed the rag and lifted it up to his nose:

"That stinks," he screamed as he threw the rag away.

"We can call for an ambulance," Tsknors suggested as he burst into laughter.

"What ambulance," the other screamed, "you want my fist in your face?"

The four men soon recovered. The rag pickers continued rummaging through the trash as they approached the men—business as usual—in anticipation of listening to what Dro would say to them. The tenor of their everyday lives might depend on what he said to them. Dro had turned off his machine. All that remained was of the sound of the seagulls squawking overhead as they flew back and forth like winged ghosts. Then complete silence. Dro spat his tobacco-filled saliva in the direction of the four men:

"You guys come to do some gardening or what?" he asked them. The rag pickers laughed and made fun of their new guests.

"In case you have the wrong address, and you want to do some digging, I can lend you some *lapatka*." A pause set in. The smoke and stench continued to tickle and itch the four strangers' bodies; Dro's pigs rummaged at their feet with their snouts, and flies buzzed in their faces.

"Dro, is that you?" the largest of the four finally asked, adjusting his glasses.

"At your service. Dro, administrator of public excrement. Administrator in charge, to be precise. I live here 24/7, year-round. The city drops its crap here like horses on the loose. And me, I burn it up."

"Are these pigs yours?"

"Yeah, they're mine. Like those other three guys over there belong to you."

"And you feed them this shit?"

"What about you?"

"What about us?"

"You have names, don't you?"

"My name is Apsos, and this is Toros, Aramais and Lusignan."

"I see. Apsos, Toros, Aramais, Lusignan ..."

"We're brothers. And I'm the eldest. My father wanted a girl. That's why he called me *Apsos*.[76] The other three came after me. That's all. Now that you're up to date on everything, let's talk business. We're looking for someone who goes by the name of Gam," he said as he removed a picture from his back pocket.

"So, you guys are police?" Dro ignored the photo completely.

"We are who we are. And we do what we do."

"Gam, you say? Well, Gam[77] may or not be here. In any case, whoever says that he's here isn't all there."

"But he must be somewhere, since he pretends to be here, with a name like his."

"Well then have a look, be my guest."

Dro started to turn to get back on his digger. The four brothers immediately surrounded him. They were so close to him that they could smell his breath, a mixture of alcohol, tobacco, smoked flesh, sweat of sow and oil, while he could smell their eau de toilette (Hugo Boss, care of a *tzanot*[78] working in customs at Zvartnots airport). The *quattuor* immediately became enraged and began to interrogate the administrator of public crap, Kalashnikov-style:

Apsos: "We searched the whole City down to the last rat hole. No rat.

---

76   *Apsos*: Unfortunately. Too bad.

77   As a recall, *gam'/kam'* means *or,* or *or else*. But it can also mean *I am, I exist, I am present*. See footnote 2 for a short explanation on its pronunciation.

78   A relative.

And if he's not there, where can he be? With the rats in the trash dump."

Toros: "Because to know where a rat might hide, you have to be a bona fide rat."

Aramaïs: "Wherever this rat is hiding, we'll bring him back, dead or alive."

Lusignan: "We've got all the time in the world."

Apsos: "Maybe he goes into the City sometimes to see his girlfriend?"

Toros: "Everyone needs a *yar* or a *seksot' bala*. Why would he be any different?"

Aramais: "That *bitch*! How does he like to *kéf*? Which of the City's *nanarnots*[79] does he prefer?

Lusignan: "Maybe the Sebastia whorehouse?"

Apsos: "That's the best one. Those *poutanka*[80] have asses like poker tables and they make you come like nobody's business."

Toros: "Makes sense. Our Minister of Education owns the one in Sebastia."

Aramais: "How does Gam like to do it, huh?"

Lusignan: "With or without a condom?"

Apsos: "And what type of condoms does he like? Did he tell you?"

Toros: "Foreign brands? *Durex? Manix? Protex? Lubrix? Sadix? Technix? Love Light?*"

Aramais: (addressing Toros) "You're forming alliances with *otars, now?* No? So don't advertise their products, *djanikess*! Our country makes the best condoms, safer, unrippable, tested on mechanical bulls. For example, Ararat condoms, in two sizes; *Small Massis* and *Big Massis*, as needed. Etchmiadzin brand, specially made for members of the church.

---

79   *Kèf:* party; *Nanarnots:* whorehouse.

80   Whores.

Geghart, for those who like to dig into virgins. Ani for those who come apart at the end. And the latest brand, Arax, especially made for those who travel a lot and often cross borders."

Lusignan: "Our Idi Gago, by the way, only uses domestic brands. That says a lot. A real patriot always uses Armenian condoms. And you can't to find a bigger fucker than him."

Apsos (to Dro): "So you have no idea if Gam uses condoms or not? We don't use any. Membership has its privileges."

Toros: "Otherwise the country will never make up for our losses during the Genocide."

Apsos: "The most fertile men have no right to block the way to their sacred sperm when the homeland is headed towards demographic anorexia."

Lusignan: "Even with a foreigner. Transferring our know-how to other nations, that's what we do best. But who knows, maybe this guy Gam is a *gomik*, who knows? A *galouboy*? A *pidr*? A *pédof*? A *sissér*? A *grab*? A *shrtib*? A *brzzee*?[81] Huh, who knows?"

Apsos: "And why is it exactly that he doesn't work in the City anymore like everyone else?"

Toros: "Maybe the City is too dirty for him, is that it?"

Aramais: "If that's the case, why doesn't he just emigrate, like any other honest person in this country?

Lusignan: "Like all our cousins. Piloting patched up airplanes in Africa, or cutting down birch trees in Siberia, or even shining shoes in Los Angeles, huh?"

Apsos: "He likes it better here? Is that it? How on earth can you like this shit so much?"

---

81   *Gomik, galouboy:* fag. *Pidr, pédof:* pedophile. *Sissér, grab, shrtib, brzzee:* uncertain meanings and pronunciations.

Toros: "By the way" (staring at Dro, then turning around towards the other rag pickers), "who do you think the President is prouder of, one of you or one of us?"

Aramais: "Truth be told, you blacken the country's image by wanting to consume consommé."

Lusignan: "And what will westerners think of us?"

Apsos: "That our President feeds his own the way you feed your pigs?"

Toros: "That he forces them to gorge themselves on rot?"

Aramais: "And why stay here when so many countries in the world are opening their arms to you?"

Lusignan: "Turkey, for example? You can find good, honest work there."

Apsos: "Turkey may be a slaughterhouse, but that's better than a trash dump, isn't it?"

Toros: "Why don't you go buy your meat in their butcher shops?"

Aramais: "One might find it fishy that you prefer a trash dump to Turkey."

Lusignan: "Yes, I suspect."

Apsos: "Gam's never been there. That much we know for a fact. We keep track of who comes and goes."

Toros: "And did he ever help his mother? A good son always helps his mother. Especially as she gets older and falls back into childhood. So why didn't he do the same?"

Aramais: "By helping his mother from abroad he would have helped his motherland as well, no?"

Dro: "His mother died."

Lusignan: "She died. Oh, she died! That makes sense, he killed her. He killed her by not helping her."

Apsos: "Our task is to help everyone's common mother. Our mother of all mothers. And that's why ..."

Toros: "We'd really like to know what he was doing attending Opposition meetings."

Aramais: "He was having someone nibble in his ears while we were throwing up over the good people's elected leader and he cheered when that *méret kouném* of a first President held his arms spread wide above his head as if he were showing you the size of his wiener. I'm telling you that guy is more of a fisherman than a messiah."

Lusignan: "Now maybe you're going to ask us why we're after Gam and not all the others? To make an example of him, of course."

Apsos: "And also, he's suspected of having written a certain article that's keeping our boss up at night. The Palace lights stayed on a few nights in a row. He couldn't sleep anymore."

Toros: "In this article our leader has been transformed into the Samourai. Why a Samourai? Because of his military background?"

Aramais: "And who is this Gam who dares to pass himself off as the Hedgehog?"

Lusignan: "Maybe he thinks that he can hide beneath his forest of quills."

Apsos: "But we recognized his style. We had fun with it for an entire night. Well, it has style, I'll admit that much. Yes, we all admit it. A mix of hot pepper and itching powder. It's the same author as the one who wrote about the Loulian affair."

Toros: "He wants to blacken the name of our *militsa* [82] or what?"

Aramais: "If he's working for a country, then let him live in it as well, that *khdr!* [83]

Lusignan: "And stop looking into the Loulian affair."

---

82   Police.

83   That bastard.

Apsos: "The guy's dead. His wife's a widow. His boys are orphans. Now let's plan for the future."

Toros: "Because you recognize his writing style, that Gam."

Aramais: "A mixture of hot pepper and itching powder."

Lusignan: "Our *militsa's* got nothing to do with this."

Apsos: "Just because he died inside a police station doesn't mean that the police killed him. Many have gone in, and few have come out. So what?"

Toros: "Many were called in, few died there."

Aramais: "Our police, it's not like our church which absolves everyone of everything."

Lusignan: "We don't have to answer to God."

Apsos: "So be sure and tell this Gam. Either Gam is on the Samourai's team. I mean on our President's. Or Gam is against him. But we're going to nab him either way."

Toros: "And we'll get him."

Aramais: "That rat."

Lusignan and Apsos: "Yeah, we'll get him, that rat."

Dro mounted his digger again and started the motor. The explosions coming from his machine signaled the end of recess. The rag pickers went back to work enthusiastically, leaving the four men like lost souls among the trash. Gam had followed the goings on from afar. That's when one of the mastodons gave one of the sows that was crowding his feet a swift kick in the stomach. The pigs surrounded the four elephantine men, teeming on all sides, nibbling on their boots, spurring them with their snouts. Squeezed in on all sides, they couldn't make enough room to kick the hideous monsters that were harassing them in the stomach. Dro was concentrating on the contents of a dump truck that he had to spread out as quickly as possible, and he couldn't hear anything due to the explosions that were filling the air around him. A first colossus lost his balance and collapsed onto a recently deposited pile of trash. The others tried to help him back up, but he also slipped. The moment they were on the same level, Idi Gago charged into them like a Panzer tank crushing toy soldiers, while the rest of the herd, encouraged by his initiative, began to trample over them as they jostled each other, screeching like witches and grumbling like ogres. Bella even dragged her teats over the face of one of the fallen men, as Cobra followed suit. The ensuing mêlée that took place within the empty trash bags was such that man and beast became indistinguishable. The former only managed to get up again once the pigs had dispersed, dirty, stinking, and covered in phlegm. The men had no choice but to give up on their search and clear out of the dump as quickly as possible. They walked back down the path with their shoulders hunched and disappeared into the dust that the passing trucks spread into the air and onto their sticky clothing. The gulls laughed as they cut the air with their sinister antics. In a foul mood and covered in shit, the Four Musketeers dove into their Hummer. The car sped back to the City with its windows wide open. Lousso picked up the picture that had fallen to the ground during the pig mêlée. It was none other than Gam, indeed. He tore the picture into little pieces and threw it onto the trash.

30.

*I*t was a real waste for your mother's tomb to be located in some godforsaken cemetery with a view on a trash dump and a road that's used to transferring lunatics and criminals to jail and children whose spirits and bodies are broken and if that weren't enough they stuck me in between some innocent guy that they assassinated and a drunkard,that poor Loulian who's screaming in his hole for anyone who can hear him that they defenestrated him except for his very sensible wife because it's his wife whose sensitive to underground waves, are you are listening to me they stole my life tell the journalists that it's my country that made me commit suicide and on the other side I've got that Djilo who dropped dead suddenly at the entrance of Paplavok that restaurant that plays Jazz music so loud that one night it actually drowned out the sound of the cries of a man who one of the Cobra's henchmen who beating to death the pirate president the piranha president of our darkest years but Djilo was still during the red years when he got drunk to blind himself to the ugliness of an era when people did everything in spite of themselves and he is screaming I need a drink give me back my Paplavok so restless that he seems burnt from the inside, and so on without any end in sight so that it looks as if his vices from when he was alive have followed him into death and what did I ever do to have to listen to these screams having never been a nurse or a midwife or a nun at Sacred Heart or a barmaid at Paplavok and how can one hope to ever rest in peace here, maybe by changing location for example at least if they had buried me somewhere over there at the bottom of the cemetery with the first tombs I would have been surrounded by dead people reduced to silent dust but the newly dead are everywhere these days, car crash victims and political assassinations or everyday people who jump off the Kiev bridge or that are made to fall off that bridge, you can tell who's guilty by the way they come by here at great lengths Loulian's wife comes by here some-times as well with her two boys that are as little as you were but usually she's alone in a black suit, a blond in a black mourning and totally dignified, no tears solid as a rock and doesn't accept that the investigation into her husband's death's is also buried: INNOCENT CITIZEN DIED AT THE HANDS OF HIS OWN COUNTRY she had that engraved on the tombstone as a slap in the face of the au-thorities and the police her Levon died within police headquarters like many others before him but how do you know anything about that, she comes here and spends hours on end just staring at those letters INNOCENT CITIZEN DIED AT THE HANDS OF HIS OWN COUNTRY, it must give her the strength to go on well of course she must come to re-energize her disheartened self which is tired of fac-ing the lies and bad faith of those who deny her need for truth the need to know more about what happened that day and which goon pushed her husband which hands did it, as if her Levon could have done that all by himself he screams out his innocence it but she doesn't hear anything above the silence well I guess an energy that comes from behind the wall because they were simple people who loved each other like normal people and worked like normal people the two of them didn't bother a soul they ran a restaurant so it had to happen that a bunch of schemers killed each other in the street one night for Levon to be called to the police station as a witness and end up suicided and now his wife has to deal with all of this alone and suffer alone blindly but in the end she's stayed strong when I see her standing above her husband's tomb with lips pursed and her hands squeezing something after leaving a bouquet of flowers on his tomb daisies or sometimes gladioli and for how much time still who knows if love doesn't get tired of frequenting death so often and if one day she won't finally turn in her black clothes for a happier existence and forget without being able to forget with another man a new one at the same time as the old one unjustly assassinated and thrown on the trash heap of time and I wonder if she feel like I do, abandoned, you had me to make you forget because of what you were writing probably about that Loulian affair. You always wanted to understand to get to the bottom of all the crap that's your profession you used to say that you had a hole within you and you were too curious, you had to push your way through tunnels and underground lives, appear in the depths that you dive into, the unlikely obscurity where the shadows scare you the black menace black everywhere someone's been watching you for a long time and so late one night when you were working on your investigation in your newspaper's offices you got a call on your cell phone some guy asked you to meet him at the café in the lobby of the office building he says he has information for you so you leave your office you walk towards the elevator and all of sudden three guys jump you and beat you up they'd already broken all the lights in the hallway one hard hit to the head another one cracked your skull against the wall you'd touched on sensitive issues other journalists had also been attacked before you police inquiries and then nothing but that wasn't going to frighten you you'd need a lot more than that no you didn't stop when you were writing you stayed clean but now that your hands don't play with all that assassins' filth your hands stayed buried in the mold to look for whatever scrap metal empty bottles or some treasure perhaps so *adios* to the trash dump you clean yourself you scrub your hands those same hands that I saw so delicate over piano keys black ones white ones that danced on top of them danced along with mine and our fingers together on the keys and our souls joyously together before the great quake because nothing was ever the same afterwards and since that day your hands have started digging, digging always deeper and deeper with Haïk as a guide down to the bottom and yet the music was the hardest and most mysterious that your eyes didn't need to see anything and your hands didn't need to touch the depths with your Anna that taught it to you in the first place but you insisted on digging into politics into the chaos the dirt and the blood and that's where it brought you to that trash dump to shake up the most corrupt layers can anyone reasonably take pleasure in going so low where instincts are at work where it swarms and devours now that it's here your exile this dump the most rotten corner of our lands but which corner of our lands weren't defiled worse than pigs we are on the shores of pure Lake Dilijan or Sevan and all of our rivers congested with trash sewers cesspits and you that's what you dig into like in Gyumri when you were searching for Garen under the ruins of our house you dig thinking that you'll reach us, the layer of dead people but the dead wander about in all directions lost souls each one burns their former obsession and will only see light of day if I may say when they wake up from their vice and what led them astray into delinquency and I am like the other and you are like the others who insist on probing the inhuman in men and without knowing it you make yourself a stranger to these lands but what's the use what's the use Gam of obsessing over other people's absurdities when we're all victims of our own destiny neither the earth nor man's time on this good earth and since our house in Gyumri collapsed not only because of the quake, its structure had been unstable and worm eaten for a long time and since then you've never stopped thinking that the entire country itself was also worm eaten and that it was built on the waste of lost stories, soft piled up cadavers unstable ways of life unstable mentally corrupt and that you wanted to know, to bring it all to light and show it so that life could thrive on life, but Gam that's why you isolated yourself from others thinking that you could fix everything all by yourself and that's how you abandoned me your own mother who cries thinking about your hands now, your lost hands that left the Krasny Oktyobr or when you'd promised to take her to Dilijan to buy her bouquets of flowers its hills dotted with wild flowers and buzzing with insects where she would so much have liked to drink all day from the purest air your mother and the clouds that pass overhead to watch them go by or the sky that smiles down on men to see him smile as well.

Sometimes Gam instinctively turned towards the cemetery and looked deep into the heart of those tombs to search for his mother's tomb, to lay his head on it and each time it was as if he heard Anna moan and he regretted that he'd broken his promise to bring her to Dilijan.

31.

A foursome silently broke away from the rest of the pack, as if propelled by the sun's position, towards an unknown destination, and without aim: Bertha, Nara, Lili et Ano.

Ah!

But where were they headed and why? And what could they have found to compete with the digs where they made their usual money? They must have felt some irrepressible need to leave these sterile surroundings behind. Had they simply been looking to empty their bladders they would have headed in another direction. Instead, they converged on the path then hurtled down the slope all the way to Dro's house, they dropped off their hooks and their *meshogs* in a corner before crossing the cemetery entrance. Gam wasn't surprised to see them changing locales to answer the call of their mysterious physiologies. It was three o'clock. They were gossiping away. Ano complained that she been a tomb for the child that died within her after only three months. Nara went on about her husband Vazo, tired exemplar of laziness itself and wrecked by a bad case of the shakes. Lili commented on her husband Raffi's rare appearances when he wasn't working in Odessa. And Bertha complained about her pencil-pushing Dono, who was already sliding into his twilight years and still dying to have a beautiful child in his own image:

"So much so that I was resigned to not taking a drop from his liquor stash. Not that it wouldn't happen in the end. He's the one who's holding back. He asks me what a child would think of a corpse-like father."

"In that case," Lili suggested, "find yourself another guy! Once you've done the deed, just visualize the kid with your God's face." They laughed.

"That's right," said Bertha, "I like touching him. Only him."

"But what about the stone then?" said Nara, troubled.

"The stone standing upright on the tomb? It climbs its way up inside me. It's so smooth that it drives me to ecstasy. And then I experience this incredible feeling of peace inside my body, as if it were him, my husband that were burrowing inside it."

"That's so funny," said Lili "It does the exact same thing to me, that stone. And yet it's only a stone. It's alive, bloated with blood. It digs inside of me, and my entire body feels electric."

"Same here," confirmed Nara, "that stone throws me into a worm hole where I forget everything else, it's simply amazing. Since Vazo's stick isn't what it used to be, the stones make up for it." Ano was walking at their side, closed in on herself like the lid on a casket.

"On your way to rub the old fur?" Roubo asked as they walked by, before his ironic lips spat out a jet of nicotine-filled spittle.

The four women shrugged. They wanted to avoid any confrontation whatsoever. In case he decided to put an end to what they considered a gratuity on his part. In fact, which dead person would ever tolerate being treated as poorly as hey treated him? Even if some would consider it flattering for Djilo to have become an object of vaginal fervor from beyond the grave. Even if these things weren't alien to his experience or to his favorite vice while he was alive. Yet thanks to the women of the trash dump, Djilo had lost none of his virility. They would go to him, meandering through the cemetery's winding allies, convinced that one way or another he would finally pass on to them a tiny drop of his poetic fecundity. It made little difference how or in what form. Especially since during his lifetime, during his brief period of fertility, he had failed to ever get his partner pregnant. Not once. The alcohol that served to ignite his poetic inspiration had made his vital life force go soft. But the women still came to him, confident.

You go figure what psychological mechanism incited them to act this way. They lost all better judgment, believing in these pagan traditions. In a land and time far away, women who couldn't conceive after their men mounted them in vain, were blamed for being infertile, as if cursed. Some stone cutters probably took pity on them and looking deep into their pagan souls, crafted some stone toys that could plow deep into the recesses of their imagination. Unless someone commissioned the toys. This would explain why at the heart of the Christian era, these gland-like mushroom-capped barrels had been erected. But art was no match for nature. In the country's southern regions, entire generations of problematic spouses had chosen a protruding stone of their own, one so perfectly adapted to the wishes of their nether regions that they would immediately bend down to kiss it afterwards. They decided, by some unknown nebulous decree, that it would have the ability to give their organs back their rightful function, on condition that they crushed their stomachs against it. And indeed, these women's faith embraced the mineral mystery with such enthusiasm that the ability to give birth sometimes returned to them. And it was this same faith, mixed in with their maternal obsessions and confused sexual thrusting that made the four unlucky women circulate so nimbly among the cemetery's twists and turns. As they watched the other women sneak out, they jabbered behind them, calling them shameful, the disgrace of their respective families, useless orifices, empty stomachs, sterile mules. In the eyes of proper wives, this reproductive tardiness was a sign of bastardization. These women were unworthy, traitors to a country during a demographic war.

The day that they caught wind of the therapeutic friction being practiced by these barren, horny women on their master Djilo's tomb Axel, Valodia, Djanikof and Sourik's blood began to boil. This also had gave them another occasion to drink some memorial *oghi* on Djilo's tomb.

For too long, they had abandoned death to their hellish thirst, so badly was he dying, his mouth open in the hopes that a drop of national alcohol would embalm his tongue and moisten his throat. The four had decided on an expedition to the cemetery to rid their poet of this stone that was crushing his lower stomach, even if it meant throwing the women into a bottomless pit of unending curses.

Axel was a foot taller than the others and he resembled an American sci-fi actor. After him came Valodia, then Djanikof, and then the much shorter Sourik. As for their hair, Valodia's curls were entirely white at this point, while Axel's were just beginning to grey. Sourik appeared to be the least married of the four, a bachelor despite his basset-hound looks. They were all crazy about Djilo, and each one had their respective anecdotes that no one else was meant know about.

Their attack took place at nightfall. Informed of their plans, Roubo had opened the gate for them. He couldn't accept that these renegade women who created such a ruckus in the trash dump, should come refresh themselves at Djilo's. And so, he welcomed the Four Knights of Djilo's Sacred Hearts crusade as a sign that would restore his honor. Go do it! he told them, then left them to go to sleep. It was the gloomiest of nights. No moon or lamps to provide any light. At first, they drove on with their headlights at full blare, hesitating at a minor fork in the road.

"It's that way," said Axel.

"What the heck are you talking about? They buried him up top," said Valodia, as if he had been a better friend of Djilo than Axel. They began to search the top part of the cemetery while Djanikof and Sourik wouldn't even leave their car. Shadows passed by in front of the headlights...

"Did you see?" asked Djanikof.

"See what?" Sourik retorted.

"It's as if somehow we're not alone here in the cemetery," said the other, worried.

"Whose brilliant idea was it to do this at night?"

"Brilliant or not," answered Sourik, "you can tell that they're completely lost."

"It's also possible that the dead want to mix up the roads and make it harder to get around," Djanikof continued." You don't believe that the dead visit each other to pass the time?"

Axel and Valodia had been wandering for close to two hours and there was still no sign of Djilo. They read the names on the gravestones, pulled apart bushes, and walked on top of dead people's slabs without a qualm. And still they found nothing. Tired of their meanderings, they rejoined their friends who were seated in the car. They opened the bottle of *oghi* to warm themselves up and pealed a cucumber to fight the burn from the alcohol.

"*Ara!* I always thought that Djilo was close to the *Molokos*," Valodia noted," I'm sure of it "

"You're sure now, are you? You're sure huh?" Alex repeated, annoyed. "And I'm telling you that he's farther down. I was there at his burial, while you were chasing after whores in Moscow! And what a stupid idea to look for a gravestone on a moonless night!"

"So, was I supposed to check the weather report, or what, Mr. Know-It-All?" answered Volodia.

"In Europe," Djanikof added, attempting to make peace between the two, "they have GPS."

"What the hell are you going to do with a GPS?" Axel exploded, "in a cemetery where the alleys don't have names? And the tombs aren't numbered? Nothing, that's what! No numbers, no names. Nothing whatsoever."

"You could have checked at the Mayor's Office first," said Sourik in the voice of a practical intellectual.

"These women," Axel asked taking in a draft as he clicked his tongue and crushed pieces of cucumber, "these women, *aggh!* Where did they find the nerve to masturbate on top of Djilo? That much, I'd like to know."

Axel, who made a living editing and prefacing books, was wondering if his beloved poet hadn't hidden from him some unpublishable smut. Djilo was also a translator: for all one knew that sly fox Djilo had read some bawdy French stories. Perhaps some salacious texts that had been left abandoned somewhere?

"Djilo, erotic poetry? Get out of here!" Valodia responded. "That wasn't like him."

"You want to know what I think?" Axel answered suddenly. "I think that those limping *nanars* pasted some Charents onto our Djilo. Charents wrote some lewd poems. They remained secret, as you might imagine. But some of them landed in famous little Gevork's hands. His son let me read them. Still. Charents isn't Djilo. And vice-versa. And neither one of them should be forced to offer up their organs to those freaking *lâtchâr!*"

"After all if eroticism could stimulate their pregnancies." Djanikof had just thrown his usual restraint to the wind, "Why hold it against them? They rub their stomachs, maybe a bit of their vaginas. So what? It's true that doing it with a stone is kind of weird. But what's wrong with wanting children, especially if they're using a time-honored tradition in our culture? In the South, in Zangezur, they've been practicing this type of stimulation for ages. And it's proven to be effective. So let them give birth, and our nation will profit from it! Let them do as they as they like and let's go home." So, they went home.

"I agree," Valodia concluded as they were driving towards the City. "Let those women heat up their tummies in the hopes of putting their contraptions in order again. OK. But with them you never know. Give them an inch and they'll take a mile. Give them eight and they'll take your arm."

The men exploded in conspiratorial laughter. And that's how that night Djilo, the unfindable Djilo remained a bundle of nerves, an exposed body topped by a petrophallus stuck in his patch of earth. That same day Bertha, Nara, Lili et Ano, once again found themselves overlooking his tomb, ready to grind their insides as they massaged their stomachs on the swollen sculpture, if not another organ farther down. Beauties who—stinking like sows, smelling like repugnant, fetid rot—threw off their clothes and sparkled in black, purple, and mauve undergarments. Lilit pulled a round bottle marked *Hermès* from her bag. "Djilo should like this," she said. "It's French. Found it in the trash dump. We're going to smell Parisian. You'd like that, wouldn't you, Djilo *djan?*" And *pschitt* behind their ears! *Pschitt* again between their breasts! Pschitt-pschitt one last time on her wrists. And their mischievous laughter fused with the radiant sky, haunted by a crow from the necropolis below.

Scantily clad, their eyes alive and their flesh excited, they surrounded the stone. The sculptor had carved it the old way. Not an exact replica of the original but close enough to be unmistakable. A column with a rounded tip and a circular fold. And just the right size so that a woman of average stature didn't need to jump up to kiss it, sprawl herself on it or squeeze it between her legs. And so smoothed over by so many rounds of filing down and rubbing of skin that it could be mistaken for an intended collaboration between artist and female frottage. But amorous rubbing required words. Lubricating words. Words to bedevil the body. Poems by Djilo, as they thought, handwritten by them on a sheet they kept as a talisman.

And that's when the four shameless women one after the other read out loud in crazed voices their copulatory *djiloteries.*

Underfoot, Djilo was hammering on his wooden coffin. In death he screamed like a lizard thrown onto an open flame. His neighbors in adjoining tombs heard him clearly. Like Anna, Gam's mother, whom this clucking foursome were disturbing as surely as a pointed knife shucking a clam: "*Harbadz*[84] harpies!" Djilo screamed." *Hechtotsanka! Poutanka! Bellatanka! Bella-parkir-là!*[85] *Poshetstsich!* [86] *Maïtochka! Minetchitsa!*[87] Bunch of sterile *lâtchâr*! I've got nothing to do with these worms! I've got enough of my own! They're not mine, you understand? Not mine! And for God's sake get rid of that stone. It's crushing my carcass! Is this some type of just retribution? I'm innocent, I tell you! Innocent! I want a drink, that's all! Valodia! Djanikof! *Oghi! Oghi!* Axel! Sourik! *Oghi! Oghi!* Please! Save me from these dead wombs! From these slushy mussels! Where the hell are you! Help!"

He was bent over, yelling in pain. But the gaps of deliverance weren't opening. Because what's up is up, and what's down is down. And if the two spheres,

---

84   Drunk.

85   Or Bella-Lay-Down-Here.

86   From *poshi,* dust. Used to describe women who practice oral sex, fellatio. (Alludes to a vacuum cleaner).

87   From the Russian, same as previous footnote.

the finite and the infinite, the ancient and the new meet, then they talk to each other without hearing or talking to each other. But time must go by for the weight to be lifted. Light are the men who, having lost their animal heritage, can lift themselves up in peace. Light...

Djilo feared the worst. That the women would add their weight to that of the stone by impaling themselves on it. It was their intention after all to straddle it. If not, why did they ever leave the trash dump? To tan the back of their necks? To air out their bodies? To masturbate to poetry? To play the bumblebee foraging in the perfumes of the world and death? To crack their slits simply at the idea of coming together? No, what they needed to do, they'd do.

And so, they did...

When the time arrived Lili and Nara and Ano, having already come, decided to stop their friend, who was the last one to hop onto the stone dildo. Bertha stood dazed, then pulled up her knickers and adjusted her bra. Then a burp from the dump passed over the women. A murmur of dirty air and bursts of fetidness. A chorus of croaking.

They got dressed in silence and rejoined the road to the trash dump. Underground Djilo was crying like a turtle without a shell. Crying...

32.

*T*here, where matter and spirit meet, top and bottom no longer exist, superior and inferior are no longer separated. Instead, they form a unified whole. Man's blood circulates like sap in a plant, and *happiness* promises to blossom forth. From the old comes the new. And the man who smiles at his fellow man erects a bridge on top of the one who already exists. And smiling, it lifts one up to the sky above. And he who doesn't smile is no more than a mask dirtied by the world's mud. Let every face learn to smile inwardly then, and ...

These words were written on a piece of paper that the wind had blown all the way to Roubo. He had seen it hover in the air like a butterfly. To make certain that it wouldn't escape his grasp, Roubo crushed it underfoot, leaned over, picked it up and read. *There, in the place where...*

ROUBO

I was reading these crazy words as the four turtle doves were about to cross my doorstep and, inevitably, walk right by me. I lifted my head because the paper and text were torn. *And he...* that was it. An abyss, a hole, and then I noticed my pretty women, cackling cheerfully as they left the dead behind. They had finished their ablutions and God knows what else. But what topic of discussion could be putting them in such a happy mood? Exuberant in their old rags instead of making a stink out of the tragedy as they slaved away, the *kaqavik.*[88] Are they perhaps in love with him? I asked myself. This flea bag has its own harem it turns out. But let him keep his pigs to himself, oh most accomplished cleaner of patriotic toilets! *Pouah!*

---

88   Little partridge. Young hen.

I was lost. Especially after that ridiculous sheet of paper. The four women crossed the road. A black car of the dubious official type preceded them in the parking lot. I was intrigued. So I kept my eye on the car to see who would get out. No one. The girls passed by. Then the chauffeur, a bulky guy with a shaved head, hailed one of the four bitches. They are talking about God knows what. The chauffeur started to use his hands to be more persuasive. Finally, he opened the back door. The four women stood outside and listened. They didn't force them into the vehicle, of course, smoky and flea ridden as they were. I couldn't hear any of this either. But my eyes didn't miss a single detail of what was going on in front of me. The chauffeur drove close by, his stony look fixed on the gravel in the parking lot. From time to time, he went to sit under a small tree, sickened by the shit-filled air that clogged everything up. Whatever the other guy saying must have been serious, grave even, as their faces darkened. He took a step back, put one foot down, then the other. A pudgy, jowly, stocky guy in a suit appeared out of nowhere and lit a cigar, probably to kill the odor of the burning trash that made it hard to breathe. He said something to the chauffeur who went back into the car and parked it right in front of the entrance, ready to roll. Meanwhile Bertha whispered a few words to the three others, as if she were saying something shameful or important, I suppose, as serious as a passage from the Bible. It sounded like *truthfully, I am telling you truthfully, the one who etc...* But what exactly? I couldn't make out what she was saying. It was horrible for me not to know what was going on. A dog would have heard everything, with its big ears. Not me though. But a dog wouldn't have understood anything either. So why wasn't I made with dog ears? And suddenly Bertha led the guy into Dro's house. And they disappeared... What was she going to do him, I wondered? It's true that he's clean, more than I am. While I've got the merchandise right here under my nose every time they go by. Well, no. They have to play around with strangers because they're all done up and roll around in big old fancy cars. I'm going to complain to Dro. They can put it all in order. A good blow job, you don't turn that down. I also have my secret place. Oh, the ingrates! I measured the amount of time that Bertha sucked the big one. Five minutes and more. Maybe longer. While that was going on, Nara, Ano and Lili went to the other side of Dro's house. Suddenly, what did Roubo see with his tobacco, alcohol, and smoke-reddened eyes? He saw that the four women were pushing the fat guy on the path to the trash yard. His hands tied to his stomach, a rope around his neck and Bertha pulling him forward. The fat one forced to follow. Pulled along, he struggled, stumbled, but moved forward towards the shit. The poor snazzed-up guy went straight toward it. A kidnapping! They're not going to cut off his penis after servicing him, are they, I asked myself? Dro's the one who's going to go nuts. The chauffeur didn't see a thing. Everything took place behind his back. But now I lost sight of them on the path that the trucks use to empty their cargo.

I could have warned the chauffeur. But he was at Dro's. I saw those tigresses pulling the other guy along and showing no pity as they turned him into a slave like a black man being swept along towards the Americas. Sure that they were going to have their way with him. Not to feel any pleasure. They're too bitter for that. But to torment him instead. I had never seen such a vendetta before unleashed by furies. Cherished creatures. Ah! Ah! Actresses who pretend to love one minute, then become killers the next minute. Hungry enough to eat their lover...

A few long minutes went by.

The worried chauffeur left the car and tried to find his boss. He panicked and ran towards Dro's shed. Nothing. And suddenly he sprinted towards the truck drivers' path and disappeared. A few more minutes went by before the chauffeur came back, filthy. He was carrying the fat one along, disheveled with his shirt open, his vest under his arm, as if he were crying. Once he reached the car, I could see that he was really sobbing and trembling. He must have been scared shitless. The chauffeur took off quickly, scraping the road, making his motor scream.

BERTHA

Peuh! That Roubo! Miserable Roubo. Guardian of the dead. He was getting a look at us from above. Too bad for him. We were wearing pants and boots under our old dresses. Well, that didn't seem to bother him one bit. Thankfully, we crossed the street. The dead belong to him, the trash dump to us. A large car appeared on the parking lot. Black, so black that you couldn't see inside it. The chauffeur came out."

"Hey! Little sisters?" he said. We turned around. "My boss would like to have a word with you. You have a minute, don't you?

"Talk, talk... Probably to throw us out of here," I answered. "What man could do that anyway? I assume it's not the President who's in the back of the car. We're in a hurry. We have to go by the cemetery. Now we must go straight to our paradise."

The guy, half-chauffeur, half-bodyguard, with a huge chest and cut like a Swiss pocketknife, insisted. He poured his syrupy flatteries on us and his handbook of threats. Something to the effect that his boss could either be a bearer of good news or else chase us from the dump. We agreed on one condition. That we'd stay on the parking lot premises during the entire talk. From atop his stool, Roubo was scrutinizing every detail of our conversation. The chauffeur opened the back door. A fat short guy was seated, wedged in his seat, dressed like a nabob. "Hello, my pretties!" Pretties? We were anything but, in our rags. If he'd seen us on top of Djilo's tomb, let's not even get started ...

"What names do you go by?"

We told him our names "Lili, Nara, Ano and you're Bertha, right? Great. Here's what this is all about, he said." Then he changed tone. From a clergyman he became a businessman.

"The garbage dump will be mine soon. I'll do exactly what I want with it. A park? A golf course? Time will tell. But before that, you rag pickers will have to pay me to go digging about. A part of what you make will go into my coffers. That's normal now, isn't it? I must be repaid now, don't I? But I'm not sure if I'll keep all of you. I may want to replace you with some of my people. The others, it's out in the street for them, it is. I know. Times are harsh. The world isn't a party, what can I say? Some are on their way up while others are on their way down. And I'm no miracle maker. Just a gardener who cuts and grafts. In fact. I'm not really the one who is making the decisions in this case, you know. They put me in charge of the preliminaries. Except with the four of you, I could be nice, if you know what I mean. Make an exception... Especially if you offer me a glass of water. Can one get a glass of water around here?"

He stuck his nose outside. I told him that he could find some at Dro's place. Then he pulled his chauffeur towards him to give him some instructions. We stood aside. I took advantage of the situation to talk things over with my sisters.

"Wait for me on the other side of the house. I'm going to make him think that I'm going to slurp his gherkin. We'll push him all the way to the dump. We're going to drag his hide through the mud and beat his ass so that he slaves away a bit the way we do here."

Then addressing the fat runt: "Well, follow me since you're thirsty. We're going to wet your throat a bit. Around here, the air isn't a benediction, but the water can be a deliverance."

We headed towards the shack. The chauffeur was busy turning his car around to face the road. We headed towards the shack.

"Hey beautiful!" The despot had become gallant. "What a fun meeting! So, we run into people like you in this type of sordid place?

"As you can see," I answered.

"And you live around here?"

"I survive here," I'd say.

"Ah!" exclaimed the fat man in the suit. "And your eyes are so intense!"

"I'm confused."

"No need to be."

"Nothing more lovely than a pretty little waist! How can one not fall in love with such pearly white teeth and edible lips?"

I pushed the door open. It was time. He took a last puff on his cigarette, the crushed it against the wall. I was at the water tap. It was running. I cleaned the glass and filled it up.

"Drink! Your thirst is making you crazy!" He greeted the glass with both hands. "Oh, life source!" he said, taking on the voice of a monk lost in the shadows of Haghpat Monastery.

"Thanks. It's like manna from heaven, receiving this cup from you. Nothing is better than water, you know. Wine doesn't measure up, except for large feasts. As for *oghi,* bah! Fire. But water stimulates the body. All the organs rejoice and give it thanks. You feel rejuvenated. Fever subsides."

"Drink!" he began to drink. Dro kept his ropes here to tie up his pigs. But first, I took advantage of the fact that the other one was still happy just to be drinking and so I walked behind him. I removed my scarf from around my neck and once his glass was barely down from his lips, I gagged him. He started to burp, and his head reddened. Then I took out a rope and tied his hands on top of his stomach so quickly that he didn't have time to put up a struggle. I tied another one around his neck and pulled. I opened the back door. My trio had awaited him with joy. We recovered our hooks and our *meshogs.*

"We're going to have some fun!" said Lili, hopping around and clapping her hands." They kicked him in the ass. We were on the path that leads up to the descending slopes.

"Well now! You wanted to play dictator of the excrements, did you?" said Nara. "Well then, we're going to rub your nose in it." A flock of seagulls, perched on some old trash, had laughter in their eyes and hatred on the tip of their beaks:

"You assassinated my son all the way inside my stomach," Ano whispered into the guy's ear. "Now you're going to repay me, you little two-legged big wig!"

"And it's your fault that my Raffi left me," Lilli added, "to find work abroad. Given that you're the one who gives work and takes it away here. Mister the big jeepster ..."

"Yes, it's true," Nara confirmed." And that's why our men are so weak. Because of you vermin, they've lost all ability to reach coitus. Now, my little bunny we're going to emasculate you. *Couic!*"

I was pulling on the rope as if a weight were holding my shoulders down.

"Eh, mister big shot lover! You need to walk a bit. You wanted to get your kiki polished? And remove us from your group of sacrificial lambs? Well, the sacrificial lambs are going to make you king of the trash dump. Why don't you wear this as a crown in the meantime!"

I dug up an old shoe box and crushed it on his head. And added my hook as a scepter.

"Squeeze it, otherwise, beware! And while we're at it," said Lili, "you're going to wear this as well." She threw her two *meshogs* on his shoulder, one in the front, the other behind. The little fatty was sweating blood and pissing water, his eyes red with fear. He bent over and crushed himself against the ground, dove into a pile of junk. Nara was kicking him left and right so that he'd get back on his feet. Feeling sorry for him, Lili took out his gag for a moment. Our pharaoh was so stupefied that he couldn't even call for help. He panted, abandoned by God, and whined, petrified at the idea of dying on the spot. We rejoined the rag pickers and explained our anger, while they expressed their admiration.

"Now pop some bags! And grovel for a living!" I said to him as I let go of his ropes and his *meshog*. "Dig with your hook. Dig!"

The man fell backwards, then got up clumsily.

"Better than that!" said Lili.

The others got on their knees in front of him and made fun of his chic clothes and pot belly like a bunch of vulgar soldiers. They screamed: "Hello to you, King of the Damned! Have you come to visit our people? Not at all! He was on his way to a costume ball and he just stopped by to say hello to us. Isn't that so, my fat rat?" Dro had stopped his machine. Paralyzed at the sight of our efforts. I saw him raise his hands up in the air. Thinking he was quieting everything down. I heard him say: "As God is my witness, I have nothing to do with this mess." He was behind the scenes. The yelling from the others was louder than his voice of reason. As for what happened, it wasn't planned.

GAM

They were all wading through that syrup-like trash. They were laughing hysterically, circling the guy, and throwing anything they found at him: boxes, cans—even bottles. He wasn't even trying to protect himself. Bertha had left him at their mercy. Haïk and I were seated, horrified. I, much more so than he. The others were so crazed, their hatred unleashed. They needed this outlet. So much bitterness pent up over so many days, months, and years. Yes, they needed this live prey and like famished lionesses they brutally cut down a wild boar that providence had placed on their path. At the risk of going blind in an instant, of endangering their world and their sustenance. It was such a huge relief as they harassed him and unleashed abominations on their detested scapegoat. *"Takavor! Kakavor! Takavor! Kakavor! Crowned King! Shit ass! Crowned King! Shit ass!"* Tsknors was screaming, dancing in a circle his arms in the air, his index fingers pointing straight up, like spikes that were about to be stuck into the beast's neck area. It was like a circus, especially once Lousso led Idi Gago into the improvised arena. The pig went crazy from the warrior-like giddiness surrounding him. He guessed that he was being pushed into a confrontation with the nabob. It was fat on four legs versus fat on two legs. This man was his enemy. He was meant to run into him and make him stumble. To make him roll under this swine. He plowed straight into his legs, which were already wobbling. The guy tried to avoid the attack, but he had no way out. The bitter ones were having a ball and closed ranks on him. The grunting resonated within the porcine fat. "Hercules knock that column down! Knock that column down! Go on my brave Idi!" they said. The man slipped and fell face first into the molasses. *Hourra! Hourra!* screamed the flea-ridden rag pickers. Haïk suddenly undid the circle and came to help the fallen man stand up. That's when the chauffeur showed up. A misunderstanding occurred. The other one had already lifted his fist at him, but his boss held his arm back. "Let's go home, he said." The rag pickers woke up. Each one returned to his task. The two men hurtled down the path, the fat one stumbling as his larger friend held him up.

Let every face learn how to smile at itself and it will be at one with itself and with the world. So read the rest of the paper that Roubo held in his hands. *For man is greater than man.* And when the terrifying *Light* fills the world to complete its mission, no one will be able to escape it. Hate will search for a hiding place but won't find any shelter. The new spirit will enlighten everything down to one's very soul. And the one who won't have chosen it will be chilled to the bone.

33.

*A*nd if... all of this... why? Gam asked himself. Your entire life... is... in this country's ass? His soul was a labyrinth and couldn't help getting lost in it. To leave! Like someone from here who always want to be someplace else and who instead is constantly beaten down. And now his eye pushed up against this fishbowl. He felt as if he were stuck in an octopus's stomach.

With the trash permanently stirred up, his hopes faded of ever seeing the light of day. Hopes of getting away from this hole. But the rampant streaming fumes were pointed straight at him. What prevented him from crossing the bottom of this pit? Can one easily abandon the sky that gave birth to you, the earth that gives you sustenance? And abandon your own people to their decay?

(This is what Gam feared the most. To be overcome by a storm of remorse. What he called the symptom of the trap. In the hole. In the fumes. In the terminus of this dead stomach. To feel nothing else except the fact that there is no tomorrow... The soul feels tangled up in cause and effect. Forever stuck. He saw the City but never visited it anymore. The farthest that he ventured out from the dump now was his shed, on the outskirts of the first suburbs. Beyond that, he awaited the time that he would be thrown in a worse spot that his current backwater. He loved his City in spite of its arrogance and vanity. He liked it for its girls that independence had suddenly made more beautiful. Like flowers that had blossomed from the deep freeze of totalitarianism. It was to safeguard its charm that he had fought its two-legged dogs tooth and nail. And now those dogs were on his trail. But here the overwhelming stench would throw them off. This cesspit was like a security blanket of sorts. But for how much longer?)

Who knows, he said. Who knows if they won't descend on me one day? They may well suicide me in their offices the way they did with that Levon Loulian. Or throw me over the Kiev bridge one night the way they did Zara. And in the best of cases, throw me in prison or in an insane asylum. Nubarashen is OK as far as neutralization asylums are concerned. That's what they do when someone embarrasses them. The judges lend them a hand in the shadows. They're all indentured to those in power. Fear makes them bend over, like gum that's been chewed, over an d over again. And which citizen can still live without the fear of being snatched haphazardly for the most minor misunderstanding or suspicion?

(Gam had a whole list of people who died the way Levon Loulian did inside police headquarters. Published, it went nowhere. One day in January 1993 the parents of Roudik Vardanian, aged 22, came to pick up his dead body. That morning, he had been summoned by the police in a theft case. Two cops were charged with abuse of power. One day in April 1995, Artavzd Manoukian died within security headquarters. Officially from an attack of hemorrhoids... One day in April 1997, the Virabians, parents of young Samuel, age 17, were summoned to come pick up his corpse. They were provided with no official explanation. One August day in 1997 the Dilanians received their 23-year-old son Galoust's body. Suicide by hanging. But the parents wouldn't let the matter go. Four policemen were charged and sentenced to two to five years in prison... 1998 in Abovian, Edouard Vardanian died in police headquarters. He's said to have tried to escape by jumping out the second-floor window. His case was filed without ever being investigated. April 2, 1998, Shahumian district: Stepan Gevorkian and Oleg Arishin were arrested, beaten, and then transferred to Artik. On April 5th Stepan lost consciousness after being beaten and died in the hospital. Oleg's turn will come on April 27th. Wounds were found on both men's bodies. Their cases were filed but never investigated. July 23rd, 1999, Arsen Stepanian was transferred to the Arabkir commissioner's office then beaten. He came home and died two hours later from a heart attack. His body was covered in

bruises. His case filed without investigation. In 1999, in the Vanadzor security offices, Artousha Ghazarian went on hunger strike in protest. Five cops tied him to a bed and forced him to eat. He died of cerebral hemorrhaging. June 30th, 2000, in Nubarashen, Babken Soghomonian, suspected of murder was transferred to Artashat. On July 5th, his father was informed that he hung himself. Case filed, no investigation. Other such cases abound; they never seem to stop).

Even the poor, he said to himself, even those in our garbage dump, aren't wise enough to save their people. Today their misery prevents them from speaking out. But give them a little bit of wealth like the rich and they too would become like wolves. Enough to make one believe that kindness isn't a human trait. Here, everyone digs his own grave. How can one go any lower? Spitting on the nabob wasn't a question of fatigue. Humiliated, the women in turn became humiliators. The insane made fun of the monstrous. That's how the taste for eternity was lost ...

(Truth be told the guy that the rag pickers had humiliated was not completely unknown to him. His name was Kamo, one of the toughest among the tough. Since his first days observing the city, Gam had witnessed his one-man terror campaign. This Kamo was a whore from the Cobra's bordello. Up to the hilt he was with him in his aghberoutioun,[89] his predatory brotherhood. All his lot had united to grab as many financial assets as possible and steal valuable real estate. The Cobra President of the Democrashitic Republic hadn't quite arrived at the end of his second and last term that Kamo was already changing over to his protégé the Samourai's team. Present for the Godfather's heists, he will be as well for the latter's protégé. A Russian journalist had conducted an inquiry. He listed companies for Gam where the Cobra took his daily bread: Artsakhbank, Armeksimbank, Unibank, Bella Bank, Renko Construction, Zanguezur copper and molybdenum, Ardshininvestbank, Converse Bank, the Sevan Kaputan Complex, The Ararat Condom Company, the Naïri

---

89   Mafia-like clan ; from the word *aghber/yeghbayr*, brother.

Medical Center, and a few random brands (Armani, Ricci, Khachapu-
ri, etc.), the Dickin' Construction Corp, Urinal City Center, «Downtown
Erevan» Construction Company (via his son, Cobra Jr.), Ararat Tobacco
Factory, the Anti-Tobacco Center, «H2» TV Company, SOS supermar-
ket chain, «Tsar» boutiques (via Cobra Jr.), Zvartnots International Air-
port, portable phones, diamond polishing, pipe polishing, large malls in
Moscos, post-Earthquake construction centers, a Moscow casino... The
Cobra's business interests were everywhere. But the Samurai as well,
though the relative scope of his list was more limited only because he
was still in his first term as President. These two weren't about to settle
for the small profits made at Vernissage.) [90]

---

90   But what is Vernissage? Ah! The Vernissage. The capital's flea market. At
the beginning painters, all educated in art schools, exhibited their kistch
there. Patriotic tourists go shopping here. Each one looking to Araratize
their living rooms. But Independence threw the country's workers onto the
streets, suddenly exposed to tomorrow's uncertainties. From the worker to the
engineer, the country's entire muscle and brainpower became factory vomit.
The currency devalued. Savings were lost overnight. The more nimble tried
their luck in the American paradise. The unresolved, those who were stuck,
trapped, who couldn't escape the every-man-for-himself hellosphere, could
only survive by dreaming of elsewhere. The Vernissage saw the rejects and
the rubbish of the newly-liberated national alienation. Tempted to sell their
superfluous possessions to be able to make enough money for a bit to eat
and drink. But what to sell and to whom ? Everyone swallowed their dignity.
People traded in their self-esteem. And so it went every Saturday and Sunday.
Family libraries, crystal antiques, old silverware sets, all the rococo and the
out-of-date, the obsolete and the expired, the overwrought and the second
hand, all to respond to the need for survival. Others began to knit, to make
lace doilies, jewelry, objects sculpted in obsidian, local curisosities, souvenirs
without memories, animal sculpted in wood, shawls, bags, string and wind
instruments, miniature churches, patriotacky or westernized paintings,
spare parts from radios, old wire, gordian knots, pipes, wooden wicks,
annoying old razors, manual and electric, old cameras, obsolete currencies,
yellowed bills with waxy Lenins on them, dried insects, unreadable books,
films in cannisters, post cards of Massis seated in majesty, rugs suspended
like old laundry, shapkas and old regime military uniforms, and even fake
teeth: molars, canines, incisors. Some lining the streets in the main square,
others in dried basins to align their products neatly along the edges. The
vernissage exposes an infinite number of articles of poverty cleverly disguised
as artisanry, all the forms that an ingenious people can give to their measly
possessions to save face in public. And now this produce of a society left to

There it is. The City stood firm, a vast pit, smoky and satanical. So close yet so far. Different from the morning when he let loose his bladder on the ant-hill. A bustling city that hid its anxiety. Buildings that burst forth from an orchestrated center towards suburban anarchy. And inside these buildings, men. In the streets, men as well. Milling about in every direction, effervescent. Bodies that thought. And swarming thoughts that masked their anxiety. Black ones, rebellious ones, erect or hung, abominable, shameful, wobbly, necessary, foreign, loved. And what if, Gam said to himself, every thought had an odor, stronger than every odor and capable of hiding ordinary ones, the more covetous ones spitting on the dirty ones, and the drab ones on the lustful ones, then the City would begin to stink, worse than the garbage dump, to smell like eviscerated intestines. It reeked of death, of the slaughterhouse, of snickering and cynicism. It stank of contempt. And the smell of dogs, fighting dogs, of fanged devouring. Like the foster mother who developed boils, buttons, lumps. Those buildings on Northern Avenue. Empty vanities which encase the worst in speculative arrogance. Gam tripped on some shit. He smiled, then grew sad. Condemned to have his nose shoved in corruption. We'll never get rid of it. Here neither grass nor wheat can grow. Only intoxicating futility.

> *You lose blood, obscure is your rage*
>
> *Obscure the fire, the massive rot*
>
> *Hell vomits forth its entrails onto me*
>
> *Then I weep from the grave and out of fear.*
>
> *Like those that yesterday were pushed on the paths*
>
> *Of the golden desert to the dying desert*
>
> *All are cursed by men and the world around*

itself has transformed itself into an institution. Desperation-turned-tourist-attraction. The lace maker trying to offload her doilies was once a scientific researcher. The guy selling yesterday's medals was once an engineer in the aluminum factory. The artisan selling the necklaces, bracelets and pendants is a writer. No one is in their rightful place anymore. Vocations have been crushed, rolled over by the leaders of all the country's chaotic wheeling and dealing. Everyone has been colonized in his own country. Every citizen a prisoner of the republic. Every member of the nation, a slave to his own nation.

And cursed so that they will never recover
From the fact that God abandoned them at a whim

To the cruelty of thirst and wild dogs. And that's when Gam, buried in trash, eye-to-eye with vermin and fleeing under a pig's stomach, noticed the mountain's winged crest: immense, intense, calm against a mystical background, perched as if from its own enigma. That's when he felt... Felt... his spirit hidden under all that splendor. Hidden. That's when he felt...

34.

Since he was accustomed to counting his pigs from time to time, on that particular night Dro was out counting. And he noticed that Bella was missing in action. Where could Bella be, his sow of sows, his sweet sow with the gorgeous ass and pink flesh tone, and such sexy eyes that you would have thought they were connected to her nose? And where was her lover, Cobra? Also missing. Maybe they were fornicating, he thought. Yes, that must be it, they're rubbing lard. Bella is pigging out on me again! But then Dro thought better of things. He had a hard time imagining them going at it in the trash. Usually, they did that in the pigsty, he reminded himself—they need their own smells to get turned on. The odor of cinders that wafted on top of the garbage dump wasn't exactly ideal for lovemaking. It didn't make them go into heat, and their ruts lay dormant within them. His heart aching, Dro searched the trash from morning to night, flashlight in hand. All for naught. He couldn't sleep. His sow's disappearance, more so that Cobra's, had rattled his brain. The next day, at the crack of dawn, standing on his terrace, he examined his sea of trash with a pair of binoculars. In one corner the dogs, crows, seagulls, and rats were working their way through some irresistible treat, like a colony of maggots. They stuck together, fought and sometimes scattered. It was Cobra who was wearing himself out by fighting against them. Dro guessed what had happened. Suddenly, he ran to a dark corner from where his pain was emanating. And there lay Bella on her side, her stomach riddled with wounds and bites, her teats all torn apart. And Cobra was squealing in distress... Dro turned the cadaver over and examined it closely. It bore no wounds on this side. Someone must have poisoned her, he thought. The rag pickers, he thought instantly. He went over their names in his head one after the other. None of them would have had the nerve to commit such a crime, even to wound him, Dro. The mystery remained whole. Dro knew that you don't kill a pig without it defending itself. It grunts, it fights back, it flees and it even attacks nastily. An yet he hadn't found any deep wounds. Who could have done this, then? And why?

THE LAMENTATIONS OF DRO

My sweet Bella, I mourn your death. Who hit you in the lard? Which *bôzi tegha* wanted your skin, oh innocent mother, who thought of nothing else besides nourishing herself and multiplying? Night and day you and your friend Cobra stuffing yourselves. You, my fat one, who knew that you don't die from overeating, only from going hungry. You knew this instinctively... Today your death has made your birth complete. This marks the end of what is finished. A pig doesn't die twice. Just as she cannot be born again after having passed away. Except if some human quality resides within her. Given this fact, inside every pig, a human lies dormant. Who knows? And the fact is that your death feels a bit as if I had died myself. Your death just adds to the horror of all these things that have expired in the trash dump. And the more I stir these things, the more I burn them, the more the feeling overcomes me that death is my master. How many ganged up on you to slaughter you? Two? Three? Surely more than that. They no doubt attacked you from behind, those *shouni tsak*.[91] Like death that comes in secret to claim both weak and strong with impunity. And even if they had to wait for the last rag pickers to depart. You were probably hanging around still, eating leftovers. Because for a pig, leftovers should never be left over. Everything that he eats is a victory over hunger. Everything that produces some fat is divine grace. But those bandits got you from behind. And they ganged up on you, several of them. Because there's safety in numbers when you're trying to knock out a pig. They isolated you... Just to make sure. But

---

91   Child of a dog.

a carcass like yours, overflowing like a baby whale, you don't get rid of it without trying pretty damn hard. Your death involved one hell of a push and pull. They needed some muscle to get you off the ground. Especially to haul you all the way up to the high parts of the road. You were too exhausting for those brainless predators. But when you realized what was happening, you let loose of your intestines. Because any living being produces waste. But this time, it was your last. You became waste yourself. The dogs, crows and rats weren't mistaken. Who knows? Oh, my sweet Bella, if it wasn't just to punish me that those *kâki ktôr* took it out on you! You, innocent as you are! Who had hurt no one. Never so much as crushed a fly. They slaughtered you in order to bring me to my knees. So that I kiss their feet. That much I know, *shan tsaker!* [92] This entire massacre to teach me a lesson. And to make me understand that after my pigs they would come after me. That you would throw me in the trash like my Bella, without even letting my remains cross the road, letting me rot in place instead. I know all these things.

BELLA'S SOLILOQUY

Bella. I am in the world beyond. Where I am still hungry, but I have nothing left to eat. And hunger holds me in its grip. I am trapped inside my own hunger. I have a pit in my stomach. Nothing left for my snout to sniff. No smells respond to its call. Everything here is mourning and deception. And my Cobra who is no longer here. I hope he doesn't see me like this because it will make me cry. We had the same smell. Who then will take care of my fat? But there you go, I didn't know that you could die just from feeding yourself. I swallowed, sucked, noshed, sucked, gobbled up, feasted... I ate so much that I died from it. Can one die from overeating? Well for Bella, the gig's up. I guzzled down so much food that day that I didn't even notice what I was swallowing. My vision was so poor

---

92   Sons of bitches.

as night fell, that my eyes couldn't distinguish between wholesome and deadly. My tongue was used to shoveling things up, drowning in the flesh of things. And I, glutton that I am, ended up by choking as I gluttoned away. But my throat still worked. I was squealing. Cobra was going crazy trying to pull on that piece of bag which tasted so evil. But our huge protruding snouts made Cobra useless. I had less and less air and collapsed onto the trash. I squealed so that Dro might hear me. But the squeals died inside my flesh. I was alive and now I am only a dead, naked body. But not completely dead, in the end. You can be completely dead otherwise, but still be hungry. What hell!

A DISCOVERY

Gam arrived in the corner of the dump earlier than usual that day and found Dro still roaring and crying over his deceased sow. He immediately waded towards him through the trash, with all sorts of horrible, outlandish, frightening images in his head. And what if Dro had uncovered another woman's body? What if he were obliged to stay silent once again? Gam sighed with relief when he spotted the dead pig: "If I get my hands on the *kekhtot* [93] who did this to her!" said Dro, as if he were talking to himself. "I had them in my hands. The pigs, they suicided my most beautiful sow. But to what end? To bring me to my knees? Let them come get me! Come on, I dare you! Dro doesn't give up easily. And anyway, I'm going to sell my pigs. One at a time. Cobra, Samouraï. Even Idi Gago. All of them. Let them turn them all into pâté, sausages, shish kebabs, I don't give a damn... I'm going to sell them. Or exchange them for some doves. White ones, preferably. And that way, I'll see them flying in the air like the spirit of my boars. Flying ...flying ...flighting high, and flying low." Gam didn't notice any blood anywhere on Bella's body. She'd just soiled her ass. He lifted one of her eyelids. The life was definitely

---

93   Bastards.

gone from her eyes. That's when he noticed the piece of blue plastic in her mouth. "What is that?" He asked. "Your sow swallowed some plastic thinking it was edible? How strange. Weird." A pig's thoughts really are inscrutable. Gam proposed to hold the pig's mouth wide open so that he could pull out the intruding and fatal item with his hand. They proceeded to do so. The carcass immediately burped up some stale smelling air that made the two men step backwards. "Let go of me, beautiful! Let go of me!" said Dro. The dead have all the rights in the world. Including the right to burp up their internal odors. So that's it then, he said. Bella had lost all sense of what could be fatal to her. But then the world wasn't the world anymore? If pigs started to lose their common sense, how many other animals were also doomed as they were? And who knows if we weren't also ...Already... Before Gam had arrived, Dro had thought of bringing Bella home with him. Retrieve his digger? The problem was that the scavengers would take advantage of even that short interval to swoop down on his sow. Unbearable. All those mouths and beaks plunging into his sweet one's entrails. As if it were his own body that was being torn apart for fun. They placed Bella on a large piece of cardboard to make pulling her easier. They made her cross the garbage dump one last time, that garden of odors and trash where she had built up her fleshiness her entire life without ever letting up. Poor sow who finally seemed at ease in her frenetic ravenousness. You would have sworn that she was about to wake up during the trip. Yet she was well and dead, a cadaver, like an animate being from whom one had suddenly extinguished the life force. And what was left of her would still serve to feed the living. Dro wasn't crazy enough to let his poor Bella's carcass be torn apart and consumed. Even if he was drowning in pain, a pain born of rage and helplessness, he wasn't someone who would bury her at a loss.

WORRIES

Once Bella was dead, the spirits began to boil up. "Good riddance!" some people spat out. The other's black imagination remained clouded by the idea of the bag that had obstructed her throat.

"Naturally, it asphyxiated her," said Lousso.

"The issue though is what on earth got into her so that she swallowed some plastic," Tsknors asked himself.

"She must have gotten it confused with something good to eat," one of the women suggested, adding that this had never happened before. "Either this sow was so hungry that she felt forced to swallow some plastic, or else she was so whacked out that she forgot exactly what it was that she was shoving down her own throat."

"Worrisome, if what one eats becomes a trap," concluded Lousso.

Indeed, what had occurred in Bella's labyrinthine physiology for her to confuse a plastic bag for a cabbage leaf? And why not a 100-dollar American bill for a slice of ham without rind, or vice-versa? Undoubtedly, a mixture of excessive gluttony combined with an absolute refusal to share. You swallow everything so quickly that your warning signals no longer function properly. And why would Bella's have stopped working properly, one might ask? Perhaps because she had become a vacuum pump so powerful, one which sucked in the refuse of refuse, so as to become such that her body had stuffed itself to the point that its most basic sense reactions no longer worked properly. It was Roubo, that completely misled Roubo, who offered the most biblical scientific explanation:

"Bella's fate awaits all of you rag pickers, he told Gam. An animal who dies because his instincts have been so disrupted marks the beginning of the destruction of our Jerusalem. In truth, I tell you, the trash dump's farts enter your body like needles, slyly and silently sneaking into every pore in your body and through your nostrils, making their way into your lungs, and mixing in with your blood. You think that you can destroy the trash dump by setting it on fire. Keep believing that! You'll never get to the real heart of its matter. And it's the trash dump that, little by little, will kill you instead. The dump will. Just look around a bit.

And even look at yourselves. The smell of corruption has already contaminated your blood. And blood throws your clocks out of order. A day will come where—hey, why not? Artemis will give some eau-de-vie to her Artem whom she considers to be the source of life. But worse than that even, old Shusho will prostitute herself up and down Abovian street. I'm even afraid that Sako will begin to sing pornographic opera tunes in Sourp Krikor Loussavoritch Cathedral in the middle of mass. And suppose that Tsknors wanted to bring his proverbs to life! Can you imagine him reading the Book of Luke on the head of a wolf? Ah! Like the story of demons who took over some boars and drove them into the ocean. And you Gam, praying that the Samourai will take you under his wing. I can imagine you working as his bodyguard... Ah! Ah! Gam as the Samourai's *vôr lzogh*! Or the Papolikos transforming his priest's gowns into a mini skirt. Raise those family jewels into the air! And that way men would start to function backwards. Their asses would be in their heads. Or maybe not. They're acting and thinking like a bunch of real *vôri tsak* as it is, as if they'd come out of their mother's ass. And what if all the things that are already all messed up here became even more unhinged due to a general fouling up, who knows if life might not actually finally go back to normal. We'd finally lead a normal existence again.

The president would be working for the people and citizens would see their wishes materialize in the president's actions. The Papolikos would share his fortune with the poor and would wash the rest of your feet, like Christ. And the rest would be a matter of course. For example, our Idi Gago's mule would be venerated and belong to all. And instead of offering up the mule to a lion's carnivorous instincts, he'd be in the cage himself! While on the outside the three animals would be getting into some crazy heavy petting. But I'm just babbling. Incoherently. There! Your air charms me to the max, I'm losing my mind. Help! Save me from this world! Give me back my virginity! What do you want Gam *djan,* with someone like me, stuck on the side of a road between a trash dump and a cemetery the game's over before it even begins. Over, I tell you."

No, Roubo wasn't hallucinating. Another pig had croaked before Bella. Its life—usurped—is taken away by an unknown demonic force. Not one of his piglets, fallen victim to the dogs or too weak to fight off disease. The rag pickers sometimes fell onto their carrion once it had already been devoured by rats, torn apart by crows, or hollowed out by maggots and necrophagic insects and still other creatures invisible to the eye. Not a pig that one would have bled to death. But dead from the same mysterious causes that had felled Bella. A well-fed pig with all its fat and one that promised to bring in major cash. At first this didn't disturb him. But how to take measure of the unjust forces that were rising within him? Deaf, unknowable ones. They quickly replaced his indolence. Lost, he even tried to hide the incident from others. To avoid the rag pickers being gripped with fear. But buried alive just trying to survive, they were far from thinking that the obscure death of a mere pig would lead to anything of the order of the trash dump being closed. If Dro was afraid that eventuality it might close, it was because he knew who he was dealing with. On this particular day, the chain of cause and effect completely escaped him.

"I need to understand," he confessed to Gam. "Things are spinning increasingly out of control. I can feel it. If my digger's motor doesn't start, I just open it up and fix the problem with my own two hands. But with this... What can you do to fix a trash dump that is starting to show signs of being annoyed with you?"

Yes indeed. As if the picture of the chaos that emerged on a regular basis from this trash-filled crater were beginning to move and exist autonomously, as if it had a life of its own. Not satisfied with simply taking in dead leftovers, the trash dump was reveling its own murderous powers today. It had long hidden this power that had taken form deep within its entrails.

For a long time, it had incubated its inner monstrosity until the day when it had become sufficiently mature to strike out in different directions. And all the while feeding its own mold, it was trying to expand by contaminating everything around and even outside of its boundaries. Some of the rag pickers would occasionally take time off because they were intoxicated or suffering from some random illness. Like Gam at the beginning when he would feel invisible poisons entering his body. But who would ever have imagined that the trash dump, that maternal matrix, would hide within its bosom a dark desire to harm or even kill?

Already Dro saw the trash dump differently from before. And a previously unknown anxiety wrapped him in fear of a world full of despair. And during the day, this anxiety ate away at his thoughts.

Dro spent too much time maneuvering his machine around and spreading the garbage at the bottom of the dump, to realize that neither the crows nor the seagulls were spared its subtle voraciousness. Gam sometimes found their bodies, their heads hanging to the side, their tongues hanging out of their mouths. Broken in mid-flight and fallen like rocks to the ground. A true godsend for the rag pickers who would roast the cadavers on the spot rather than abandon them to the rats and insects. But blind to these strange manifestations of an upheaval taking place within the earth's secret depths below. Their work now completed, they gathered around Lousso's old bathtub to light a fire. As for Gam, he had already noted Dro's rising anxiety. Well before Bella's death, the increasing number of dead birds had put him on alert. More than ever, he scanned the sky and the trees, instead of keeping continual watch over his plastic bags. Already the crows that were in the cemetery's poplar trees would return at night looking weakened. They bickered less often. Some were missing from their usual branches. But where had they gone instead? Only the jackdaws that haunted the vegetation around the tombs and who fed themselves on insects, snails and grains seemed to be spared. But the moving flows of sparrows seemed to be thinning out, as if the trash dump were picking them off at random as they flew by. Gam didn't think it would do any good to explain his observations to Dro. What would be the point in adding his own cataclysmic observations to Dro's current worries? "Imagine if you will," he told him one day, as he was grinding his coffee beans. "If our birds disappeared, I don't think we'd survive very long afterwards. Yes, slaughter is coming. And what if that were to take place, huh? Yerevan without swallows." What would Yerevan be, indeed, deprived of its swallows, of their graceful flight as they land in their nests like those nestled beneath the ledge of our roof in Gyumri? And suppose that were to happen to us as well, he mused. And what if the evil trash dump were really a reflection of ourselves? These were the questions that Gam asked himself as he began to dig again and descend into the pit where he still hoped to find something. To willingly remain blind to reality's inexorable drum roll. As if the country's unpunished crimes didn't have something to do with the organic changes that people were undergoing ... It isn't for naught that he had started to plant his *lapatka* amidst the darkest pessimism, to search the earth for things that might life more bearable. He was digging into his own cowardice with his shovel, the one that had led him to choose to isolate himself far away in the city's anus rather than stay and though his writings openly fight the people who were really ruining everyone's lives. Those people lied to you from morning to night while he was content to scratch the dead ground. They deliberately obstructed the truth while he cracked open mounds of dead earth. They tortured those who resisted while he had decided to ignore the cries of help that came from their bodies as they were pounded by boot or fist. It's true that even from the great beyond Anna could never have withstood seeing her son bloodied up, or his hands broken, the same hands that played Komitas along with hers on Krassniy Oktyobr. He had cut his investigation short. Had he done so out of a fear of digging too deep into things that made one's head spin? No, he knew that the causes were inextricable, and as a result he could never finish his investigation. That people would keep their mouths shut out of fear of reprisals. Truth will never win out because man... He had decided not to trouble Anna's peace... And yet, she inspired him to bring more peace to the world, as she had while she was alive.

35.

s Dro wasn't the type of man to bury his sow at a loss, he decided to share her with others. Lousso spread the news throughout the garbage dump. "*Khorovadz* Saturday! *Khoooorovadz* Saturday! Bella, Bella for everyone, Saturday! Saturday, Bella belongs to everyone!" Like a God announcing promised flesh to his people, he pierced the smoke and then disappeared.

"What do you mean, Bella for everyone?" Old Shusho asked, intrigued as she searched the insides of a plastic bag. She swiveled her head around a quarter-turn.

"Are you talking about fate or a fiesta?"

"About a fiesta, Shusho," Lousso corrected. "As for fate, we're already experiencing it. We're up to our necks in it, we are. Dro's going to offer up his Bella for us to nibble on."

"No way!" said Shusho. "No way! We're going to have ourselves some *bella* while we nibble on Bella! Because all that shit she swallowed she's going to end up in our bodies during this *khorovadz*, that's for sure."

Dro didn't even wince when he stuck his knife into his sow's flesh for the first time. Of course, he might as well have been dead as he tweaked her ribs with his knife or struck her with an ax. But the idea of distributing all his gluttonous sow's stored up lard to the starving masses sent him into paroxysms of joy. It made him categorically drunk to be a purveyor of miracles to a humanity beset by dead things.

"Where will you find meat to serve to the little people?" Tsknors had asked him. "It's your choice if you want to transform Bella into a *madagh*.[94] Because

---

94   Part of an animal generally a lamb, offered to friends and to the needy during

believe you me on that day, it's not just the rag pickers that will come to screw around here, but their entire families, strangers passing by, and vagabonds who'll follow their dogs alerted by their truffles. Let's not even talk about Roubo. If he abandons his gate, who knows if he won't be entitled to some refugees come to accompany the deceased. The buried may even send their souls back up to take a bath in a nostalgic smell fest. All they would have to do is cross the street. You know perfectly well that with us you can hop without any moral qualms from the *souk* to the *kef,* from funerals to sumptuous feats."

"Taratata," Dro answered. Bella will see to it, oh unbeliever... "...

Her meats were placed in a few pots to macerate with some onions, vinegar, and spices (red peppers, blue peppers, orange peppers). Gam even caught him adding some pomegranate seeds. No one was as adept as Dro at making a barbecue tasty and national in flavor.

Quite a few people were surprised to receive an invitation. Who would have believed that Dro was eager to put his mourning on fire, to have his love chewed up by humans?

"In truth," people were saying, "he just wants to prove that his hogs are edible. And that they taste good despite being nourished on the dump's shit and manure."

"The main thing," he explained, "is that the pig be free range and eat at will. And that you give it lots of space to roam around. Lots. And what space is bigger than this rotting Eden? There's everything you could possibly want here. You just have to know where to find it. Only pigs who are fenced in produce poison! A pig is as sensitive as a little girl. Behind its massive fat and beady little eyes, an energy close to consciousness pulsates. That's why I don't like people to hit my pigs. It kills their meat to beat them ..."

But who could be sure that Dro wasn't offering up his Bella as a sacrifice so that the rag pickers left the other ones alone? It was still to be seen if they would happily participate in the feast. Those who were truly starving would come, of

a celebration.

course. And who wasn't starving, after all, among those that made their living in the godsend? Even if the pigs ate everything on their path, including excrement as well as what was comestible, rotten and harmful, from dead insects to prescription drugs, if it contributed to their fat reserves. Some people just didn't care. Meat had become so expensive that they lost all desire for it. Overlooking the fact that a free meal open to all had become as rare as a social reform, they would have been wrong to snub the animal, questionable as she may or may not have been. And anyway, was their flesh any less modified that that of the pigs? That day was long and busy. The sky had lost its usual cynicism. And near the entrance to the parking lot, the smell from the barbecue had overwhelmed the terrible odors. It carried all the way to the cemetery. The happy smell touched everything along its way. And both the dogs and the men's bodies were sated with dreams of gustatory excitement. Roubo, whose days marinated in the boredom of death, found himself away from his usual stool. He crossed the road to join the feast. His barbecue master Dro, a big but generous Satan, wouldn't hold it against him if he crossed the border. The night before Dro had given away part of his sow to Ardoush, buyer of carcasses. He received a fistful of drams in exchange. The day's blazing air made one want to party, and an entire truck had to be driven down to Yerevan to bring back bottles of *oghi,* cognac, Djermouk and lemonade, cases of Kilikia bear, cheese, bouquets of *khod* [95] and bundles of *lavash*. Standing before his makeshift barbecue (a 200-liter container of gas, cut in half, and covered in rust), Dro was turning over pieces of his Bella in rows on metal sticks. From time to time, his throat would get excited by a swig of alcohol or a perfectly brined cornichon. He would lick his tongue in satisfaction and manipulate his kebabs like a foosball player touched by divine grace.

"To Gam!" he said "Every morning, barely out of my pew, I go out to my terrace. Like where you are now. My view has been for same for years: on one side, Roubo's cemetery, on the other the garbage dump, and straight in front the same Yerevan where the Samourai fucks everything in sight. Nothing changes except the sky. If I fall sick, that's where I'd like to end up stuck forever. Not in

---

95   Aromatic herbs.

a hospital. For me, Yerevan is a foreign country. And anyway, who would want some old smelly guy like Dro? And who'd become that way because of her, the city! That whore sleeps with whoever pays her the most. But in the end the men who reproduce there and live there are wading around in the same quagmire as I am. I mean that the ability to live somewhere pleasing to both body and soul has been stolen from both of us."

"I don't understand," said Gam.

"Ah!" said Dro, surprised. "You don't understand."

Dro wiped the sweat from his brow.

"Let me help you understand. For example, how can you explain that you and your friends must pick through trash to stay alive? Difficult but true? But blind as you are, the entire country slaves away the same way you do. And I do the same. What do you think? If we aren't free, it's because neither our bodies nor our souls can find human sustenance here. It's become humiliating to feed ourselves. Food has become a trick and calm an illusion. One poisons you, the other strangles you. We have nothing to envy pigs, even if I've pretended that they're happy. But our space will keep growing smaller. Because our spirit doesn't walk around on all fours. It vibrates, it flies. It wants to become immense by injecting itself with the infinite. From here, everything seems open. The view extends beyond the City. Don't be fooled Gam! We are unrepentant travelers, and blind ones at that. What do we know about the world? Nothing. We think that the world belongs inside ours. What's the point in being curious about foreign countries? Our own country hasn't even met the dawn of some obscure democracy. And that's why I am in this toilet going on about my anxieties. My acts, my desires and all that I endure have finally trapped me and thrown me into this catastrophe. It's impossible after that to settle down and establish oneself. What woman would want someone as contaminated as I am?"

He pulled a piece of meat from his thick fingers and nibbled on it, burning his lips in the process. He chewed a bit, then decided that it was time to remove the skewers from the fire.

"But Dro, don't try to make me believe that you've never had a woman of your own," Gam dared to say. "Before the dump, I mean."

A question which troubled the intimacy of things that had been poorly repressed. Dro carefully placed the skewers on a dish decorated in lavash, which he then covered in more strips of lavash. He swallowed what was left at the bottom of his glass and smacked his tongue.

"Since you must know, like you, I made the cardinal mistake of getting married. Dro married to a *Natasha*. A Russian can understand other Russians, but not people like us. Our story is nothing but an endless skewering of fanatic contempt and insidious hatred, made to harm us. I needed caresses, she mistook me for a Soviet colony. It was almost to the point where I had to dream in her language and march to the international. To get some skin, I had to wait for as long as a beggar on the corner of an abandoned street asking for some coin. And if she ever let me pull her legs apart, it was only so that she could sleep in peace afterwards. A pleasure for me, but an unpleasant duty for her, as if she were undergoing an operation. Except that she'd have fallen asleep before the surgeon's scalpel in order not to feel anything during an operation... My grandparents came from Urdu. Their throats were slit in a nearby valley along with so many others. What had they done to deserve this? Nothing. My father was lucky enough to be able to cross the border. He fought to keep this country. And even to make sure that I was born here. To be born free in our own country. Right! Ideological terror, that yes. Instead of bread, I sucked on stones. Then came independence. Painful independence. At first, I told myself that no one would ruin my life and my sustenance anymore. But our liberators soon managed to organize a new version of contempt. The contempt that one brother has for another. I got into some anxiety-filled verbal attacks with others during meetings. Then I exiled myself in this pigsty. Shit governs the world, Gam. Shit. Now bring this meat over to the tables. Don't make those beaks wait any longer!"

Next to the bottles, goblets and cheeses, plates full of the type of *khod* that put the country's smells on your palate: *hamem, samit, tarkhoum* and purple-leafed *rehan*.

"Help yourselves! Go ahead, dig in!" Dro insisted, walking by Gam, his glass in hand. "Haïk *djan,* serve everyone!"

In fact, everything was unusual. Dressed differently from when they were sorting, the rag pickers were rag pickers no longer, enshrouded in a limpid simplicity like ordinary citizens dressed for an ordinary day. And rid of the smoke that turned them into ephemeral silhouettes. They had found their human forms again. And this was the day where the sky made its luminous grace descend on men. A sky that only this country can produce: subtle, discreet and powerful, making illnesses sweet and the everyday astonishing. In the background, nervous seagulls beat the indolent vapors that mounted and spread out into the air. And Gam, son of Anna and Garen, felt cured of the everyday events that he shared with his friends. The sight of the food and drinks had made them suddenly forget their condition. All dressed up for the feast, inwardly and outwardly. And the bitterness that usually disfigured them had been so joyfully thrown in the trash that they even gave off a certain air of elegance. Astonished, Tsknors made jokes with the women who had worn skirts for the first time, as if he had never met them before. "Ah," he told Sako, "you can see yourself *shineling*[96] one of our fuckers. They look like ballerinas today ..." But some hadn't dared to feminize themselves to the point of showing their legs. The eldest hid their deformities to void visual scorn. These women were horrified that they had rubbed their calves against dogs with dirty fur. Even if they chased them away on a regular basis, they hung out nearby in the hopes that someone would throw them a bone. Only the most courageous managed to snake in and out. Dressed like a boy in pale blue pants and a white shirt, Lala was filled with wonder as lemonade bubbles danced in her throat. It wasn't by chance that she found herself standing right in front of Gam when he placed the meat on the table.

"*Opal*[97] *djan,* uncover them! I'm dying to see them!"

Dro, whose eyes were shining and whose mouth was in ecstasy that day, signaled for him to move the lavash. The others, whose stomachs were growling, some of them

---

96   Fucking.

97   *Uncle*, term used as a mark of respect.

since the night before, were suddenly gripped with the gastronomic ecstasy that was about to offer itself up to them. The solemn moment when the sow's braised flesh would scatter the smoked radiance of its incarnation like the pure effect of a revelation. The first lavash removed, *ahs* and *ohs* fused together, blown with gusto, kept within, or barely murmured. To see them so dumbstruck, the men gave off the impression that they had seen a woman's leg through the slit in skirt. As for the physical ecstasy that the women were displaying, one wouldn't even know what to compare it to. With her dark eyes, Lala was already staring at the parts sitting next to each other that still seemed to be sizzling. As Gam uncovered the platter completely, the others stared down at it magnetically. Their eyes luxuriated on it, their heads gone crazy from the proximity of such pleasures, their internal organs secretly sweating. Everyone was trying to take in its beauty. They were knocking each other over as if they were in church waiting for the Papolikos to walk by, that bearer of centuries and giver of eternal life. Roubo was standing in front, his eyes inside his old teeth. And old Garo as well, trembling at the mere idea that he was entitled to a piece. Or Shousho, so bent over from old age that her eyesight came up to the height of the table, joyful at the thought of the taste on her tongue, since she couldn't chew them. She kept repeating: "A rag picker, that's what's become of me. And proof that this country is a disaster." And Gam, with all those faces leaning over onto the miracle of these cooked meats, suddenly felt frightened. They all wore the look of wild animals on their faces, garbage collectors with beat up faces, young innocents ravaged by uncertainty, dreamers who had lost all illusions, the degraded and the vulnerable, the tough ones who fended off incoming storms, imps like Tsknors or nasty ones like Mouk. But in the end the monstrous sense of excitement wasn't the result of hunger. It came rather from the pleasure that each one would throw himself into. And it made their senses go off in the direction of strange bliss. And it appeased them as well. Gam pushed the meat using a *lavash* to loosen then from their skewers. Then he felt the jealous pressure from the onlooking faces on his fingers. Now everyone had a cup in hand, filled to the top and raised in honor.

"Long live Dro *djan*! Long live Dro!" But it was Haïk's job to speak on behalf of the guests."

"Today," he started, in his hoarse voice that towered over all the others, "we are assembled around you, Dro *djan*. It's thanks to you that we're all here. But especially thanks to Bella, your favorite pig amongst pigs. To share your grief surrounding this death that affects us all. As we all know, it's not an everyday animal that has left us, but a sow and a mother. Through her, we honor all the mothers here today and all the mothers in our country without whom our country would be nothing. And if today you've decided to give us her flesh to eat, it's so that in her death she become a part of our life. We were hungry and you will fill our hunger. Even if this death was accidental, it remains shrouded in mystery. Who would believe that a pig can't tell the difference between a plastic bag and a salad leaf? If our animals are dying today from such cases of mistaken identity, of what troubles will men die of tomorrow, I ask you? The future is troublesome. This is no ordinary death, but a murder, I tell you. In whose interest was it to see such a peaceful animal disappear form the face of the earth? An animal who had devoted her life to feeding herself and to giving birth? And to say that some people today would even give themselves the right to prevent us from having enough food to eat. Dro *djan,* defend the rest of your herd! Defend its right to eat! We'll fight on your side in this combat. Your life hasn't always been easy. For a long time, you've chosen solitude and hard work. And not just any work! The most ungrateful work there exists, but always for the good of everyone. And we know that your pigs keep you company when the rest of us are already back home. You don't know each one, but you protect them all. And you're right to do so. Thanks to you, they live happily, free to come and go as they please, and to eat what they want when they want to. And today, thanks to you, Yerevan isn't collapsing under its own weight in waste. Your trucks crisscross the streets, and the garbage doesn't pile up for more than four days, and never more than a week. If people in our cities and villages have forgotten, we know with what care you carry out your mission. A sacred mission, a humanitarian mission. We know that thanks to your daily presence in this garbage dump for years, our citizens live in dignity and our industry prospers. It's thanks to your perseverance, your sacrifice, your exceptional way of managing every family's garbage, as well and those of all the markets and boutiques in the capital, from the most modest to the most luxurious. For all these things, we say: long live Dro *djan*! For if you're alive, then we will be as well. Long live Dro!"

And everyone repeated in unison: "Long live Dro *djan*!" and held their cups high in the air and drank. But since *oghi* scratches your throat as it goes down, everyone quickly followed it up with some food to put out the fire in their mouths.

Winding its way down from Noubarashen, a minibus stopped in front of the entrance where Roubo stood guard. Some passengers got out and the chauffeur, also attracted by the smell, and happy to see people who seemed tipsy, pulled hard on the brake of his old buggy, and followed these pretenders who had forgotten their trip to hang out with the rag pickers:

"When you have enough for ten, then you have enough for twenty," said Dro. From worthless Dro's mouth, the more the merrier!

"Come this way. Have a glass! Bella ate for four," Tsknors noted, "never seen anything like it. She took from the people, now we give her back to the people. If other people's religion is humanity, ours is hospitality, a religion of kings."

"Of kings or schwings?" Lousso said ironically, before she started to laugh and guffaw. The cups passed from hand to hand, filled with beer, *oghi*, and cognac, Djermouk or lemonade. But the sounds, mixed in with the smells awoke the ears and noses of everyone nearby. Emerging from a fresh inhumation, the mourners could stand it no longer and crossed the road. Seeing all those mouths advancing like funnels, Gam turned to Dro

"They're going to finish off our Bella, he said. A few more mouthfuls and we'll have nothing left to give out."

"What? You're a doubter?" Dro replied. "Let them come! Their flesh is hungry and you're trying to count things out. I've kept a lot of Bella's reserves in reserve, don't you worry. I'll put them on the grill ..."

But there were others at hand, hiding among the crowd, playing hide and go seek in search of nourishment. Roubo who usually obstructed the entrance to the cemetery with his smoke, had left his stool during the first minutes of the stampede, as the meat's lovely smells wended their way from tomb to tomb, awaking lost nostalgias and gustatory memories. Hence Gam saw the friends whom he recognized, gave life to and then quickly lost, looks that they had long forgotten. And smiles. And expressions. All belonging to the property across the road. They were portraits engraved in marble that let all the way to Anna's tomb. Like the little Marianna, four years old, who was reflected in Lala's smile. Or her aunt Seda, who burned in Maya's eyes, both in their thirties. Didn't one see Azad, who had died in 1988, on Sako's face? Or three-star general Ardashes Ghazarian on Garo's mug? And his wife Victoria who seemed to have lost her teeth, reflected in old Shusho's mouth? But these living people, in Gam's eyes, stuffed food down their throats and drank like two. Proof... But it was on Ano, Lili, Nara and especially Bertha that he saw Djilo wreak havoc. They had started to drink *eau-de-vie* and were knocking back one glass after another. No Anna, however. Did this disappoint or reassure him? Regardless, Gam didn't see her in any of the carnivores, known or unknown, who were working their jaws off to swallow Bella's most recalcitrant parts. The rush for meat followed suit on the alcohol consumption. The person drinking would grimace and appease the burning feeling in his throat. But also satisfy a hunger that had been held back for too long. Without warning the hands would appear out of nowhere and dig into the meats, or they would grab the *lavash,* all in response to the feast at hand. Rough hands with the dirty fingernails of garbage men and chauffeurs, grasping hands still grabbing on to their hooks, fat hands belonging to those who search through the jumble of the trash, and those who had been preserved with gloves, like Lala and Anoush, who gave off a modest grace compared to the others who seemed carried away like some unchained horde. Things were going so quickly in this predatory effervescence that the less alert were in danger of coming away empty-handed. Thankfully, he was careful to remove some pieces occasionally to give to the less valiant, like Roubo and old Garo, who were both submerged by the swell. Dro who had hawk-like eyes, could see what distress they seemed to be enveloped in, and signaled for him to bring them the meat himself. But others close by had handed them some pieces wrapped in *lavash*, from their own skewers. Tsknors was serving Garo and Haïk was asking Roubo to open his hands. Each one received their due and lit up in thanks. Edik received some pieces that Gam had prepared.

"*Spasiba*, comrade Gam," he said, thanking him.

The time had come to stop talking and simply chew instead. Mouths were pulling on the meat, tearing it apart with their teeth, sucking on perfectly cooked sow juice, searching out pieces of flesh in the grilled fat. They were used to working under the odor of burnt-out trash, and now for the first time the smell of something smoked mixed into their saliva. And they enjoyed it, as if they suddenly felt a primordial satisfaction in their bodies. A brief happiness, from a wildlife long past. That was why they didn't discuss it, they mixed it until it formed a type of broth inside their mouths, forgotten memories from a time when they didn't form a nation yet, only a group of people unified in some obscure need for survival. And Gam could hardly chew anything completely. In order not to wake any suspicions. Something had spoiled his appetite. Probably the pathetic nature of this collective frenzy. A need that had bored itself within them, that they tried to fill in a crazed manner, even to the point of choking. Some just gulped their meat down and forgot to chew it, so that it would arrive in their stomachs all the quicker. Trying to outdo the others in speed. And when the meat wouldn't go down, they would try to make it slide with the help of some beer or Djermouk.

But suddenly Maya made a false move. She was holding onto her throat and could barely breathe or make a sound:

"Maya! Maya! What's happening to you?" Her neighbor asked, frightened.

"Do something! Can't you see can that she's leaving us?" another one begged.

It was bound to happen, thought Gam, trying to swallow twice as much as a normal human being. Panic spread among the picnickers. As if a devastating shadow had broken out over their festivities. Some hadn't taken to Roubo crossing the street and spreading this rancid death on them.

"Who sent us this *kaki ktor?*... Why did he ever leave his stool?" the most suspicious among them asked. His Maccabees would have taken advantage of things to double our intake of liquor? Even before she had collapsed, Gam was holding Maya up. Haïk had lent a hand as well. But neither of them knew how to go about removing the piece that was stuck in her throat. Maya closed her eyes and was sinking in Gam's arms. Then Haïk grabbed her and asked the others to back up. Tall and strong, he picked her up and turned over the young woman's limp body. Hands tight around her calves. He shook the poor woman like a spring. Shook her as hard as he could, thinking that her organs would push the piece through. Of course, it was still that pig who was pulling Maya on her side until she choked. Or who wouldn't let anyone forget her by playing the troublemaker, thought the others. It was as if they were all at a fair. The revelers were treated to an acrobatic spectacle, as the threshing machine happily continued to frighten them. And since Maya, wearing a dress, was hanging upside down with her feet in the air, her naked legs were suddenly exposed. You could also see her hips, in black sparkling panties from which a few rolls of fat escaped. But the most surprising thing that Gam could see, lay at the confluence of her thighs under her panties where he noticed a small seemingly hidden gleaming mound. Like a little nose under a mask. There there, he said to himself. And what if Maya were another member of the club? As far as the legs were concerned, they were definitely legs! Made for stockings and garters, so smooth and velvety. Ideal legs, that you get through genetic happenstance or divine intervention. It was a real pity to think that they spent their time going through garbage all day when their true vocation was no doubt to regale some Arab prince or inspire a Persian poet. Yet now they offered themselves up to everyone to see. The men were secreting confused coital tears, their eyes wide open in order not to lose a drop of this manna from heaven. But if the eldest, who were waiting in vain for some virile physiological reaction to this sight, fell into the martyrdom of some deaf nostalgia, the others were getting hard in their pants. As if the small flames of their physical beings had suddenly become a blaze after so many days starvation. While Haïk continued to shake the victim piston-like back-and-forth, no one knew whether they should be frightened by the oncoming death or abandon themselves to the ballet that was taking place, and which reminded one of a frenetic exotic dance. And no one was sure either, whether it was acceptable or not to watch this half-nude woman being tossed around as she hung between life and death, while others of her gender looked on disapprovingly as if they themselves were being gawked at by these impudent eyes. But the men wanted to show that they were more interested in Maya's destiny rather than her charming thighs. For every dead person in this country has a right to be treated compassionately. Here and there some people suggested that it did no good to shake poor Maya like a bottle of Djermouk. And that's when Mouk intervened. Why so late, as she was starting to turn blue from top to bottom? He no doubt had something in mind because he asked Haïk to stop bouncing the young woman up and down and put her back on her two feet. Mouk took over without waiting. He got behind her and pulled her back onto his chest. Everyone stayed frozen on the spot. Would Mouk be the hero to save Maya? Would he really? Mouk grabbed the victim like a belt. Taking prisoner with his arms visions that he had already formed inside his head. Enter into eternal peace! Enter eternal peace! He made a ball with his hands on the victim's stomach. Waited a minute. Then pushed down hard. The piece of meat dislodged itself instantly and went flying. The rag pickers, garbage collectors, travelers, bereaved let out a series of *oufs*! and *akhs*! while a stray dog, the red one with the motley tail, grabbed the meat in mid-air and swallowed it. People clapped at this last trick. Laughter and words proffered loosened people's jaws and untied their hearts. Maya was laid out on a bench. Dro had already called an ambulance. A blanket was brought. Everyone went back to gnawing on their meat while commenting on Mouk's know-how, even if their heart was no longer in it. Haïk, however, remained humiliated. A defeat that you could read in people's faces for a long time coming. But for Gam, Haïk hadn't lost any of his past authority. He approached him with his arm extended, carrying a glass of *oghi* as an offering, a means of getting him to feel good about himself again.

"Haïk *djan*," he told him "drink this and think for a bit! Did you attempt the impossible? Yes, you did. Before Mouk? Yes, again. And if Mouk was successful, he knew that he would be before he started. He'd probably tried the trick before. Where is the merit in that? And it's not as if he hurried. And what's more, he left you out there drowning all by yourself for quite a while. He wanted to make you look ridiculous before saving a life. His lack of alacrity in helping us out will remain a stain on his performance."

"But he did it," Gam, answered Haïk. "And well. Why see a plot in it?"

Warm under her covers, Maya was slowly emerging from her deep suffocation. The sip of water that she had drunk to dislodge the piece of meat had flown through her lungs. And now that she was exposed to the open air, the transition was going well.

"You escaped from us quickly," said Maro. "You passed out in an instant. We called out to you, yelled, but you were beyond our reach. It was as if you'd left us for another world."

"If only you knew how good I felt!" answered Maya, still half asleep from her rapture. "I sat down on a bench, surrounded by flowers. I felt so light, so light, and completely detached form everything! I would have liked to have remained that way, it was calm and luminous. I wasn't the least bit afraid. And then suddenly I felt heavy. My flesh found its bearings again. And then I felt like a cold blow. The hardness of the bench was piercing my bones. And I heard voices. At first simply murmurs, then they came closer and closer."

So, she declared. And Gam listened, he who had always wanted to ignore the happy trip that his Anna was currently experiencing. Truth be told, he knew nothing about the things that Maya was talking about. The earth had always been enough for him, without having to go on about all the fanciful dreams that patriotic preachers used to disguise it as paradise. And he didn't like that paradise to be soiled. Still, as Maya kept describing image after image of felicity, a smile slowly emerged on Gam's lips. An ironic smile, mixed in with a measure of astonishment. Who knows, after all? And so, Gam lifted his eyes up towards the hill where his mother's remains were located. And it seemed to him as if that hill were suddenly ridding itself of its shadows and was inundated by an all-powerful light. The hill of the dead was flowing with a harmless fire and Maya was revealing to him that which his mother on her own would never have been able to make him understand.

The rag pickers and garbage collectors had rarely seen an emergency ambulance anywhere near the dump. White like an angel that had descended into a pigsty. It clashed completely with the usual smelly and dented up trucks. A young woman emerged from the truck—in a perfectly white coat and raven black hair. The chauffeur followed her, identically dressed.

"Where's the patient?" the woman asked.

People made way for her to get by. Haïk briefly explained what had occurred.

"You probably got water caught in your lungs. We'll have to examine you and keep you for a bit," the angel nurse said to the young woman who had come back to life.

They brought a stretcher. When the door to the ambulance closed, people's eyes teared up. The ambulance went on its way down the road until it became a white dot on the horizon among the clouds and the capital's brouhaha. Everyone remained baffled for a while, crushed. Dro then raised his glass in a toast to their colleague's health. They all drank with joy, which gave them a pretext to free themselves from the guilt they felt. Two hours later they had gone home already. The minibus was back on the road. The only thing left were the tables, the chairs, and the bench. And on the plates enough meats, herbs, and leaves of lavash to feed a small army regiment.

"Let's gather up these leftovers, and make sure nothing goes to waste," Dro told Gam."

Dogs milled about in the distance under the watchful eye of some crows.

36.

W hat do you mean, dead?" Dro exclaimed.

"Dead as dead can be," Khatcho answered. "Finished, extinguished, rigid, ruined, flat, but no necrosis yet. Well, dead as I see you. He looks like he's taking a nap. Laid out on his side, I'm telling you, at the left of the entrance, on the side of the road."

"He got hit by a car, that's all," Dro concluded. "And after all, it's only a dog. He'll decompose all by himself. Let's leave him here to shit up Roubo's nostrils, that way he'll end up by throwing him in one of his holes. Even if the cadaver isn't on his side of the road."

"Ah, so that's what you think?" Khatcho protested. "A suicidal dog? And who played with the wheels on the cars? Except that's it's the red dog with the motley tail!"

"What red dog with a motley tail?" Dro worried.

"The red dog with a motley tail," confirmed Khatcho. "I'd bet my life on it. The one who grabbed the piece that flew out of pretty Maya's belly into the air. Ah those legs!"

"And what about me," Dro said annoyed, "that leaves me in quite a position!"

"Yep," Khatcho said ironically, "not as nice a position as Maya's legs. But just imagine how it must make our own think well and hard, this death. Especially the women."

"Sure!" said Dro, astonished, "that will leave a bad impression."

Dro didn't care for this type of morbid reminder of the feast that Maya had ruined. What on earth had gotten into her that she should choke that way? And right after his sow! And now that this... it smelled like a plot. And now that this stray dog had bit the dust, it would seem like a plot were at hand. The rag pickers would believe that his sow had poison running through her veins, even when she was cooked. He hurried to find the dead dog. He was happy to take care of the trash, but the Maccabees weren't his concern. The beast was there indeed, lying on the concrete, not far from the hillock that separated the road from the parking lot. Dro noticed that next to the animal, the gravel was red with blood. Hit by a car, he said to himself. People stay too close to the side of the road when they turn here. But go explain that to the rag pickers! That it was an accident. It won't stop people's imaginations from running crazy. And the crazy ones will see an evil omen. He stopped one of the trucks and threw the dog onto it. "And no matter what you do, he told the driver, you get rid of it before you get to the back of the dump. And you never saw anything, understood?" He went back his shack to drink a cup of coffee. A few seconds later, someone knocked on his door. The old Garo with his air of the end of the world having arrived. Everything was drooping on his face: his features, his eyes, his hair, his nose, his features. He was huffing from walking up the stairs. Trembling from a fear that was devouring him whole.

"What's going on, Garo *djan?*" Dro asked before he'd even regained his breath. "If you dragged your carcass all the way to my door, it's not to let me know that you're getting married!"

"So, what happened with Roubo?" asked Garo.

"And so Roubo?" exclaimed Dro. "Maybe I'm his mother, that *vor lzogh*! Should I not have let him join us at our table? Me, the dump, I invited Roubo, the cemetery. Who would have done any better? So don't go telling me that my meat killed him! That meat, I cut it up myself, seasoned it, cooked it on the flame. And I know when it's cooked enough to be served.

"He's not on his stool anymore," said Garo.

"So, if he's not there anymore then he's somewhere else! Give him the time to empty out his!"

"No," answered Garo. "I saw him put his stool down, but he didn't have time to sit. They took him away."

"Took him away?" Dro asked, "But who took him away? The Samourai's men? The angel of death? Who?"

"The white emergency ambulance," answered Garo.

"Her again!" Dro said annoyed." And why, may I ask? That guy stays stuck on his stool all day and manages to contract a disease!"

"Because of the water," explained Garo. "The water that he drank at the fountain. He vomited it up. And then he fainted. Now it's forbidden to drink the cemetery water. The word *killing* is written on the wall. That means dead. Better to know these things. But when you're thirsty, you're thirsty. They even added a sign."

"Don't worry about that Roubo," said Dro to reassure him. "His stool won't stay empty for very long."

"But if we can't drink the cemetery water," Gam concluded, "what will we drink when it's scorching hot out? Maybe yours is also compromised?"

Roubo was absent an entire week. There was no more sign of his famous stool in the third entrance. Who knows if he hadn't wanted to leave with him simply because he liked Roubo's ass so much? They made themselves at home under a window in the hospital and watched the world as they waited to take up their rightful places once again. But at the end of a week Roubo was still missing. Someone else was taking over his seat. A clumsy guy assigned by interview. When they asked this other person how much time he intended to stay there, he answered that Roubo was sick etc. For Gam, something was starting to change. This pillar of the third entrance without its Roubo, who resembled his cemetery so remarkably. His skin the same coppered ocher as the dirt, his teeth like the tombs that had moved. And so thin that one saw the dead man beneath the live one. And so it happened that the killer water had led him to the City hospital. Then came an uncertain time. Would he regain his former spot or take his place in one of the holes in this same cemetery that he had guarded for so long?

"I've been living with this stool under my ass for years now, he was telling Gam. We're inseparable."

For years, Roubo, straddling two worlds, taken care of on one side but sucked into another. And who knows if being forced to live in the cemetery for so long hadn't forced him to become more of a philosopher than a *semoushka* [98] *seller*, a bank employee, a budget minister, priest, or taxi driver? If inside his head the deadly air hadn't ended up by contaminating his vital forces? Besides which vital forces did he have left? Passion had long deserted him.

Even if when he passed sterile women or ecologists, the memories of past thrills resurged within his body. His fires vegetated in a form of reduced existence of minimal pleasure. And his cigarettes served as a damper. With all these flowering Maccabees that crossed his threshold, he found it perfectly normal to die. So normal that he was surprised to see the people in the procession crying. The first ones especially, their spirits turned upside down and their faces withered, overtaken by a powerful catastrophe. Out of common decency, Roubo didn't smoke in front of the bereaved, walking or otherwise. At the beginning, contrite and sympathetic, he held back. But in reality, he thought about these mortuary processions every day.

As they never ended, he sometimes lost patience. And as his lungs couldn't bear everyday, normal air, he lit a cigarette. After that, he only did as he pleased. He let go of any qualms or restraint. The mourners looked at him with a crooked eye. But no one dared say anything to his face. And his face, like that of the living dead, didn't make one want to engage him in conversation. Closed in like a tomb. And his unshaven beard made him look like a diabolical Cerberus. The dangers of smoking? *Peuh!* If he were going to die, it would be from smoke inhalation. His and Dro's. But mostly Dro's. Those invisible and foul-smelling clouds that the wind blew back on him in droves. He was the first to be exposed, but he was also the only one to complain about it, as the dead no longer fear anyone or anything, at peace in their boxes and slabs. Any official car that parked in the parking lot he took as a call to law and order. Proof that his neighbor's

---

98   Sunflower seed.

toxic excesses required appropriate measures. In the best of all worlds, a definite condemnation. Dro knew what he was really thinking. To taunt him he stood on his terrace facing him. Which signified that he was there, really there. That he would be hard to get rid of. One day he was drinking a cup of coffee with Gam, and Dro signaled to that Roubo guy to join them. A good cup of coffee is stronger than any grudge for Roubo.

"You see, Roubo *djan*," Dro started as he filled his cup, "you and I, you can consider us like this place's veterans, no?"

"You could say that." said Roubo.

"We each have an official position," Dro continued. "Even if mine makes me run around everywhere and yours makes you stay in place. But that's not the point. But we must admit that you and I we don't have much respect for our respective bosses. They pull our strings from somewhere way above our heads. They decide everything, on whether we live or die. What can we do to change things? Nothing. They let us believe that we control our own lives. But our life is nothing but the result of their whims. Today we're here, but tomorrow we won't be anymore. Today, I collect your garbage and one day you'll guard my grave. I intend to end up in your cemetery in the end. There's no better place for my corpse, there isn't. My hole is ready and waiting. I bought it from you-know-who. And I even paid a steep price for the shade that the tree I've been allowed to plant will provide me. I dug the hole deep. Except with all these stories about toxic products, seismic tremors, and lack of space, I'm afraid that the dead will want to be buried somewhere else or that they'll simply close your rabbit hutch. And then, where will I be buried, I ask you?"

"Dude, it's your shit hole they'll close down first," Roubo exploded." And that way, I won't have to smell those horrific odors every time the wind changes. You understand that much, *ptsi maz!* [99] Your dump stops me from breathing."

"Your dump stops me from breathing," Dro repeated annoyed. "*Voritset mi*

---

99   Literally : hair on a vulva.

khossa! [100] If you stopped smoking, your lungs would start to breathe again, *chan lakot!* It's not my garbage dump that's asphyxiating you. You are! You smoke like a chimney, and you sweat like a pig from each one of your pores!"

"I smoke!" answered Roubo. "Yes, I smoke! And so what! That's my business! Did we win our independence or not? And anyway, when it comes to that, you're a fine one to talk! Your saliva has become like tobacco syrup, you tug on those Erebouni [101] so often! You think I smoke like a chimney, but you spit out more than your digger! In any case your garbage dump, Dro, is killing me. And that, I suffer from," Roubo concluded.

"I smoke as much as you do, I admit it," Dro conceded. "I'm also overcome with fumes all the time. I slave away at the heart of that inferno, I do. What other choice do I have except to burn your garbage! Is it my fault if the wind blows your way? They didn't nominate me Head of Wind Currents after all, did they?"

"Here's why," Dro *djan,* said Roubo with a cutting tone, "your gas factory has to be closed down, covered in earth or else they have to build incinerators."

"Incinerators!" Dro exploded. "And where would the smoke from your incinerators go exactly? In Baron [102] Roubo's nostrils. Without mentioning the fact that you would put all the rag pickers out of work. But I'll tell you Roubik, your cemetery will fall out of favor with both our Supreme Leaders and our baksheesh collectors. Your graves are dancing like waves and your dead disappear without trace."

"And yet," Roubo said ironically, "that's where you prepared your hole. But Dro *djan,* if the graves in my cemetery dance the way you say they do, why are you in such a hurry to bury yourself in one?"

"Precisely so I can be near my garbage dump," said Dro."

This explanation exasperated Roubo.

"Your dump! Your dump! It's not exactly Etchmiadzin, your dump! Unless

---

100   Stop talking out of your ass.

101   Cigarette brand and Yerevan's original name.

102   Mister/Monsieur.

you think of yourself as the pope of public excrement! You know in the old days the corpses of priests were placed under a slab with their name written on it inside their own churches. So why don't you ask the Samourai if he'll grant you a corner somewhere in the middle of your dump? Eh! For good and loyal services rendered to the homeland. And if they make it into a park after you're gone, it'll become your pantheon. People strolling by will leave flowers on your square of old weeds. You'll have a black marble headstone with your pig keeper's muzzle on it, and your name written out in our country's alphabet. As the years go by, the ignorant would think you were an important historical figure. Dro become the General Antranik[103] of the public sewage! And you'd have this same landscape in front of you that you see now when you have your daily coffee. A park, I tell you, with free benches for lovers to fuck on. Or a golf course, why not? With thick green turf as soft as a carpet. And so no more smoke. You hear? No more smoke!"

Gam recognized in Roubo's words the insane asylum director's long-winded speech. As if he had planted his idea for a park inside his head, to reach stubborn Dro indirectly. Hence the project was on its merry way. Among the most exasperated, but also with those pragmatic wolves that lurked in the shadows.

Before this entire story took place, Roubo began to follow not because of his crusted-over lungs, but because of the killer water, the subterranean terror having already made its way. The women ecologists had tried to throw their terror onto him, but he had turned a deaf ear to them. A woman's word was still only a woman's word. For this gruff guy shielded from any matrimonial dealings, his feelings had little to do with reality. And those gossips that ferreted around in a corner drove him crazy

"But why," he would say upset, "don't you go poke around the garbage dump? You harass my cemetery, while the garbage dump spreads the plague, destroys everything on its path with its dust that glides over your heads and end ends up in our lungs."

---

103   National hero.

They then pointed out to him that the emergency at this current time was on this side of the road, and that it was easier to close a cemetery than move an entire garbage dump.

"And you really believe that?" answered Roubo. "You have to bury the dead somewhere, after all, don't you? And you girls, tell me where you will be buried if we get rid of my dead during their hibernation? New Maccabees arrive every day. You see them knocking on the entrance to get to their graves? Every day, I tell you. And much more so during periods when there are lots of shootouts. I'm not talking about our soldiers who have their Yerablur, a hillside just for themselves. But of the innocents and the thugs that get gunned down right in the heart of the City. As for when it gets excruciatingly hot in the summer, and they are getting more and more frequent, old people arrive by the shovel full. Summers, it gets busy in here. A veritable dying diarrhea. And when in a couple, a husband dies from the heat, the wife dies soon thereafter of solitude. She doesn't wait very long, you know. And conversely, should she go first. They follow in each other's footsteps and so there are twice as many arrivals. Here I still have enough room to put them. I make them climb the hills. Each one gets their own plot. It's a matter of good business practices and respect. No, I'm telling you. It's the dump that you must condemn. In its place, you could install a huge incinerator and you'd be done."

Roubo was careful not to let the women know about Japanese who wanted to kill two birds with one stone by adding a crematorium to the incinerator. But hello, then came the funerary processions, the slow processions on the road, the defunct drowning in his flowered casket while he watched the sky glide above, just before his last night on earth! Surely, no dead person in this country would have put up with being made into a *khorovadz*, like Bella. And what family would accept such a fate, whether the defunct were a child or an elderly person? None. Here, it's all about the land, the millennial land, the land which produces men and trees, only she's supposed to work on the decomposition of the dead. Here a dead person isn't just some vulgar waste product. It must be buried with care, in a place where it can be found. Like the living give the name to the land that carries them, the dead give it its meaning ...

And now Roubo was swallowed up by the hospital. His being simply disappeared! The irreplaceable replaced by a trophy wife. And Dro lost on the terrace every morning, searching for him. When would that old rug of a Roubo be sent back to his cemetery? he asked himself. But especially when would he be returned to all those corpses that he was guarding with such jealousy that you would have thought that someone wanted to whisk them away from humor that they themselves were trying to get away to take in a few gulps of city air. Roubo, who filtered everything, all comings and goings, had let the water play this dirty trick on him. And what if the water started to kill! Thought Dro. Starting with the person who walks in a puddle in the street. The minnows who bathe in it. But also, the wild beasts who came for the humans. It would even go after his pigs who swallowed anything in their paths. So much so that they seemed invulnerable. From that day onwards, Dro even began to doubt his own faucet. He saw himself on the floor frothing at the mouth, unable to reach for his phone to call the white emergency ambulance. Usually, the rag pickers drank their water either at the cemetery fountain or at Dro's. And suddenly they were bringing in their own personal bottles ...

The morning where Dro, smoking on his terrace, saw Roubo's familiar shape on his stool again was as auspicious as the day when he's found his poor departed sow giving birth. Life was returning to its regular course, even if it meant that the fights would start up once again.

"You're back, you old carcass?" Dro yelled. "I hope they fixed your pipes a bit."

"You can imagine that they wanted to keep me," answered Roubo." And no more smoking cigarettes. Forbidden. I was roasting on the spot. Two inches away from dying, if you can imagine! I had one foot in the land of the dead. I missed my cemetery. So, I came home."

"Too bad," said Dro. "I would have been the one to bury you."

"You?" said Roubo, to emphasize his superiority. "But look at yourself in your tiny piece of a mirror, for God's sake! You'll see that between the two of us, you're more worn out. A Moushetsi is tough as nails. I have the mountain air that my parents used to breathe in my lungs. The air from Moush it stays with you for generations."

"Except if you spit out as much smoke as your Alaverdi chimney, you run the risk of pushing yourself into your own hole," answered Dro. "And without ever going to the hospital," he added.

"Dro, make sure that you don't turn into some old ruin before I do! You look more and more like the remains of Erebouni."

"And what are you going to drink, moving forward?" asked Dro, worried.

"What am I going to drink? A glass of *oghi*, like every other morning. It kills all the germs, and it cleans out your lungs. I'd advise you to do the same thing. As for water, from now on, I'll boil mine and filter it, thank you."

During the day, the good news that Roubo had returned had spread among the rag pickers:

"... Have you seen Roubo?"

"... Did he come home?"

"... Roubo the guardian is still guardian."

"... He was stronger than the hospital."

"... It's his stool that must be happy."

"... It found him again, his ass."

Everyone came to congratulate the returnee, one by one. Gam did so as well, on his way to visiting Ann's tomb. He told Roubo how much he missed filling his bottle at the fountain. Because his water was fresh.

"It's a new age," Roubo conceded. "The wine has turned to vinegar. Everything changes and sometimes in the wrong direction. You search but you don't find the original good. I wonder when I'll be able to look at my fountain water again and think of it as healthy and wild. Probably never. And this water looks the same as yesterday. But I've lost all confidence in her. We've killed its innocence. And I am ashamed to be sitting here all day, a man sullying its body. In the end, Gam, I am my own water's killer."

Yes, the rag pickers were reassured: Roubo had returned. They were also finding their own place again. But the water... You can feel triumphant, but your everyday lives have already been altered, it seemed to be saying. And from now on Gam would drink his water from Niko's place, two kilometers down the hill. And who knew if the contamination hadn't reached his café already. And with it the outskirts of the limits. The land sent men back, defeated and poor. The rag pickers were so preoccupied with survival that they didn't see things the way death makes you see them. You could read in Anna's eyes and those of all the dead like her, what the living couldn't see. And those that were above both the dead and the living knew the links that exist between all things, and they cried the catastrophes yet to come...

37.

They came one random morning, dressed up for the event, in purely geometric fashion. The Japanese. Clean from top to bottom, helmets, jackets, and boots. Their hands gloved. Silent. They unloaded case after case. Piled them up in one of the two cabins on the garbage dump premises, to the left of the parking lot. They were immaculate. Standing in front of Dro, the smoking God who had just appeared from within the city's entrails, the master Nippon took off his helmet, bowed slightly and said *"Barev Baron,"*[104] his eyes masked in politeness, showing off rows of teeth lined up like books on a shelf, his hair short and Zen. The large potbellied Dro, who suddenly felt encroached upon by these animal-like gesticulations, remained stiff as a flagpole. Firmly planted, legs spread, like a man ready to pee. Dro was in fact thinking of peeing on these exotic ants who had come to control the garbage dump in their own way, contemptuous as they were of organized chaos.

Roubo was gloating. After years of being smoked out, he was celebrating, triumphant.

"They're going to install an incinerator for you, Dro!" he screamed from atop his stool!

"It's about time! It couldn't go on like this. The more time goes by, the more your garbage increases. I could see it with the comings and goings of all those trucks. Otherwise, they were going to have to find somewhere else to empty out all this bazar."

The Japanese had already showed up discretely a few times before.

Periodically, the authorities quibbled over details, as a way of pretending to be making a point. But accustomed to defeating bombs, tidal waves, and earthquakes, the Japanese always came back. It wasn't some simple monster with a gangrened soul that would make them throw in the towel. Wearing masks to combat the poisonous odors, they advanced carefully into the heart and the margins of the filthy graveyard. From the heights of their tripods that they had planted in different places, they measured things on the cliff and the dead parts as well. Hunched over their instruments' viewfinders, they took notes. It was a proliferation of insects leaving their holes like devils or diving in one place to come out of another. They were so applied to their tasks that their faces appeared cold and scientific. The rag pickers began to feel as if a saber were ready to descend on them and chop their heads off. Especially when the climbers disappeared for a while. What were they plotting behind our backs, they wondered? They even suggested that Dro send them his pigs as an offering. All these measurements and pointing above their heads were like invisible strings meant to wrap up the dump, once and for all. Like a spider that captures its prey after paralyzing it only to come back later and eat it.

"They think the dump's like an old ship that they can moor with chains and cords," Haïk said annoyed, in front of Gam. "But it's actually a living ocean. One that inflates, retracts, moves, produces, eats, spits, pisses, shits, hisses, blows, explodes, multiplies, relaxes, stretches out, what else do I know?... You go take control of such a temperamental mass!"

"You mean an ogre that demands its five hundred daily tons of waste," Gam clarified.

"The City produces that fresh every day," Haïk continued. "Because it fears its wrath, the underground ones and the ones that burn above ground. Otherwise, it would turn against her. Judgment day! Judgment day!"

"But that's precisely the point," Gam went on, "That Japanese know-how will prevent that type of explosion. I scoped out one of their engineers. They're fastidious and they do things ceremoniously. They'll cut a grain of rice in four and again in four. With blades as thin as razors. Their study is dividing the site into three twenty-hectare sectors. Zone A is for the oldest section, from its creation in 1960 until 1986. Zone B is for where it spreads out to this day. And Zone C is devoted to future projects."

The Japanese set up a knowing web of pipes connected to tubes with holes in them that they plunged into deep layers to trap the methane. The engineer let Gam listen to the hissing of the gas that was devouring things as it made its way upwards.

"I thought I heard the monster breathing," he said to Haïk.

"Just think of it," Haïk answered in a disappointed tone, "It ate at our lungs without anyone ever warning us. God knows what evil we don't know about today that will surface tomorrow!"

"And don't you think that methane just disappears into the atmosphere," Gam interrupted him. "The blue sky, so pure, so calm, is also being pathologized and one day it'll all fall back down storm-like on our heads."

"And then," said Haïk, "Judgment Day! There will be no place to save oneself, on earth or in heaven. We'll all be trapped in our petty joys. Here our masters already rape us daily. And every day, I'm a slave to my own hunger. What chance can grace can time possibly offer me."

"But in the future," Gam said, to sound reassuring, "with methane combustion, we'll produce electricity that will serve hundreds of homes."

"That's right," answered Haïk. "And then we'll put in an incinerator. But where will all the toxic smoke go that will come out of all the chimneys? Man invents things that eventually kill him, that's all I know. The day that the City begins to sort its own waste, we'll be useless here. Let's get ready to confront that challenge. Because that will be the end of the world. Our world, that is. We'll leave it without even being chased out of it, simply victims of the times. Hunger doesn't look at what it devours. As for us we'll be like a bunch of ants gone crazy from some malevolent person's blow."

"People sorting their own trash?" Added Gam "that's a long way from now. We're not the Japanese."

"Oh no we're not!" Haïk repeated, "We're not Japanese, nor Papuans nor Eskimos. And yet we had our bomb dropped on us, and all our cities and villages were like Hiroshima or Nagasaki. And that's why we are who we are. Look at the result," he said as he touched his chest with his two index fingers.

38.

Now, as the day drew long, all that remained was an obscure agonizing sensation. All the effort and frenetic activity that usually took place, its sad and tiring course, was absent. The pickers were finishing up the last movements of their daily litany, begun earlier that morning. Soon the trucks would drop off their last loads, and the rag pickers would fill their meshogs as they had the others, with bottles and scrap metal, to transport them to their various points of sale. Today like yesterday, the bags contained whatever they could. And if Anna knew more and saw farther than he did, she had no way to show or explain any of it to her son. Her hand didn't have the power to rip apart the veil that covered the world's fatalities. Or to move the lines on the map of human hours to conjure up some hope and offer it to the chosen one and make him a reaper of the heavens above rather being merely exalted down below on earth. Then a fleeting image would come and lighten up one's mind, the time for an eruption to graze the unreal. Anna was crying under her son's tired gaze, not daring to let him understand that there were more important things in this world than that hypothetical booty to which he attached so much importance. But as the desperate like to say, fortune only visits you once in life... That's how, suddenly enlightened out of nowhere, Gam turned around looking in Lousso's direction, eyes fixed on a bag like all the others which contained the usual trash. But the bag had suddenly become as valuable as a diamond. Why suddenly this one? A gleaming ray of light on the white piece of plastic. Like the *sig* [105] during a picnic by the shores of Lake Sevan with Anna, one that had come close to the bait and leapt out of the water into the clear azure, as quick as a silver thunder bolt. Lousso was blindly hitting

---

105   Fish from Lake Sevan.

other pockets that lay in front of him. For Lousso hadn't experienced this lightning flash, followed by a profound and irresistible magnetization of one's entire body. Gam harpooned the envelope that seemed to be waiting to be found among all the others. It was his from now on. Lousso was surprised to see Gam go pick his targets in his back when he had so many at his own feet. Was Gam perhaps trying to steal something from him on his own hunting grounds? Of course, not? That land belonged to everyone. No reason for Lousso to think of Gam as a rival. And in any case, it wasn't the time for either jealousy or rivalries. But whatever was hidden in Gam's plastic bag was attracting her. Lousso watched Gam ripped apart the plastic until it was just a fine skin-like membrane. And noticing his indifference to everything that would usually have attracted his attention—those bottles of plastic and that book—he expressed his astonishment out loud:

"What—you've worked so hard all day, that now you're ignoring your find? "

"You're right," said Gam, "fatigue is clouding my judgment."

"Open that book at least," Lousso proposed. "Who knows? It might be interesting."

"Lala..."

A book, surrounded by a rubber band with a cardboard cover, originally white, but covered in jam and yogurt onto which some dirt had stuck. Gam wiped it off with a piece of cloth. A title appeared, sullied by some moisture. Like some type of truth lying under untruth. Beauty asphyxiated by the absurd, made fun of by cynical laughter:

ASK HRECHDAGUI: THE ANGEL'S WORDS

... Should he open it up? Why bother? Who knew what this book might hold within it? Who knew what path it might set one on? Gam decided to give it to Lala as he had found it, the next day. He rejoiced at the thought of placing the spirit of this bouquet of words in those young hands. Yet Anna was doing everything in her power to make him open it:

"Open it! Come on now, open it already!"

But why was the book imprisoned with elastic force by that rubber band?

"It's the first time," said Lousso, "that I've ever seen a book closed that way. Its owner must have been hiding something inside it. If I were you, I'd check it out."

"What do you think could possibly be in it?" answered Gam, jaded. "Images or pictures? I'll leave the surprise for Lala. A discovery that will give us the opportunity to discuss."

"In the meantime, pop off that rubber band!" Lousso insisted, in an annoyed tone that didn't quite seem its usual self to Gam: "I can do it for you, if you'd like."

"That's great, since you won't give up." said Gam.

The rubber band was stuck to the book cover. Once it was released, it left a mark, a white band, its edges perfectly outlined by the dirt. The pages of the book now seemed liberated from their straitjacket. Who knows? Gam said to himself. Maybe someone put some pictures in between them. The type that you hope won't fall into just anybody's hands. Gam was sorry that Haïk had gone down to the city. He had begged him not to follow him, adding that it was preferable that no one find him there. Any image that he'd found here would have been enough to open his eyes wide. Gam was leafing through the pages one by one at present. They came apart automatically under his gaze, one after another, releasing the same nectar that they buzzed around. And as he went from one discovery to another, his restless fingers carefully parted each sullied but graceful petal. Anna was staring at her son's face, devastated by the delightfulness of his distress. Fear and joy alternated and the sensation of a new source, the wonderful flowering of a desert, of life suddenly unresolved, and the intimate certainty of a lost tranquility. Gam was trying to add things up as he turned the pages. He was hoping that they would never stop delivering their gift, each one with its own number, always the same, the large one, the sublime, the supreme. He barely noticed the sentences that were printed on each page of a brave new world, that would suddenly begin to produce enough to survive on, a pure force, fresh and immaterial. *Give and you will be forgiven... Everything that is life giveth... Giving is the great law around here... The world's heart beats to renew itself by giving... The blood that doesn't give coagulates...* And here was Gam, counting and re-counting each page, one after another. So much so that he saw himself jumping repeatedly, huge leaps from the garbage dump to the cemetery and from the cemetery to the hills, without respite to the rhythm of his imagination. Jumping while he blessed the sun with this manna, not knowing whether he should suspect Anna of having something to do with things or if the world had suddenly decided to even itself out through the force of some mysterious justice. Yes, he could legitimately ask himself how such a book, stuffed like a fat wallet, had made its way through the chaos of this waste to end up in his hands. What crazy person had thrown it into his trash can? Some freak, one had to assume. How angry or vengeful must someone have been for this luminous, used book, to end up stuffed with inserts, for the profit of someone unknown who had always dreamed of such a find?

"So?" Lousso said worried. "What are the pictures? You're going from one page to another, jubilant, but you're remaining silent."

"I was wondering," said Gam, "if I was dreaming or still in real life."

"But can't you feel your real life?" Lousso exclaimed. "Smell how it stinks! You're right in the middle of it. But can you answer me, which images?"

"Which images," Gam answered. "Which images, huh? Always the same. Benjamin Franklin's bald pate, with his fur collar and all green."

That's when Lousso stopped moving, paralyzed. Standing on a pile of bags, stiff as the virile Motherland statue on its quadrangular tower:

"Are you kidding me?"

"Do I have the face of an actor?" answered Gam. "Hundred-dollar inserts, Lousso *djana.* And I counted ten of them. That's a thousand dollars. You hear? A thousand dollars!"

"I heard, I heard," said Lousso, annoyed. "What's the use of you screaming your pleasure as if you were *shineling* [106] some Chinese woman?" So that all the envious, flea ridden, and wily people turn and buzz like bees."

"But Lousso *djana*, it's exactly as you're saying!"

"And you want the entire country to hear the good news?" Lousso countered in a low voice.

"So that all the envious, flea ridden, and wily people turn and buzz like bees around your honey? I can't believe it. You didn't even want to open the book. And now you're rich! You have enough to leave the garbage dump. And it's all thanks to me, really. If I hadn't insisted, that gift would have landed in Lal's hands. I deserve my share, don't I? So, you owe me a *magharitch*,[107] no?"

As he said these words, a rat which had leapt from within a box, snuck in between Gam's legs, followed by a whole pack that cleared a path for itself in the middle of the trash until it disappeared under some cardboard. And Gam looked up at Lousso. In a nanosecond, the image of the first rat appeared still stuck in his gaze like some troublesome image. It transposed to Lousso's face, with his little black eyes, his hairy mustache, and his thin lips like some wily animal.

"Yes of course," answered Gam. *The grace of knowledge lies in knowing how to give.*

"We're like brothers, aren't we," said Lousso? "We share everything in the dump, hard times and good ones alike. And today this gift from heaven that's just fallen in your hands, it belongs to us both, wouldn't you agree?"

His speech was threaded with as many pearls, artificial and flattering, as that of a politician during an electoral campaign. And delivered in a tone of false modesty and somber recklessness. How should Gam answer Lousso? One day he'd surprised him stuffing into his *meshog* a pair of shoes that old Garo, who was limping around in his, could have used. But now another image flitted across his circus of feelings. It was Anna giving a pair of new slippers to an elderly neighbor who would beg every passer-by, seated against a plane tree on

---

106   From *shinel*, to screw.

107   Gift, reward.

Komitas Avenue. And Gam took out a green bill from his ASK HRECHDAGUI and handed it over to Lousso.

"Take it!" he told him. And Lousso, holding it by the edges, brought the Benjamin Franklin up to his lips.

"Hum! he said. What a smell! America! It's the scent of America that you just offered me."

"You think? More like mold, yeah. Stuck in their grave of a book. The green seems to have run onto the printed pages over time. But a dollar is still a dollar. I'm going to take them all out of their grave so they can get some air and color again."

"Good for you," Lousso approved. "I'll do the same with that bill that you gave me, a tenth of what God lent you... A tenth of what God lent you."

Gam had never thought of Lousso as being the brightest bulb. Not enough to send really pointed barbs. His words were *made in the garbage dump.* But this time, Gam worried... Lousso wasn't used to making such observations, so someone must have dictated them to him. Words that augured cruel interior combats. And these inert but powerful bills would eventually win out over his conscience. Gam already felt torn between the desire to finish his day normally and to abandon everything and start off on the road back. But Artemis, always with her little Artem, had appeared in the area. Who knows if she hadn't overheard? His eyes kept looking at Gam, who had suddenly become an object of singular attention. And suddenly she started to pull her little boy towards her to indicate her distress more clearly. Instinctively, Gam walked over to her side. And as he moved towards her, his smile illuminated the young woman. Give with an open heart... A gull, perched on a box, surveyed the scene before flying off, its white wing melting into the azure blue in a calm, cold beat. Gam stood next to her now. Artemis straightened herself out holding on to her hips, her eyes looking straight at Gam's. Timid and firm under a few meshes of hair that emerged from beneath her scarf. Without saying a word, Gam opened his ASK HRECHDAGUI. He took out a bill.

"Here!" he said to her. "Take this and go buy your little one some of the happiness that was stolen from him."

Artemis lost her breath. She wanted to grab his hands and kiss them in thanks. Gam removed them just in time.

"No. Not that," he said annoyed.

"But!" said Artemis.

"But nothing," answered Gam. "That's all. Put it to good use. It isn't always a holiday in our part of the world ..."

Soon thereafter, he walked toward the trucks with his *meshog*. The others inside were waiting to sell theirs.

"I'm leaving you," said Gam. "You'll give this money to Artemis."

"You supposedly won the lottery?" One guy dared. "The wheel of fortune keeps turning, as they say."

"They also say," another one added, "that bald guys are always lucky. But don't wait to lose your hair to get married!"

And they all started to laugh like crazed people despite their long day. The truck began to lurch forward on the dirt path, forcing the rag pickers to hold on to the sideboards while they kept an eye on their *meshogs*. The good news flew behind them with the dust that came from the truck, and on the road with the plumes of black smoke that were escaping from it, not to mention all the chit-chatting that the wind would carry down all the way to the City.

Gam walked down the road alone, his ASK HRECHDAGUI held firm against his chest, triumphant, light, indifferent to the yellowish powder that was sticking to his boots. In back, the acid stench that had scratched his lungs for months on end. And the croaking crows. And the screaming gulls. Gam on the hill that joined the area right before the entrance. His exalted Anna awaited him like a lover. A soul that felt her son's steps making their way towards her. And her breath took in the air of a true renewal. Her eyes even poked out at the different parts of the cemetery, looking from her tomb. This earth on top of Anna represented a small source of serenity and for him now, a fixed point from which the two worlds flared. Gam flowed as alert as water in its riverbed, thrilled to be free after years of stagnation and of falling asleep in the same slump. Blessed moment that would make you brave the blaze despite all its obstacles. In the air a flight of swallows trapped in the gilded embers of the falling sun. Their colony punctuated the increasingly vast silence of the rust-colored sky with their cries. The pleasure they took in being alive was his as well. Blood that had remained stagnant for too long had suddenly come alive. And the oft-asked question that took on the face of a miracle at present. I give you fire... I give you fire...

Two policemen, one under the entrance to the garbage dump, the other in the middle of the road, were directing traffic. A nighttime procession was blocking the entrance to the dead. A petty people that passed by in a black silence on the main road, led by its priest who resembled a shepherd guiding his flock towards the hills. The deceased's car was slowly rolling by, followed close behind by the moaning choir of the families. From time to time the two cops threw a wild look in Gam's direction, as if they wanted to grab him at the exit. The procession seemed to annoy them so much that they tried to hurry people along: "Come on! Hurry up! Hurry up!" They repeated. "You can see that you're blocking the pavement! It'll be nighttime soon..." Having left his guard zone, Roubo had planted himself on the sidewalk, taking drags on his cigarette, one eye fixed on Gam so as not to lose him. During the time that the truck had stayed parked before starting up again on the road, its driver or someone else hadn't been able to resist making a report to the police, to try and sour the good luck that had befallen one of theirs.

The last members of the procession were barely inside the necropolis when the two cap-wearing predators descended on Gam.

"So, our brother discovers a treasure and doesn't bother to report it to the authorities, whose only mission is to find its rightful owner?" one of the officers in black sunglasses and matching mustache scolded him.

"I see that the gentleman likes books," said the other cop, a potbellied giant. "ASK HRECHDAGUI... Imagine that! People come to the garbage dump to listen to angels speak. Can we see what's inside?"

The policeman read one the open pages, which Gam held firmly in place.

"Giving makes the world grow... Giving makes the world grow," the other one repeated, with the look of a simpleton functionary etched on his face: "Illustrated with pictures, probably. I like pictures a lot."

Then switching to the razor-like voice that he used to intimidate people, the mustachioed policeman in glasses attacked from an opposite tact:

"Listen, my man! We can cart you off for all sorts of reasons, confiscate your ASK HRECHDAGUI and throw you in the brig like an apricot pit. But times are hard for everyone. For you as well as for us. Every day our kids wait to be fed with their held mouths wide open. So, keep the bulk of what you found and just offer us a *magharitch*. And that way, we'll forget about everything. You can go home. Buy yourself some cognac. Invite the girls from Sebastia Avenue. We can even make some introductions for you. I mean, go have some fun! And that way we can go home and give our little chicks some food ..."

What should he answer to keep from getting arrested? Should he try to fight them, and finish suicided under their watch? On the other side of the road, Roubo was looking for his smallest movements and occasionally spat onto the concrete from. Two crows were fighting, croaking at one another.

"It's fine," said Gam. "You're cleaning me out. That's the way things go, isn't it?" The two were frothing at the mouth and Gam opened his angel's wings. He took out a bill and handed it over to the fat one.

"You can split it!" he said disdainfully.

"What do you mean, split it? Such a beautiful bill! Cut it in half?" The man in the glasses was annoyed. "I want one exactly like it."

Gam handed him one as well.

"God be with you, my brother!" added the latter, having pocketed their manna, and rejoined their car, starting up right away to return towards Noubarashen. They probably went to celebrate their earnings a bit later Proshian

Street and then masticated some *khorovadz* while swigging one beer bottle after another, before going home to give anything to their hungry chicks.

"*Giving makes the world grow.* You must be kidding!" the fat one had said.

"Makes what grow?" his acolyte had asked, feigning innocence. "The world?"

"Yes, the world," the other one confirmed in a scholarly tone. "Giving makes the world grow— grow. Ah! The world. The world ..."

But in the grave among graves, Anna was waiting for her son. She wanted to feel his light step touch the earth and the earth vibrate happily. Gam crossed the road under Roubo's contemptuous gaze. And decided not to be taken in by his flattery. When you spend time with dogs, you start stinking like them too. He was still on the road when the other attacked

"You don't say hello to your brother?" Roubo said, pretending to be surprised.

"Now that a magic wand has made us rich, we forget our friends. That's it. Throw your anger on Roubo! The cops rip you off and he's the one who takes the blame. Go on! Go find Anna's tomb! And pretend not to see the down and outs that you could help without being all the poorer for it. You have so many bills in that book of yours. You wouldn't even notice, say... You're running away from me as if I had the plague, now? Isn't it thanks to me perhaps that you even have them within your hands in the first place? Ah the *kekhtot!* Isn't it thanks to me that your family was given this beautiful corner for Anna's tomb? A sunny place with a panoramic view on the dump? And from which she can observe you. But now you turn your back to me. Not even a smile. Not even a *magharitch* ..."

Gam was already on the central road as that old dog of a Roubo continued to negotiate for his bone. But how could he resist the challenge that his own compassion was throwing his way? Be the hand that opens and the grain that gives... Why Artemis and not this old bloke, after all? The man's salary was so scant that he could barely live, and he didn't even dream of escaping towards a life that he could only dream of. Gam walked back towards him, contrite. Roubo was already wondering what vengeful words he'd have to endure. But no. He saw him smile, his lips open and his body relax:

"Forgive me, Roubo *djana*, I have nothing against you, but you saw those *tarakan*? They extorted two hundred dollars from me ..." then taking out a bill from his book, he added: "Take it. I give it to you with open heart!"

Roubo lit up. He'd never held on to a bill so spanking green in his entire life. He started to caress it with his index finger like a woman's skin, then against his stubbly cheek; his body became electric at its touch.

"I wasn't asking for so much," he protested. "But at my age, this bill is really precious. I'm certainly not going to frame it like that Cobra's mug in our office. This portrait is worth a lot. And I must take care of my retirement days, you know *djanikes.*"

"Where I come from they say that money dirties one's hands," said Gam.

"That's true, they do say that," confirmed Roubo. "They say a lot of things. But when you have money, everything's jolly ..."

Gam was striding on the asphalt path that descends slowly to the waterway buried beneath a labyrinth of bulrushes. The air was chirping and cawing as the light slowly fell. The members of the procession were grouped around a grave pit. The cover was slowly being screwed on to the coffin. The priest was as rigid as a somber pipe, as he chanted some nasal prayers. He held his gold crucifix in one hand from which a rust-colored light emanated, and in the other his book whence he found the mourner's spiritual pittance. The gem on his ring shone intermittently. A jackdaw traced a nocturnal cross in the night air, which was saturated with liturgical chanting. The priest's eyes, when they weren't looking down at his book, was fixated on Gam, suspicious and slightly accusatory. And as Gam came closer to the group, heads began to turn one by one in his direction, guided by the priest's gaze *"For unconscious death is death. Conscious death is immortality,"* he was saying, a triumphal prophet blessing the mortuary casket without his gaze ever once being distracted from his own self.

"Man, his days are like grass, like the flowers in a field he blossoms; a breath blows on him, he is no more and never again will he know his place ..."

Gam didn't know these people and the deceased was a total stranger to him.

He took a side path that led to the road towards Anna's tomb. He was being judged from the side of people's gaze due to the dirt that covered his clothes. People sniffed the air as he walked by. And yet suddenly, under the effect of the priest's injunction, Gam felt that his humanity was being made to choose between his eternal suicide and eternal life. But who tomorrow would remember this indictment that the passing days had swallowed up? While avoiding the group, his attention was drawn to a milky stain that was dripping on the shimmering black of the priest's cone-headed coif which transformed him into a practitioner of white magic. Which bird had dared to let go in mid-flight with such a benediction. The priest turned around while Gam was smiling at this manna fallen from heaven. It encouraged one to follow him. Stuffing his book and his cross inside his large pockets, the religious man picked his robes up and cinched it to avoid it trailing in the dust. It was encouragement enough for him to follow. He joined the side road as quickly as possible without for a second worrying about abandoning some of his flock to their wailing and others to their sadness. What did they want from him anyway? He followed Gam's footsteps closely. Not used to such steep climbs, he started to huff and puff:

"Just one minute my son, one minute," he begged. "I'm having trouble catching up to you and I'd very much like to talk to you."

"But someone is waiting for me," said Gam. "My mother."

And Gam continued on his way in the hope that the other would give up. Soon he sat down on a low wall that adjoined Anna's tomb. The violence of the effort had dazed him. The priest was huffing and puffing below. The loud breathing of a sedentary soul used to exercise... Finally his willpower managed to move his body forward and he arrived:

"These robes," he said in muffled voice, "are as heavy as armor. Now I'm here and I have my reward, so grand is the panorama. And so powerful. The garbage dump, the City and Mount Massis in the background... And that sun that drowns everything in its blood."

A moment of silence, enough time to catch his breath again, his eye on the horizon, unleashing all its fires, he began to recite his visions using Narek's febrile words:

"The sky is my home, and my home is the sky, the deepest depths, the highest ascent, sky, sky, flowing with gold again."

Then, changing his tone, he turned towards the tomb.

"This is where your mother is lying, I assume. And you'd like to come more often, wouldn't you? To speak to her. But... she speaks to you from the depths of her silence. A breath inside your soul, not even a murmur. In truth, she never stopped talking. She lives in words, so long as you can't hear her voice. A breath within your spirit, not even a murmur. What else can one say except that we have a duty to be honest. A charitable duty. Isn't that right? One day, on the altar of one of our churches in Thessaloniki, dedicated to God's Sainted Mather, I read, let me give you a new commandment: *Love one another.* Written in our language: *Love one another.*"

He sat next to Gam on the low wall, then looked at him searchingly. A scalpel looking for uncertainty, a need that he seemed to know well.

"You are from the garbage dump, no?" he asked Gam.

"What makes you think that?" Cam protested. "I could work in the cemetery."

"One doesn't get dirty in quite the same way," the priest corrected. "Here one makes holes for the departed. There to look for treasure."

He was smoothing out his pointy black beard.

"So, tell me! What did you find that is so exciting that you are in a hurry to share your joy with your mother? You know that God lends us things so that we can give to others. Take and give as it is said one should, instead of taking and swallowing. You will be able to leave the garbage dump for good and be comforted a bit. Whoever has money is an *agha*,[108] who has none is just a rat. That's what the people think. But in truth it is the rich man who is a slave to his riches. These dollars will turn you into prey for your predators. And in our country, there are plenty

---

108   Master, Sir.

of predators! Bitter crones, children covered in soot with pimply cheeks, red eyes, and their gaze too deadened to even beg, who run around the countryside trying to feed themselves, searching the earth or the garbage like animals, chewing on bones like dogs. Who will give them enough food for them to lead dignified lives, if not the Church? The one national compassionate Church? Thanks to us, our miserable eat. We open free soup kitchens for them when this government multiplies casinos and banks. God has chosen you. He's let you find so that you can share your find with others. That's the meaning of the good news!"

And with these words, as he leaned forward to wipe the speck of dust that was otherwise dirtying his shoe polish, and a stream of light emanated from his ring. Gam kept quiet. The sermon giver's words had thrown onto his joy the somber irony of intimate knots that squeeze you tightly in their grip. In a few words, the man had revived within him the indignation that he shared with Haïk. The darkness that his inquiry had uncovered returned. And Garo's silhouette, staggering in his old shoes. And Artem's. And the mouths chewing on Bella's braised meat, Dro's sow who was so missed and appreciated by the others. And in front of him the garbage dump bathed in a wine-red light, with smoking shadows rising, and red and mauve wings piercing the space above it under the flames of the first darkness... *Give if you want to save the world...*

"I understood what you meant to say," said Gam. "You are the one Church, national and compassionate. But what do I hear? That your property is richer than the state budget? And what do I see? That you wear holy clothes richly woven, chalices and crucifixes made of solid gold... Massive objects... Sacred objects, you would tell me. But what is more sacred in the eyes of God that his living and suffering creatures? If you sell only one of these objects, you'll be able to feed a lot more people that with the few dollars that you want to extort from me. In this republic those who have possess a duty towards those who have not. Don't you think?"

And for the third time, as the priest stood up, his ring threw out a ray of fire.

"Beware!" He answered him. "Our finest objects made by man's hand are symbols of our devotion to the divine greatness. Imperfect as we are imperfect.

And the same goes for our country. Absolute ideas applied by men who love only themselves ..."

Then, waiting to go down the hill:

"You must have not heard me correctly, my son. No one is more fooled by our own contradictions than we are. Your soul must be stuck in a vein of egotism in order not to share some of your bounty with our poor ..."

And he started to leave. Gam caught him by the sleeve. Then opening his ASK HRECHDAGUI, he took out a bill:

"Here!" he said, for the love of God.

"I wouldn't turn a second one down," the servant of God added quickly. And Gam opened two other pages to remit the bills asleep within them.

"*Der voghormia!*" The priest chanted to the sky. "*Der voghormia!* I can recite a prayer on your mother's tomb ..." Gam held up his hand to signify that he didn't want any.

"So, I am going to rejoin my flock," said the priest. "The cars are waiting. And I'm afraid of falling because of the darkness ..."

He made his decision quickly. But Gam wanted to have a clear conscience. Despite the declining light, he leafed through his book page by page. Sometimes he'd missed a bill. He had three bills left. He intended to add them to a roll of drams in a minute. Then thought better of it. Better to keep them warm inside the book that had brought him luck. Then he had an idea. To place on Anna's tomb one of the bills that had survived so many misadventures. The bottle of *khoung* that was buried in a corner would do the trick. He rolled one of the bills against himself. Wrapped them in a piece of newspaper that he found nearby and enclosed it in the bottle before placing it back in its hole. A blind conviction led him to think that Anna at least would know how to protect this one while other predators would no doubt emerge along his way. He got ready to go down to her tomb. *If you want to save the world, give... If you want to save the world, give...* Gam turned around. Nothing, he saw nothing. But... but what? He took the bill that he had just hidden in the bottle and started on his way, using the tombs that he knew well by now as reference points. Everyone was gone. The dead man was now alone in his subterranean solitude. Fresh earth that the night would sow with its peaceful embrace, and which was already keeping Anna snug.

He was on the road that hugged the wall to the cemetery when heard the entrance gate which Roubo was closing squeak.

"Have a good night, my brother!" he yelled.

And Gam attempted to answer him by raising his right hand, but he felt the weight of the difficult day that had just gone by.

39.

*T*he smoke rose fuming into the sky. Torn on its crest, a silhouette floated by, its profile swollen by a large bag on its backside. And now it stopped between two black trees on the cliff that served as a wall for the garbage dump. From these heights saturated with quiet lights and vapors, with Mount Massis' pearly crest in the background, the man searched for something downhill... Or for someone, as Gam thought, watching him. He put down his bag, squatted and sat on his knees. He opened a large bag and took out a precious instrument which he fixed on a support. Then he lay down on the grass, taking on the contour of the ground below him. The flow of trucks coming up from the City had slowed to a trickle, as if they had been stopped somewhere far below in the first suburbs. In their place, so that they had free access, identical armored cars ready for battle had come and parked on the lot. Like a neighbor excited by the sudden commotion, Roubo abandoned his stool and planted himself in the middle of the road to feed his curiosity. His mouth and eyes wide open, paralyzed by the surprise invasion, he was unable to take even one drag from his cigarette. From inside the cars, a platoon of cold-blooded soldiers emerged, as silent as well-oiled machines. Not a single bark could be heard to protest this uncommon presence, only ordinary squawking. Harnesses in anticipation of their confrontation with the rioters, helmets with low visors, bullet-proof vests, knee pads and boots, men carrying billy clubs in their hands, giant translucent shields pressed against their bodies. They formed one black and compact mass that immediately took the dirt path. Their steps lifted clouds of dirt and made the sparrows and seagulls scatter. Their battle cry was strong and confident, soon drowned out by the spitting sounds emanating from Dro's digger. The rag pickers began to move all around him. Right before the big loop in the trail, the troops broke up. They formed a front for several dozen meters... Other armored cars were parked higher up at the first turn in the road and other men with similar equipment had deployed themselves over the dead parts of the garbage dump. In turn they advanced in one line in the same direction. They crossed the pits and the hillock on the field in front of them. They knocked over Lousso's shed made up of the old zhigouli, threw the bathtub into the pits and smashed the old, broken sofas. They advanced, impassible, their only aim to join themselves to the other group. Hence, there was no retreat possible, the dump having been transformed into a net; the prey had no choice but to accept the trap that it found itself in. The only exit was the western part of the dump which abruptly ended at the house with the red roof. Still only the most agile would be able to reach it before they were encircled... For a moment, the panicked flight of the gulls made the pairs of eyes that were used to staring at the floor for pickings look up into the air. But suddenly the boots' rhythmic rumble on the path created irritations among the pigs. The dogs turned their heads from time to time. Some whined, while others instinctively felt pushed forward to find their daily fare. The first troop faced the dump as far as it could see. A debacle of destroyed cardboard, ripped- open bags, empty abandoned boxes and bottles, all sorts of cadavers, gravel, scrap metal, rags, unending paper, and a rancid odor in the air that irritated the eyes and lungs. These men had never confronted such a diarrhea of waste. They knew the hardness of urban sidewalks, how to conquer barricades, but for the first time they hesitated on this large mattress of filth that made their bodies reel. They pushed in anyway, strong, heartless automatons, straight to the heart of this vast shithole where game animals were wandering. With the appearance of the first helmets, the pigs began to growl and to make their way towards Dro's digger. In a few seconds their nervousness extended to the dogs. Some gulls flew away to find refuge in the heights, beyond the sky's grey emanations. When the rag pickers farthest away from the center saw the first black forms appear they called the alarm: "Look who's coming! They're coming to hunt us down!" Dro stopped his machine, the motor's cracking sounds followed by the confused silence of footsteps. That's when the rag pickers recognized the second troop that suddenly appeared at the top of the dump. Some dropped their meshogs and hooks and dove to the bottom where the refuse was always burning... From atop the cliff the sound of gunfire... Dro stood on his machine and couldn't believe his eyes or his ears. Some of the wiser rag pickers risked moving towards the side of the red house to escape being surrounded, like Tsknors, who encouraged Sako to follow him. They hurtled down the slopes, slowed by the sticky refuse and collided with unexpected obstacles that they had to step over, bypassed, crushed. Tsknors arrived first, and without any fear of hurting himself, rolled on the garbage. Sako followed suit. Another rag picker managed to plunge right behind them and fell all the way down. Only a few meters remained before they could jump the wall surrounding the dump. Free now in the owner's garden. Haïk pushed the women and the youngest ones to move in the same direction. But Artemis stayed fixed in place, her child pressed against her body. And little Lala stuck to both. Others joined and pressed themselves against them. What good would it do to flee like mere criminals? The old men trailed behind, paralyzed by the fear of being hit. They knew they were powerless. Some let themselves fall to the ground. Like old Garo. A second shot. A crimson hole amidst the smoky veil, and Garo fell to the ground. His pink parka suddenly started to bleed, his body hunched over a pile of waste and his meshog thrown on the ground that vomited forth its last trash. Haïk could do nothing for him. He lifted his gaze to the top of the cliff and noticed the shooter's head and shoulders in a gap. During that time, the men in the first troop had attacked Dro's pigs. They hit them blindly to open a path before them. But the pigs resisted. A moving, unshakable mass, they made it impossible to pass. Behind them the dogs were ready to attack, all teeth, to defend their daily fare. The bludgeons, excited by these attempts at intimidation, came down twice as hard. They came down on their skin and hit their heads. And the panicked pigs screamed a thousand times as they began to run, falling over and onto one another and making a path despite themselves towards the dogs. The latter, their hair on end and spitting with rage, jumped onto the men but slid down their shields. Blows which shattered them. And whimpering with pain, they walked away or lay down like soft things on the ground. Now the two troops formed semi-circles which slowly closed. Lousso didn't have the time to jump into the empty space behind Tsknors. Bludgeoned, he collapsed onto the cardboard. After that, the men made a loop of the entire space and tightened their vice. They advanced on the rag pickers and forced them to back up against the bottom of the cliff, along the line where the trash was burning. Seeing the troop approach, Dro took refuge inside his digger's cabin. The lack of a door made him vulnerable. He tried to protest, but they came down on him brutally. Once, then ten times on his arms which he'd folded around his head for protection. The men went by and walked towards Haïk and the other rag pickers that were grouped around him. Some were ready to defend themselves. They brandished their hooks, their meshog held tight against their bodies to absorb the hits.

"What?" screamed Haïk! "You want us dead? You're even going to hit women, is that it?"

The forty rag pickers were now at the mercy of these dark automatons. Hooks against shields, bludgeons against *meshogs*. Screams, breaths, spit in their mouths, blood all over the bodies and the trash.

"What have we done to hurt you? Who ordered you to strike down your brothers and sisters? Shame on you! Shame!"

And another shot from on high. The air crackled in the distance. A pig dove into the bags, stunned. Then another shot, a second pig, a loud noise, stopped dead in its tracks. Seagull wings climbed into the sky and sliced through the fatty smoke. Dro began to cry at seeing his pigs shot at like rabbits. The most aggressive of the rag pickers threw their hooks onto the shields and pounded on the helmets. The men in black multiplied and attacked the other men and demolished them as quickly as they could. They all bent under the assault. Donatello had stayed in place without fighting back, convinced that he could stop the mechanical attack of the bludgeons simply by offering no resistance. His forehead exploded and he fell to his knees in the trash. They quickly encircled Haïk and attacked him; he curled up and awaited the end. He dove to the ground, his nose in the bags that were only recently discharged. Khatcho fired from his truck then was thrown into the ruckus. They slew him by kicking him with their boots. The entire attack lasted a whole ten minutes. Dro was astounded. The bludgeoned moaned. The women cried without even protesting. The young ones, lost, hunkered down and tried to understand why people wanted their skin. No one could raise their voice. They formed one large, bruised pile, awaiting their fate. Everyone searched around them, without their hooks. Haïk more meticulously than the others. And quickly they took his Tokarev away. They knew. Haïk was silent but noticed everything.

"Is this to shoot at the police, huh?" the mustachioed officer who led the attack asked him.

"Found it here," Haïk protested, "When I was searching in the old parts. You can check if you want anyway, there are no bullets anywhere, not here or at my home either. I'll keep it as a souvenir."

"It's still a firearm, my man," said the officer. "Not to mention the fact that the metal bars that you all carry say a lot about your intentions."

The bars were gathered and laid in a row so that they could be filmed and the television report could invent all sorts of murderous intentions.

"No one wants you here. You give our country a bad name. And you know it very well."

"But you shot at us! Like in a war!" Haïk exploded. "You killed our friend Garo. Look at what you've done!"

"We never used any firearms," the police chief asserted. "And anyway, we'd like to know who it was who shot him. Maybe it was you. In any case, we're taking you with us. You'll have a lot of explaining to do. Let the women get out of my sight. I don't want to see you again. As for the men, get in the truck. And let no one sully our country's reputation anymore!"

"We're not worth less that the city folk," a voice protested. "We find food here, in the dump. Otherwise let the guy who gives you orders find us some work."

"Yes, some work!" added another.

And suddenly, Dro who was vomiting, stood up on his machine:

"*Bozi lakotner!* You massacred my pigs! And you assassinated old Garo! I say assassinated! The rag pickers will never abandon the trash! You hear us? Never! They're not hurting anyone. And neither are my pigs. Or the dogs. Take care of the City!"

"You, *kaki ktor*," answered the chief, "shut your mouth otherwise we'll take you in as well!"

"Take me in!" Dro answered ironically. "Well go right ahead! And how will you evacuate all your crap? I don't know a single person who'd want to take my place! Not one, you hear! I could even teach the president a lesson. Because that's what this country needs, a giant garbage collector!"

"You fatten your pigs with our waste and then we find it in our plates," the officer tells him. "You should be happy that we didn't call the sanitation services! Because we know your trade. Today, I'll close my eyes to it. But tomorrow, you get rid of all of this for me. Raise some doves instead since you like animals so much!"

Hard at work, Dro's pigs pretended not to hear anything, their heads held low, their muzzles out in front like pumps. Above the cloud, the seagulls soared, carried along by the plumes of some secret music. They spread their wings, spun around and then bounced back, their eyes trained on the men, the hard ones, the hurt ones, so small from high above, stuck in the jumbled waste. Two worlds that never embraced. The women had already taken the dirt path. The men in black surrounded the other rag pickers who were destined to climb, but the latter asked if they could carry old Garo themselves up to the parking lot. They let them put together a cardboard stretcher. And Garo would take the path to the exit lying down, his motionless body carried by his last family on earth. The crows and the gulls melded their scythe-like wings above, slicing the soft vapors that the wind pushed forward without malice until the cemetery doors, to the other side of the road where Roubo was standing. Garo had just died. Who knows how and at who's hand? Haïk turned his head once more to see the dump's smoking heart, that which had given him so much in life. That's when he saw the man on the crest again, leaving his mark, and the bag stuck to his back suddenly disappeared like magic behind a veil. Haïk quickly walked backwards now on the same path that he'd taken so many times to kiss his poisonous flower, and rejoined the company of his errant dogs, Dro's pigs, the gulls, and the rats. To go to work with all the others. And here he found himself walking with men as thick as walls. And as they approached the entrance, the dust began to fall, and the ground became firm. He could knock over his guards and go lose himself in the cemetery, laughing at the thought of being followed by crazed packs. But he kept his place with the others. Something within him was stopping him. He moved towards the vans, a hostage of his own country, of his own blood brothers. And all these independence movements would forever remain dreams of physical and childish joy, like people jumping, running, and swimming in the image of Lousso, bludgeoned in mid-air and now being dragged towards the parking lot. After work was over, so that his body would forget the hours spent bent over the plastic bags, Lousso would run around his shelter as quickly as he could jumping onto its hillocks and falling into its holes and coming right back up, like a kid who plays at life in order to forget it.

Surrounded by the troop, the rag pickers reached the armored trucks parked in the lot. Some carried Garo's soft body lost in his pink bloodstained parka on an improvised stretcher, sneakers on his feet, stained in filth. The officer who orchestrated the attack, potbellied with a mustache that cascaded down to his mouth, asked if the cadaver had any family. Who could answer that question? Nobody. Garo, short for Garabed, a name as used up as an old piece of cloth, and the shortened version of his official name. The rag pickers, his only tribe, emotional and fickle, in a living pigsty that smoked up his days and nights. The officer had carried out his duty. All he had to do was get rid of this package now. He took a few steps toward the road and asked Roubo:

"Do you have any room for one more dead person?"

"There must be a hole somewhere on the hill," answered Roubo. "It's for someone who's supposed to arrive tomorrow."

"You're gonna take it for me," the officer ordered.

"Take who?" asked Roubo.

"His friends will take care of putting his dirt over him," the mustachioed officer contented himself to answer: "But not a trace. And no name on it either. Understood? And anyway, he doesn't even have one."

Then addressing the rag pickers who were carrying Garo:

"Go on," he ordered.

A few women who had remained near the portal and had decided to cross the street despite the bizarre clothing that they were wearing for a burial, followed the strange procession composed of men in combat wear holding five or six outcasts whom they had just crushed with their clubs. Roubo hobbled ahead dragging an iron shovel that squeaked on the ground. Despite his weakness due to age and to his sedentary smoker's health, he was determined to climb the fifty meters up to the pit. He paid for his stubbornness early. The air that his lungs were searching for made his body go topsy turvy.

"It's right here," said a random voice pointing to a freshly dug hole." They lay Garo's body down nearby. The men from the troop formed a circle. The rag pickers copied Haïk's attitude. Their eyes fixed on their Garo's body. Dead indeed, Garo, curled up on his bloodied red cardboard, erect when before he was aways trembling year-round. Haïk took off his own windbreaker and placed it over his friend's remains. Then dared to say in a grave voice:

"There are so many things that we could say today. But we will keep them to ourselves ..."

The women standing in the back had a hard time hiding their tears. But what were they crying about? About the disappearance of one of their friends or the death of their livelihood? Then that heaviest of moments arrived where the dreaming is rent, when one knows that the earth's dark mouth awaits its prey and is asking that this body which it carried for so long be returned to the earth. Roubo had taken out two thick ropes from a corner. They slid it under the cardboard that had transported the cadaver. Thanks to them four men were able to slowly descend into the trench. Earth was already coming loose at the sides to take possession of its goods. Each person threw in a farewell handful. Haïk, whom Roubo had given his shovel to as well as the difficult task of erasing Garo from this world, began to fill in the trench. At the end, they pat down the fresh earth. Roubo took back his shovel and his ropes. He began to head down. The rag pickers were placed into groups by the men in black and led back to the parking lot. All in all, the burial lasted less than an hour. And the armored cars took to the road. Towards Noubarashen...

40.

Gam was the third man to escape by the side of the house with the red roof, behind Tsknors and Sako. A long moment after the violent combat where humans came to blows in a paroxysm of man-to-man combat and the clubs of the law began to beat down on the workers of despair. The heavy weights came down on men who were defeated long in advance! And without mercy! A military avalanche on helpless, unarmed souls! Der voghormia! Der! Your sons, what did they do to your sons? And what has man done to help his fellow man? And the homeland is one unending ruin. And what about the race's future? Nothing but a dream destined to end up in death's stomach. So, it is. So, it's always been. Punches on people's mouths so that their mouths stop opening! And who'd want to scream after something like that? Who would dare to still have the desire to live? Let the weak finish up, caught in the ropes! Let them finish with bloody noses stuck to the ground after the first round! Defeated, suffocated, their stomachs bruised.

Gam had seen his friends encircled by the troop from afar and had cried for his friend Garo. He'd also seen his friends carried away in armored trucks. He'd seen Haïk climb into them as well, resigned and confused. He'd seen the cars take off in the direction of Noubarashen, where the Samourai president's prisons lay. The endpoint for any offense committed against the prince's goodness. And Gam—that was his greatest flaw—wanted to know everything.

He asked Roubo if he'd noticed any blood on Garo's windbreaker.

"And how!" said Roubo. "On the windbreaker and on the cardboard. And it wasn't a hit from some club that put a hole through Garo. His blood was coming out of a hole. They also shot Dro's pigs. Anyway, what's he going to do with his pigs now, Dro? Those that they killed and the ones that are still alive?" And while Gam was walking away he said, "I didn't see Mouk on that day. You didn't either, I suppose. So, you tell me, huh?"

A man who worried, Gam had things to verify after what he'd seen and heard. That unknown man on the cliff who'd lain down in the grass. The sound of shots that had exploded behind him as he fled, tearing apart the haze, the burning vapors, then Garo's windbreaker then Garo's skin, and then finally Garo's flesh. For a while Gam walked alone up the hill road, a completely typical road leading up to Noubarashen, an insipid and stupid road. But he feared that at any moment a car with black windows and dark intentions would gobble him up before spitting him back out into some hole. Gam distanced himself from this road, the steepest in the country, which carried uninterrupted its democratic messiahs towards their Golgotha and cut across the dump's dead zones. He was hoping to reach the cliff and the trees under which the man in black had lain down. Lively, stubborn, he ascended with that one idea in mind. Garo had been shot just like Dro's pigs.

He reached the two trees. A few cartridges lay strewn about, pell-mell. Gam found the spot for the gun stand, a tripod, and behind it the shape that a body had made in the grass. These reference points indicated a direction, that of the digger around which the rag pickers were huddled during the mêlée. He lay down in the same space. And hence entered the criminal's soul.

Vai! [109] my brother, Gam said to himself. You did it. You let go of your rage. Hell added onto hell. Cold, you spat fire onto these poor derelicts who only asked for justice. They were already less human than others. Instead of finding some peace for them, you unleashed evil upon them. What courage is there in crushing those whose misfortune should inspire impartial justice? But there you have it. You fired on justice itself. On the beauty of the nation. The beauty of his eternal spirit. You committed the act that sanctifies a flag against beings whose blood was too weak to survive. You killed and you destroyed. You put metal inside their bodies. You killed a brother who felt no remorse against you, apart

---

109   Interjection.

from the anger of suffering more than anyone else in the land. A land where justice doesn't exist. Where the one whom one calls Great violates the heavenly truths and teaches his fellow men to do the same. And whose scribes write that there is no other God besides himself. Hence you threw your strength onto those who had given their last clothes to the Lord who crushed their lives. Instead of being unfaithful to him, you found an advantage in seeing these bodies which sullied his image fall. You did it. Instead of loving the persecuted, those that are forced to feed themselves in indignity, who received excrement when all they asked for was bread, you cursed him. Instead of being at peace with yourself, you chose the path of untruth. And this will forever more be your burden, at night as during the day. At night as during the day...

And so, Gam let the light slowly slide to places far away, to places known only to itself. The dump was still smoking continuously. The fire was doing its job, eating away at the bad and the worse still, consuming everything that offered itself up to its joyous consumption. Invulnerable winner after the violent mêlée, and the percussion, the chaos, while Dro's last pigs were rummaging here and there amidst the crows, the gulls and the dogs who were finishing off leftovers. Now there was peace... High above, at Gam's eye level, elegant birds flew across the air's innocence, where everything seemed untouched, safe from the hard lies in which human breath loses itself. Gam looked west. And saw Mount Ararat's eternal snows turn pink and then black. And the dust from the sun dissolved softly into the immensity.

Suddenly red, a glimmer of light. Like on the roofs in the city center. And the echoes from explosions started to shatter the air all the way to Gam's ears. Probably near the Main Market, he thought. Red, suddenly... Darkness fell and violent flashes with long tails of fire on Mashdots Avenue. Then the sound of gongs resonated through the soft peaceful sky. Suddenly, a flash of light. Groups of loud sound carried by the wind all the way to Gam. But those explosions. *They're firing guns*, said Gam. *Yes, they're firing.* Then everything became confused. Gam saw. Gam imagined the contagion spreading towards the south and extending its dominion over the embassy neighborhood. A flash of crimson red blood spreading its tentacles out as quickly as a powerful wave. The black crest of the buildings. The fire searched out the pink building entrances as well as the slightest hovels with its tongues. Devouring the Circus. Then it spread hungry to Central Square, then to Abovian Street and took with it the museum of natural history along the way, and the vestiges and other vulnerable ancient things that had become one large fire. Farther to the east and caught in between old houses, the covered market was also in flames. Judging from the height of the flames, Gam guessed that the clothes that they were selling there were also feeding the fire. The fire won't stop at anything anymore, Gam thought, and after it has ravaged the City's center, it will attack the neighborhoods on the hill. And no one will be protected, neither the citizens down low nor the ones on high. Women's lamentations, lost in front of the red menace, the elderly too limp, the young too naive, a crowd where everyone tried to save themselves, or to save others along with oneself, the strong pulling aside the impotent, a crowd besieged on all sides. While some unknown people helped the fire to burn where it has lost strength or pillaged stores. A red glimmer. Suddenly a river flooding everywhere like a destructive ogre, able to climb trees and reach the heights. Not far from the Circus, flames licked the skin of the beige tuffa that covered the information tower. They inserted themselves everywhere, a thousand fiery fingertips. A giant torch that consumed newspapers and journalists alike, and now fell back onto the vast Arshakouniats Avenue. Gam imagined the flames jumping from car to car, from street to street with the wind's complicity. The heat from the last weeks having dried out the small woods surrounding the pantheon, it would also quickly go up in flames, he thought. Then it would attack the illustrious dead, blackening their milky marble slabs, obfuscating their names and effigies. Suddenly red, the glimmer illuminated the entire Mashdots Avenue on its way to devastating violence. Who knows if the assault would spare the manuscript conservatory, a grey building whose esplanade served the leaders from the Opposition to harangue the crowds gathered below. Yerevan is ablaze, exploding, Gam said to himself. And probably committing suicide. And soon the blaze spread to Tzitzernakaberd hill and submerge the flame at the heart of the Memorial ...

41.

What was this blaze that Gam had just invented inside his head? Traces of light dotted the night that overlay the city. He got up. But for God knows what reason, instead of following the easy road back to his shack, he decided to cut through the garbage dump. Chance often takes its own course and decisions are made for unknown reasons. Gam plunged into the valley using a steep path. After taking a few steps in the mounds of grass and earth, he reached the demarcation line of the burnt land. He walked through the trash, his eyes fixed on the digger's black outline. Sometimes he heard the sounds coming from the monster at work, blowing, sighing, snoring. Deaf scratching. The chit-chat of a somber mass. Whining laughter. The beating of wings. And what if evil spirits came here to frolic and lie in the trash? Roubo could close the entrance to his cemetery all he wanted, who knew if the darkest of the dead didn't walk along its walls looking to inhale the odors of agony? Gam felt reassured as he touched the digger's hood. Dro's soul was locked inside that piece of scrap metal worn out by its daily labor. And Zara's soul was buried somewhere nearby. "Zara!" Gam said aloud, what monster ordered your death? And what type of a monster am I that I didn't denounce it? I should never have listened to Dro. Should never have... Tears welled up in his eyes. The gas, he thought. Waves of vertigo passed through him. He remembered that he'd left his hook near the digger as he fled. He patted down the trash with his feet. In the process he awakened some hoarse groans. Dro's pigs, Gam said to himself. They're still foraging. His eyes having gotten used to the dark, he could make out backs moving around him. He slipped on some sticky things and landed on his haunches, unleashing a huge quake in the bodies and some horrible groans, fearful and aggressive. The memory of the killings that had swept away a few of them became more excited at the smell of human flesh. They shoved Gam. He felt the woolen stench of the pigs on his face. His hand grabbed the digger's caterpillar track. Touching its cold metal which had been fashioned by man comforted him. He managed to find refuge in Dro's cabin. Then he remembered that Dro was in the habit of hiding his lighter underneath his seat. He lit it and extended his arm outside the cabin. Its small light made his eyes sparkle. Gam saw that the pigs had formed a circle around him along with the other animals, the rats most probably, and on the fringe of the halo gulls were perched on boxes... A hook would have certainly been useful for him to defend himself. He waited a few moments. To leave the cabin and try to pass these irritated masses was risky. He recognized Idi Gago and the Samourai. They seemed to be waiting for him, to rough him up. Having become wild again since Bella's death, the Cobra was probably waiting in ambush in a corner somewhere. Gam came down anyway, carrying his flame at the end of his extended arm. He'd barely put his feet on the ground that he found himself scratched by dark roars, pulled downwards, and pushed until he fell. Collapsed. Stomachs immediately crushed him. Snouts ripped his clothes. Hideous odors assaulted his senses. Muddy asses, hairy rats turned him over repeatedly in the morass. And somewhere beyond this world, Anna was crying as she watched her son on the ground: she wanted to take his pain away, but she remained stuck inside her box... Implore higher powers as she might, the world had been left all alone to fulfill itself... Anna! Gam moaned in his choked voice. And suddenly, using a pig to balance himself, he stood back up again. He had lost Dro's lighter. The night had returned to surround them. The beasts didn't seem to have given up on the idea of murdering him. Gam took a few steps in the direction of the truck path, when Idi Gago knocked him over with the full brunt of his body weight, while the Cobra pushed him as well. Gam stumbled and put out his hand looking in vain for support, then collapsed like a dead weight. Suffocated. He was running out of oxygen. For a moment he thought he was disappearing into the moon. Then he heard clicking and panting. The dogs, he thought. He made out the sounds of the gulls. He lost his head again, asphyxiating, panting, and panting, then he murmured, *Der voghormia! Der...* until the moment when the night's darkness, the stench of the garbage dump, the crushing that his body disappeared. Forever disappeared... And God only knows where Gam ended up.

42.

A Storybook Ending

The sky was so pure and boundless that it filled men with joy. On this morning, which seems to bookend our story, it set the country ablaze. The colors appeared even more alive than usual. The yellows shone yellower and the grays grayer than ever before. And sounds reverberated blissfully off one another in every direction. The cemetery itself, usually such a gloomy place, bathed in this glow as well. If anyone had been buried today, the skies would have sent down such sweet winds to the grieving that people would have been certain that their dear departed ones were on their way up to the Kingdom of Heaven. The road, which wound its way from Yerevan to Nubarashen prison, usually so tough on old motors, seemed easy to cover, even for those who were on their way to jail. But the truck driver was the most astonished of all. Accustomed to this itinerary, he made sure to look at Dro's house along the way. Sure, it was the same old group of desolate barracks. And the large rusty old bucket out back remained the same as always. And the dump trucks kept picking up dirt as in the past, as they made their way to the heart of the garbage dump. But instead, the driver seemed stunned by what he did not see. Where had everyone gone? Had Dro's pigs and dogs, the rag pickers and Dro himself, not to mention his digger, just disappeared into thin air? Doves swirled in the newfound stillness that emanated from the trash dump. So many doves, fluttering into the air for the sheer pleasure of it, for the ecstasy of feeling the wind's light currents before gliding gently back down and alighting on the rooftops. The man he was taking to jail witnessed the same spectacle. But men see the world only through their own personal anguish and so the wretch didn't marvel at what he witnessed, ignoring everything that went into the making of this novel—one which may get lost in time or on the other hand become eternal, this novel where the guard at a trash dump curses the businessman responsible for a nation's woes, where an old tractor mills about in the middle of an ocean of filth, where a mother nourishes her child with a thousand breasts swelling of milk, where women ecologists lament the skies, where feminists break down and cry, where infertile women get turned on, where feral pigs bear the names of presidents, where the dead flee their tombs to smell life's fresh air, where a buried woman still suffers from the slightest harm committed against her son and where her son, a certain Gam, dead or alive, fights valiantly in one world before falling inexorably into another, whispering on the way down *Der Voghormia. Der...*

Acknowledgments

My thanks for their encouragement, for reading my manuscript and for their sage counsel go Christa Nitsch, Anne-Sophie Monglon et Daniel Arsand. Thanks go as well to sociologist Hranoush Kharadian, whose on-the-spot research was the impetus for this book in the first place. To Georges Festa, for his unstinting support over so many years. My thanks and gratitude go out as well to Anahit Avetissian, Yvette Vartanian, Seda Mavian and Vahan Ishkhanian who shared their knowledge and advice with me. And special thanks to Mkrtitch Matevossian for his drawing in Chapter 15 and to Gerard Torikian for his music in Chapter 19. Thanks as well to the artists who painted the aquarelle in Chapter 2. 2.

Finally, my infinite gratitude extends as well to Myriam Anderson, my editor whose confidence in me and enthusiasm provided much comfort even when she did not realize it. *—Denis Donikian*

The translator would like to thank the Calouste Gulbenkian Foundation in Lisbon for the generous grant that made the English translation of this book possible. He is indebted as well to Actes Sud for granting him the English translation rights for the book.

—*Christopher Atamian*